LEGENDS
OF THE
FALLEN

JACOB THE CHOSEN

Aaron Stillwater

AARON STILLWATER

Printed in the United States of America.

Edited by Xulon Press.

ISBN 9781498481090

www.xulonpress.com

CHAPTER I

M aybe it was fate, or it could just be that the boy had bad luck. No rock was more jagged, and no hard place was as unyielding as the two he was pinned between. The small caves behind his home provided entertainment during the long summer days. It was cool beneath the earth, and he had a particular inkling for adventure. He was a boy, and for now he could wiggle between the tough spots, but soon he would grow up, and already he feared how the weight of the world, much like the walls of this small cave, would come pressing in on him as he grew into the man he would be—the man so many people hoped he would be. Hope, for most, empowers one to persevere, and to have hope brings a feeling of security even in the darkest times. But to *be* the hope in those dark times brings a smothering feeling of inadequacy. It was not literally said to him, but he was old enough now to understand the overt tones of the hope that he filled a particular part in the lore of his family.

As he wiggled through the crevasses back toward the light and the voice calling him from the other side, he only had the vaguest sense of his place in the future. He was not like most boys who had wild fantasies of what life would be like in the real world. No, his calling was much more exciting than that of an athlete or doctor or a nuclear physicist; the future that peeked over his horizon would make even the war heroes of old seem mundane and common.

He was a half-breed fallen angel of his mother's damned bloodline, and his father's heritage was cursed. Every firstborn from his father's line would always live in literal strife against the forces of evil. Fate had dealt him cruelly; his father had passed him a curse—one that he would then pass to his firstborn offspring— and his mother's entire bloodline was doomed to stand among the Fallen angels and be judged with them as they were cast into Hell. The hope of a people placed in a lad who was barely one meter tall seemed ridiculous. He still had substantial growing to do, and not all of it was vertical. Part of him was excited, but in reality he was terrified of his future.

Though he was young, Jacob understood too well that he would receive double torment in the end. His mother's blood, the blood of Nephilim, carried the mark of

5

Hell, and his father's blood ensured he would spend his future on earth brushing with death and confronting the demons he would later have to suffer again in the afterlife. He did not yet understand how close he stood to the threshold of Hell or how he was expected to escape not only from his curse, but also to rescue the fallen before him. The Promise had been given long ago: "One shall come from the stars as you have but shall bear not Hell and walk among the Fallen of this world and raise them up." Jacob had not yet figured out how they determined he was the fulfillment of this prophecy, but he knew he was expected to carry this weight. Perhaps the only reason this expectation had not been said outright to him was because of his tender age. But he knew, though the full weight had not been realized, that he was chosen to carry the burden of the Nephilim.

Through the years, the bloodline of the Nephilim had thinned; most had been wiped out by Israel when they conquered the Promised Land. But the few who remained passed on their enriched genes through the centuries. The blood protected itself and steeled its power away, only emerging in a select few members of the family. Jacob had enough of their blood in him to condemn him as a bastard son of one of the Fallen. Only a trace was required to condemn him, but he had a special portion and some might say he was not from this world. Some might say he was gifted, but most would call him evil. A father's sins will pass to the son, and for Jacob, there was a clear blood line straight back to the demons that assaulted the Mercy Seat of God. The blood was spread to millions, and most never even knew they were cursed. The special powers of his bloodline were only granted to every tenth generation because the line had preserved itself to do so. He was in a peculiar situation, though. His mother was the child of a ninth- and eighth-generation Nephilim line. She inherited the powers of her ninth-generation father but had also passed her powers from her mother to him.

Part of him wanted the powers that his grandmother would give him, and part of him was afraid. His mother's bloodline was always looking to their tenth-generation demigods to redeem their cursed blood. For every hero that rose among them, nine generations of evil would undo their work and then a corrupt narcissist would inherit the gifts and sink them further into the damnation of their fathers. Jacob was expected to prove his family was human enough to receive salvation. He was already forced to spend the rest of his breathing days, fighting things no man should ever live to see. Sometimes his father would come home beat and bleeding, but he always got back up the next night and put on his trench coat and marched out the door with his Bible in hand. Some days nothing happened, and others Jacob feared his father might not return.

His mother was unable to help him in this endeavor; the fact that the demons his father fought were kin to her ancestors made his father doubt she could do anything against them. But Jacob was special; he had inherited *both* curses. He knew he would inherit his father's cures. Already he knew that the monsters under his bed were real. Unlike most children though, his fear would not grow any less as he got older; rather, the nightmares would become real, and he would have to face them. Today was the day he would find out if he had his mother's curse, or gifts, as she often called them.

He scrambled out in to the brightness. Despite the tight fit, he relished every moment he spent in the dim caves. It was partly the adventure, but what he really enjoyed was the smell of the undisturbed dirt beneath his feet. The scent of old, forgotten places that nobody else could reach or understand gave his small mind a certain thrill of discovery. To him, somewhere in the dim, moist earth was the smell of knowledge. As he emerged into the open air of the hillside and brushed the loose strands of his hair away from the sticky sweat on his face, he beheld the dirt upon his cloths and was instantly gripped with paralyzing fear. The voice that called him out of the darkness was his mother's. Normally she was amused by his curiosity, but today she had particularly instructed him *not* to soil his clothes.

It was his twelfth birthday today. It was the age that his mother's family deemed the beginning of adulthood, typically because that was the age that the ones who had powers began to use them. His mother didn't have much family. They did not have very many children, trying not to spread their tainted blood too far among the nations, but also to try not to thin it in an attempt to breed a savior. For this reason, his mother was often criticized for marrying a man who was not from the Fallen. On the other hand, his father had many relatives. His father's family usually lost the firstborn to the curse, and it became imperative to have many children. And the children were all close in age because one of their parents would usually die young—it took a lot of strength to hunt demons. His father's line considered thirteen to be the beginning of adulthood, and next year he would begin go with his father when he hunted spirits in the dark hours.

"Jacob?" His mother called again. Her normally calm and soothing voice was brimming with irritation. He looked up the gentle hill and saw her staring down at him, quite cross. Her blue eyes pierced him like lightening.

"Jacob! How did I know you would be here?" She exclaimed, "Of all days for you to go wandering in those dirty caves, you chose today!" She folded her arms and gave him the most serious condescending scowl a mother could ever deliver to a child. "Bring yourself up here now! I must get you ready for the trials tonight."

Jacob didn't say anything, he just hung his head, fixed his shame-filled eyes on his muddy boots, and wandered up the hill to his mother. He didn't intend on getting dirty. He wasn't even going to go in the caves at first; he really just wanted to look. But then he had to go in, just a little. Then he had to go past the first bend and then the second, and then through that first tight spot. He hadn't even gone as far as the small stream that he normally crawled through, and somehow he was covered in dirt. *How did he get so dirty?*

It seemed trivial to Jacob that he should have to endure a test of his powers. His mother had already taught him and his two younger siblings how to tap into the supernatural aura in their blood. But this was the way of his family, and in two years his sister, and in three years his brother, would have to do the same.

His mother cleaned him up and redressed him and then they left to meet the council, delayed because of his adventures. She took him to a place he had become familiar with since it was of importance to her family. He had become acquainted with many ruins and odd sites in his short life and knew more of the true history behind them than most historians would ever amass. She led him to a secret chamber, that until today he had never seen, and then, instructed him to wait and disappeared behind an impossibly heavy stone door.

The room he had been waiting in was solid stone, a massive granite fortress beneath the ancient Stirling Castle in the middle of Scotland. The passage he stood in outdated the fortress above him by at least two hundred years. His mother had taught him well about the history of ruins such as these. Growing up in Ireland, he had visited nearly all of the ruined castles and megalithic constructions throughout his homeland and the neighboring Scotland and England. He had never seen this passage, but he knew it was built into the hill underneath the castle long before the castle was constructed. It had a very strategic position, and before the castle topped it, the entire facility was underground. Apparently there were not many people who did know about this passage because the air was stale, and the dim torchlight revealed layers of undisturbed dust upon ancient relics. Massive tangles of webs hung in the corners of the ceiling.

His mother had disappeared into a large room to partake in some kind of family council before his test began. He had already tried listening in, but the stone door was at least two feet thick, and he could hear nothing. The dim, cold, dusty air was beginning to give him the creeps. Surely his mother had been in there for an hour already. Was she trying to get the council to wave the test? Was the test supposed to have started already? He could not think what the delay was about. Just when he had made up his mind that he was being tested already and was about to grab a torch from the wall and make his way down one of the dark passages, he heard the door scraping against the floor. He turned and saw a man he did not recognize at all.

"It's good to meet you, lad." The man said. He was clearly Scottish. Jacob couldn't see well in the dim light, but his accent was unmistakable. "I'm your cousin, Malcolm. You've got a very important day ahead of you." Then he stepped out of the doorway and motioned for him to enter. "There's a few of your kin folk to meet before you begin your test. Come on, they're waiting for you." Jacob had never met any of his mother's family. From the way his mother talked about the family, keeping the blood from getting thin or spreading and some of the horrible feuds that had killed some of his cousins, he figured there was no family on his mother's side.

Jacob nervously took one step forward. He had powers; he knew that, but what if this was a different kind of test? He caught a glimmer in Malcolm's eye as he entered the room. Once he had stepped in, Malcolm followed him, and the great stone door scraped shut behind him. *Malcolm must have powers, too.* Jacob inferred. *There's no way a normal man would have the strength to use that door.*

The room was dark except for a small circle, what Jacob assumed was the center of the room. The circle appeared to be moonlight coming from a hole in the ceiling— perhaps this is what they were waiting for. His mother was standing in the light waiting for him.

"Go on lad, into the circle." Malcolm said and gave him a firm, enthused push.

Jacob nearly fell from the unexpected contact but kept his composure and walked with deliberation to his mother's side. It was eerie, Lucile looked so much different in the silver light; she wasn't his mother in that light. Her features were hard and perfected, and she no longer seemed so gentle, just powerful. The warm, motherly look of her eyes was dimmed, serious, and cold. Jacob couldn't remember ever seeing her expression like this, even when she was angry. Her silky blond hair seemed silver in the moonlight, and it fell around her shoulders and draped down her back like a waterfall.

He looked carefully, wondering if it was a trick with the pale light or if this was who she really was. Just a moment before he entered the light, he stopped and wondered if he would look different, too; perhaps this was a different kind of test. Would he suddenly become hard and cold? He took a breath as if he were jumping into a cold pool and stepped into the pale silver glow. The light seemed cold. His mother still looked sharp and hard, and he still looked like a child. Was it a trick with the light? Then why did he still look the same? He felt weird—cold and nervous. His mother reached for him to take her hand. It was not inviting as if she meant to guide him but demanding as if he had no choice.

Jacob reached and took her hand and felt it was very cold as well. Everything about this moment was chilling. She turned him so that he was facing the blackness on his left instead of the blackness that he had been facing a moment ago.

"This is my son, Jacob." His mother said. Her soothing Irish voice wasn't so smooth. It was not irritated and angry as it was when he stumbled out of the cave earlier. There was something about it he could not place; it seemed otherworldly. Jacob shivered as he heard it, not sure if it was the room or if his mother was somehow different. "I think you'll find him more than kin to you. He's a strong lad, a good head on his shoulders."

"I take you at your word when you say he's your own, Lucile." Another Scottish voice answered from the darkness. This voice was a man, and it had an equally creepy tone. Perhaps it was just that he could not see the man's face, but it seemed to ring with a condescending menace. "But only time will tell if he's the one, and you can't help that case for him."

There was that tone again. It was less overt now, it was almost obvious that expectations about him were substantially higher than he was able to understand.

"Can't I brag a little on my own son without you assuming I mean to make him an idol?" His mother answered. The question she asked seemed as if it were a condemnation of the remark the other voice had made, while at the same time an affirmation of her intention to make him an idol. "He's a good lad, is all."

"I suppose you're entitled by right of being the boy's mother." The voice replied, "Now come up here, and let us begin."

Jacob's mother looked down at him and smiled. It was a smile he had never seen before; it wasn't really a happy smile, but it wasn't a forced smile, either. "You'll do fine." And then she walked out of the light and vanished in the direction of the voice.

"Jacob, how are you boy'o? It's been nearly twelve years since I last saw you." A new voice said. The voice was rich and resonated through the empty chamber.

"Good sir." Jacob answered a little shy and kind of quiet. He noticed that his voice fell flat in the darkness as if the vibrations of the others' voices still lingered in the stale air and ate up his words.

"I don't suppose you remember me, do you, boy'o? I'm your grandfather, your very own mother's father. Aye, what a noble-looking grandson she made for me." Jacob didn't sense any kind of compliment in his voice, but he managed a nervous smile into the shadows.

"Henry, the boy is here to be tested." The first voice replied.

"Wait 'til your granddaughter stands up here, you don't know how it feels to see them all grown up when it's been so long since you last laid your eyes on them, William."

"I'm only saying, what good does it do the lad who has no memory of you if you introduce yourself when there isn't any light for the boy to see your wrinkled face?" Jacob could tell the remark was half in jest and half meant to sting, and he got a vibe that his family wasn't at all close knit like a family should be.

"Well we shall have to remedy that." There was a shuffle, and Jacob heard shoes hit the ground, "Malcolm, fetch us some light." He heard one of the men stepping toward him. The footsteps came into the light, and a tall man with deep brown eyes and soft grey hair that hung about his shoulders and a full beard of fading black hair stood before him, "You look just like your mother, lad." Jacob could not tell if he was being complimented or appraised. "And I'm in there somewhere, I hope. Your mother says I am. I reckon she knows; she raised you!" The man stroked his fading beard and furrowed his wrinkled brow. Even the wrinkles in his skin seemed sharp and flawless in this light. He examined Jacob from head to toe and then broke into a smile; his white teeth gleamed like mirrors in the silver light.

The man opened up his arms and embraced the little boy. Jacob felt like he was going to be crushed under his powerful arms. It took him a moment to get the composure and the courage to return the gesture. Henry held him there for a few moments and then released him. "A strong lad you are, my boy. One day you'll be sitting in my place in this council."

Jacob wasn't sure if that was a good thing. Henry smiled and clapped Jacob on the shoulder, and his legs nearly buckled under him. He firmly grabbed Jacob's shoulder and gave a proud shake and then turned to go back to his seat. Malcolm had returned with three torches by now and was placing them around the council.

Now Jacob could see that he stood before his mother, his grandfather, and two other people, one of whom had to be William, and the other was rather old—extremely old.

The old man used to be very large and still looked imposing, but he also looked to be over one hundred years old. His mother had mentioned him before; the old man was the leader, not just of his clan, but of all the clans that were scattered around the globe. His name was Roth. Supposedly Roth was eight hundred years old. No one really knew for sure, but his mother said he had outlived his great grandchildren and had seen his entire line fall to ruin. There was no one to vouch for his actual age, and he would not mention it or how he had gained his longevity.

Malcolm and Henry took their seats, and the meeting resumed. Henry sat between Lucile and the old man, and Malcolm sat beside the man Jacob had assumed was William.

"Jacob, I am your great uncle, William. Henry is my older brother, and Malcolm is my boy." Jacob took a moment to remember that; he guessed that the really old man sitting in the middle of them was Roth but had no clue how he was related. If he really was that old, did it matter?

"The elder is of no special relation to you." William clarified for him as if he had read his mind.

"My name is Roth, William." The old man spoke in a condescending tone of archaic superiority. "You have lived long, but you still have elders. Just because I'm as old as dirt doesn't mean I cannot break you in half."

"You're slower than you think, Roth. I wouldn't challenge you, but I'd not be about challenging people myself if I had one foot in the grave." William replied.

"Careful boy!" Roth bellowed. His voice was dry, but it was deep and the air seemed to shift at his warning. "I've got more than enough fight left in me to bring all of Stirling down on you."

"But could you do it before we all get through the megalith port?" William shot back.

Malcolm gave a slight chuckle.

"Careful you don't take after your father, lad. He's not a good one to be taking after." Roth gestured to them both as if drunk. He was feeble in his appearance, but his voice was full of power and secrets.

"No disrespect Roth, I find the prospect of you and my father getting into it and sending both your souls to an early damnation a wee bit funny."

Roth sat back in his seat and forced himself to ease up. His eyes were yellow from age, and Jacob wondered how they still worked. He had talked about bringing down the whole castle; could he be a tenth generation of his family as well? Perhaps that's where his longevity came from. Often tenth generation members lived to be one hundred and fifty years old or better.

"Jacob," Roth said, "Do you know what it is you're standing in?"

Jacob looked around and noticed that the room was a lot bigger then he had thought. He was in the center, but the council was sitting in a set of stone chairs that marked the edge of one of many circles. The last circle in the ring was about forty meters from him and was marked by erect stones. He was standing in the center of an underground megalithic construction.

"It's a megalith sir." He replied after looking around a bit.

"Good, and do you know what it's good for?" Roth asked.

"No sir, I'm afraid I don't." Jacob answered.

"Some megaliths were built to protect, and some can be used to travel." Roth said, "Did you know that lad?"

"No sir." Jacob thought he had answered that question already, but to keep with formality he answered anyway.

"Avebury is surrounded by a large megalith that used to keep evil spirits out of the town. It's broken now, and that art has been lost. It was a place our ancestors set up to live in, and they had a bit of a problem with demons wanting to claim them as kin." Roth paused and drew a long dry breath. "Most of these are used to take you places, and some have other more esoteric uses that have been forgotten in the generations. Like the one in Avebury, for example; no one knows how to use it or how it once worked."

"What is this one made for?" Jacob asked.

"This one is a portal, lad. It can take you anywhere, granted you've been there before." Roth replied.

"How does it work?" Normally he would not have asked such a question, but Roth had brought this up and with this new knowledge Jacob assumed this would be used as part of the test.

"Any one of our bloodline can use it. The blood in your veins is the key, lad. The megaliths mark the doors—you just need a knob to open it with." The feeble old man got up from his seat and ambled into the light. He looked frailer once the moonlight showed on him—frail but terrifyingly wise.

Roth reached his withered hand into his cloak and pulled out a ring that had a fascinating symbol on it. Jacob tried to make out the symbol, but the light was too illusive and he could not focus on the emblem. "This is the door knob, lad. Not everyone in the family gets to have one. The magic to make such things has been lost. I'm giving this to you, son, but if you cannot prove you know how to use the family's magic, then I cannot let you keep it." He held it next to one that was identical on his white bony finger and then offered it to Jacob.

Jacob looked at the gold ring in the palm of Roth's hand and tried to study the pattern, but looking at it made his head hurt. The symbol, no, the *symbols* overlapped and seemed to move. Was this another trick of the light? Jacob reached out and took the ring from Roth. When he held it, he thought he heard whispers like someone chanting, but it was faint and nonsensical. The more he focused on the symbols, the more tangled they became, and the harder he tried to listen to the whispers, the less he could hear. It was almost like the thing was alive somehow and speaking to a part of him that he was not aware of. The more he tried to be aware of it and understand it, the more distant and obscure it seemed.

With a curious finger he traced the knot of symbols. In some places, the gold seemed red, and it almost felt warm to the touch. Then he remembered that he had seen the pattern before on a ring his mother sometimes wore. It had been a long time since she had worn it. He was probably five years old, and the pattern caught the same fascination as it was now.

He gave up on figuring it out and brought his eyes up to meet the Roth's faded gaze. "Thank you, sir."

"Now I suppose we might tell you what it is we expect," Roth said as he moved weakly to return to his seat.

"We've got two challenges for you, lad," William said as Roth took his seat. "Your first lies in Orkney, and the other is in Wilshire. If you make it through those tests, you'll need to find some way to make it to Newgrange. Once we're done explaining what you have to do, you'll only have until dawn to get it done, and it's already pushing midnight."

Jacob swallowed hard, trying to draw his attention away from the strange ring and pay attention. "What do I have to do?"

"Prove you can use the family's magic," Henry said, "And I don't mean the powers you got from your mother. We're talking about things like that ring you just got. You'll find what you need when you get to where you'll need it. And if you can use it right, you'll get to keep it."

"What am I looking for?" Jacob asked still not sure what they wanted him to do.

"You're looking for more door knobs. I cannot tell you what they look like, but that ring turns red when there's family magic around that's not in your possession," Henry explained. "You might have to wander around a bit to find these items, but once you learn to use the portals, you should be able to get into the general area by using the megaliths."

"Alright." Jacob said a little nervous, "How do I get started then?"

"We'll show you how to open a portal and get to where you're going, but you'll have to figure the rest out for yourself."

Jacob looked about the room. He had no idea what he was to do, but he understood that he was going to be on his own once he left the room. Before, he was very cold; now the light seemed to drain his warmth away. Shivering, he thought back on how many children had stood in his spot before; he reckoned he was not unique. He had known his whole life that his blood held a particular magic. Tonight he would find out how much he understood.

"Well," Jacob finally said after a moment of hesitation, the shivering had more or less forced it out before he meant to say it. "How do I get started?" The men seemed a bit surprised by how quickly the small boy had resolved to meet the task, but his mother only nodded stoically in approval.

After looking at each of the others for confirmation, Henry stepped down and came toward him, "First you have to put the ring on your finger."

Jacob looked down at the mysterious pattern once again and then gently slid the ring on. It was a little loose but he was not yet fully grown.

"Then you have to know what makes the magic work." Henry said as he came closer. "This one's simple, boy; the ring will open the portal if you speak a phrase. Others aren't so simple. Some of our magic has been sealed from us by the sands of time, and even Roth doesn't know how to use some of the relics."

"I just tell it to open the portal?" Jacob asked as if it could really be that simple.

"Well you're almost right, boy. You have to command it. Then the ring thinks you are opening a gate." Henry replied. "Your mother taught you to speak Latin, did she not?"

"Yes." Jacob replied.

He thought for a moment and put the clues together. He had to tell the ring to open a "gate," and he had to use Latin. That wasn't so hard. "Patefacio porta." He spoke softly.

"What's that, my boy? I can barely hear you." Henry asked. "You have to speak up; that little ring is old as time. It doesn't hear so well. You'll just have to speak louder." He grinned as he spoke. Henry was his grandfather, and the glimmer in his eyes was pure pride of the young boy standing in the moonlight.

"Patefacio porta!" Jacob said a bit stronger.

The room filled with a dim, silver light that emitted from an orb now in the center of the room instead of the small hole in the ceiling, and Jacob realized that he was not in the center of the room as he had thought. Just behind him a white circle covered in runes and symbols had appeared. "There's the portal, son." Henry pointed. "It came when you called for it. The longer you have that ring, the less you will have to command it. Eventually it will anticipate your orders."

"Where does it go?" Jacob asked as he stepped closer in amazement. For so long he had known this was possible, but now he could finally use it.

"This'll take you anywhere you want to go so long as you have been there once before." Henry explained. "You can't call a portal just anywhere, you understand. There has to already be one there, and you have to open it. But any open portal can take you to any location you can picture in your head."

"So if I go somewhere that isn't a portal?" Jacob asked.

"Well, there's tricks around that, boy, but until you learn a bit, you'll be stranded wherever you go that isn't a portal," Henry explained.

"And I have to go to Wilshire and Avebury?" Jacob confirmed.

"Aye, my boy. You know the way?"

"Aye. I know the way."

"Then off you go." Henry gestured to the glowing circle. "You need only think of the place you want to go, and it'll take you."

"Stonehenge, the Standing Stones of Stenness, the Ring of Brodgar? They're all portals?"

"I cannot tell you what they do, son." Henry replied. "You'll have to figure the rest out for yourself now. Remember, the ring will tell you when there's magic about. Listen to the little trinket."

"And I have until sunup?" Jacob asked. "Is that in Ireland, Scotland, or England?"

"You have until the first ray of sweet sunshine wakes Newgrange." Henry answered.

"I'll be there." Jacob said and then nodded. He looked up at his mother before he stepped into the portal. She gave a slight nod, and then he placed one foot at a time in the glowing circle and thought of the hillsides of Orkney, the Ring of Brodgar would be where he began his search.

CHAPTER 2

J acob had experienced some odd things in his life, but nothing was quite the
same as being hurled across the globe. Teleporting wasn't exactly the word for
it; it was more like flying—or flinging. Jacob had traveled so fast that it seemed
instantaneous, but he definitely knew that he had basically been thrown the whole
way, in some form other than his body. He got up from the soft grass. At least the
landing had been soft—it was certainly not smooth. As Jacob brushed off some of
the grass and tried to recover from the vertigo, he hoped that he would get better
at the landing part.

He stood up and looked around at the strange sight. The fluid in his inner ear
had not settled, and he stumbled as he tried to walk, and then he felt as if he might
vomit. He took a deep breath and steadied himself, trying to get his bearings. He
had managed to land in the center of the megalith. At night, the Ring of Brodgar
appeared quite different; he hardly recognized the place. Jacob stumbled forward
and found that his legs were just as confused as his head. Nearly falling, he managed his way to a large rock and leaned against it to get a grip. He took in a few
more deep breaths as he surveyed the menacing and eerie landscape. Once the
air had cooled him down, he looked at his ring and noticed that it was glowing a
faint red. Then he remembered that he was supposed to be looking for something.

Jacob searched for anything visible first and didn't see anything obvious. Of
course, if all these relics were going to be as small as the ring, it could take a while.
Not finding any obvious sign, he began to wonder in which direction he should go
first. His mind seemed to be set on east before he had even given much thought
on the matter. Something seemed to be murmuring inside his head. He could not
understand it, but he was somehow compelled to a certain direction. Jacob got the
feeling the ring was guiding his senses and thought it best to go with the feeling.
Hopefully, this was part of the test: to see if he could interact with the heirlooms
he was searching for. Or perhaps he was just hearing things.

He had not gone far when he found the relic. Down a gentle hill, lodged in
a large boulder was a sword. The weapon was beautiful and glinted in the moonlight as he approached it. Jacob knew it was what he had come to find as soon as

he saw it. The ring had changed to a bright red now, and the humming in his head had changed. He still didn't understand the hushed words, but the vibe was pleased. Maybe he wasn't hearing things. First he checked to make sure there were no traps or triggers; he had figured this would be harder. Assured it was safe, he stepped up on the large rock and grasped the sword by the hilt. He pulled on it and found it was firmly established. He tried once more with both hands, squatting and pulling on it with the force of his legs, but the blade didn't budge.

Remembering the phrase, the ring responded to Jacob began to conjure his Latin vocabulary. "Prodire!" *Come out.* And he tried again, but the blade either didn't respond to words or he was using the wrong one.

"Gladis!" *Sword.* Nothing.

"Setrucke!" *Cut.* He tugged on it and felt the blade slide and then caught again.

There was a subtle snap in the air, the glow of the ring dissipated and something in the sword seemed to react.

"Setrucke!" He commanded louder. Jacob took both hands and yanked the blade. Nothing happened. With both hands he clenched the blade's handle, and he felt the sword protest. "You're coming out," he declared as sweat dripped off his forehead. He focused, and felt something touch his mind, or rather, his mind escaped his body for a moment. Jacob gritted his teeth and forced the sword through the rock, as if he could cleave the boulder in two since the blade would not let go of it. There was a loud scraping sound, and the blade slid out of the rock, leaving a rather large gash where it had carved its way out. Jacob fell down as the sword cut through the side of the boulder, and he crashed to the ground.

He sat up slowly and shook off the fall. Then he grabbed the blade and examined it, comparing the mirror-smooth metal to the perfectly cleaved rock.

"So you can cut?" he asked the blade as he stood up. "But words don't work on you so how do I make you work?" Jacob stood and held it in the moonlight. It glimmered with a kind of raw power he had seen just a few minutes ago when his mother stood in the circle with him. Taking it with both hands above his head, he brought it down on the boulder. It clanged off sparking as it hit, only scraping the rock's surface. Looking at the blade Jacob noted that there was no damage at all. He thought to try again. Jacob lifted the blade once again. His mother had taught him how to use a sword, but this was a blade for a grown man, a tall and stout man, and the excess weight threw him off balance slightly.

He tried to recreate the feeling that had occurred before he cut through the rock. He willed the blade to cut and felt as if it had suddenly become an extension of him. As he brought it down, he focused hard on cutting the rock. This time, the cleaving sound of a guillotine rang out, and the blade went straight through the rock and hit the ground beneath it. A large part of the boulder fell off and thudded to the ground. Jacob had nearly cut it in half. And it was smooth—perfectly smooth.

Observing the cut, Jacob was impressed by the precision of the blade. The edges of the rock were so cleanly hewn that it could cut someone if they touched it. He curiously pressed his fingers against the side of the rock and found it was warm to the touch. Just to be sure he had not missed anything Jacob walked around the rock, and he found a sheath on the other side. The sheath was very plain at first glance, but Jacob could make out faded symbols that had been painted and pressed into the leather a very long time ago.

Thinking it best to put the blade away, he put it back in its place and then fastened the sheath around his torso. It had one strap that went over his shoulder and another that went around his waist. After tightening the straps as much as he possibly could—leaving the ends dangling about his knees—he headed back to the gate. Returning up the gentle incline was much more difficult now that he had the cumbersome package. He had to lean forward to keep the tip of the sword from hitting his ankles as he picked up his feet. But the walk didn't really seem like a challenge to Jacob. He wondered if the next task would be just as simple. All he had to do now was go to Stonehenge and search there. If the last relic was like these two, then this should be simple. He felt pretty confident that he could use these tools, though it was going to take a little getting used to.

The walk seemed longer on the return, but soon Jacob was back at the Ring of Brodgar. However, something felt wrong, and Jacob got a disturbing feeling that the test wasn't over. Reaching high to grasp the blade and awkwardly pulling it out Jacob cautiously approached the monument. He scanned the area but could not see anything that might threaten him. The feeling was still there, though. He wished his father were here. The curse had come early to him, and he had been attacked by demons in the middle of the night before.

His father knew how to handle them though. He had taught Jacob a few things, but he said that there were things he couldn't know about until he was old enough. Jacob tugged on an amulet his father had given him as he stepped closer. He wasn't sure what it was, but it was supposed to help keep evil spirits away. The small gem wasn't always effective, and Jacob wondered if being part demon nullified any power it may have had. As he began to enter the ring he felt a force repelling him. It was subtle at first, but it amplified as soon as he stepped past the towering rock and threw him back out of the ring.

Jacob rolled across the ground, dropping the sword so it wouldn't hurt him. Once he had stopped he looked around frantically. He was certain that a demon was after him and the only thing he had was that sword. *The sword!* Jacob thought. It was forged by his ancestors, and they were more demon than he was. Maybe he could cleave it in two. He scrambled back to the sword and picked it up with both hands.

Trembling and drawing panicky breaths, he looked side to side for an attacker. But still, he didn't see anything. He hesitated for a moment and decided to try to get out before the spirit could attack him again. He sprinted for the circle, but once again, an invisible force threw him back. Jacob did not roll this time. Instead, he landed flat on his back with his arms and legs spread out. He coughed a few times and drew in a rough breath. He rolled over and picked up the sword again. As he stood up, the thought crossed his mind that this wasn't a demon, but rather a spell that he had to break.

For a moment he was relived, and then he realized that he didn't know the first thing about spells.

It's okay . . . maybe this will be as simple as teleporting, Jacob thought. *But what is the doorknob?*

Then he realized the sword was the only thing he had that could work. Perhaps the spell was a force field and he simply needed to cut it. *Can this sword really cut anything?* It was worth a shot.

Jacob got to the edge of the stones and readied the blade with both hands. He focused on cutting and poured all the rage of his little body into his motions and assaulted the thin air. His charge was thwarted, and he was again pushed back. The third time was more surprising than the first had been. He was sure he had figured out the riddle and having the same thing happen was a bit disappointing. The impact might have been what jarred his mind, *You're not cutting rocks anymore, Jacob.* He laid there a moment and thought of the simplicity of this notion. He already knew what he was going to do. Jacob didn't really know how he understood, but he knew this time he would make it work.

Jacob collected himself and walked up to the edge of the circle where the force was gently pushing against him. He paused for a moment and focused; he inched a little further until he could feel the energy around him attempting to force him back again. Then he lifted the sword as if he was blocking another blade, forcing his will into it and whirled himself into the circle. The air in front of him turned to a thin blue mist that came hurling at him. There was a whipping sound that was followed by a crack like a gunshot as the blade met the air and whatever was pushing him back before had missed. The sword glowed white, and the fine vapor disappeared. This time Jacob was standing inside the circle, and there was no invisible force flinging him around like a rag doll. Satisfied with his accomplishment, he summoned the portal and strode toward it. He stepped in and set his heart on Stonehenge.

That same instant he was there. This time he did not fall, but his head was still swimming, and this time a strong feeling of nausea welled up in his stomach. Jacob quenched the urge to puke and took a deep breath to calm his nerves. He gained his composure and looked down at his ring. It was glowing faintly again, not as bright as it had before, but there was something near. Again, the feeling came upon him, accompanied by a whisper, to take a specific direction to find the relic. This time, it was not such a short walk, however. He inspected the fence that surrounded the ancient site and decided that it was not made to be climbed. He took his new sword and thought about how much trouble he might get in for cutting through the fence, but he didn't have any other way out. He needed to get to Avebury, and this was the closest portal.

He slowly lifted the sword and focused. Jacob forced his will into the sword and swung through the fence like it was tin foil. Then he swung it again to create a hole he could crawl through. He stepped out to the tourist side of the fence and peered into the distance. This was going to be a long walk. Jacob continued for some hours until he could see the light of the sun peering over the horizon, pinkening the sky. He was further east than his final destination in Newgrange, but his time was running out. The ring was glowing stronger now, but unless he could manage a portal back to Stonehenge, he was going to be stranded.

Looking over the gentle grassland, he noticed a large boulder in a peculiarly upright position. Scanning the area, he saw more in like fashion. He had walked all the way to Avebury. There was no way he could get back in time, even the instantaneous transport from Stonehenge to Newgrange couldn't help him. It had been a long night, and lugging that sword around had become a chore.

There must be a way or else they wouldn't have set this up. Jacob thought. Rather than give up, he walked to the stone that marked the edge of the town and thought for a second. He looked out and followed the ring to the east. About fifty meters away on another standing stone, something caught his eye. The illusive voice in his head chimed, and he knew it was what he was looking for. It could have easily been nothing, but the ring granted him special discernment and understanding. It was almost as if he recognized the trinket that rested on the boulder.

He hustled to get to it, shifting the sword to a more comfortable position. Getting there, he found a pendent on a gold chain that had been hung around the top of the rock. "I've gotcha now," he whispered as he took it off the rock. He slipped it over his head and then looked toward the horizon to behold the sun struggling to peer over the edge of the world.

He didn't have much time left, just minutes before the sun would rise in Newgrange. He looked at the pendant and noticed it had the same twisting, illusive pattern that was on the ring. "I've got to make it to Newgrange." He sighed and turned back in the direction he had come from. He paused a moment and looked down at the ring. "Perhaps you can help me," he suggested. It was inert. Then he thought hard and forced his will into the ring like he had with the sword. If it could show him where magic was, then maybe he could get it to show him where another portal might be.

Both to his surprise and dismay it worked. The ring triggered a compass in him that pointed to the nearest gate. Unfortunately, it urged him toward Stonehenge. "Can you just take me to Stonehenge?" He asked sarcastically to the ring.

Then he stopped and thought about what he was had just done. He took the medallion and compared the symbols, still unable to make out what they really were. Henry's words echoed, *"There are tricks around that."* Jacob grinned, "The ring can't, but you can, can't you?" He had the sense that if he could force his will into the ring and the sword that he could force his will into this thing, too. And since it had the same symbol as the ring, perhaps they were supposed to be used together. He focused on where the ring was telling him to go and commanded that the amulet bring him there.

Before he really knew what was happening, a brilliant flash emitted from the amulet, and when he could see again, he was rolling in the odd circle of ancient stones. It was a neat trick, but it was more nauseating than teleporting, also unexpected. He looked around just to be sure he was where he thought he was. A small group of tourists, who had gathered to watch the sun rise, had gathered around the hole he had cut through the fence and were staring open-mouthed and wide-eyed at the small boy and his brilliant appearance.

Jacob felt sick again, worse this time, but he didn't have time to wait around, and these people who had seen him would have questions that he didn't care to answer. Some of them would be questions he'd rather like to ask. Scrambling to his feet, he stepped in the center of the monument trying to move quickly before anyone had the chance to ask questions or get a good look at him. His head was spinning from the jump he had just made, his stomach was in knots, and his legs were shaking. Holding his right hand with his ring up, he summoned the portal. As he jumped in, he recalled all the images from the inner rooms of Newgrange, and one sickening moment later, he was there in the dark, cold, stone room.

The floor was cold, and he did not manage to land standing up. This time his stomach had had enough; he heaved, and bile splashed on the tile in front of him.

"I told you the boy would make it!" He heard Henry exclaim.

"Well done, lad." The stale voice of Roth trickled through the room.

He looked up. The room was spinning, and his watering eyes were not helping.

There was a faint light and then a brighter light as someone lit a torch. It was Malcom; he carried the torch around the room and began to light others that were hanging on the wall.

Jacob coughed and spat to remove the lingering bile and mucus out of his throat and mouth and stood up, shaking, as the room spun around him. Slowly he wiped the water from his eyes and the remaining bile from his chin. He was sure he did not look impressive, but he didn't really care right now. He wanted to lay back down on the floor where it was cold and didn't move so much.

"The teleporting takes some getting used to." Henry commented, "Just shake it off and practice a bit later."

"He figured out how to use the amulet, and he brought back the blade." William said, "But the lad cut it pretty close on the time limit."

"Has anyone ever made it before there was twilight in the sky?" Henry answered.

"Aye, if you don't remember; it was I." William retorted.

"And if you didn't remember, boy, you had set out at dusk, and it took you almost till dawn to get back." Roth said in his superior manner. Jacob would have thought him arrogant, but just by looking at the feeble old man, he knew Roth had the authority to put his words just how he wanted.

"Forgive me for being normal, old man. I didn't have the advantage of powers like you and the lad there." William argued back. "That's why he made it. He's got more power in his blood than most of us."

"What are you getting at?" His mother asked.

"It comes more natural to him; he should have made it shorter."

His mother raised an eyebrow and took on a lecturing posture, "The ability to command these tools is not dependent on tenth-generation powers! Quit being jealous, William; you always have been. You're even jealous of your own son when it was you who gave him the gift. Jacob made it, he made it faster than you, and so did everyone else in this room."

"You all have the powers." William tried.

"I don't," Henry said. "You better close your mouth, brother, before it gets you in trouble."

That was the end of the debate. Roth stood up and held his hand up in a silencing gesture. "You see why we don't have much family?" He said. "You're always at each other's throats, and that's how the killing starts. That's why we never get together. You've got to put the past behind you and get the chip of your shoulder. Move on! We have more problems than either of your clans can solve, but you both sure helped in making them."

Then he lowered his hand, "Jacob passed the trial. He's of our blood, and he knows how to use the family's magic. The lad is entitled to have access to our magic. Barring any objections, I'm bestowing on him the power of a member of the council."

"I object," William said.

"Overruled." Roth spat back, dragging out the last syllable.

"You have become stubborn in your old age, Roth, that you would so quickly disregard my opinion," William shot back.

"I disregard you because you disrespect me. And you don't even have grounds for your objection except petty bickering between you and your brother. If you were capable of producing a legitimate issue, I would hear it, but I already know your case! Even your own son agrees he should be on the council." Roth silenced him.

"The council must be balanced." William made one final attempt.

"And next year your granddaughter will be taking the trial and, if she passes, shall be installed to balance it. Or don't you have faith in her?" Roth said with exhausted irritation, turning away from him and approaching Jacob.

"Lad, the council is a great responsibility. You understand that, but you don't yet know what it is for, do you?"

"No, sir, I don't," Jacob answered.

"The council is selected and chosen to try to right the wrongs of our past. We're only half human and the grace of God only goes so far on our souls. The father of our wretched clan is a son of Satan himself. Our fathers spent an eternity in Heaven before the world was created, and they are doomed to spend a second eternity in Hell for their treachery. Alas, a father's sins pass to his son. We cannot be redeemed unless we can find a way to renounce the blood of our fathers. But the prophesy was given that: 'One who is like us, who has been divine in mortal form, shall kneel before the Judge and remove the mark of shame and sin, which our fathers bore unto us and which we bare by our nature, and cleanse our transgressions from us so that we may stand as righteous men in the presence of a Holy God.'"

Jacob was familiar with this prophesy. He understood this ceremony, but he also understood, for some of the people in this room, he was the answer to that prophesy.

"Our entire line has to be paid for, and that's what the council works for." Roth continued in his sharp, ancient whisper of a voice. "One man can't be saved from our line unless we all go with him. Rumors and ancient prophecies tell of a savior for our kind, but until he is revealed, the council is our only hope to have salvation. Hell isn't a pleasant place, lad, and I don't want to see my kinfolk burn just because they were born of a demon, do you?"

"No, sir."

"Then do you solemnly swear by the blood of your fathers that you'll do everything in your power to pay the blood debt that they owe? That you will live your life so as not to incur any advancement of the debt already on your shoulders and those of your kinsmen? And do you swear that you'll be dedicated during your life on earth to prove your forefathers have no claim on your blood nor your soul nor any stake on the rest of your family?"

Jacob knew it went without saying; they wanted him to be their savior. Nobody would say it, but he knew that they were all hoping. The signs of the end-of-times were beginning to appear, and their family had one foot stuck in the doorway to Hell while time was running out. It was a great responsibility to be on the council, and rarely did they offer the position to new blood. He swallowed before answering the question. He was being asked no more than those before him, but the weight of their expectations beyond what they were willing to ask pressed the air around him.

Finally, after only a few moments that seemed like hours, Jacob delivered his answer, "I swear." He said it so cold and resolutely, you would have thought he was the savior for their blood.

"Welcome to the family." Roth said, "And congratulations on becoming a member of the council at such a young age."

"We had best be moving." Henry said. "I've had about enough of this crowd as I can stand for one night. Unless more urgent business works up, the council will reconvene under the second full moon from now." With that he waved his hand and opened a portal in the middle of the room much like the ones Jacob had used the night before.

His mother stepped down and embraced him. She wasn't cold; she looked like his mother again. Her features were soft again and her voice was warm. "I'm proud of you, son. Let's go home and rest. We can talk about this later." Then she turned him toward the portal. "Just think of your back yard out by the porch." Then she gently urged him forward and followed with one hand on his shoulder. He entered and found himself standing in his own yard with his mother as the sun was peering over the horizon. All the colors blurred in his head, and he felt as if he would vomit again. He began to wonder how long it would take to get used to this.

CHAPTER 3

One year to the day had passed. He was thirteen now, or would be tomorrow. This was the age his father deemed the beginning of adulthood. Historically, in his family, it was also the age when the demonic attacks started to get worse and more frequent. Since the trial of his mother's family last year, he had learned a lot about using certain powers and two or three spells pretty well. The thought of more demons coming after him was intimidating. He had a slight advantage over his father and his father's fathers. But that advantage could also prove to be a great weakness as well. Contemplating his future and the road ahead, he lay in his bed and gazed at the dark ceiling above him. The last year had gone by so fast.

He had learned so much about his mother's magic. She had been very urgent in teaching him the tricks and spells and various alchemies that her people used. It was odd sometimes, and a lot of the rules didn't make sense. Some spells could be used by any man and others could only be used by tenth-generation family members. Some of the relics worked for all his family, and some only worked for certain bloodlines or for tenth-generation members.

Most of the spells were lost magic of old and not specific to his family. He had learned a lot of old alchemy magic. But more important, he had learned a lot of family patents for enchanting items, and he had taken a fascination for the lost art of enchanted forgery of weapons. Once he was fifteen he would be allowed into the library to do his own research. His mother had taught him so much, but there was far more locked away in the history of his family than even Roth knew. Jacob was just itching to try his hand at some of the forgery he had been learning about.

Jacob had heard stories of his aunts, uncles, and cousins who had spent their entire lives sealed away trying to unlock part of the forgotten knowledge. Some of the ancient texts were written in codes and languages that died with the authors. Others had magic seals that only opened to the presence of a particular division of their bloodline. Some texts were spells, and others were instructions to use certain relics. The problem with the relics was that they had an array of uses, and many were missing instructions—or were just missing. There were also large volumes of history that told where some of these were, or a general idea of where they had been lost. But time has a way of moving things. Many of the relics were not where they should be. Some that were secure were lost, and others that were lost were now in museums. And to make matters worse, these histories were written in the language of the Fallen.

He had been excited about today, the coming of age of his father's side. But there had been nothing special. His father had never talked about it like his mother had, and he was beginning to wonder if it was simply an increase of demonic activity in his life. Shuddering at the thought, he rolled over and tried to sleep. Even with all the magic he had learned, he felt so inadequate to fight hordes of demons. As he began to slip away into an uncomfortable dream, his door slid open. Jacob jumped out of his semi-slumber and met the source of this new fear with determination and collection that surprised himself.

"Are you going to cut me?" His father, Drake, asked, nodding at Jacob's hand that had instinctively gone for Jade, the blade he had received last year from his mother's family.

"No, sir." He answered and relaxed. "I was just startled a bit."

"I was the same way." He stepped in and Jacob saw the familiar coat his father always wore into battle. "It's time, son."

He tossed him a lump of something. Jacob could not see well enough in the dim light that crept through the doorway to make it out. It expanded and landed in a heap beside him on the bed. Running his hands over it, he felt cool leather. He smelled leather also. It was old, really old. He picked it up and turned on a lamp. It was an old brown leather jacket, very well worn.

"It belonged to your great-grandfather, Jacob. Our family had been bound to servitude to Satan for many generations, and he severed that bond, but it was replaced by a new curse. We were being used as tools to traverse between the realm of darkness and the world we stand in. Our forefathers took blood in the name of evil. They were Wraiths, long-lived and terrifying."

In the dim light, he could tell his father had just finished shaving. Drake went through razors faster than most men shaved. Each night before his father went to bed, he would shave and every evening at supper Drake appeared to have a three-day growth of his wild red beard around his face.

"The servitude passed to every firstborn. But your forefather Jacob, who I named you after, would not turn." And there was sign that his father's family had placed their hope of salvation in him as well. "He would not give in to the darkness; he hunted down and killed his ancient ancestors. Jacob killed as many as he could find, and the Curse of the Servant became the Curse of the Defiant. Just as the sin of his father's passed to him, it passes to us. By ancient contract, we are the servants of darkness, but by the new pact, we may fight to regain our place in eternity.

"Satan sent his demons to retrieve what had been deeded to him, but they failed. Though he carried the mark of his fathers, God took pity on him and gave him the strength to stand against the evil. The demons feared him, and so it is custom to give his jacket to the next warrior. It will protect you for now, but not forever. It's

25

time you get to see what you're up against." Drake's steel-colored eyes peered out from beneath his furrowing red brows as he introduced Jacob to the next step in his life. They boy was scared, but as long as his father was there, he knew he was safe.

"What are we doing?" Jacob asked part in excitement and part in hesitation.

"The forces of darkness are all around us." His father replied. "They prey on men, and they have a grudge with our family. In your future, you will have to do battle. Sometimes you may have to throw out demons from men or homes. Other times, your life may be directly attacked. It's a terrible curse, but all we have to do is live. We keep the blood alive until Judgment Day, and we will be set free. God can pardon our forefathers' sin, but their deal with the Devil must not be fulfilled. As of yet, we remain in debt to the Devil by virtue of being our fathers' sons. The end is near though; the Devil is anxious, and he has been trying hard to bring settlement. Our house is forced to shoulder the responsibility of our fathers' folly, but we are also granted great strength so long as we defy the evil our fathers bound us to.

"Tonight I'm going to teach you how to survive."

The words fell on him like a large weight. Jacob was about to carry the torch of his family's curse. It wasn't something he had a choice in, there was no upside, and failure would be worse than death. He nodded, slid out of his bed, and put on a thick pair of pants. He threw on a shirt and then slid into the jacket. It was a little big for him. As he went to put Jade over his shoulder his father stopped him.

"I know you've got power from your mother's side son, but these monsters use worse than that blade, and that ring will light up like a beacon and bring them right to you. You'd better leave that here."

Jacob let Jade rest against the wall where it had been, "So what do we use?"

"It's almost like the stories of hunting vampires." His father began, "They are mostly creatures of the night, but every once in a while, one will become emboldened or even summoned to wreak havoc during the day. Water helps keep them at bay." He reached into his coat and brought out a small orb of glass that contained water. "There is no such thing as 'holy water' son, all things in God's creation are clean." He handed the orb to Jacob

"The water is a symbol of cleansing. Applied to yourself, it will protect you; or splashed on a demon, it can drive them away. I wish I could say this was all we needed, but in this kind of fight, nothing is guaranteed to work.

"A second defense we have is incense." He continued as he held out a small iron ball with holes bored in it that was attached to a chain. "The design is mine, a button on the bottom ignites the incense. It is a pleasing smell to God, and it carries your prayers to Heaven. We are cut off because of our sin, a contract that we are bound to, but our Father still loves us. He will listen in times of need.

"Another method, a last method, you can stab their heart with a silver stake." He again presented the tool to his son, it was like a nail, but sharp on both ends. "The stakes are like the nails used to crucify the Son of God, and the silver is a symbol of purity. The objects themselves have no real power, but the demons have a degree of respect for them.

"Finally—and most important—the Word." He gave the small leather Bible he had always carried to Jacob with reverence. The book was tattered and very worn. "The book itself has no power; it won't frighten them away or send them to Hell. You must learn it and keep it in your heart. Carry the book as your guide, but it will only help you if it's in your heart. These creatures know this book better than you ever will. It is important to know the truths contained in it so that you can see through the lies they will assault you with.

"We have been cut off from God by our forefathers, but this Word is true no matter who speaks it. And it is the way He speaks to us even when we can't speak to him. Learn it, use it, and let it light the darkness. Son this is the most important thing you can have, but you have to understand you've been born with a curse. For most, faith and this Word will stop a demon dead in his tracks, but for you and me and for your firstborn, it is only a barrier. It can and it will be broken by those bold enough to challenge you. But God has shown grace on us. We do not suffer this burden ill equipped, but because the sins of a father pass to his sons, we are still cut off from mercy until the day of Return. We have been given a small portion of power to compensate for the curse and that, son, is our grace. Our souls are not under the protection of mercy, but our bodies have keener senses, and we are more able to face their attacks. You will be able to withstand attacks that would crush a normal man. Our bodies have been made strong because our souls are nearly lost."

Jacob looked at the orb of water and the stake. They seemed ordinary. The orb was smaller than a cue ball and the stake was a six-inch, double-sided nail made of silver. He took the incense ball and looked at his father, "I designed the chain so that you can wrap it around your waist and clip one of the links like a belt." He placed the orb in his jacket pocket, and then he reached out to accept the Bible.

"Why do we hunt them if they are already looking for us?" He asked as he situated the incense around his waist.

"We have been cursed to always have conflict, but as a small protection we are given power. It is only right to use that power to help the weak and stand between the forces of darkness and those they would wish to harm," Drake explained.

"Doesn't God have angels to do that?" Jacob asked.

"Angels come in many different forms, son. God uses many people, even unlikely people to do great things. Even as you will see angels, so those God gives you to protect will call you an angel. Satan owned our family, and now we are the first line between him and those around us. They will use that against you, they will attack people to draw you out, and they will attack those close to you. It is a terrible thing, son, but this is your future." He paused for a moment, "This may be your future, but it is not your hope. Your hope is not in this life but the next. We will make it to Heaven, son; be strong, and one day we will stand before God and claim our part of salvation. Just as He was made to bear scars for our sakes, we must also bear scars for His name."

Jacob took a second for the weight of this duty to set in. It wasn't really fair. His mother's side of the family was looking to him for redemption, and his father's line depended on him to carry the torch. So much responsibility—the weight of human lives had been placed on his shoulders—and at such a young age. He was barely thirteen, and he already felt more weight of responsibility than most ever would.

"What if I ca . . ." Jacob started, but he couldn't finish. What if he failed? He knew what would happen. His mother's side would be disappointed, but they could still look for a savior. But his father and all the ancestors before him would burn.

"Son, I don't ask you for a miracle," his father said bringing himself eye level with his son. "I only ask that you try your best. Don't give in when you feel like quitting, and you'll be fine."

He stood up and opened his jacket and showed a place where he carried his own stake in the inside of the coat. "The stake goes on your left side and Bible goes on your right. You'll do fine, son."

CHAPTER 4

Two years of demon hunting has a chilling effect on a child. He was still young, somewhere between leaving his boyhood and becoming a man. All of his features had darkened. He wasn't sure if it was because of the crazy late nights he was always pulling with his father or the amount of time he spent dealing with magic and evil or if it was simply growing up. His fair boyish skin was becoming rough and oily, and his hair was courser now, but he was still far from rugged.

Jacob had learned how to handle himself and knew how do perform a "simple" exorcism. Simple meant that a malicious spirit had entered a person or a place on its own volition. It got a bit more complicated if the person invited or did something to provoke it into residing within their body or home.

But today he was furthering his knowledge of his mother's family. Jacob had finally grown into the heirlooms of his mother's side and now wore them often. Last month when he had turned fifteen, he had been given access to the archives. There were so many questions in so many old books. It was a pity that there were nearly two hundred different languages in them, some so unique that the only known sample of the language was in just one book.

He did enjoy the library; he had outgrown the small caves he once explored, but the smell of the books also enticed his sense of adventure with a similar aroma of oldness. Reading the books gave him the same feeling of discovering something that had been forgotten. In some ways it was just like crawling in the darkness of the earth; the books had an earthy scent about them, and working his way through translations was like wiggling through the small spaces he had outgrown not so long ago. The library was massive. Like the secret tunnels under the Stirling Castle he had been in the night he had passed the trial, this place was secluded underground. The entrance was the ruined Donnotar Castle that had not been restored to the capacity that Stirling had. This place once served as a fortress, isolated on the North Sea and connected to the mainland by a thin strip of earth. Now it housed an extensive collection of his clan's history.

On the north side of the cliff there was a large cave that overlooked the sea. This area was known as the upper study. There were several stone tables in the room; all had checkerboard patterns carved into them. The ones near the opening had chess pieces on them. Some of the pieces were out of place in ongoing games. You might find two people playing a game, or you might see a piece move every once in a while. Someone who wanted to play might move a white piece to start a game, and anyone else who wished to challenge them would move a black piece. In this particular method of playing, the opponents might never know who they were playing against, and a single game could take months.

Deep under him in the basement of the castle, the forge was still intact, and beneath that, in the secret passages, was where the actual library was located. The library consisted of the lower study and the archives sort of joined together. Many more passages lay under the castle, but Jacob had no clue where they went.

The only other place he had been was to the Oasis. One of the tunnels surfaced in a magic garden on the main land. It was a small collection of rare trees and flowers. It was very beautiful, one of the few places in the facility that was outside. In the middle was a still pond with a willow growing out of the center. Steppingstones to the tiny island under the willow lay throughout the pond. On the far side was another construction that descended again into the dark underground. Jacob did not know what was under there, but he had been told not to meddle with it.

Still unfamiliar with the facility, he remained in the lower study, partly because it was close to the books and partly for the help the librarian gave him in his studies. He had begun studying the Scripts of Bolor, a collection of incantations and charms. Bolor had gathered and collected knowledge of the fading and now lost arts, and had compiled his research in Latin. Not only were the spells very useful, but in Bolor's collection were many keys to understanding far older works by great wizards. Most of the family scholars used his collection as a guide to studying all else in the library. One thing Bolor was unable to scratch was the language of the angels. Each of the Fallen had written books of either spells or prophecies or dark forgery. But very little was known about the content of these books. Out of the alleged two hundred and thirty-three Books of the Fallen, only one hundred and forty-nine had been found, and only sixty had been opened. The fact that they knew so very little about the Books of the Fallen fascinated Jacob and he intended to decode the language and unlock the full potential of his family's power. The *Book of Anzel* was the only one to have been translated completely.

The funny thing about the language of the angels is that there are five hundred and eighty-eight symbols much like an alphabet. Many of the symbols have the same sound, and some cannot be pronounced by humans. Consequently, there could be seven different ways to write one word. But each spelling gave it a new meaning, sometimes opposite and sometimes not related. For example, the word for "rope" and "tree" in the language of the angels sounded the same, but on paper, they had none of the same symbols. This being the case, there were only eighty-four known words (seventy-seven that were pronounceable), and each word could be spelled up to seven different ways. Thus eighty-four same-sounding words became five hundred and eighty-eight words with different meanings.

The vocabulary was small, and it was odd that the language had just as many symbols as it had words. However, none of the symbols could form a word alone. The spelling of the word and the context of the word and the preceding word(s) and following word(s) often changed the meaning completely, and so the study of the Fallen was something left for more advanced scholars. For now, there was much Jacob was learning from the simple lessons of Bolor. He would love to take one of the volumes home, but all of the books had to stay in the library. He would spend his weekends in the great stone hall, researching and copying down symbols and directions to practice at home. Nearly every night now he had to go with his father on a hunt, and that took time away from his studies.

More often than not they would find nothing, but the encounters they did find were terrifying. A few weeks ago a spirit singled him out as he was walking the hillside near the Stonehenge portal. It was his first encounter without his father there to protect him. He broke the orb of water on his chest and prayed the creature would not touch him. It stopped, but it would not leave so he pulled out Jade and found out that the blade worked quite well even though its forgery was from the darker side of magic.

He had learned about the different types of evil spirits. There were Shadows, like the one that had attacked him, that lurked in dark spaces and clung to the night. The Shadows did not so much have a physical form, but Jade was made to cut non-physical things. There were Wraiths also. Wraiths used to be human, and for lack of a better term, sold their souls to the devil. Many of his ancestors had been made into Wraiths, but most of them had been killed by his fathers before him.

It was rare to see a full-fledged demon. They were all considered "demons," but demon was like a rank somewhat like a commander. They were the first to fall with Satan, and a full-fledged demon was impossible to kill. Defeating them meant you survived. Demons plotted and schemed with their master and walked the earth when they pleased. They were responsible to maintain their own legion of Wraiths and Shadows, and each Wraith or Shadow was called by the name of the demon it was bound to. Finding out which demon had dominion over a given area was difficult because the records were obscure, and the minions didn't give out names freely. Jacob was hoping to be able to look in the ancient histories one day and puzzle out which demon his line came from.

The librarian, Rain, had spent many, many years studying in these dark halls. She knew more than most in the family; sometimes it seemed she knew more than Roth. Her job was credited to only the wisest, and she had proven to be that. Though she had been in the library for nearly two centuries, she had not aged a day. The halls had a way of slowing time for the one entrusted with its care. It was common for a librarian to remain in the position for several centuries. Rain was barely older than Jacob when she was appointed to the position. She was now nearly two hundred years old, but she still had the look and energy of a youth. Her history was obscure, and no one really knew how she fit into the clan's bloodline. Jacob had known her for a brief time and envied the eternal youth she possessed; when he died she would still not have aged a day. But then he would think about how dreadfully lonely it would be to live that long and to see all your friends and family pass away while you were stuck within the confines of the castle.

Being so used to the grounds and all the contents of the books, Rain was very helpful in understanding some of the more complex ideas behind the ancient magic. Her mastery was due partly to studying so long and part because she actually knew the magic inside and out. The process was as much science as it was art. There were many spells that were strict about how and when they were used, but there were others for which one could substitute ingredients and use nearly anywhere. Rain did a good job explaining these when he had questions. His mother, of course, had a wide knowledge of these arts, and she helped him at home, but he found that he got much more help from the books and having the resources at hand to practice.

He closed the book and picked it up to return it. It was time to go home again, and he would have to wait a week before he could come back. He could not wait until his sister, Sarah, would be old enough to come study with him. She had been inducted last year, and their younger brother, Dominick, was going to face the trial in two months. He could not wait to bring them here to show them the wonders of their ancestors. However, Sarah had almost two more years and Dom still had to pass the indoctrination and reach the age of maturity. In the meantime, he was enjoying learning, and he spent many hours practicing things he had learned. He still had to attend school, but he learned to work quickly and stay ahead so he could use his time at home for learning family secrets.

It was also important to stay ahead because often he would miss a day of school due to being out chasing spirits until it was nearly dawn. School was important, but there were other things that took a higher priority. His teachers would have been stricter about his attendance, but he was at the top of his class. Jacob loved learning and was far beyond his peers. Despite not having the proper study hours, he always made the top grade. It was this same enthusiasm that drove him to learn the forgotten secrets of his mother's family.

The council had already declared him the chosen one to redeem them. They had been impressed with his abilities, and the fact that he was a demon hunter by blood gave them hope that he would be the great hero to bring virtue to their blood. Jacob understood the honor it was to carry the burden, but he also wished he could be normal. So many children fanaticized about being something great. Well, he was, and he'd have given anything just to be normal. He loved studying the arts and magic of his mother's family, but he'd even give that up just to be normal. In truth, he had grown up too fast, something he would never have the chance to repeat. Childhood was something he never really could experience.

It was wrong for so much responsibility to be thrust onto a boy so young, and it was wrong that he was expected to lift two curses. It was wrong, it wasn't fair, but Jacob understood that quitting held worse consequences. For him, it was imperative that he fulfill both curses; it was his only way to live, the only way he could escape eternal fire. It was a grim fact, but he was bound to Hell twice, once from each of his parents' bloodlines. He and his progeny now shared a double curse of part man, part demon, demon hunter. Jacob was the first to carry the double burden, and he vowed he would be the last. It would be years before he would have a family, but he had already sworn to protect them, which that meant he had to clear any hold Hell had to his blood.

"Are you finished?" Rain asked as he walked up to the stone table that mostly blocked the entrance to the area of the library where the books and scrolls were kept. She had not aged a day in almost two centuries, and she was very friendly, impossibly pleasant to look at, and helpful. There was, though, an invisible wall around her that whispered of secrets. Rain had a curious appearance and always seemed fey and stoic, almost like his mother except a lot more secluded. Her hair was white-blond; at least that is the color Jacob decided it was. It was rather hard to tell. It was not a faded white from age, rather a pure white that blended all the colors of light together and at the same time divided the spectrum into ambiguous shades of reds, pinks, and blues.

In the torchlight of the halls, her hair seemed a bold blond with red streaks of the evening sky, and when the sun shown on it her locks, they turned platinum and became tinged with blue and gold. But the way she appeared now it had a watery copper hue to it, absorbing and reflecting the light from the furnace on the far side of the room when it swayed. The dress she wore was said to have been woven by angels, and it behaved much like her hair; reflecting the attitude of the air around her.

Jacob placed the large book on the table and withdrew himself with a sigh. He looked up and saw her golden eyes turned down on him. It was nearly impossible to know what she was thinking, she hid her expressions exceptionally well and never smiled. "No, I'll be back next weekend." It was the same thing he had said every Sunday night since he was allowed into the archives. All week long he would look forward to the smell of the old dusty books, he had a fascination with the lost arts of his family, but he also found some of the knowledge was useful against the spirits he would have to fight. Then he did feel like it was his job to know all he could about his ancestors, being deemed the savior he had to . . .

So he studied; he studied ahead of his classes in school, and he studied through his legendary history. Every weekend he dutifully spent in the library, studying under Rain's instruction; it was not long before they became quite close friends. By the time he was eighteen, he could craft a blade like Jade, and he could work calculus equations in his head. Fighting Wraiths and Shadows had become second nature, and Roth had deemed that his deeds would surely bring their blood the honor of pleading their lives before God. As the leader of the clans, Roth gave Jacob the title of the "Chosen One."

For such an astounding young man, he had his own problems. Pretending to be normal was a problem. Everyone else in his classes were worrying about what to do once school was over, which universities they should attend, or what they should do with their lives. As much as Jacob wanted to choose his course, he did not have that problem. His life had been set in stone. It was impossible to explain to his teachers that he had no plans to go to a university. He told them that he had just not decided on his career, and they hurried him to make a choice.

Being such a unique individual he had several unique habits. He always wore a little red, dried up flower on his jacket collar, and he always wore the same jacket his father had given him. The flower was a sign of life, the color was a symbol of the blood of the Son of God, and the particular type of extremely rare flower produced seeds that cured many different illnesses. It was a Vita Lily, said to have grown under the shade of the Tree of Life. The flower was incredibly hard to grow, and the only known place it would grow naturally was in remote Chinese mountains. It was so rare that scientists almost did not even know of its existence. Some of the more skilled potion-makers in his family had managed to grow some in Ireland in their secret garden. But the people who knew about this blossom were few and far between.

Because he always spent his time studying, he had very few friends to speak of, and he used the term *friend* loosely. Truthfully, the closer someone was to him, the more they would risk, but Jacob feared a long and lonely life more so than his constant waking to face of evil. He was a young man now, almost an adult. The last thing that remained of his boyish face was his grin and the wide-eyed expression of curiosity when he found something new in an old book or relic. The definition in his face had become sharp, and his stare now carried authority beyond his years. He was nearly rugged.

As he sat outside enjoying the fresh air of the hillside flowing in on a breeze, his mind began to wonder. At the moment he was at lunch, and the outdoor lunch area of the school was crowded. The weather was nice in early September, the air was crisp, and the summer heat was gone but not too cold yet. Often Jacob though about what he would do if a spirit attacked his school. What would he do? How would he save this many people? It was fortunate that they were reclusive. But what if one decided to attack him here?

A soft voice pulled him back from his worry. "Excuse me?" He replied, looking to see who had called him. He was almost startled to see that someone was standing with a lunch tray next to him. He was particularly surprised that it was a girl. The tables in the courtyard were stone and could fit four people at each. Jacob was more often than not the only person at his table, by his own choosing.

"Hi." She repeated, "Can I sit here?"

Jacob stared for a moment. She was cute, her wavy brown hair danced around her face in the gentle wind, and she smiled like she was greeting an old friend. "Oh, sure." He answered and closed one of his notebooks to make a spot for her tray. "Sure." He added gesturing to the new vacancy.

He didn't really know how to act around people, much less a girl. Battling evil and studying the notes from the archives was more of his thing, but he gladly put that notebook aside to let her sit down. Suddenly he felt as if he wished he hadn't spent so much time in the archives and prepared a little more for social encounters like the one at his table right now.

"Thanks." She said and placed her tray down beside his. The girl sat down and then turned to him, "Hi, I'm Emily." She said with a sort of happiness that made him glad she spoke.

He forgot how to talk for a moment. Something about her eyes made him unable to think. Her eyes were a brilliant green, and they seemed familiar as if he had seen them before. Surely he would remember someone with eyes like that, but he couldn't figure out what they reminded him of.

He blinked and recalled his name, "Jacob." He offered his hand to shake and halfway stood up to greet her.

"It's nice to meet you." She replied and took his hand and the seat.

Emily picked up the ham-and-cheese sandwich they all had received a moment before and took a short bite. Jacob swore he had seen her before, but he thought she must be new since nobody ever bothered him. "I'm sorry, are you new here?" He asked, those people skills he never built were showing. *That wasn't a good conversation starter.*

"No," she laughed, "I've been going to this school my whole life." She looked at him with a grin and added. "I've been one year behind you the entire time."

"Oh." Jacob tried not to sound dumb—it was a dumb question. "I just thought you were because nobody here ever says anything to me. I've kind of made my place, and people tend to stay out of it."

"Why is that?" she asked. Most people implied, "What's wrong with you?" when they asked that question, but she seemed to say "how sad" when she asked.

"Probably because I don't talk much." Jacob replied.

"Does it hurt to talk to people?" she asked and then took a bite out of the sandwich.

"Well, no," Jacob answered. "I just get caught up in . . ." He really didn't want to bring up his studies because he really did not want her to think he was some crazy person who believed in magic.

"So then, why don't you?" She asked and looked at him curiously.

"Well," Jacob didn't have an answer that he wanted to give. He had one and a good reason to exile himself, but the details were too—extravagant—for anyone to believe. Instead he would change topics, "Why are you talking to me?" *And another wrong thing to say. Now she's going to get up and leave.* Jacob kicked himself.

"It's a silly reason." She said and took another bite of the sandwich.

"What is it?" Jacob asked.

"I asked you first," she demanded in the nicest way possible.

"It's a silly reason," Jacob answered. "You would not believe me if I told you."

"Okay," Emily said and continued to finish her sandwich.

Once she had finished and taken a few sips of the juice the cafeteria served, she turned to face him again. "So why don't you talk much?"

Jacob laughed on the inside from her persistence. "Well, the things I know . . . are dangerous. People get hurt when they get involved in what I do."

"But you said it doesn't hurt to talk," Emily replied.

"I'm not the best person to hang around." Jacob answered, "My life is a bit . . . different than most, and strange things happen that most people never experience."

"Like what?" She asked.

Jacob just paused for a moment and thought of all the wrong things to say, and the worst thing he could say right now would be the truth. And following his record so far he said just that, "If you want the honest truth, I am a half-demon cursed to fight and hunt demons."

"Fascinating!" She answered. "That sounds like a terrific adventure."

"Adventure . . ." Jacob skewed his gaze wondering if this girl was sane or if she was trying to be polite. "Terrible is more like it."

"But just think how lucky you are to be so unique." Emily smiled as if demon hunting was a coveted career.

Jacob laughed a little bit to himself and they fell silent for a moment.

"So?" Jacob asked, trying to continue this conversation even while his instincts to protect told him it was better left in silence.

"So, what?" Emily replied.

"Now you," Jacob continued. "Why did you sit down to talk to me?"

"Well, my reason is not nearly as good as yours," she said and looked away trying to hide a laugh.

"I'd still like to hear it."

"Well, don't laugh," Emily urged.

"I promise; you didn't laugh at mine. What could be as bad as my excuse?"

She turned her celadon eyes away and smiled as if about to laugh and then she looked back up at him. "A fortune cookie," she whispered sheepishly.

Jacob suppressed his laugh and wished he had thought of that. "I see. What did it say?"

"It said," she adjusted herself as if she were a professor addressing a class, "'Make a new friend tomorrow. You never know what the future holds.'" Then she looked him straight in the eye for a full three seconds and then doubled over giggling.

Jacob started to chuckle and leaned forward with his elbows on the table and placed his hand over his face to hide the laugh.

"Stop laughing; you promised," she said still laughing herself.

"You laughed first," he replied and turned away to hide the grin and the red on his face.

"I'm serious," she continued. "I always try to do what the fortune says."

"You really believe you will get something out of a cookie?" Jacob asked as he gathered his composure and turned back to face her.

"No," she replied and cocked her head to the side. "They never tell you that you are supposed to get anything. They just give you general good advice."

"Well, it sounds like you had a bad cookie," Jacob replied and began to laugh again, "if you crossed paths with me."

"No, it was a good cookie," She said and then smiled, "I'm glad I met you."

Jacob smiled, "Thanks, it was nice sharing lunch with you."

The rest of the day was normal, but Jacob could not manage to stay focused. Emily's sweet voice and friendly smile kept running through his mind.

After he got home, he promptly completed his homework before dinner. Jacob enjoyed the meal with his family and afterward did some studying of the ancient powers his blood possessed.

CHAPTER 5

J acob finished his studies, did some recreational research on the language of the angels, and then went to bed. It was not long before he woke up. The clock beside his bed displayed 03:12 in big red numbers. Part of his father's curse was sensing when and where these evil spirits entered the world. When they came in, they lit up like a beacon, and over the short years Jacob had become quite keen on this, keen enough to wake up when one appeared.

This had happened in the past when they would get home and he would go to bed. His father usually stayed up later and would wake Jacob up to get redressed and go back out. He knew the drill, and he began readying himself. A few short minutes later, he opened the door to his room and stepped out into the hall. A click and creek came from the far end of the hall as the door to his parent's bedroom opened, and his father emerged. "You're getting slow, Dad." Jacob smirked. It was the second time in a row Jacob had gotten ready first.

His father smiled, "You'll make me proud, son. If I could retire I'd do it. You can handle yourself, and I *am* getting slower." Jacob never understood why his father felt the need to dress for church when he was on duty, but he had made him do the same. They both stood in the hall in boots, black slacks, shirts, and leather jackets. On occasion, Drake would also deem that a black tie and wide brim hat were necessary.

Jacob fidgeted with the sleeve of his jacket, he didn't like the way his father responded to his effort at a joke. "It was just a joke, Dad." Jacob replied after an awkward moment.

"I am getting slower, son." His father said in a somber tone. "But I didn't say I was dead," he continued, "or dying!" He added that with emphasis and slapped his hand on Jacob's back. "So let's get out there."

The grim reality was that his father was considered old in his family. Battling evil can make a youth strong, but it takes its toll in the long run, and most of the firstborn, the curse-bearers, died before they were forty. His father was forty-two. He knew he would have to face his death soon, but he did not want to think about it. Jacob could fight these forces just as well if not better than his father, but it just seemed unreal that he would have to go it alone one day.

Jacob still wore the jacket his father had given him years ago, not because he was still training but because he liked the feel and style. It had grown on him, and he now filled it better than he had when he was thirteen. Drake had seen what the weapons of Lucile's family could do in the hands of their son and allowed him to bring them now and even encouraged him to use them. He was unsure about them before, but they had proven effective, at least in Jacob's hands. Perhaps it was having both curses that allowed him to turn the tools of one against the other. Drake still insisted that the old ways of his fathers were the best ways, and it would be a great asset for Jacob to use the knowledge he had raised him in.

They stepped out the door, Jacob following his father into the cold night. A dark, thin mist covered the grassy hills of their wide-open yard. The place had been in the family for a long time, passed down to the firstborn child. It was off the beaten path, and there was enough room on the land to put a small subdivision. But since there was an abnormal amount of spiritual activity associated with his family, it was best that they stay secluded.

Jacob looked out in the direction the sun would be coming from in a few hours. "He's in the east," he said, predicting what it was doing was impossible, but the evil was not far in that direction, probably about three or four kilometers. It was a Shadow. Jacob's senses were now keen enough to locate spirits within a fifty-kilometer distance. They could hide, but he would know if they entered the world or if they left, and if they were active, he would be able to sense them.

More often than not, a Shadow entered the world to reside over a place, what a normal person would call "haunting." But really, they just chose the place to rest, and as long as they were not active Jacob wouldn't know where they were. However, sometimes they bothered the people who lived in or visited the place, most of the time after being provoked. It was much easier for a spirit to disturb and harass a person if it had been invited or contacted. In those cases, Jacob could sense them a long way off and often would have to become the exorcist to get rid of the spirit.

Tonight he did not know what they would encounter, but Shadows were easy to deal with. A Wraith on the other hand, was a lot stronger and could not hide as well when it was inactive. That was a good thing, too, because they were much more dangerous that the Shadows. To normal people, they looked like normal people, but to people like Jacob and Drake, they were infused with a demonic aura that shrouded their features, hiding their faces and forms. This made them difficult to fight because it was like fighting a black fog, and you could never read their footwork or see where an attack was coming from.

A Wraith could pass between Earth and Hell and sometimes even open additional portals or persuade mortals to do so. Not that a mortal had to be persuaded; they dabbled often and some opened portals out of ignorance and some in a misguided attempt to control demons. Fortunately, they seldom succeeded because the art of conjuring had all but died.

The Shadow they were now after may or may not have been invited in. No side of his family in all of their knowledge knew how Shadows sometimes passed between worlds without being called. However, it was a lot simpler to cast them out if they came over on their own accord. If one just comes over itself, Jacob could simply command it to go back, and it would do so. If it had been invited, then they would have to fight it. It had taken him a long time to learn all the odd rules, but he had caught on and now knew the process like a fine art.

Jacob jumped in the back of his father's truck; his father cranked it up, and they departed. It helped a lot now that Jacob was a bit older and more experienced; he would ride in the bed of the truck and would not have to wait for the truck to stop to engage the spirit. Tonight was the first time he had thought that soon he would be driving the truck, and there would be no one in the back until his firstborn was of age. They drove off into the fog and toward their destination. It was cold in the wind, but Jacob was brimming with adrenaline. Though this had become normal, his heart always sped up when he was about to face a spirit.

They got to where they were going—a large open field that had odd stones erected in it. The truck turned off the road and headed to the source of the aura. There was a dim glow of a fire about two stone throws away. Jacob got ready to deploy when he saw the glow. That meant there were people, and usually these Shadows did not show up in fields unless they were summoned. A fight was inevitable, and there would possibly be a possession to deal with. The truck rolled over the grass and bumped and shook on the uneven ground as it approached the camp.

Once they got closer Jacob could see one person, a girl, standing in the light. Something was wrong; she was not normal. His senses told him this, but any normal person could look at her and tell. Drake drove the truck straight for her. Before he stopped, Jacob jumped on the roof and ran down the windshield and across the hood and jumped off. He hit the ground and rolled up to the disturbed figure. She glared at him with an evil that a human could not possess. He stood up and commanded in a tone of authority, "Get out of her!" He continued with his momentum and tackled the girl to the ground. The girl laughed and another much deeper tone echoed and overpowered her own voice. The girl flung him off like he was a leaf. While he rolled, she rushed at him with surprising speed, but Jacob's reflexes were accustomed to such things.

He drew Jade in an instant and commanded his will into it, a technique he had discovered recently came in handy at times like this. Still lying on his back, he stabbed the girl in the chest and the sword went straight through her. She screamed and a piercing cry of true agony and rang out into the darkness.

"Get out!" He yelled again, twisting the sword and rocking it. He drove the blade in, grabbing onto the girl's shoulder and pulling himself to his feet. There was another scream, but it was not the girl screaming; it was the spirit. It was a shriek of bitterness and pain, fear and hate. The girl collapsed, and the sword melted through her flesh as if it was nothing but an illusion. She fell to the ground unconscious, but otherwise uninjured. Jacob still didn't fully understand the physics of what he did, but he had discovered how to strike the spirit and leave the flesh of a person unscathed.

A grotesque shadowy creature hung on the blade. Shadows did not have physical bodies, but Jade had been crafted to kill their kind back in the ancient times. He had stabbed the monster through the chest but had not killed it. The creature reeled from pain it had never felt before as it clawed at the steel that magically pierced its ghostly figure. Jacob pulled the blade out of the Shadow and whirled it around to sever the creature in two. But just as the blade met the vapors of the spirit, it vanished. He had not killed it; it simply recoiled into the shadows of the night and was very angry.

Jacob looked around the camp as his father ran to his side. Two bodies, dead men's bodies, were near the fire. The three of them had come out here, probably meaning no harm and there it was—a dead animal, a sacrifice. The kids didn't look like they knew what they were doing here; they were probably thrill seekers and thought this was a bunch of hocus. They thought it would be harmless fun, but no one should ever test the spirits. He could not make out what the animal was, usually they were dogs or goats. Usually these rituals summoned worse than one Shadow. Jacob immediately scanned for something else. The Shadow was not far, but he knew there had to be more out here.

Drake started a chant to force the creature to show itself. "Wait, Dad."

"What's wrong?" he replied.

"This is not right; there's got to be something else here." Jacob said and walked over to the man who was lying on a board that was open and active. He smashed the board with his sword and threw it into the fire. It was a bold move, knowing that there had been some contact with a spirit there, and breaking and burning the board would provoke the spirit. The board was its portal, and Jacob had no intentions of letting it return unscathed.

He looked at his father, "There is only one spirit, just a Shadow, but that board was active, and there is the summoning circle. There should be something worse." Just as he said that, the Shadow reappeared and drove at him. He pulled up the blade, and the Shadow whipped around him on both sides as if the blade had divided it. He turned to cut it, but it had gone.

"Perhaps the summon did not work," his father said, "They may not have completed it."

They both understood that the Shadow was not particularly pleased with Jacob. "This one was summoned," Jacob said as he looked around for where it might come from next. "We would already be done with it if it had only appeared to taunt their efforts." Just before Jacob had a chance to search for others, the small fire blazed much greater than it had before. The flames that had been a comfortable heat of a dying fire now scorched the air and soared eight feet high.

Jacob stepped back and shielded his face from the heat; the grass around him blackened and caught fire, and he smelt the stench of burning hair. He crushed one of the orbs of water that he carried, and he was able to withstand the heat without backing away further. Drake grabbed the girl and carried her body away, so she would not burn as Jacob stood in the doorway to hell to face whatever might emerge. Out of the inferno, a dark figure started to form. Jacob was relieved to see it was not a full-fledged demon. Certainly the creature had emerged from a portal to Hell; it reeked of evil, but it was not a true demon. It was a Wraith, a glorified pawn. Wraiths were strong but not invincible. Jacob had only fought a handful before with his father but never one *and* a Shadow at the same time.

The dark figure stepped out of the flames, and the fire slowly lost its brilliance and the air around Jacob cooled, but the dry grass continued to burn. The Wraith wore black armor that glowed red at the hinges, and from every crack, a black fog exuded and masked the Wraith's form and movements. All that Jacob could make out was the outline of a tall man where red glows managed to pierce the black aura. The foulness of death and destruction surrounded it. It looked at Jacob, and he felt it jab his heart as its gaze pierced his feelings, thoughts, and emotions. Then it turned to his father and drew a long black sword; even the blade it wielded was like a ghost.

"Jacob, give me some time." His father said quickly and he prepared his best defense against the black knight. Jacob knew what he had to do to send it back to Hell and stepped between the Wraith and his father. The Wraith unleashed a furious stroke at the boy. Jacob barely blocked it, and the force sent him rolling to his right. His father was still scrambling to get the procedure together. Jacob regained his footing and rushed to get back between the demon-man and his father. The Wraith swung at him again, but this time Jacob evaded the blow and sliced at the evil. He stepped back to assess the damage and noted that he had not phased the creature in the slightest. Had he hit it at all? It was hard to tell.

"You might want to hurry, Dad!" Jacob insisted, realizing the difficulty this would bring.

Just then the Shadow showed up again. The beast ran into Jacob and pushed him over. It came after him while he was down, but Jacob instinctively threw a vile of water at it, and it recoiled. But not for long, once Jacob had regained his footing the Shadow had regained its composure. Jacob glanced over at his father who was backing down from a one-sided fight. He had to take down this Shadow first before they could fight the Wraith. "Jacob!" his father yelled, "If anything happens, run!"

Jacob understood, but he wasn't going to leave his father behind, so he didn't respond and barely remembered the instruction. The Shadow rushed at him as before, but Jacob brought up Jade and the beast turned into vapor to avoid being impaled by the mystic blade. It instantly reappeared behind him. The tricky thing about using his weapons against the Shadows was that they had impeccable reflexes and could literally vanish into thin air and thus avoid injuries. Most people tend to think they have no physical bodies at all, but that is not entirely true; there are only certain things that can hurt them, and then you must be quick enough to catch them with their guard down.

Jacob turned swinging, and the same vanishing trick occurred. He looked at his father who was now all-out running, never mind trying to create the charm. He had to get over there; he had to get this Shadow off his back and help his father. The beast came back and rushed him again. Jacob only had time to roll out of the way. He reached into his pocket and drew another vile of water and waited for the creature to come back. It did, from behind him. He rolled out of the way again and quickly stood. It kept attacking from his blind side, good. It was afraid of him, and now it was predictable.

It came at him once more, and Jacob turned to face it. He let it hit him and broke the vile against the Shadow's face. It reeled back as steam curled around its vaporous, translucent face, and it clawed at the spot the water had burned. Jacob wasted no time; he had landed too far to strike with his sword but he quickly pulled out a stake and threw it with years of skill. It hit the beast in the chest and caused new anguish.

The silver in the stake is what actually helped a man kill it but was not the cause of death. The purity of the silver disabled the creature from using the dark magic inside it and kept the beast from turning into a vapor, allowing any normal tool to kill it. For this reason, stakes worked better than bullets. Bullets hurt the creature but often passed through and lost the effect. And once the silver had passed through the creature's body, the wound would heal quickly.

Jacob stood up and approached the beast, which was now flailing in pain on the dirt. He raised Jade and with a forceful, quick stab, he pinned the creature to the ground. Then he took another stake and accurately plunged it into the beast's heart. It wailed a thousand screams of terror and anguish. The horrid shriek lasted for three seconds before the creature fell silent. The superior Wraith took no notice of the lesser pawn's struggle and continued to pursue Drake. The Shadow wriggled in the pain and shrieked in hateful spite while Jacob pulled the sword out of the creature. He raised the gleaming blade high and dropped the enchanted Jade on its neck like a guillotine and erased it from the face of the earth.

Jacob picked up his stakes and placed one back in his coat and held the other in a reverse grip in his left hand. He turned to face the remaining opponent and ran at the Wraith, bold and stupid. He could never hope to take it on in melee combat. The Wraith either did not notice Jacob charging from behind, or it did not care. Jacob reached his target and slashed the Wraith across the back with his enchanted blade. For a moment the black shroud rolled back, and Jacob could see the full terror of the Wraith's form as Jade pierced through the armor. The evil creature spun around with fury and anger, and in one smooth motion swung its sword at Jacob. Ducking under the blow, Jacob moved in closer and jammed the stake into the shoulder joint of the Wraith. A shriek and a sharp jab from the Wraith's left arm sent him nearly back to the ground. He stumbled away, leaving the stake in the Wraith's flesh.

Jacob managed to stay on his feet, the Wraith had punched him in the chest with enough force to shatter a brick wall. He looked at the demonic figure that now stood before him. The stake caused the evil aura to disappear, and Jacob could see all the grotesque features of the thing that was once human. The face was burnt and distorted; it looked as if the man had been dead for a long time. With the fog rolled back, Jacob could see that his shoulders were uneven, and his armor was riddled with cracks where he had been struck many times. The cracks glowed red and flames dripped out of the wounds that never healed like blood.

The Wraith grabbed the stake and pulled it free. The creature examined it as the fog returned to hide it once more. The end of the silver was glowing yellow like it had been in a furnace. The Wraith focused all its hate and fury at Jacob; the explosion of wrath heated the air again and caused more grass to blaze. But it quickly turned and threw the stake the other way at his father. It was a good throw, and it made its mark. His father had his back turned, trying to finish the charm as he hurried to a safe distance.

Drake screamed as he fell to the ground. The small spell book flew from his hand, and he grabbed at the stake in his back. The metal was hot, and he could not grab it as it seared and cauterized the wound it had created.

It was not fatal wound. but it was going to keep him down for the fight and a bit longer. And worse, Jacob did not know how to finish the charm.

"Jacob!" His father yelled. "Get out of here!"

"No, I can't leave you here." Jacob yelled back and focused for the fight of his life. Even if he did run, the Wraith would come for him; he had drawn blood and had become the object of its wrath.

Though it ran, it seemed like slow motion. The wound he had inflicted did not appear to hinder the beast at all, and all the hate exploding form the creature was terrible. Every stride left a black and burning hole in the grass. Jacob forced his footing and gritted his teeth and met blades. There was one thing he had left, something dangerous but just might save his life. A trick that only the tenth generation of his mother's family could use; he could draw on the power of his own demon. His mother had taught him this and had warned him to never use it. To do so was to risk rousing a monster within him. But why would she teach him something he wasn't supposed to use? There had to be a time he would need to know how.

A spark ignited in him and his demon blood made his veins boil. New strength welled up in him, dark strength. He wasn't as strong as the Wraith, but he was stronger than any normal man. He stepped out of the way and countered, which was blocked, and then he took several steps backward while narrowly avoiding decapitation and severed limbs.

"Can you finish the charm?" Jacob asked as he blocked a furious blow at his head. His voice seemed both distant, and overwhelming at the same time like it wasn't really his. "I know how to apply it if you can finish it for me." He had only drawn this power once under his mother's supervision, and he hadn't been under pressure when he had done so. This was intimidating; the Wraith seemed to move slower, his perception of his environment was keener, and his strength was tenfold. The initial feeling was overpowering confidence, but realizing his full strength came with a certain fear, and curiosity, of what he might do. The warning his mother had given him was not to fully wake his "demon" or it would consume him.

Jacob had seen his father seal away a few Wraiths and never really wanted to have the duty of doing the same thing. But eventually he would have to, and well . . . this might as well be his first endeavor. Applying the seal was tricky and dangerous but no less tricky and dangerous than locking blades with a Wraith.

Drake did not answer, but he looked up and blinked the pain out of his eyes and fumbled for his book.

Jacob heard his father begin blessing the spell for the seal, and his adrenaline skyrocketed. This was real. For some reason it had not set in until now, but this was his life. He had always accepted it, but he just now realized that he would live for this moment again and again. The energy of his own demon blood flowed over him, and he felt as if he could not die. His inner demon was invincible but he knew he was very much mortal. Good, he still feared—he was still in control.

Rolling his opponent's blade off and swiping his sword around, he found purchase on the Wraith's sword arm. Quickly, he adjusted the angle of his blade and lunged in to stab its torso. He moved out of the way as the new wounds clearly had no effect on the opponent. He stumbled back into a defensive position. Jacob leaned out of the way of the next attack and turned to run. As he ran, he put Jade in her sheath and drew his last vile of water and a stake. He ran like mad to the truck in the appearance of fleeing and once he reached the door he turned and threw first the water to no effect and then the stake, catching his opponent in the throat.

The Wraith was thrown off by the shock, and Jacob took the moment to get closer while he pulled Jade out again. The blade of his enemy was already descending, and he moved under it, not to block the stroke, but it dismembered the arm. This maneuver worked, but Jacob was disappointed when he saw the arm regenerate from the elbow with a new phantom blade in hand. Marching on, the Wraith continued to attack and Jacob backed up slowly. "Jacob!" His father yelled to get his attention, "It's finished!" He held up a small notebook. It was full of blank paper, and he used it to inscribe the charms and notes. Jacob knew what to look for, two pages, one to stun him and the other to port him back to the dark recesses of Hell where it had come from.

"Good, toss it!" Jacob yelled and turned and ran straight to him. In midstride he caught the small book and fumbled through the pages to find the diagram he needed. He could no longer focus on defending himself so he dropped Jade in the charred grass and flipped through the tattered pages while he ran. He found the page with the symbol on it and ripped it out. This was the page to immobilize the evil, and right behind it was the page that would port it back to Hell.

Jacob turned the next page and found the incantation he needed. Stopping abruptly, he turned to face the Wraith and began reading the ancient text. His father had memorized it, but he had written it for Jacob to repeat. It was written in ancient Hebrew and was quite hard to read. But he managed; somehow between evading the strokes of the Demon's blade and stumbling through his father's hurried, and frantic handwriting, he managed to get it finished. As soon as he reached the last line the page in his other hand began to glow and he threw it up in front of the creature and finished the last phrase.

It lingered in the air as if it had been tacked to an invisible wall, and a burst of light shot out of the symbol that his father had encrypted on the page and the evil froze. Jacob removed the other page and flipped the next to find the proper incantation. He checked it to make sure it was what he had heard his father use, and he read it off quickly. The page also contained a diagram which turned blood red once he finished. Under the diagram, it had a brief text that Jacob had to recite in a moment. Boldly stepping closer to the creature, he palmed the paper to the Wraith's face. Once again the dark fog rolled away while the whole page turned to fire. Jacob stepped back and spoke the last phrase. The Wraith convulsed and was absorbed into the page as it burned.

The paper lingered in the air, flaming for a few moments before it vanished without so much as a trace of ash to know it had been in existence. The page and the Wraith were now in a much greater fire, one that would never be quenched. As soon as the light had faded, Jacob's blood cooled and he felt tired like he had never felt before. Tapping that energy had drained him more than he realized. He remembered his father, and his natural adrenalin brought him back as ran to aid him. Drake was trying to stand, assisting himself with one of the large rocks in the field. Jacob grabbed his father and attempted to help him up, but his father's strength gave out and he grunted in pain.

"I can't stand up," he muttered.

As he reached for the source of the pain, Jacob realized that the stake was still lodged in his lower back. His father fumbled around it with trembling fingers for a moment and then dropped his hand. "You have to take it out." He panted.

"Out?" Jacob asked not sure if that was the best idea.

Drake looked up at him and locked eyes so his son knew he was serious. "You have to take it out. I can't go anywhere like this."

Jacob nodded and gently grabbed the silver handle. His father flinched from the stake moving but gritted his teeth and bared the discomfort.

"On three." Jacob said, "one . . . two . . ."

"Don't.'" Drake gasped, "Don't . . . don't." He grunted and took a deep breath, "Don't count . . . just do it." He grabbed the collar of his leather coat and bit down on it bracing for the pain.

Jacob tightened his grip on the stake and counted in his mind . . . *Three*. The stake slid out, and his father gave a muffled scream through his teeth clenched against the leather collar. Drake dropped from one knee to the fetal position and twisted in pain. Jacob placed the stake in his coat where it belonged, and then helped his father to a sitting position against the bolder. The stake had cauterized the wound, and fortunately it was not very deep or near any of his organs, so there was actually very little bleeding. Jacob wondered if his father was just lucky, or if God hadn't really turned his back on this tainted bloodline. He let Drake catch his breath for a moment and then helped him to his feet and shouldered his weight back to the truck.

Drake fell against the side of the truck and rested while Jacob reached in the cab for their first aid kit. He pulled out a bandage and some surgical tape, enough to stop the bleeding for now. Once they got home they would have to clean the wound and redress it, but for now stopping the blood was the important thing.

One bad part about getting injured on the job in this field was that you could not explain many injuries, so medical attention was not always practical. Thus, his mother had become skilled at stitching flesh and cleaning wounds. On rare occasions, his father would see a doctor if he managed a wound that threatened his life, but he preferred not trying to explain his injuries to those who did not understand.

"Okayay, Dad, let's get home." Jacob said as he finished applying the bandage. He handed his father his coat and got in the driver's seat. Drake walked around and opened the passenger side door. He paused and fumbled in his pocket for the keys. Sliding gently into the seat he handed his son the key and rested against the old, worn leather seat.

The truck rumbled to life and they departed. The girl would wake up, but chances were she would not remember much. It was just as well; she probably murdered the two men while she was out of her mind. As much as people would like to believe, demons just don't kill. She might get scared and keep quiet or she might go straight to the police, but in order for Drake and Jacob to keep doing their job, they could not afford to give her any help. She was still possessed at the time they found her, so the chances she would remember them were slim. Seldom, however, one of the people they saved would reference an angel, or pair of angels when they recounted their stories. Sometimes Jacob thought those references were to him and his father; other times he wanted to believe they were real angels.

Jacob never understood why anyone would try to play with spirits, perhaps having an inside look on the creatures deterred his curiosity. It just seemed like too much of a risk to invite spirits, and why anyone would try just baffled him. Ignorance was probably the main reason or maybe a misplaced curiosity. He doubted anyone would get into that kind of trouble if they actually knew what they were dabbling in. As for him, he didn't really have a choice; he was going to have to live it for the rest of his life. This was one way to spend Friday nights . . .

CHAPTER 6

U nable to return to sleep after the encounter, Jacob headed to the library before the sun was up. His normal routine was to spend the whole weekend by studying in the library. His sister started coming with him once she was old enough to go, and he spent a lot of time teaching her. Sarah was still asleep when he left, but she would be here later. Jacob used the time to study on his own. Rain knew something was wrong immediately. It was not uncommon for Jacob to rise early and get a head start on studying, but no one could match her intuition. She asked about it and offered to listen, but Jacob declined. She had the ability to touch minds, and she could feel a person's thoughts by touching them, understand their pain, and sometimes predict futures.

The communication went both ways; only one person needed to have knowledge to open the link of minds, and both participants could see each other's secrets, past, present, and future. The futures were often skewed by the desires of the reader or the one being read. Through this magic, one could become very persuasive, and that was something Jacob was uneasy with.

Many of the family members who had this gift had read him before to see his deepest thoughts his fears, hopes, and dreams, but his future had always been veiled to them. That was probably because their desire for him to be a savior leaned so strongly, and he didn't have the slightest clue what he really wanted. Rain had read him several times before. He liked her, and they had become friends, but it had not felt right when their minds touched. The metaphors that their minds generated to be read like dreams were hard to interpret. He could feel her secrets but dared not open them. Her mind was a little bit different from the others, and when she read him, he found it difficult to withdraw from her.

For now, he just wanted to study. He kept the Scripts of Bolor as a reference though he had mostly memorized all three volumes of his work. He was studying *The Lost Mages: Magic of Old*. Last year he had studied the *Book of Forgotten Forgery* and learned to craft enchanted weapons. The mages of old and their spells could be used to further enhance these already-mystic weapons, and this had pricked his interest for the past several months. In his spare time, when he could not go into the forge to practice what he was learning, he worked through translating the *Book of Anzel*. Though it was already translated, and the only book of the angels to be translated fully, he thought it would be good practice to translate it himself and compare what he understood to what had been interpreted previously. The *Book of Anzel* was one of the Lesser Works, and it contained may insights about the nature of demons and explained a lot about the differences between Wraiths, Shadows, and demons. His father taught him a lot about the technical side of encountering them, but he did not know much about how they exist.

Jacob hoped that by translating the book, he would get a better understanding of his enemy and possibly understand his demon. It was something that scared him; he had been taught to tap the power, but some of his family had accidentally awakened their demons and that had led to their destruction. There was a fine line between unleashing the power and waking the being that resided in him, and he was hesitant to tap his full power and possibly lose control. He also wanted to better understand the language of the angels in the hope of completing the translation of Denomoi, one of the Infernal Records, which concerned Heaven and Hell from a fallen angel's perspective and would explain volumes of his family's nature if the *Book of Anzel* left him wanting. Perhaps one day he would be able to fully translate one of the books that had yet to be unlocked, a lofty ambition.

Another good idea would be to research how to make better use of his sleeping demon. If it was part of him, he needed to understand it. For that he didn't know where to start, but something helpful had to be in this library. However, today he was particularly searching for a spell that would help him avoid encounters like the night before. The Shadow should have been eliminated before the Wraith ever came through the portal. But he was not able to move quick enough to get the kill stroke in after he pulled the creature out of the girl. Searching for most of the morning yielded no results that were practical, and just as he was becoming frustrated, Sarah arrived. "Good morning, Jacob." Her light-hearted voice broke the irritating silence around his mind.

"Oh, hey, Sarah," he said looking up with a weary face. He saw her smiling and eager to learn, and then his tired expression melted into the same cheerful smile she was wearing. Sarah had that kind of ability; not only was she the person who could empathize and feel what others were feeling but she could almost make people feel something different from what they were feeling. Something about her piercing blue eyes could change the tension in the air. She looked a lot like their mother, with the exception of having their father's bright red hair.

She stepped closer, and the smile almost left her face, "Mother told me what happened," she said hesitantly.

"It was a rough night," Jacob replied as he stood up to give his sister a hug. "Is Dad any better?"

"He's still sleeping," she answered, returning the embrace. "I hate it that you two have to always be out there."

"That's how it's always been," Jacob sighed as he let her go. "And that is how it will always be, I suppose." He shrugged and sat back down. "Somehow I'm supposed to be the one who changes that."

"I wish I could help," Sarah said. She did not know what that meant, but she was sincere.

"It is much different than you think, Sarah." Jacob answered. "I know you would help if you could, but it's not your burden and you should not want it."

"But it's just not fair that you have to do it alone," she continued.

"Father is with me." Jacob paused. After what had happened last night he would be alone soon. He was prepared to go alone, but he was not prepared to lose his father.

"For now, Jacob, and hopefully for a long time." Sarah added her smile fading to worry. "But even for both of you, it's such a large burden."

"Sarah, you know there is nothing you can do." He replied. There was awkward pause, "Sorry, I don't mean to sound like I don't appreciate your concern. I know, even if you could help I would want you as far away from this as possible. It is dangerous out there, and I can't have my little sister getting hurt."

The smile came back to her face gently, and she sat down opposite of him at the desk, "That is why you teach me." Jacob opened the third volume of Bolor as Sarah got situated.

"You know, you moved through the Bolor scripts quite fast, and we are nearly done with the last volume." Jacob said flipping to the last quarter of the thick book.

"You do such a good job of explaining it." Sarah replied.

"I think you have a natural ability for this stuff," Jacob continued. "What do you think you would like to study next?"

"Well I'd like to learn more about incantations and enchantments." Sarah answered with a bit of excitement. "I was thinking the works of Stephen the wizard would be fun."

Jacob frowned slightly in thoughtful consideration.

"I know you have not studied that yet, so I thought maybe we could study it together." Sarah added.

"I'll see where I'm at with my own studies and maybe," Jacob said. "It would be good for you, I think, but I'm not sure I can teach you as much as I have with Bolor."

"It's okay if you can't." Sarah said, "I'd like to try to study by myself. I just thought it might be fun to study something new together."

"Well, you do that then." Jacob replied. "I think it would be fun for the three of us, once Dom get old enough, to crack open the *Ancient Nimba*."

"Oh yes; that would be fun!" Sarah exclaimed, the lightening sparked in her eyes at the prospect.

"I thought you would like that." Jacob smiled. "But first, we must finish Bolor." He said patting the musty old pages. "Then you can take up a private study of Stephen, and by the time Dom is with us, you shall be a master of sorcery."

"Okay, so what is next from Bolor?" Sarah asked brimming with enthusiasm.

The lesson was Bolor's usual: basics. He was brilliant for dissecting and simplifying the art and science of magic, and having a thorough grasp of the concepts he laid down made learning much easier once you moved on the advanced works like the Forgotten series he was working on, or Stephen's works like Sarah would soon embark on.

After the lesson, the previous night finally caught up to Jacob, and he left early that day. Sarah stayed behind to continue studying Bolor. Her class on Seracata, the fighting style of the angels, began in an hour, so until then she would keep occupied with studies. Jacob got home a little after lunch. Drake was still asleep, recovering from his injury, but his mother assured him that he was fine and gave him some of the leftover chowder the family had for lunch. After he ate a little, he retired to his room to catch up on some of the sleep he had missed last night.

After just a few hours he woke up. It was not often he had nightmares about his work, but what woke him was the image of the Shadow escaping. The first mistake of last night was made when he missed the Shadow the first time, and that kept repeating in his dreams, each time ending differently. Neither of the endings were good; he had images of it vanishing and then coming back and catching him with his guard down and images of it killing his father. It was uncomfortable. He knew that everything had worked out, but he should have handled it better. He got out of his bed and saw that there was still some daylight left. The barn in the back yard had a practice dummy Jacob had made to hone his sword skills. He redressed and took up Jade to go shake the sleep off.

Jacob threw open the large heavy door, and the dark barn filled with the last rays of sun. The dummy stood in the middle of the floor. Jacob walked up to it and placed his sword beside its chest as if he had the Shadow once again, and he pulled back and swung the blade as he had before. The blade thudded into the thick wood and leather.

He did it again.

Repetition was the only way to get a skill mastered. He had to be quicker; those things were very quick, and last night one had nearly gotten away, which almost cost them their lives. Because he missed the creature the first time, his father almost died, and he knew he had to get better at this—especially if he was ever going to be out there on his own.

Jacob diligently tried to improve his speed for nearly half an hour before he turned to look out at the evening rays of sun. A figure leaned on the frame; his father had finally gotten up.

"You have that much energy after what we went through?" Drake asked.

"I couldn't rest."

"So you just keep working," his father said, easing off the wall and taking slow, anguished steps toward him.

Jacob walked to meet him halfway. "Are you feeling better?"

"A little," he said as he took a rather heavy step. It was his right side that hurt most. He could bear weight, but Jacob could tell it hurt.

"I suppose I'm going to be on my own tonight?" Jacob asked.

"For two weeks at least," his father said as he placed a hand on his shoulder and walked past. He moved slowly across the floor to the wall and gently allowed himself to sit on some of the equipment, resting against it.

"You'll do fine, son. Don't worry about it." He said looking up with his steely eyes as if to assess him. "You're almost ready to take over this operation anyway. It looks like my age is catching up."

"I'm sorry." Jacob felt like he was responsible somehow.

Drake looked at him curiously, "For what? It's not your fault. It's a dangerous job, Jacob. How many times have I come home half alive before?"

"I had it, and it got away," Jacob explained. "If I had taken care of it when I had it, then when the Wraith showed up, we would have been ready."

"Well, I'm glad that things turned out this way." Drake said, running his hand over his short red hair.

Jacob looked curiously at his father sitting on a table resting his arm on an anvil. He was not wearing a shirt, and he had a large bandage around his torso. He had slept all day long, but he still looked beat, "How?"

"You did well." Drake responded with a smile. "You finished the spell, and you sent the creature back."

Jacob was not so sure he understood. "Son, when it was my time to learn these things, my father had already died." He looked down, frowning at the bits of straw on the dirt floor mingled with small chips of wood form the practice dummy his son had hacked off. "This will be good for you, Jacob. It took me three weeks to take down my first Wraith. I had no idea what I was up against. You might not know how to make the spell yet, but that's actually the easy part. What you did last night was impressive. You will be out on your own, and you will do fine. I'll be back on my feet in no time." He paused, "But you know as well as I do, son, that I'm not going to be here forever."

"I don't want it to be my mistake that causes it, though," Jacob said somberly and sat down beside his father.

"Go rest, son." Drake said, "Tomorrow is the Sabbath, and you ought not to have to wake. Get a full night sleep and return to your studies." He sighed and clasped his hand against his son's shoulder. The hand felt weak. Jacob worried about his father now; he had seen him beat and bruised before but never weak. Could it be nearing his end? How would he continue without him? There was still so much he needed to learn.

"I'll need the Sabbath to rest if I'm supposed to be out there alone these next weeks." Jacob said and placed his arm on his father's shoulder. "Tomorrow I will look into healing research."

"Thanks, son. I believe you could do it, but you know how I feel about that." He removed his hand from Jacob's shoulder and mock slapped him across the face.

"I'm at ease with life, and when it is time for me to go, I don't want to linger. I'm proud of you, and I'm sure you can do better than your old man."

"But there is so much for me to learn," Jacob protested, "How will I learn if you aren't here to teach me?"

"You already know more than me, son." Drake replied. "The things you seek to know will come to you as life goes on. I cannot teach you any more."

"I'd still feel better, knowing you're here."

"It's not a job you can retire from, lad," Drake replied. "Go rest," he added, changing the subject and giving his son a tap on the back to get him moving. There was that weakness again. Jacob barely felt the contact.

He stood up and hugged his father before he left. Neither of them said another word.

Jacob lay down on his bed and tried to take his father's advice and rest, but he kept thinking. His reflexes were too slow; compared to the average person, they were actually quicker, but that still wasn't good enough. He needed to be quicker in the confrontations, not just to protect his father who was now weakened, but to protect himself from getting injured. Even going to be alone for only two weeks, he would need to be sharper. If only there was another way to injure these things.

That was it! He needed another weapon like Jade. His mind began to fill with all the tools and weapons his mother's side of the family possessed. There were so many applications. But they would never let him take them out of the library. He would have to craft his own, then. He knew enough about forging, and he knew the spells. It was a project to begin researching in the morning. But he was now filled with energy at the prospect of making this device. So he would only rest for a few hours—that should be enough.

He set his clock to wake him just after 3:30 in the morning, and he would get an early start again at the library.

Jacob rose early and felt no hesitation in rising up to start his new project. He put on his hunting attire, ready for anything to happen. It was the Sabbath, and the chance of any evil crossing over tonight was greatly reduced, but Jacob would hate to have to return home if something did happen. Also, being the Sabbath, he had learned this day always merited adding the black tie and wide hat to his attire by his father's rules.

He arrived at the library before Rain woke and found Naff, the keeper, over-seeing the facility. They recognized one another but seldom had any contact. Naff was not quite as good at teaching as Rain, but he still knew his way around the library as one of Rain's assistants. Jacob explained the craft he desired, and Naff retrieved the proper guidelines for the project. Naff had long, blond hair that he wore in a ponytail, and his blue eyes sparkled out of his pale face. His complexion and the silky shimmer of his hair reminded Jacob of an elf from old lore. Naff did not have the magic age-defying perks like Rain, but he had aged quite well. The man was older than he appeared, but compared to Rain, he was a child.

After two hours of work, Jacob knew what he wanted and had a good idea how he should make it, it being an ancient weapon, one that no one had actually recovered or recreated: a Light Shard. Part of the reason no weapon like this had ever been created was due to the fact that the only examples known to have ever existed belonged to the angels who fell from Heaven. According to the legend, they had to be created in Heaven itself, but Jacob was confident he could use a method that would suffice. He knew where to look for all of the previous attempts and how different processes had turned out.

A Light Shard was called such because of the power it held. Theoretically, it didn't matter what kind of weapon it was, only how it was made. Jacob wished to make a dagger. He suspected he would have to endure several failed attempts before he perfected the technique. That could take weeks, especially since he was only here on the weekends. He still had all day. Perhaps there would be enough time for a first attempt. Sarah would be here in two hours for her lesson. She would be capable of studying while he worked.

Jacob called over Naff and submitted a list of materials he desired for the project. Naff half laughed when he realized what the materials were for: repurified silver, black marble from the quarries of Eastern China, obsidian from the underwater volcanoes in the center of the Pacific Ocean, hammered gold from Solomon's temple, two diamonds from the Valley of the Fallen, and Arctic cedar. "You do realize that this is beyond your scope?" Naff asked.

"How would I know?" Jacob replied, looking up with a scowl at Naff for belittling his request. "I've not yet tried it."

"Very well," Naff said, "I shall gather this for you in the forge, but you shall only succeed in making a pretty blade. The powers you seek have been lost to the sands of time."

"I suspect not the powers, but a missing ingredient has been lost."

"Oh?" Naff asked, checking the list curiously, "And what might that be?"

"That is why I need to these items, Naff." Jacob said as if it should have been obvious. "I'm looking for it," he added with a smirk.

"Of course, that makes sense." Naff did not seem convinced, but he did as requested and fetched the ingredients.

Jacob headed to the forge and began to heat the furnace. Soon Naff appeared and presented the objects, all to Jacob's specifications.

"Thanks, Naff," Jacob said as he looked them over.

"Is there anything else you require?" Naff asked.

"I'm going to need more cedar." Jacob said looking at the single bough Naff had brought.

"Will not this one suffice for the handle of your creation?" Naff asked.

"I said I thought something was missing. I also think the procedure is flawed." Jacob said and tossed the bough into the furnace, "It is to be forged of cedar, no? That is what the text translates."

"Ah, you may have an idea there. I shall load the cart and bring you one load, but it is nearing my time to depart," Naff said and disappeared from his presence.

Jacob studied the tools he had arranged and the molds for his project. He could see two flaws. First, there was a missing ingredient and, second, the process was not perfect. He would work on the process first, and then perhaps next week he could figure out what was missing.

Naff delivered the cart of cedar to fuel the forge, and Jacob began to burn it in the fire. The strange wood seemed cool to the touch. The forge was already hot enough, but he waited a few minutes to make sure the cedar was burning well.

The smooth scent of cedar soon filled the forge with a pleasant aroma of fresh forests.

An hour later, Rain came in to see what he was up to. "A new project?" she inquired in her ever-young soothing voice as she looked over at a cast iron pot full of molten silver that had been placed carefully in the fire. It was delicately balanced to keep the silver liquid, but not so far it that it should burn and boil and flaw the metal.

Jacob looked up briefly to make eye contact. The librarian stood in the doorway, gazing at him. Her hair was tinged with red and gold when it moved, matching her eyes as they reflected the furnace. A subtle air of curiosity was about her youth-filled golden eyes. Jacob returned his gaze to the crafting of the handle. "Hello Rain, I'm attempting to learn the secrets of the Light Shards."

She stepped closer, "If anyone can, it is you." She was so much more optimistic than Naff.

"Some people don't even think they exist," Jacob shrugged.

"They certainly do exist." Rain assured. She walked beside him and placed one hand against his shoulder as she examined the work. "But the ability to create them is a legend that was possessed by certain angels."

"Then how do you believe I can craft one?" he asked as he frowned at his progress.

She looked at him with her golden gaze, "It is not the knowledge of the craft that holds us back; the secret is in the heart of he who crafts it."

"Perhaps," Jacob said, and wondered if she had just equated him to a true angel. "You sound like you know something about that."

"There was a time when the world was ruled by these things; not all of them fell from Heaven." Rain replied.

"How do you know that?" Jacob asked, giving her a curious glance, "The histories are full of the failures, but there is no mention of success."

"When you do create this art, you will understand why it was lost." She stated, "It will be one of the greatest discoveries of our lineage."

Jacob paused for a moment. He had not started this research for this side of his family. He was more interested in keeping his father safe. Was it wrong to use the magic hidden in his mother's family to fight the curse of his father's family? No, not really. They were both his curses now; he could use the leverage of one against the other if he wanted, right? But he still needed to think about this side of his family, as well. He had almost forgotten that they depended on him, too.

"Yes, it would." He sighed and continued to work with the blade's handle. The marble served to anchor the blade, and obsidian encased it with black glass. Laid into the glassy surface was fine gold fashioned in a spiral to provide better grip. He had not finished it yet, but it was beautiful craftsmanship and at least looked authentic like it *should* be imbued with holy light.

"I'll leave you to your work." Rain said, "I've never been any good at forgery, so I doubt you'll need my help." She let her hand brush across his back as she turned to go. She stopped in the doorway, "You look good." She remarked of his clothing. It was an odd sort of comment coming from Rain; she seldom gave compliments to anyone. Her manner was so stoic, she normally refrained from stating anything other than subjective facts.

"You wouldn't be in the way if that is what you mean." Jacob said, breaking his gaze from his own tantalizing craft. Rain had spent so much time here and had never studied forgery, but she and Jacob were both scholars. He also needed something to distract him from the real reason he was down here. This work only reminded him of the things he was trying to prevent, and he wanted her company. And Rain also understood what it was like to be alone. Jacob was alone in the sense he had the world on his shoulders and no one to help him, and she had seen her family fade away with the sands of time while she remained young.

"I have other business to take care of." Rain replied, lingering her glance over her shoulder a bit longer. Jacob never could tell what she was thinking, but he got the feeling from her look that there was something she wanted to tell him. Her hair shifted and now appeared to be made of light pinks and faint highlights of purple. She turned and stepped across the threshold.

"Rain," Jacob stopped her, "Tell Sarah her lesson will be in here today."

"Of course. You know she is almost as fast of a learner as you." Rain said. "Perhaps it is not just you, but your whole family who will save us." She turned to face him and leaned against the door at the start of a new conversation.

"I'm 'The Savior' for now. But saviors have been named before." Jacob replied and turned his focus back to his work. That wasn't what he had wanted to talk about. Perhaps that was not a bad idea, though. He was forced to face his father's curse, but his sister and brother were not. Could they shoulder this one? How could he think that? He would never push this responsibility on them. Even if he doubted his own strength, there was no way he could ask for their help. They were under the same curse, and he had to find a way to break it for them, as well as the many others who were half-breed children of the Fallen in his mother's family. Even if he didn't know how, he had to do it.

"This is true," Rain answered, "but none of the ones we looked up to as a savior had felled demons as you have."

"Are the others as hopeful as you?" Jacob asked. He did not like this topic; it made him uncomfortable to think about the weight of each life. The few family members he saw regularly, even the ones he didn't like much, and all the clans spread across the globe, all put their hope in him. He still wanted Rain's company and conversation, but he hated discussing how he seemed to fit into the legends and prophesies of his people.

"We have had our hope broken before; each time we hope it will not be broken again." She returned to his side and sat down on the smith's chair Jacob was not using. She took her hand and gently turned his gaze from his work to her eyes. His eyes met with her eyes, and as they captured him like a trap, he felt his mind falling into hers. Rain's hair shimmered and shifted between the illusions of many different colors as the flood of information passed between their minds. Jacob wasn't sure if it shifted color in the light or if Rain had some kind of control over it. He often wasn't sure it changed color, but then again he never could tell just what color it was to begin with.

She meant to read him, to feel what he felt and see what he saw, but Jacob could tell she empathized with his fear of failure. But there was something else behind her wise, golden stare. Every once in a while, Rain would read his thoughts, which was how he had learned so much about her and why he was the only one who could see the subtle marks of emotion in her stoic features.

"I don't want to break that hope for everyone." If this was his future, then he would do his best, but with everyone holding him up to this standard, he feared to disappoint them.

"I believe in you," She answered not breaking eye contact with him. The feeling of her in his mind grew stronger, and he felt her eyes on his soul. The feeling was warm and full of life. For someone that never showed any outward emotions Rain's feelings were very strong. She had learned to hide her feelings over the years. Or, perhaps she forgot how to show outward emotions since she lacked real social contact for so long.

Jacob almost lost himself in her gaze. He had declined this contact yesterday, but he could not bring himself to refuse her this time. This helped him understand who he was sometimes, and right now he needed affirmation. That old prophecy hummed in his head as if Rain had spoken it: *One shall come from the stars as you have but shall bear not Hell and walk among the Fallen of this world and raise them up.* "Did you believe in the others before me?" Jacob felt her presence washing over him, it was not a feeling he was unfamiliar with or afraid of; many sages of his family had done this. Her touch seemed to fill him and search his soul. It was neither unpleasant or desirable, but liquid and curious.

She thought for a moment, contemplated his question and then replied, "No." Jacob didn't hear the word so much as felt the meaning through the fledging connection of their thoughts. Nearly two hundred years of wisdom were held in her single word, shared perceptions from part of her mind being in his. It was meant to reassure him of her confidence, and it did, somewhat. But at the same time that one syllable hefted the huge burden on him of being the one she thought he was.

"Then why believe in me?" Jacob asked, halfway whispering and halfway lost in Rain's mind. He pushed into her mind ever so gently as she sank deeper into his thoughts. She would be alive long after he was dead, and what story would she tell of him if he should fail? His hand reached for hers against his face. She pulled her hand away suddenly as if her searching in his mind had frightened her. Her eyes fell down, and she hesitated to look back up.

Jacob felt slightly dizzy from her mind rushing out of his so quickly.

Rain rose slowly and reached for him but recoiled her arm. She turned to go, "I'm sorry."

Jacob was baffled by her reaction. What had she found? That link could have shown her anything from his secrets to his future or any metaphor, simple or complex. But why didn't he know what she had seen? Both parties saw what the other was thinking and seeing. Before he could stop her to ask, she had vanished around the corner, and all that was left was the sound of her footsteps in the long, empty corridor. He stared through the doorway for a few moments before he was convinced she was not coming back to tell him what the problem was. Then he sat down for a minute to convince himself not to go after her. If Rain didn't want to say something, she wasn't going to. Just as old people were set in their ways, Rain had learned to be stubborn. But her body, mind, and spirit were still young; perhaps he could convince her to speak about it.

Jacob decided to try to pry it out later and returned to his work. An hour later as Jacob continued to work the gold into the handle he heard Sarah's footsteps in the hall.

"Good morning, Jacob," she grinned, her blue eyes teemed with energy.

Jacob looked up and smiled, "Hello, Sarah. I think we can finish up the Scripts today, and you can start on Stephen next week."

"Oh?" She asked, "I thought you were busy today."

"Why?" Jacob replied, "I just moved our study in here so I could work while we talk."

"Rain said you would be busy," she explained, brushing her auburn braids over her shoulder. "She said you were working on something."

"Nothing I intend to finish anytime soon," he replied.

Sarah looked at the tools and materials. "It looks like you are nearly done."

"I'll have to study my own work once it's finished." Jacob said and looked over the handle he was working on. "This method has not been perfected yet, and something is missing from the recipe."

"Method? Recipe? What?" Sarah asked. Apparently, Rain had not told her what he was doing, just that he was busy.

"I'm trying to create a Light Shard." Jacob explained. "The silver is there in the pot, and I'm working on the handle while it is sitting. I had to crush a diamond and the dust is bonding to the silver, I hope."

Sarah's eyes filled with a marveling curiosity. "A Light Shard? You can make one? You know how?"

"I'm trying," Jacob said.

"Jacob, I want one." She said and gently reached for the unfinished handle. "If you made one for me, I could help you and father."

"You know I would not ask for your help, even if you could." Jacob was uncomfortable with how eager Sarah was to try to help him; Dom was also a bit too interested. He couldn't expect them to not be curious about what he and his father did. But Jacob, like Drake, didn't want them to be remotely envious of their duty. "It's my job, my curse, so let me do it. I appreciate your sentiment, but do not get involved." Wanting to help him find his quest to save the Fallen would have been different, it was not as dangerous. Jacob still had no idea what the quest was. But somehow Sarah thought that the two jobs were the same.

She sighed at the familiar lecture that Jacob and Drake had both given her before she said, "I still want one."

Jacob paused, "Well, first I have to figure out what's wrong with the method. Then getting permission to use it would be . . ." He realized he had not taken into account that the Council decided what magic could and could not be used outside of their controlled areas. He would have to get their approval or hide it if he did make one.

"Oh right, the Council." Sarah had also forgot for a moment.

Jacob took back the incomplete handle, "But I have time yet before this is ready. For now, we can study. I'm going to keep working, so you teach me the last lesson. See if I can learn something new from you today."

Jacob fashioned a mold for the blade from a cast and prepared it to make his blade. The large caster would hurl the molten silver into an iron case that was shaped like the blade on the inside. Once it was cooled, he would then attach it to the handle and assess what worked and what did not work.

He hoped it would work, but he knew there were more problems with the method, and he would end up with a "pretty blade." At least it would make a nice ornament. The handle was done. The core was black marble, a heavy, secure anchor for the blade. It was wrapped in obsidian that caught light and reflected it like fire, and fine gold was laid in a spiral into the glassy stone bringing the gleam to life. At the bottom end, the gold strands met and formed a claw that held the second diamond in place at the base of the handle. All that was missing was the blade.

Jacob prepared the cast and then put on the smith's gloves and transported the molten silver over to the mold, filling the mold ever so carefully and then releasing the cast. It spun around, using centripetal force to throw the liquid into the back of the mold and hold it there while it cooled.

After it was done spinning, Jacob retrieved it and submerged it in water to cool. Once satisfied it would not burn him, he removed the gloves and opened the mold to reveal a perfect cast.

The silver would need to be cleaned and the edge of the blade sharpened, but it was the shape he desired with no defects.

After filing and brushing the silver until one edge was sharp and the rest was shining bright as the fire it came from, he went to join the blade to the base. He had left room in the cast for the silver blade to have a handle that would extend into a hole he had cut in the marble core of the hilt. He assembled all the necessary ingredients to get the blade to adhere to the handle and got ready to focus on the very detailed work that this particular blade required. Normally all that was needed was to clean the surfaces, apply the adhesive, and put the parts together. This process was painfully detailed in how to clean, apply, and place, and much more time-consuming than a normal weapon.

Before he began, he inserted the shaft of the blade into the slot in the marble it would soon join, testing to see if his measurements fit. There was a clicking sound and then the sound of an electric buzz and the shaft slid in. Jacob thought he was hearing things, but the blade would not come loose.

It had sealed itself.

Jacob looked at the self-adhering blade and then at the pile of unused instructions and cleaning materials and adhesives on the table. "Well, that is interesting," he said out loud.

He did not feel anything special in the blade; it did not respond like any of the enchanted blades he had forged in the past. But apparently his tweak to the process had been in the right direction. Perhaps next time he should try the appropriate cleanings first, and then apply the two ends together. Maybe there was not a missing piece but only a flawed design? In all the research he had compiled, this had not been mentioned. He wasn't entirely sure what he had done differently, but he knew he had stumbled on to the right path. He had a good place to start from, so he would cool the forge and take his prototype blade to his personal vault for later inspection.

Jacob collected all the books and stacked them neatly and then gathered all the remaining supplies and brought them all with his new creation to Rain. He would have been capable of putting them up himself, but the rule stood that only the librarian could take anything from its place and put a thing back in its place. She looked at the blade and picked it up, "It is incomplete, but it makes a fine example of your skills. I dare say you shall find the secrets you are seeking." Rain pulled her gaze from the new blade, and her gentle eyes fell on Jacob. They complimented him with words that could not be spoken. Jacob wondered for a moment if she was talking about the weapon or what she had hidden from him earlier.

"I have not looked at it to see where I erred yet, please keep it with my private collection." Jacob instructed.

"Of course," she answered and took the books and tools that Naff had gathered for him.

"Would it help if I took some of those for you?" Jacob asked.

"You know the rules; I cannot let you take or put anything back," she replied.

"But I could carry it for you, and then you could put it back," Jacob suggested. "It's a good armload, I nearly dropped a few items on my way from the forge."

She set the tools down, "Very well; take those, and follow me," she consented and then turned and walked away.

He picked them up and followed her through the maze of dusty shelves, "I was wondering if there were any good books on healing arts back here."

Rain was quiet for a brief moment while she summoned her vast knowledge, "Zarien has many ancient works on surgery." She began, "but for healing, you might consider Herbaria, whom herbs have been named after. They are good at curing what ails you and ideal for rejuvenation. Then Master Ronk was good at repairing bodily damage, healing bones and wounds. The lesser known practices of Zor and Burner include some methods of necromancy and soul raising."

She paused as she turned sharply down a corner and waited until Jacob had caught up to continue speaking. "But I think I good place to start is with Ellen. She studied all of these and has come up with many methods that combine techniques of the former three." She halted and turned to her right, ran a finger along the shelf, and then grabbed a three-inch thick book. "Here we are." She pulled it off and handed it to Jacob, "Her works require little understanding to operate, so it is a good place to start. If you desire to know more of the science behind the methods you should look up Zarien, Herbaria, and Ronk individually, but Ellen should give you good direction for that which you wish to pursue."

"You are so good at these things." Jacob answered almost blown over by how well and how fast she had explained the basics and found exactly what he was looking for.

"It's my job, Jacob." She said like it was superfluous of him to compliment her. All the worry and apprehension she had just a few hours ago was gone now. Jacob wondered where it went. How had she buried it so well? He studied her features for a moment, trying to find a trace of her thoughts, but he only saw golden eyes and faint pricks of lavender and sky blue in her hair.

"Well, thanks." Jacob thought about probing for what had frightened her; now might be a good time. They continued to walk, and she came to the place where the books on the Light Shards belonged, and she placed them on the shelves. "I'll take those now," she said gesturing to the tools he carried.

"Sure." Jacob handed them over and then followed her to the workshop.

Perhaps it wasn't the best time, but he had to say something, "So back in the forge when you tried to read me," Jacob began, "did you see something?"

"Like what?" she asked. There were many things she could conceal from other people, but Jacob knew her well enough to realize she was hiding something. He should have been aware of what she saw or felt but he couldn't. The only thing he felt was her liquid touch against his mind.

"You seemed frightened or upset by something, but I didn't see anything, only your touch." Jacob didn't know if that might have been the problem or if something else was wrong.

"You didn't know?" She shrugged off his concern and kept her pace. Her voice became serious, and she did not look at him.

"Should I have?" Jacob wasn't sure what she meant. He took two quick steps to get abreast of her, and he looked into her eyes that were now full of fiery confusion and locked straight forward. It was hard to detect, but Jacob saw unmistakable fear in her gaze.

"Then we will hope something was wrong with the link." She said. She blinked, and the expression was gone. "If you could not see what I saw, then the contact was incomplete."

Jacob thought for a second about the implications of that. If the link was incomplete, then she should not have been able to read him, and he should not have been aware of any contact deeper than his skin. "What does that mean?"

"I was reading, but not, there was no connection, and so my mind read something that was not there." She lied—he knew it. There was a connection; he felt her in his mind. She had flipped over a rock that she didn't want to, and somehow he didn't know what it was.

"Are you sure?" he asked.

"Yes," Rain answered looking straight forward, not blinking and still walking.

"Then just out of curiosity, what did you see?"

"It doesn't matter, Jacob; it was nonsense," she told him, still not blinking still fixing her gaze on the far wall. Then she fell silent.

Jacob knew she lied; he had felt the contact and saw the expression on her face. For someone like Rain that was a telltale sign. Something was wrong, and she wasn't telling him. He had never seen her falter from her stoic expression before, and right now she would not look him in the eye. He tried not to think about it. Later he would pry again. He would learn what it was, maybe not soon, but he would pull out the information. For now, it was clear that Rain did not want to talk about it.

CHAPTER 7

The next day was back to pretending to be normal, but that was a challenge for the boy in the top of the advanced classes who showed no interest in furthering his education. The fact that he was so smart, often absent from classes, rarely spoke, and nobody really knew him caused most people to believe he was crazy. It bothered his teachers to no end that he had no plans after graduation. They would always tell him how much of his intellect he was wasting. They'd never understand, or even believe, what his future would be and that it was already set in stone. Sometimes he even struggled to believe it, even though it was already upon him, and the events of his life were already unfolding.

But for now, for today at least, he was "normal."

Jacob enjoyed the lunch break he had outside in the open fresh air. It let the noise of the ambient conversation disperse so he could think. But today it was raining, and he was forced, along with the other multitude of students to cram into the cafeteria. The noise blasted off the walls and ceiling, and his thoughts turned to vapor. Uneasy because of the noise, he finished his meal quickly and made his way to his next classroom. The room was empty and quiet, perfect. He sat his books down on his desk and took out the homework from his last class, already half finished. The lunch break here was fifty-five minutes, and he still had a good forty before the bell rang. That should be plenty of time to finish the exercises and leave him with some brief research for the class once he got home. The project was not due until next week, but he had to stay ahead with his lifestyle.

The minutes ticked by, and the exercises diminished. Jacob's mind sank into his work, and his thoughts ran deep, half his mind worked through the exercises while the other half absently pondered his place in the future. The work ahead of him was immense and terrifying, and so many people were placing their faith in him. The half of his mind that was at work on his lesson meandered back to what he had studied the night before, the medicinal chapter of Ellen's compilation. She used techniques from both Herbiria and Ronk to explain different things. Herbiria found uses for herbs and such that escaped modern medicine, and Ronk worked in channeling energy. Ellen had pioneered the synergy of the two and thus made techniques to extract energy from the herbs and apply it as a normal healing energy.

In effect, this amplified the herbs' potency and greatly reduced the time needed to heal a wound or mend a bone.

Eventually he was roused from his meandering thoughts by a soft rap on the door. It was Emily. He had never noticed, until now, that she was in this class. She was also early by ten minutes, something most students tried to avoid.

"Hello," Jacob said it, slightly perturbed that his thoughts had been broken and partially excited by the revelation that she would be here every day.

She walked in and sat at the desk on his left; it had been empty the entire school year. "So you're in class early," she smiled—she always smiled. Now that he thought about it, he did remember seeing her around the school, and she always smiled. "You left the lunch hall early. Doing some more studying?" She asked nodding at his textbooks from last class open.

"The only way to stay ahead." He replied looking up to meet her gaze. Her hair was pulled back in a neat ponytail today, showing her features more fully. Her eyes were the same shade of green as the grass of the rainy hillside outside the window. He still couldn't place what they reminded him of. They seemed like they held the world and reflected what the earth felt, the green in her eyes shimmered like the fields of wet grass in the slow breeze. Jacob almost thought she would cry and start gushing water like the sky, but her eyes, like the grass, were pleased with the rain.

"So, what do you do if you finish all your homework at school?" she asked and leaned forward, anticipating an answer.

Jacob looked down for a moment and then back at Emily. "I told you last time what I do."

She raised her eyebrow with interest rather that scrutiny, "That's right! You did tell me." She scooted the desk a few inches closer, "Did you have any adventures this weekend?"

She thinks I'm joking, but she is willing to humor me. Jacob was trying to think; he didn't want to tell anyone, but somehow he felt comfortable with Emily. He also had never really had a friend he could talk to about his life. Whether she thought it was a joke or not, he would be glad to have someone to discuss things with.

"More adventure than I'd care to repeat." Jacob said remembering getting thrown by that Wraith and his father's brush with death.

"Sounds exciting." She was pushing for details; he could tell. She was either genuinely interested or trying to see how well he lied. So he continued with the truth.

"I'm a demon hunter, like my father and his father," he began, "It runs in the family." Before he could continue with the events Emily had asked about she stopped him.

"How does someone become a demon hunter? That sounds like so much fun." She appeared convinced, but Jacob knew any sane person would have called him nuts for what he just said. Perhaps she had a very vivid imagination and felt inspired by the things he said and his reclusive traits.

"Well, your ancestors have to make a pact with the Devil to give the blood of their firstborns into his service. Then one bold man has to break the pact. The Devil still owns part of me. Being a demon hunter is more of being hunted really; they come to try and claim me." Jacob gave a nutshell of his curse.

"The only way to survive is to strike first. I can sense when they cross over into this world, and if I want to stay alive, I have to face them. It's a bit of a paradox really. I have to find that which tries to kill me to remain alive."

Emily stared for a second, her brow wrinkled under her thoughts, and her eyes scanned the room as if she were reading a hidden message scribbled all over the walls. "So it's even more exciting than I thought. That might be too much for me, though." She lowered her eyes, "I guess that must be pretty tough."

"It is tough," Jacob replied, "Especially since no one understands."

She frowned and tilted her head to the side, "I would like to understand. Sometimes I wish my life had more adventure, but if you don't want to talk about it, you don't have to." Then the smile jumped back to her face, "But if you ever need someone to talk to I'll listen."

"Thanks," Jacob said. He was still not sure if she was playing along, expecting it to be a game or if she just went out on a limb and believed him. It did give him a small piece of a comfort that he had never had: companionship.

Emily sat forward in her desk and folded her hands on top of her books, "So last weekend must have been tough if it was something you don't want to happen again." Then she jerked her head to face him and had a very sad and petrified look on her face. "I'm really sorry!" she gasped. "I don't mean to pry; I'm just curious by nature. I mean I really want to know, I really do. But if I make you uncomfortable, just tell me, and I'll stop asking."

Jacob was struck by her sudden awareness of his feelings and concern. Emily was sweet, pretty, smart, and had an odd carefree, and deeply caring personality that he found charming.

"I'm not sure I get uncomfortable anymore after all I've been through." Jacob said after a few moments of silence. "I've never even told anyone, to be honest."

"Well then, I'm here to listen." Her concern of offending him washed back into the natural smile she always wore.

"It's a long story," Jacob said and turned away and stared at the blank black board on the far wall. "Do you want to hear it?"

"Well you usually spend some time in the study hall before you leave." Emily smiled. "I have some math problems I need to work on later, so maybe I'll see you in the library."

He didn't even discuss these things with his siblings, mostly because they wanted to help in some way. "It would be nice to finally have someone to talk with." Maybe it wasn't such a bad idea to have one friend who would listen to his problems. Jacob was still not sure if she was genuinely interested in getting to know him, but Emily was the closest person to a real friend he had ever had. During the next two classes, Jacob began to wonder if something as simple as someone having knowledge about him was enough to endanger them. He barely knew Emily, but he could not help but be a little apprehensive that something would hone in on her, and he would have to protect her like he protected his sister.

Over all the excitement of having a friend, he felt conviction. By telling her these things he was making her aware of problems that were not hers to worry about. If she continued to hang out with him, it would inevitably put her in danger. That part would be the first thing he would have to tell her. He liked her, and he didn't want to see her get hurt because of him. She seemed so intrigued, but she was still unaware of the very real danger that surrounded him.

After his last class he went to the library as usual and began working on his homework. Shortly after he had begun, the chair next to him slid back and Emily sat down. "Okay, story time." She smiled like a little kid eager to hear what the storyteller would have. She slapped her math books down on the table, but she was clearly uninterested in the work she had mentioned earlier. Jacob hesitated and then replied, "Before this goes any further, I want you to know, if you get involved with me, it will bring dangerous things into your life—things you don't want and you can't control."

"Life without danger is just a waste of breath," Emily said as she folded her hands and placed her elbows on the table to make a rest for her chin. She was still smiling and still anticipating the epic tale. "I could use a little adventure."

Jacob thought about it for a moment and then proceeded. He trusted her; he doubted she understood or believed him, but he didn't have a reason not to tell her, and he really liked the idea of having a friend to talk to—even if she thought it was just a story.

"This adventure . . .," he mentioned, "is not one that you can turn back from. No matter what happens, you have to move forward, and there is no rest until it's over. The kind of things that happen to me," He began, "are like living nightmares. Three nights ago, my father and I woke from the energy of a Shadow being called into the world." He paused; would she even know what that was? He'd better explain as he went along. "There are three types of entities; Shadows, Wraiths, and demons.

"Shadows are entirely spirits. They can possess a body or "haunt" a location. Shadows are the most common and are typically mistaken for ghosts. The Wraiths are the actual bodies of people who swore their lives to the Devil. They are a bit harder to kill. And a full-fledged demon . . ." he stopped and thought; he had never seen one, but he knew what they could do, "You better pray you never see one."

"Why is that?" Emily asked, "Aren't you a demon hunter?"

"Yes, that is what they call me, but a real demon is a terrible opponent, extremely powerful. A Shadow can come and go if it wants, but if it has been summoned, it is a lot harder to kill. A demon was once an angel, is immortal, and if it is summoned, it can only be sent back one way."

"How?"

"You have to drag it to Hell with you," Jacob whispered.

Emily paused for a moment, "You mean?"

"Yes," Jacob answered. "The ritual of the portal requires a soul to be freed from its body."

Emily sat back and focused, "But you only fought with a Shadow?"

Jacob nodded, "The creature was summoned, so we had to fight it. If it had appeared on its own, it would be as simple as commanding it away, but once wished into the world, it must be forced back or killed."

"Did you kill it?"

"It almost got away," Jacob said. "It was possessing a girl. I pulled it out and tried to kill it, and it vanished. Before I could make it show itself, a Wraith appeared, also summoned by the people the Shadow had . . . killed." They were in the obituaries, the bodies had been discovered, the girl is still in the hospital, and nobody knew what had happened.

"There is a way to send a Wraith back to Hell, but it takes some time. I fought with the Shadow while my father ran from the Wraith and tried to begin the incantation. Once I had killed the Shadow, I tried to occupy the Wraith so my father could finish. It took one of my own weapons, a stake, and threw it into my father's back."

Emily's face wrinkled with sympathy, "Was he hurt?"

"He's not going to be doing anything for at least another week." Jacob replied. "He did finish the charm, but I had to apply it. We managed to send him back, but it nearly killed my father."

"Oh, I'm sorry." Emily said; even if she thought this was all made up, she was good at pretending she believed him.

"This will be my first time out alone. Until now he's always been with me." Jacob sighed, "And I just don't know what I'm going to do when he's really gone. These kind of encounters happen often, but this last one has been the worst I've ever seen."

Emily seemed to take a mental step backward, "Often? How often does this happen—things crossing over?"

"More often than you think, but people are only aware of them in extreme cases." Jacob thought for a moment and came up with a quick average. "The encounters vary, sometimes two weeks apart and ones like this most recent one, the ones that get attention—that is the first I've seen in my lifetime."

Emily pondered the story for a moment, "Do you write?" she asked.

"About what?"

"You're really sharp," she said, "You took that story from the papers and filled in all the details like you were there. You have an outstanding imagination, and I think you would be great at writing. You know, like books: fiction and stuff."

Jacob lowered his eyes, and his chest sank, realizing she had thought his interpretation of the mystery of the murders that had happened was farce,. But in a way, he was glad that she had not taken it seriously; perhaps she would not get too involved that way and not get any attention from his curse.

"I mean I liked your story," she said. "If I believed in that kind of stuff, I would have totally been convinced."

That's what it was, a ghost story. Jacob only wished it was a story. It was real, and the less people that believed the better, but he still felt a bit disappointed. He didn't realize how bad he wanted a friend until Emily started talking to him. The thought had never really crossed his mind that he was alone. It was something he always had accepted, not alone in the sense that he had no friends, but alone as in the deliverer for his people. But now the realization of both senses of the word hit him. Being without a companion hit him just as hard as being the sole hope of redemption for an entire race. He was not sure what to say. The last time he had said all the wrong things. What should he reply? "Thanks for listening" sort of slipped out between his thoughts.

"Do you know what this is?" He asked trying to change the subject. Jacob fumbled at the collar of his jacket and pulled off the flower he always wore. Not really sure what he was thinking. he showed it to her.

"It looks like a dried and preserved flower." Emily replied.

"It is a very rare flower." Jacob explained. "The only known location that it grows naturally is in remote areas of Chinese mountains."

Emily smiled, "And how did you get it?"

"My mother's side of the family has a few talents. Some of them are quite good at gardening." Jacob answered. "This is a unique flower. The seeds inside it, even if dried for fifty years, can cure almost any illness. The scent of a freshly picked flower can sooth your body and clear your mind. When burned, the smoke can cleanse skin and remove infections. The ashes used to be used in the emperor's soaps. It is called Vita Lily."

Emily looked at it in wonder, "You really are good at telling stories."

Jacob ignored the comment and acted as if it was a story and he had to finish telling it. "They say it used to grow in the shade of the Tree of Life." He paused. "I want you to have it."

Then he extended his hand out to her. He thought back over the lesson he had read the night before about simple rejuvenation of plants and other small spells. He channeled the energy into the old dried-up flower and just as Emily reached for it, the pedals began to come back to life. The color flushed back into them, and they slowly unfolded.

Emily marveled at the sight and slowly remarked, "Oh, that is really a pretty trick."

Her eyes flickered and seemed so familiar. Jacob had decided they were just pretty, but every time he looked in her eyes some part of his memory was stirred.

"It's not a trick." Jacob said and placed it between her fingers. "Smell it."

She gently took it to her face and inhaled the scent. It was faint, but what she did smell was like lilacs and aloe and a host of medicinal herbs. Her head felt tingly for a moment, and then she thought better and breathed clearer. She even saw things better, sharper, and noticed more details like the direction the grain went in the wood of the table and the way Jacob looked so isolated.

She exhaled and the sudden sharpness dissipated, and the world and her aware-ness of it was normal again. Then Emily extended the flower back to Jacob. "It's very pretty and it smells pretty, but I can't take this."

Jacob took her hand and pushed it back gently. "It's a gift." He withdrew his hands and rested them on the table. "For a friend."

"But this is something that means a lot to you." Emily replied. "And it did just like you said. It isn't something I've ever seen before, and I don't want to take it from you."

"I've had that thing dried up on my jacket for four years. If I ever had a better time to use it, I missed it when it passed by." He smiled and reclined, partly to appear relaxed and partly to get out of her reach to possibly keep her from attempting to return the gift again.

Emily looked at the blossom, "Thank you," she said and looked back up with her smile. Jacob could tell the subtle effects of the flower's scent were working, her already-bright smile seemed to radiate. She was genuinely thrilled with the gift even if she thought all of what he said was fiction. The week went by, and every day Emily found him at lunch or in the library and listened to his family history. She soaked it up like a small child at story time. Jacob knew she did not believe him, but the way she listened seemed like she wished it was true. Her imagina-tion was very active. Perhaps she just wanted to be part of his world even if she believed it was only in his mind.

He explained the history of his father's side of the family and the legend of his mother's side. Then he laid out all the events that led to his current situation with the weight of a race and the souls of his fathers in his hands.

Emily pieced it together quite well, stopped referring to it as a story, and began talking as if she had been there. She had mentioned she wanted more adventure. Was her life really that boring that she would play pretend with him? Jacob wanted to show her how real it was. That would give her adventure. But he knew that this particular adventure was one you could not turn back from once you embarked. Whether she really wanted to believe him or not, Jacob knew she was not ready. Maybe he would tell her in small steps. For him it had been second nature, even normal, because he had grown up with it. But in Emily's case, she was a normal girl, and her imagination was running at full speed with the story of his life, iron-ically blinding her from realizing it wasn't just a reality in Jacob's mind that she wanted to have adventures in; it *was his* reality.

He would have to come up with more clever tricks like he had with that flower. That might let her on to the revelation that something was different. He had come up with that so quick and on-the-spot, but he was having trouble thinking of any other things he could do. But there was no hurry. A few weeks flew by before Jacob had a chance to blink. His sister had finished her introductory studies on Bolor, and he had made some progress toward the Light Shard.

Sarah had started her own study today, so he spent the normal lesson time researching Ellen's charms, potions, and remedies. Small herbal charms and tricks were perhaps the simplest way to show Emily he really was what he said he was. Anything more might frighten her.

Once his head stopped spinning from the surge of information, he retrieved the failed Light Shard and began to analyze what might have gone wrong. It was a fair attempt, but something had not quite meshed. Jacob did not want to waste materials, so he studied his work and calculated what might be better for the next time. After making a few notes and jotting down some things to look up later, he resumed his normal studies of the *Forgotten Mages* and retranslating Anzel.

Rain had avoided talking today, which was not usual. They had become good friends, and she usually sought out his company. Something was definitely wrong with what she had seen the last time. She was probably aware that Jacob knew she had lied about it, too; he was not good at hiding his thoughts like she was. Trying to get her to talk about it was not simple, though. She had two hundred years of patience. She wasn't going to give up information if she didn't want to. However, Rain's secrets were not what was bothering him today. A council meeting had been called for tomorrow. Since Roth had decreed that Jacob was the Chosen One, there had been a lot more tension at these "family reunions." William and Malcolm didn't really like Henry's side of the family to begin with, and his mother never would explain why his grandfather and his uncle didn't get along.

Malcolm tended to think his own daughter was better suited for the job of being the Chosen, and Jacob was the only member who didn't care. He had been placed on the council because Roth intended to install him as the Chosen, and Julie had been placed on the council to balance the power of the ruling families and to pacify William.

Jacob didn't understand what the feud was about. The job looked prestigious, but he didn't feel special—just burdened. He had not spoken to Julie enough to gage her opinion, but he assumed she inherited William and Malcolm's prejudice of Henry, Lucile, and himself.

No doubt this meeting would be interesting. As far as Jacob knew, there was no reason to have a meeting so that probably meant it was about him.

CHAPTER 8

T he dark chamber had become more familiar than he had wanted. Being dragged into these council meetings was not fun. Jacob liked to imagine his entire family was supportive of him and that they all sought to help. But from what he gathered at these "meetings" was that only his direct relatives, his mother and grandfather, stood behind Roth's decision. The others were skeptical at best, and no one ever thought of how they might assist him. Seeing as it was their lives he had been appointed to save, he felt like it wasn't too much to ask if they did something every now and then. The dim room was lighted by a faint ray of sunshine coming through the hole in the ceiling. They all sat in a circle around the inner ring of the megalith where they had all come from.

Jacob really didn't want to be here. He'd rather be in the dimly lit library, studying or at home practicing calculus. Where he would really like to be was at lunch talking to Emily, the one person he thought of as a real friend. But even if he didn't have to be here, there was still no school today, so that was not possible. Unfortunately, he was forced to endure this, and as it was called to order by Roth in his dry dusty voice, Jacob tried to think of the honor it was to be on the council— it felt like another curse.

"The entire council is present." Roth began. His voice had grown weaker in the few years Jacob had known him, but it still vibrated with authority that he dared not question. "Our business of the day shall proceed."

The family had clans scattered all over the place, but this council focused on the two clans that Henry and William presided over. Jacob never figured out how the two brothers were heads of two different clans and figured there was a division in the family. At any rate, they were the ruling families, and business meant deciding laws, privileges, and punishments for all his cousins he had never met.

Jacob really didn't understand why he was on the council. He knew it was because Roth believed he was the Chosen, but that didn't make sense. He still had no idea what was really happening or who they were talking about. Perhaps that was the point, to have a completely objective perspective. He did not know these people or even which clan they belonged to. He was not part of any feud and could make moral decisions without being blinded by social situation. That was a good theory, but he was pretty sure it was just because Roth wanted him to be the savior.

The time lagged on, and Jacob gave his yay's and nay's but never brought up anything or gave his opinion. Finally, when the meeting came to an end, Roth announced the last order of business, the Chosen, just when he was thinking he would get out of the meeting without having to talk about it. Jacob thought for a moment. If he had the faintest idea of what he was actually supposed to be doing, he might be able to make up something about his progress. What was his quest? Right now he was on a quest to learn what he was supposed to do. Any progress report would be incomplete.

"I'm still struggling with the particulars of my duties." Jacob replied. It was odd that the one thing he needed help with was the one thing nobody would help him accomplish. "I can't say I'm exactly certain of how I'm supposed to proceed. I've never received any instructions."

"Perhaps he's not the one you were hoping for then, Roth." William piped in. "He doesn't even know where to start."

That remark didn't help. "Well if you know, dear uncle, please tell. Or better yet, why have you not done it yourself?" Jacob had never lashed out like that. It was common for the council to get heated, but Jacob had always stayed out of the fights.

"I beg your pardon?" William shot back in his tone of condescending resentment.

"You should respect your elders, boy." Malcolm added in his father's defense.

Jacob turned to him and glared; he didn't like it, but he was beginning to develop his own tone that showed up around these members of the family. "If anyone has the foggiest idea how it is I should do this, please let me know, and if not be silent. All I asked for was direction." His eyes burned through the dim room into the stubborn eyes of his uncle. "Respect my elders?" He laughed, "Elders are supposed to offer guidance, not ridicule, Uncle. I'll tell you when, if ever, I find an answer. If you do not wish to offer any comments of use, then stay out of my way." This was the first argument in this circle that he had started, and he was not going to back down. "As far as I can tell, you only elect a Chosen so you have someone to place the responsibility of your own failures on."

"Julie would have been a better choice, Roth." William said. "Why don't you reconsider that?"

"Shut up, William." Roth ordered and waved his tired arm dismissively. "Jacob, this is an honor, a great honor. Do you wish not to shoulder it? Are you ungrateful that this is your responsibility?"

"Roth, there have been countless others before me. What makes you think I will do better?" Jacob began careful not to disrespect the old man, but he was not willing to hide what was really on his mind. "Why should I do it alone? You place the entire family, all the clans on my shoulders. Two hundred and thirty-three demons fathered this damned bloodline, and you want to put them on one man, one man! As your means of pardon?" He paused and looked around the room. All of their faces were full of shock at this outburst from the normally calm and quiet young man.

"I don't see why there should not be one from each clan, to be frank," he continued. "But you want me to cover all the sins of our forefathers and renounce the blood of our damned fathers. What you ask is not possible. If I knew what to do, I could tell if it was in my power, but no one can tell me what my duties as the Chosen are."

Was it not enough that he had to stand before Christ and beg for his fathers? The clans wanted him to be Christ for their people. He understood the patience it took for the Son of God, and he did not have it. His people demanded him to be perfect and didn't really seem interested in helping. But he was not Christ, and he needed to get that message across; he could not do this.

"Jacob, you are strong." Henry spoke up, attempting to encourage him.

"Aye, Henry, I am." Jacob replied to his grandfather in a tone of frustration. "What of it? I'm not Jesus Christ." For a full three seconds nobody said anything. "I'm not here to break this curse; I'm only as good as any of you." He looked around the room and was surprised that no one had any remarks; they were all struck silent. "So if you would, please, find some way to help before you ask me again. It's not just my soul on the line here. It's not just your soul on the line." He added pointing at William. "You placed you own damned souls in my hands; you should think about helping in this 'quest' I'm supposed to be on. It's not just our souls on the line; it's not just our clan's souls—it's the souls of every half-breed-damned-to-Hell child of the Nephilim on the line." Just now, he realized he had stood up.

How long had he been standing? Did he give the whole speech standing or did he stand up when he talked back to Henry? He sat back down and began to mull over what had just happened. The council would probably remove his title. So what? There were far worse things they could do, though: remove him from the council, restrict his studies—he needed the access to the family's secrets to help him fight his father's curse. He placed his hand across his forehead and squeezed his temples waiting for a rebuttal.

"The boy is right," Roth finally broke the silence. "This is far too great for just one man to shoulder."

"So what?" William asked, "Are you suggesting we cannot have our hero? That every man woman and child is to fight their own battles?"

"Quiet. Why do you resent the one I appointed to redeem your soul?" Roth stated slowly. "Is it because I did not choose your son or granddaughter?" He accused as he looked wearily at Julie. "You must put aside your petty nonsense if there is to be any hope at all."

"That has nothing to do with it, but since you brought it up, my line would have been a better choice." William replied arrogantly.

Roth dismissed his comment with a wave of his hand, "He's the Chosen before all clans! He's not Christ, only a shadow who must one day stand before him and plead our case that we are not the children of evil and that we do not wish to share in the sins of our fathers. If you would rather do it yourself, please make the effort. It will be one less life the boy has to worry about."

There was silence; silence usually meant agreement had been reached, however resented it may be. "So what do you propose?" William asked, "That each clan appoint a chosen?"

"Perhaps some sort of assistant should be appointed from each clan. Or maybe a representative will do; we shall decide that in the next meeting," Roth decided. "Between now and then I shall speak with the other clans, and we shall have a meeting to discuss how we are to move forward."

An unsettling feeling filled the air around the discussion. Jacob sat with his question still unanswered, and they were going to give him an assistant to help him complete a task that he still didn't understand.

"All in favor?" Henry asked before unsettled air had a chance to lash out into another argument.

Unanimously, the room vibrated with an affirming answer.

"Are there any further topics to discuss?" Lucile asked.

Silence answered her, "I make a motion to adjourn," she added.

"Second," Jacob replied.

Once the council broke, Jacob hurried to the library to salvage what was left of the day in his research. He sat at a table in the upper study with a copy of Ellen's guide to health, potions, and other remedies. He was surprised that she included not only the magic remedies for good health but also stressed the importance of a balanced diet and good exercise, diet supplements, and natural medicine, and urged the reader to use the magic only as supplements or in cases of emergencies. Apparently, it was possible to develop addictions to the remedies and supplements. The table Jacob sat at was one of the game tables. Sometimes people didn't like it when he used one of the boards for study, so when they would make a remark, he would simply move a white piece and continue to study while he waited for a challenger. Nine times out of ten, no one could best him, and so more often than not his challenge went unmet. So in an effort to retain unbroken peace and quiet, he initiated the game when he sat down, hoping anyone who might want his table would pass him by.

As he was studying the recipes and remedies for natural elixirs, he heard the clunk of one of the small stone pieces against the polished and painted granite of the board. He looked up and saw his cousin, Julie, on the other side of the table. The way games were played here, the winner got to make a request of the loser. Normally that was the table they sat at, since he tended to occupy it for an extended period of time, but Julie had no reason to ask for his table. She was Malcolm's daughter so he doubted what she wanted was anything he cared to surrender. But she was also still a child, one year his junior, so there might yet be hope the family politics had not poisoned her mind. At any rate it was not custom for the challenger to make their demands known until they had succeeded.

He had started the game, and she had challenged, so he had to finish it. Both queens' pawns were now in the center of the board diagonal from one another. One was Jacob's polished white quartz and the other was Julie's etched obsidian. He frowned at the board and moved his king's knight to support his pawn. The game continued in silence, Jacob's only concern was why she had challenged him. If she won, he would find out and if he won, that would be the one thing he would ask. He didn't need anything from her, so why make a demand?

As the game progressed, it became clear that Julie was not accustomed to losing, either. They were a very even match. The evening sun was now setting; they had been at this board for nearly three hours. Jacob thought he had an upper hand, and Julie had been furrowing her brows at her next move for almost fifteen minutes. She sat back and relaxed, smiled, and moved her silky brown hair out of her hazel eyes, and then slowly reached for the piece she intended to move. Jacob had not noticed the bishop sitting there. She moved it into a position to attack his queen and the added, "Check," finally breaking the silence.

Jacob took a double look and realized the bishop had been between his king and her rook and kicked himself for that mistake. It was a very bad mistake to make against such a skilled opponent. She worked the mechanics of the game like Jacob worked math, and she had hidden attacks that he should have seen coming. It was a blunder on his part, but the piece he had to sacrifice was what made it worse. He thought and scowled at the board. They would now be "even" as far as the pieces counted. But as far as the position of the board—Jacob now had a gaping hole in his defense, and Julie was poised to attack. If he was going to recover, he had to be perfect—and lucky. Julie had to make the next mistake, and he would have to exploit it any way he could.

For another hour, the game drew on, and Julie never faltered. Jacob didn't go down without a fight, though. At the end just before the final stroke fell, he had recovered his queen, and so had she. Just when Jacob thought he might force a draw or possibly turn it around, when Julie seemed like she had made the mistake of resigning her second queen, he noticed it was another one of her hidden attacks. He had two options, take the queen or stall and put her in check.

If he took her queen, her next move would be the kill stroke. And if he tried to stall it was likely that would not last too long. But, better to stall and give himself more time to think and give Julie more time to make a mistake.

He slid his queen across the board to attack her king, and Julie retracted him behind a knight and a pawn, hiding him in a corner. If Julie's queen had not been there, he could have taken the knight with his one remaining bishop. And then perhaps have a chance to queen another of his remaining three pawns. But his bishop was the last line of defense between that queen and his king. It was impossible to move it because that move would leave the king in check.

He sighed and knew the game was over; it had been hard fought, but he knew he would have to face whatever his cousin wanted. He took the queen and the trap she had set. He moved his bishop to her and captured the square. Julie smiled and took her knight and danced it across the board. It landed and placed his king in a vice. Her rook and his own two pawns barricaded him from escape, and the game was finished.

Jacob reached forward to shake the hand of his opponent. It was a very good game. "Well Julie you beat me." He said, "Well done." She took his hand and returned the gesture.

"You played a good game," she replied.

"Yes, but not good enough. I must say you took me by surprise with your mastery of the board there." Jacob sat back and crossed his arms, "So . . ."

"So what?" She asked imitating his posture.

"You won, what did you want?"

She sighed heavily and looked at him with a slight exasperation, "Can't anyone around here do anything without assuming everyone is out to get something from them?"

Jacob gestured, waving his left hand in the air, "You are on the council, too. What would you expect? You see how shrewd and backstabbing the whole family is; am I wrong to watch my back?"

"I suppose not," she answered, "It doesn't make sense to me, the level of discontinuity between us." She leaned forward and folded her hands over the edge of the table just behind the back row of the board. "I mean, we're cousins for Christ's sake!" She pounded her hand against the table for emphasis. "Why shouldn't we be able to have a conversation like it?"

"If only it were so simple," Jacob sighed.

"It could be," Julie said as if it were taboo to even think it. "That's what I wanted if you must know, Jacob. I just want to talk."

"About what?"

"Well for starters, I like what you said in the meeting today. You don't have the snobbishness of the others that had come before you."

Jacob wasn't exactly sure if it was a compliment, but he wasn't sold that she wanted a normal conversation, either. There was always something. But she had won, and she wanted to talk, so he was obliged to do so. Even if he might actually get something from this himself.

"I know our two families have differences."

Jacob interrupted her, "By the way, what might those be? I can't seem to find out."

"I wish I knew; it might help to make them cooperate a bit more." She looked down at the board the pieces still arranged at the endgame scene. She began to move them back to their starting positions, except she put the white pieces on her side this time. "I was hoping you could tell me. I thought you might know since Roth did name you the Chosen. But I guess nobody is above the secret politics of the elders—that old man and our grandfathers."

Jacob watched her hands move as she reset the board. She was quick and accurate. She looked at the pieces she grabbed but not the places they went. Without looking, Julie's hands knew where each piece should be and found the proper square to rest it on. The shuffle and cluck of the pieces sliding and landing on the granite tablet had a rhythm to it like the faint sound of a djembe playing a steady beat.

She finished setting the game, and the music stopped; she looked up and connected with Jacob's stare. Without glancing down, she reached for the king's knight and set it in front of the pawn to its left. She had made the move and was now waiting for a challenger. Though it seemed much more like a challenge from Jacob's perspective.

He glanced down at the board and examined his black pieces. Jacob plucked up the queen's pawn and examined it in his hand. "What do you want?"

She smiled, "Just to talk over a game of chess and learn how we can fix things. Our parents don't seem to care, so I suppose we must."

He set the piece back down on the square it came from, "I'm not convinced," he replied. Jacob held his hand there, he wanted to let the piece go and continue this conversation without another game but he could not bring himself to release the piece. Instead he moved it one step forward. He needed to even the score.

Jacob let go and retracted his hand, folded his arms, and smiled to his cousin.

CHAPTER 9

"Well that doesn't sound so bad," Emily said, after he was done explaining the story, "You make it seem like your family is much worse."

"You have not met them then," Jacob replied, looking off to the far side of the school's cafeteria. "They are much worse in person."

Emily shrugged, "It seemed to me like she just wanted to play a game."

"It *seems* that way," Jacob emphasized, "My people do things with ulterior motives and metaphors."

"You think she could be trying to get you to relax?" Emily continued. "Maybe that game of chess could have been a metaphor for a much larger game she's playing with your mind." There it was, Emily had just carelessly explained what he was thinking. But unlike Jacob's serious concern, Emily was poking fun at his paranoia and trying to guess what was going to happen in the next chapter of the story.

"That's exactly what I was concerned about," Jacob sighed nervously.

"Why? Now that you know this is a game, you can start playing." Emily spoke as if it was as simple as the school's sports team competing against another school. "It will be easy if she doesn't know you figured it out."

"But," Jacob hesitated, "if it's a metaphor, I'm not doing so well."

Emily gave a curious look, "Why is that?"

"I lost both games."

Emily thought for a moment and then her gentle smile broke across her glaring concentration. "She didn't ask anything after she won; those games don't matter so you have not lost anything yet. It's just a metaphor for what she's up to, not the outcome."

Jacob smiled back at her, reflecting on the comment, "And now that I know what she's up to, did I really lose those games or have I still won?"

"I suppose it depends on how you use the information," Emily considered. An autumn breeze blew a stray strand of her hair into her face. She brushed it away and smiled. It was strange, he didn't know much about the girl, but the way she took an interest in him and eagerly played along made him think he might like her.

September became October, and October became November. It grew cold in the library. The hills of Scotland became covered in a thin white powder in the late end of the month. Inside the ruined castle, many fires burned to heat the rooms, but the only place a person could really be warm was the forge. But that's not why Jacob spent most of his time there. He was about to solve the mystery behind the Light Shard, he hoped. For three months he had worked out the problems, and he was at the end of his patience when Emily, who thought this was some kind of fantasy he dreamed up, suggested to put the light in it: *"If it's supposed to give light, it must have a light source right?"*

He had no idea how that was supposed to happen, but he thought he found the missing element. It's funny how she had solved this and didn't even know it was real. He had the handle perfectly crafted, and the blade had just cooled. Since the first trial, he no longer used casts, instead he used an eastern folding art to form the blade. Done this way, the blade would be much stronger. Each time, he recycled as much of the materials as he could. Getting the bits of diamond dust out of the silver was a chore, but he didn't have to crush them, so the time it took was really about the same. Most of the time he found he could reuse the handle, but this time, he was working with completely new materials.

The weapon was ready to put together, but this time he used a moonstone. It was a semiprecious rock that absorbed and emitted light. He was not sure how it was supposed to be applied, but he took a guess and used a small round stone. After holding it in the coals of the burning cedar for some time, Jacob removed it. It was glowing red hot from the fire but it also held a pure white light that beamed between the tongs he held it with. He had seen these stones glow before, but the heat of the fire made it sparkle with a kind of brilliance that only the sun held.

He dropped the small pebble into the slot where the blade should go and then slid the blade in after it. There was the clicking, buzzing sound of the metal bonding to the marble like the other attempts had. But this time the blade turned red. Jacob studied the reaction, not quite sure what was happening. The red brightened slowly to yellow, and the diamond at the bottom of the handle lit up brilliantly. Jacob watched as the yellow grew brighter and became white. Power pulsed from the light, amazing power. The silver blade was so white that he could hardly look at it. And then the diamond became so bright that the entire room filled with a flash of lightening. Only it was not so much a flash because it lingered for a while. The light was energy and power; it filled the room and washed Jacob with more power than he had ever felt before.

It faded slowly and Jacob could see again. The blade was silver again, but it seemed like it was brighter now, purer and full of energy. He had done it! But he wasn't excited like he thought he would be. What had happened was a bit terrifying. The blade had power. He could feel it in his hand; he could tell by looking at it. It would not be long before someone would ask him—everyone in the castle had to have felt that burst.

He could have guessed Rain would be the first to arrive. "Was that you just now?" she asked, half running to his side. Her hair was shimmering blond, highlighted with silver, and neatly framing her fair-skinned face in the red light of the forge. Jacob suddenly did not want to reveal what he had made; it had scared him. "Yes." But he couldn't lie about it.

"Then you did it?" She was energized and excited as she reached for the new blade he had crafted.

Jacob picked it up first, "No." He burst out; he barely understood the power of this thing, and he did not want *anyone* to touch it until he knew what it could do.

Rain withdrew her hand and looked at him as if he had just stabbed her with the blade. "Sorry," Jacob said. "It was not quite ready." He shrugged—maybe he could lie. "This one was nearly perfect, but it's not complete." Jacob hesitated; she would know he had lied.

"We felt that in the lower levels, Jacob." Rain replied, slightly put off.

Jacob looked up into her golden eyes, they were hot and wanted answers; she knew he was hiding the truth. But graciously, she was going to let him keep his secret. "I'll surely have it next time." Jacob said. "Tell Roth I'll have a gift for him at the next council meeting."

Rain raised her eyebrow, "You would create this and then give such a fine creation to Roth?"

"He is the leader of the clans." Jacob argued, "If anyone deserves to wield such a weapon, it is him."

Rain drew closer and wrapped her hand around his hand that held the blade, "Why should he have one and not the Chosen?" she whispered.

He knew she was not fooled. She knew the blade in his hand was a real Light Shard. She just didn't know how much it had scared him; she thought he wanted it for himself. She thought he *should have it for himself.*

Well he did. He started this research to try to make him more efficient in his other job. Now that he thought about it that way he wanted to hide it altogether, even from Roth. He had made this, he needed this, and it was his!

But that was not fair.

He didn't have to share the technology, but he was obligated to show off his skill. Not for his own glorification but to show that the lost secrets of his family could be found.

Rain's hand pushed his clenched fist gently to his chest and then slid up to clasp his shoulder. Jacob felt her try to read him again. He wanted to, but she had still not answered his questions from the last time, and he shut her out of his mind. "Be careful, I am not the only one who took note of you," she whispered, and continued to attempt to connect with his mind. "You are always being watched. What you have done is only a proof of the threat that you pose to the Powers of the Air."

She spoke as if the link had been confirmed, like she was seeing an event in his very near future. "They will move against you for this, already they plot from the darkness. You must keep it; protect it, just as it shall protect you, and be on your guard."

Her golden eyes tried to pry into his soul, and he could not look away. Jacob kept trying to push her out of his mind, but he nearly lost his thoughts in her unblinking stare. It was inviting, but there was a strange void behind the warm gaze. The void, Jacob picked up something from her, had he created a link? Had she? Even a faint one? But he had shut her out, he thought. He denied the communication, but he was somehow in her mind, or more like just slightly in the doorway. He should not be feeling this. Some kind of metaphor was leaking between them. Was this a secret hidden in her mind—a place he did not want to be right now? He thought of her as a friend, but two centuries of memories were stacked in here, and there were many things that she knew, which he didn't want any part of.

That void called to him. No, it clung to him, attached to him, wanting to fuse with his mind and become part of him. Was this metaphor from his mind or hers? He backed out and blinked free. Jacob had not noticed that his other hand had found rest on her shoulder. He stepped back and withdrew himself. That glimpse had startled him a bit, he was not sure what it was, if Rain even knew it was in her mind or if it wasn't Rain's mind, but his own he had been in.

"What's wrong?" Rain asked. and a fleeting wrinkle of confusion crossed her otherwise perfect face.

Any other person would not have caught the brief expression, but to Jacob, it couldn't be clearer. "You didn't feel that?" Jacob stepped toward her again and almost reached for her but stopped himself. "I was in your mind."

"No. How?" She stepped back this time as if Jacob had offended her.

"I'm not sure," he began, "I refused the connection, and the next thing I knew I was in your mind."

"What did you see?" Rain demanded.

Jacob paused, was there something he was not supposed to see? He could refuse to tell her until she finally told him what she had seen the last time. "I'm not sure."

"What was it?" she persisted; it was not like her to be so urgent.

"What did you see?" Jacob asked his question instead.

"Just as I said: nothing." Rain said, her expression was worried, on the verge of panic. "I saw nothing, I felt nothing, just you pushing my touch away." Rain replied. "You said you saw something."

"Maybe I did. But last time you never told me what you saw. You first." Jacob challenged. "If it was nothing when I could not see or feel, then it was nothing just now. If you must know, then so shall I."

Rain lowered her gaze and the stepped toward him again. She slowly looked up and stared at him. Through her fey and stoic expression, he could tell that she wasn't pleased. "I saw choices." She appeared as if she might cry suddenly, though it wasn't in her nature to show any hint of emotion.

"Choices?"

"Choices you would be faced with," Rain explained.

Jacob gently grabbed her shoulder again—it was a subconscious movement to keep her from turning her face from him. "What kind of choices? What did I do?" It wasn't a question he was supposed to ask. He wasn't really supposed to know, but the way Rain reacted had scared him.

"I only saw the choices I did not see what you chose." Rain looked away, unable to meet his gaze.

"Are they that bad?" Jacob asked.

"Your job is hard; you will be faced with many choices you should never have to face. I cannot tell you what they were, and I can't say when. Jacob, I'm sorry I wish things were different." Her voice that had always been so unyielding carried traces of remorse.

"What's that supposed to mean?" Jacob replied, "I know I'll have these choices to make; I've made some already."

"It is not my place to change your future." Rain answered. "I wish I could change—never mind, that would be both foolish and selfish."

"Then you did see my future? Selfish?" Jacob inquired and stepped toward her. "Tell me what you saw."

"I saw choices that you would receive," Rain repeated.

Jacob took another step forward, "No, Rain, you did see something; what was it?"

Rain did not answer, she only stared at him and as she did so, her normal features of stoic expression returned as if nothing had happened.

She looked back up at him, Jacob had never seen her so emotional before. Rain's golden eyes had dimmed, and she looked like she was about to burst into tears. "That is what I saw, now tell me, what did you see?"

"That's not all, is it?" Jacob asked.

"It's all I know," Rain replied, "What did you see?"

"Whatever you saw I promise you, it won't be that bad. You of all people should know that these things are not certain." Jacob gave up on getting any more information from her. She nodded at his words.

Jacob paused—no it wasn't all she had seen. Didn't he already know this? How was this a secret? He knew, Rain knew, long before anyone ever tried to look into his future knew that he would face such trials. Whatever she had seen, bothered her greatly. Either it was terrible or she was somehow involved.

"It was dark, empty," he began. "It was brief, but it called to me."

Rain did not say anything; she just kept staring at him, "It was like an empty place that needed to be filled. It was a void, seeking me in the darkness."

Rain moved back and turned her back to him. "Rain I don't know what I saw." Jacob continued. "If there's something wrong, you can tell me." He had felt the void; it touched him and brushed his soul. It wanted him, but he was afraid to let her know what he had sensed.

She made a slight sigh, and Jacob heard a whisper, "So then, you have already made your choice . . ."

Jacob didn't understand. He stepped forward, "What choice? I haven't done anything yet. I don't understand." If that was it, then that didn't seem like much to get worked up about. It didn't even make sense to Jacob. Rain was still hiding something, and that might reveal why it had particularly upset her.

Rain drew a steady breath. "I'm fine, Jacob. I'm sure it was nothing." As Jacob reached to place his hand on her shoulder, she made her way to the door and left.

Jacob was again confused by her secrets; there was something wrong, and they both knew it. Until they were both honest with each other, neither could help the other. She had to know that he wasn't stupid. Whatever was bothering her was so bad that it couldn't be kept behind her stone-cold expressions, and that said a lot.

All he had seen was an empty, dark expanse. How did that mean he had already made his choice? His attention reluctantly returned to the thriving bright blade in his hand; he had what he had labored for. Then why did he feel like something was out of place?

During lunch the next day he told Emily he had finished the project, and her idea had helped. She was thrilled when he said he wanted to show it to her, but they had to wait until after school. It would not be safe to let too many eyes grace that blade. He was surprised Rain had let him leave with it. Normally, such things had to stay hidden, but she seemed like she didn't care at all. So in the parking lot after their last class, he let Emily see the magic craft.

"Oh, that's pretty." She remarked when she saw the handle sticking out of the sheath. She reached for it. He didn't retract it as he had when Rain tried to take it; he felt more comfortable with Emily taking it. Perhaps because she was incapable of unleashing the power it contained. She pulled on it, and the shiny silver blade emerged. It beamed in the midafternoon sunlight. The snow around them was jealous of the brightness and purity of the silver. "Wow," Emily gasped, "You made this? It sure looks like magic." She examined the gold worked into the handle and the diamond on the end.

"It is magic," Jacob replied.

Just then the diamond on the end lit up and beamed with a piercing white light. Jacob had been able to do a few things with it but was not expecting Emily to be able to turn on any kind of power.

"It . . . glows?" Emily asked.

The blade began to glow as well, and Jacob took it back. The light faded. He was scared again—she should not have been able to do that. Or was this power not bound by bloodlines?

"This is a very powerful weapon," Jacob explained as if she knew the reality of it. "It must be treated with respect and handled with extreme care."

Emily smiled, "I know, you should keep it safe."

"I made this, and I'm afraid to let anyone use it or know about it." Jacob said and placed the blade back in its sheath. "But soon there will be another."

"You will make another?" She asked curiously.

"For Roth." Jacob said, "I told him I would have a gift for him next week."

"Roth?" Emily thought for a moment, "That's the really old guy that rules over all the clans right?"

Jacob smiled. She might think this was all a fairy tale, but she wanted to be part of it. "Yes."

"I should hope he would be responsible enough to use it," she said.

"He is," Jacob answered, "Probably more than I am."

"Well if he isn't, you will hold the only equalizer."

Jacob looked down at the blade in his hand, "Roth always has the clans' best interest at heart. If anyone, he should have this."

"Then why not give him that one?" Emily asked.

Jacob paused, "I think it will help when I have to fight these spirits."

"Well, it should help." Emily smiled. "That really is a magic blade."

They paused for a moment. Jacob turned and placed the blade back in a safe place. "Jacob, I really want to see one of the adventures you have."

Jacob stopped himself from laughing at the request. "It's not an adventure you want to be honest."

"Well, I was thinking since we have a break for a few weeks, I might be able to go with you." Jacob didn't like that idea at all—she still thought it was a game. And even if she knew it was real, he would never put her in that much danger.

"On an adventure?" He asked trying to act as normal as possible.

"Just once." Emily was excited just thinking about it, "It would be so much fun."

Jacob thought for a moment, how he should say no? He didn't want to because the idea of spending some time with her away from school was nice, but there was no chance he would let her near a spirit.

"An adventure?" Jacob said it as if the idea was a revelation, "Would dinner qualify as an adventure? A small one perhaps?"

Emily thought for a moment, not the adventure she thought of, but she liked that, too. She smiled, her green eyes were bright against the white background of the snow-covered hillside, sparkling with anticipation, "That sounds like a very nice adventure, Jacob."

Jacob hoped she wasn't thinking his dinners were just as dangerous as his *adventures*. "I think I have a good place in mind." Jacob said. "Friday night after school? I could pick you up." He was stunned by how simply that had just spilled out of him.

"Okay, Friday, we can have our small adventure." Emily, always smiling, was beaming with excitement. She hugged him tight, "Thanks, Jacob. I'll see you tomorrow."

Jacob barely had time to return the hug before she was skipping away. "Bye," he said and stood there for a moment before getting into the truck to return home.

CHAPTER 10

J acob's normal week dragged on endlessly as he waited for the weekend to arrive so he could study. This week had seemed as if it would never end. And finally it did. He couldn't explain why he had anticipated this so much, or why; now that the night was here, he had suddenly become nervous. He had picked Emily up from her house, and they had gone to eat. As they got out to enter the diner, Jacob noticed that the sky was exceptionally clear and crisp. The stars were very bright, even though they were just starting to shine, and they illuminated the white hills of the countryside in the distance. It was almost perfect.

Jacob made his way around the truck and opened the door for Emily. He was glad that Emily had not dressed too formally. She wore a casual dress, nice but not-over-the-top showy. It was a deep maroon, contrasting her green eyes that sparkled like the stars when she blinked. They made him forget all about the biting cold of the frozen night air. The dress was almost the same color as the dried Vitality that he had given her. She had preserved it and dried the flower again and used it to decorate her neat waves of shiny brown hair. Her dress was simple, but her presence, the way she carried herself, was what made her beautiful. She smiled like always and straightened out her coat over her shoulders as she got out of the truck. Not wanting to wrinkle the sleeves of her dress, she had crossed her arms over her chest inside the coat, one holding her purse under it and the other holding the collar of the coat together around her neck.

Jacob reached up and buttoned the top button of her coat for her. His hand brushed hers, and she clasped it. It dropped to her side still holding his. Jacob smiled and then they walked to the door. Jacob, who normally hated the cold, could have stood out here for hours. As cold as it was, he was oblivious to it.

It was a quaint little place, not too formal and not very big. The place was family owned, and so the service was more personal than most chains. A server was with them in moments to offer them complementary water and ask if they wanted anything else to drink. They both decided they were satisfied with water. The server was kind enough to point out some specials and the most popular item on the menu, as well as give descriptions of the dishes. Once he had finished, he stepped aside, promising to return in a minute to let them decide. Jacob had already made up his mind. The waiter returned promptly and gathered their requests and menus. Jacob found it hard to find something to start a conversation with. He tried not to say anything stupid like he had the day they met.

"Emily, tell me something about yourself." It wasn't the best thing he could have said, but he really didn't know much about her.

She looked up and her natural smile seemed to put him at ease, "What do you mean?"

"Anything, what you like to do, where you grew up, who your favorite or least favorite teacher is. I mean, all the time we've known each other, we've always talked about me. I don't really know anything about you."

"That's because you're so much more interesting," Emily said, "I'm very boring. For fun I like to draw, I've lived here all my life, and I like all my teachers, I can't say I like my math class though."

Jacob shrugged, "There's a start. Why not math?"

"I hate math," Emily replied. "I just don't understand most of it. I can do it, but it just takes so long."

"Well see, if I had known that, we could have spent some of this time going over that," Jacob pointed out. "I'm good with math."

Emily sighed, "I'd rather be off in my own little world. That's why I never asked."

"Well, the offer is still on the table if you ever want the help." Jacob said. "So what do you like to draw?"

Emily smiled and looked off in a different direction. "Anything really. But recently what I draw most are the adventures you tell me about." Her eyes glinted with enthusiasm, and the mysterious familiarity filled up in them.

"Oh really?" Jacob asked. "I'd like to see it."

Emily's gaze dropped to her lap and she fiddled with her napkin, "Nobody has ever seen my drawings."

"Why not?" Jacob inquired.

"Well," Emily said and the looked back up. "I just don't like people looking at my art."

Jacob thought, "I guess I understand that. I'd still like to see it."

Emily looked down again, "Maybe—if you promise not to laugh."

"Why would I?" Jacob asked and leaned forward.

"I don't know; I just don't like it when people see my art. I guess I'm afraid of criticism, and I can't stand false praise, either. I can always tell when it's sincere or not." She glanced back up at him, "It sounds silly; either way, I just don't like what people say to me."

Jacob leaned forward so he could see her green eyes better. A few stands of hair had fallen in her face—he brushed them aside, and his hand hit the dried flower in her hair. It moved slightly out of place. Emily instinctively moved her hand to correct it. Jacob stopped her. He did it himself and performed the trick he had when he gave it to her. The flower rejuvenated and the petals unfolded and regained their color, and the sweet scent of the flower danced lightly through the air.

"If your work reflects the artist in any way, I'm sure it is amazing." Jacob wasn't sure where those words came from but it actually sounded nice. She blushed a little from his comment and laughed. Laughter is a natural reaction when you don't know what to do.

"I said I could always tell when a comment was sincere or not," she replied.

"It was sincere," Jacob answered.

Emily nodded, "I know, but you've never even seen my drawings. How would you know?" she asked.

Jacob shrugged, "I'm sure you're very talented. You should consider letting someone see them."

"I'll consider it," Emily replied and sipped her water, "But that doesn't mean you can see them."

"No, it doesn't." Jacob acknowledged.

By the end of dinner Jacob was beginning to convince himself that he really like this girl. During all the time they had spent together, he had done most of the talking. It was nice to actually be his quiet self and listen to Emily for a change. Jacob didn't mean to sit there for so long; he left a nice tip since they had been in the way. They had gotten deep into conversation. Jacob learned a lot about Emily's childhood: why she stared drawing, where she had gone to school in earlier years, she had no siblings, and what her favorite ice cream flavor was: chocolate cherry.

When they stepped out, Jacob noticed the sky was overcast and dark. The crystal clear stars that were just beginning to shine when they arrived were all hidden now. He wondered if the stars were still just as bright even though he couldn't see them. Of course they were. Then a feeling slowly crept up his spine. A terrible feeling. *It's not even midnight.* Jacob thought. *No, this is for certain.* He didn't have much time, he had to get Emily home and go hunt down whatever had just entered the world.

Jacob did his best to pretend nothing was bothering him and opened the door for Emily. She slid in the truck and sat down; it was the same temperature as the air and it was freezing. Jacob hated the cold. Jacob quickly got in and turned on the heat. He felt the prick on his spine again, and again, like more were coming through the barrier; something was really wrong. Whatever it was had the worst timing possible. Suddenly the cold did not matter anymore; adrenalin flushed his veins so fast he had no sense of the temperature.

He put the truck in gear and tried to drive like he wasn't in a hurry. That was hard. When these things happened, time was important. If he told Emily what was happening, she would want to go with him. She would think it was an "adventure" or some made-up fantasy he was inventing, trying to be romantic and appeal to her adventurous nature. If he didn't get her home soon, there might actually be an adventure.

After a mile, the road became thick with a fog, and Jacob knew whatever had come through was after him. It was in the fog. The good news, if he could call it that, was that these creatures had no intention of slipping by him unnoticed.

"Oooh, that fog looks wicked." Emily said as they met the wall in the road.

You have no idea. Jacob thought, "Yes, that's . . . creepy."

"I don't think I've ever seen a fog this thick before." Emily replied.

Jacob was trying to see through the thick mist; he could barely see the road. "Yes this is a little nerve-racking driving in this."

"It's kind of exciting." Emily suggested.

Oh, no it's not! Jacob thought. *If you only knew what was hiding out there.*

He slowed down. He was anxious to get out of the fog, but he could barely see the road and was not about to take chances with Emily in the truck. After a few minutes Jacob sensed more spirits coming through. He had never heard of anything like this; his father had never told him about anything like this ever happening. Where were they all coming from? He stared to worry they might target his father as well.

They could each hold their own, but they did work better together. That and Jacob was still worried about his father after his injury a few months ago. He had recovered, but that was the only time he had ever seen Drake vulnerable.

"Did you see that?" Emily asked and strained to peer through the fog.

Jacob slowed to a stop, "What?" He asked.

"I thought I saw something." Emily said.

Jacob hesitated, "Do you think you saw something or did you see something?" The fog was darker than anything he had seen, and he could sense the evil in it. It was almost as though it wasn't just dark but actually ate the light. The headlights of the truck seemed to fall short in the veil of mist.

Emily turned to speak to him, and her gentle gaze met with the most serious face she had ever seen in her life. She paused before answering, "I *thought* I saw something."

"Okay, just making sure." Jacob knew there was something out there; there was a good chance she had caught a glance of something she should never have to look at.

Jacob drove for just a little bit further and a gale burst at the truck and left the fog in its wake a bit thinner. The dark figure of a Wraith loomed in the road ahead. Jacob stopped the car; it didn't take him an instant to realize what was in his way. His adrenaline pumped as it always did before he fought.

"What is he doing just standing there in the road?" Emily asked. "This fog is so thick, someone might hit him."

"Stay here," Jacob ordered as he opened his door. These things could mask their appearance to people who did not know any better, and the fog helped hide the evil from untrained eyes.

He got out and reached behind the seat of the truck and removed the leather jacket that had all the equipment in it.

Emily's eyes were wide with worry and confusion, "Is that a gun?" She asked panicked.

"Bullets don't work on these things," Jacob replied as he retrieved Jade and the Light Shard. He got back in the truck and removed one of the orbs of water from his coat.

"Jacob, what are you doing?" Emily asked. She recognized the Light Shard, but she had never seen Jade before, "Just leave him alone."

"I don't have time to explain; just trust me and do what I say," Jacob insisted as he began to arm himself with the orbs and stakes. And then he looked at her and locked with her stare. "Exactly as I say." Jacob added. Before she could respond, he took the orb and broke it above her head. The water sprinkled down on her, and she tried to wipe off the liquid, "It is only water." Jacob assured her. The glass cut into his palm as he crushed it, and small drops of blood rolled down his wrist.

"What's wrong?" Emily asked confused.

"I'll explain later," Jacob answered and handed her the cross pendant his father had given him, "Put that on and stay here." Jacob had to remember that what he saw as a dark figure with an oozing demonic aura Emily perceived as a normal person, shrouded in fog. Unfortunately, that would change in a moment.

He got back out and shut the door. "Jacob what are you doing?" Emily asked again and unfastened her seatbelt.

"Stay in the truck. If anything happens, run," Jacob repeated. He began to walk to the Wraith. There were multiple Shadows in the fog around him, but he could not see them yet. Jacob walked slowly and swung Jade onto his back and the Light Shard around his chest as he neared the dark figure.

He got halfway there and heard the door to the truck open. "Jacob leave him alone; come back!" Emily knew something was wrong; his behavior made that obvious. She just had no idea just how bad it was.

"Please stay in the truck," Jacob repeated.

Then he heard the door close, and he knew she was not inside the vehicle. The sound of her footsteps hurried to his side. Just as he finished fastening Jade across his shoulder, she reached his side and grabbed his hand, the one that was bleeding. "Jacob, please tell me what's going on."

Jacob started to answer, but the words never made it out of his throat. A hand appeared out of the shroud of darkness around the creature and pointed toward him. The Wraith shrieked like a thousand souls in pain.

"What's wrong?" Emily asked, now frantic as she realized the deranged man was a little worse than she originally thought. The veil was beginning to falter, and soon she would see the monster as he did.

"Please just go back to the truck," Jacob pleaded locking his stare with the hellish warrior in front of him, "Trust me." He could see the ominous, red glow beneath the cracks in his armor. Hate permeated the air, thicker than the fog that threatened to smother them.

Instead of letting go of his hand and going back she held tighter. She was no longer trying to pull him back; she clung to him out of fear. She was starting to perceive the true form of the Wraith. Before he had time to react, a Shadow appeared from the darkness between him and the Wraith. Jacob drew the Light Shard with his left hand and held up the blade in a reverse grip. He hoped this thing exceeded his expectations because there was no time to test its abilities.

Emily still clung to his right hand, scared to the point of breathlessness.

He stepped back, forcing Emily to also step back, trying to get her as far from the Wraith as possible. Another Shadow appeared behind them. Jacob wrenched his hand free from Emily and drew out Jade and pointed the sword at the spirit. He stepped close to Emily, and she buried her face in his chest and started to cry. Four more Shadows appeared around them. As the creatures materialized, the darkness seemed to press on him, the air became heavy and the fog got thicker.

Now Jacob was worried. Shadows were weaker, but so many posed a great problem. Six Shadows and a Wraith. The time he had faced the Wraith and a Shadow when Drake got injured was the most he had ever had to take on at once.

"Emily," Jacob said through his teeth, "If anything happens, I want you to run." She just cried.

"Do you understand me?" He insisted, "They are here for me; if anything happens I want you to run. They won't follow you."

Jacob stepped so that he was more or less making a cage around Emily pointing the Light Shard forward at the Wraith and Jade backward keeping her as safe as possible. If he moved, they would take her. He had to make an opening.

Jacob reached into his coat with the hand that held the Light Shard and fumbled out the two remaining orbs of water. He broke them both around Emily's feet.

It was a shot in the dark, but sometimes God even heard the prayers of the damned. Jacob summoned all his courage, swallowed hard and spoke with authority, not one of his spells, but something far older—something timeless that had power to move mountains.

"In the beginning was the Word!" He yelled, "and the Word was with God, and the Word was God. He was with God in the beginning. Through him all things were made: without him nothing was made that has been made. In him was life, and that life was the light of men. The light shines in the darkness, but the darkness has not overcome it!"

As soon as he finished the quote, the Light Shard filled with illumination. It rapidly focused to the diamond in the hilt and then it shot out like a beacon as if he held the sun in the palm of his hand. The fog rolled back, and the Shadows recoiled and shrieked. It was brighter than daylight, and the white hills and trees glistened in the pure light. Jacob was also taken by surprise, not knowing that the blade would react this way. The spirits were not stunned long, and they quickly grew bold. The light aggravated them, and they moved in to extinguish it.

Energy flowed from them, and Jacob could feed off of it. He grinned behind the light in his hand, and his demon blood became hot as he drew on the power of the beast that slumbered somewhere inside him. His muscles tensed, and he became strong like a demon. It was dangerous to feed on his hidden power, and he had to be careful he didn't wake it fully, but now, if ever, was the time to use its power; his mother would not have told him how to do this if she meant for him to leave it alone. He didn't have time to think of the paradox of a demon killing other demons with holy light. He didn't have time to think about being mortal. He only had time to think about two things: Emily and the Shadows.

Jacob dropped his hand holding Jade and swung the blade around as he stepped to connect with the first Shadow. The light made it fail to retreat, and it fell dead and burned away with dry screams. He stepped toward the second and stabbed it. He paused for a second as it wasted away at the end of his sword. Looking back at Emily, he saw two of the creatures coming from behind her. Jacob stepped forward, jumping past Emily as she stood covering her face and ran Jade through the closest one. He spun around Emily and thrust the Light Shard into the second one.

Two remained—this was going much better than he had anticipated. The power hidden in the Light Shard was certainly from heaven because these creatures of darkness succumbed to its power with ease. Adrenalin and demon fury pulsed in his veins as he took a moment to stare down his opponents. One on his left and one on his right, Jacob stepped around Emily's back and thrust Jade into the one approaching from the left. Turning around quickly, he saw the last one coming—it stopped in fear. A quick step in front of Emily and he faced the stunned opponent. Jade whistled through the air, dispatching the last Shadow just as easy as the others.

He stood in front of Emily and faced the Wraith. Ashes filled the air from the Shadows burning away as they withered. Emily was standing behind him untouched and crying. Her face was buried in her hands, and she was petrified. She slowly brought her hands down with shaky motions and saw Jacob's back.

Jacob raised his weapons in a challenge and stepped forward. The closer he got, the more he could sense the Wraith weakening; the Light Shard was draining its energy. And the more the Wraith weakened, the more he could feel his own demonic powers increase. It was curious; he had been able to tap these powers on occasion, but he was now on a surge he had never felt before. It was also odd that the holy light that pierced through these evils seemed to have no effect on the heated blood of his spirit that was now flooding his veins.

The light coming out of his blade was immense, and Jacob could only make out the Wraith by its dark outline against the whiteness. Even the asphalt of the road showed white as the snow, but the Wraith was a dingy dirty brown figure holding up its hand to shield its face. The darkness that surrounded it was dissipated and the shroud of evil no longer hid the Wraith's true form. He could tell it had the same effect for Emily, too, as she screamed as the sight was revealed. He walked with the Light Shard in front of him to light his way, and he held Jade pointed at the opponent. As the distance got close enough to fight, the Wraith drew its ghostly blade and lunged forward at him.

Jacob met the blow with Jade, blocking high. The Wraith had weakened, but it still had unearthly strength, and the blow caused him to stagger back. The blood from his palm nearly caused him to lose his grip. The Wraith quickly moved before he recovered and swung on the other side. Jacob ducked under the blow and rushed in to plant Jade in his enemy's chest. The creature was still quick enough to block the attempt, and Jacob was deflected. The ground was cold—he landed hard but kept the glowing diamond pointed at the Wraith. He stood up and focused on the light. He was still not completely sure what the blade could do. As he focused his power and energy, the light changed from a wide burst and focused the majority of its power into a beam that covered the Wraith in white light.

The Wraith marched forward and as the light bathed it, it hissed and steam began to roll off of its armor. Jacob stepped to meet it. It swung again. This time when Jacob blocked, it stayed; its strength was gone. Jacob seized the chance and lunged forward. He planted the Light Shard in his opponent's side. Fire spewed from the hole the blade had punched through the armor.

The Wraith staggered back and shrieked. The stench of burnt flesh erupted in Jacob's nostrils. Jacob followed up by plunging Jade into its chest. He let go of the Light Shard and left it hanging in the creature as he continued to push Jade harder. It fell down as embers erupted from the new wound. It dropped its weapon and hissed as Jade drove deeper into its chest and pierced through his back, "Very good, my child, but the damned will be damned, and you cannot escape what becomes of us all." Jacob was stunned. He had never heard intelligible speech from any of the creatures before. He gave one last thrust, driving Jade further into the Wraith. The wound where the Light Shard was lodged began to erupt and ashes of flesh flaked off, smoke curling from its side.

"All that lives must die, and you will meet your fate; the fight is in vain," It laughed with evil satisfaction as it contorted from the pain. Jacob took his bloody fist and rammed it into the creature's jaw and sent it flailing to the pavement. His body burned from a surge of power that was trapped in his blood. The language it spoke was of the Fallen, and Jacob understood it. Though he had never really heard it spoken, the words made sense to him. "Will you kill your own? What good will it do? How will you save a soul by destroying it?" The monster laughed.

Jacob wrenched Jade out of the Wraith's chest, the creature's insides were smoldering away, and flames came out of the wound when he removed the blade. He had heard too much, and it wanted to confuse him with its speech. Jade flashed in the night air as Jacob lifted her up for the kill stroke. A few drops of his blood fell on the Wraith's face and seared its flesh. Then he dropped the blade and cleaved the Wraith's head from its shoulders. The head rolled off and, the body collapsed and the Wraith began to burn away as the Shadows had. Within moments there was nothing left but the ashes that floated away.

A cold wind wiped around him and cooled his blood as the fog rolled away with all the ashes of the spirits, revealing the stars again. The Light Shard dimmed, and Jacob picked it up reverently. He was tired.

Wraiths were supposed to be nearly impossible to get rid of—Jacob was amazed. Typically, the only way was to deport them back to Hell. Had he just killed a Wraith? He kicked himself for that being the first thing he thought of. Emily had to be horrified. He turned and ran to her. Once he got to her side, she collapsed on him, and he had to drop to one knee to catch her.

Her face was distorted with fear, tears, and a few smears of his blood that had gotten on her hands when she clenched his. The smile he knew her for and that he liked so much was so far away, he feared it may never come back. "Jacob," She whispered. "Is it real?" Then she passed out. Jacob laid her in the truck, quickly collected all his gear, and then took her to his home. Her parents would be worried in the morning—Emily would have to decide if she wanted to tell them the truth. For tonight, though, his mother would best know how to care for her. The morning would be interesting at best.

CHAPTER II

When Jacob reached his home, his father was standing on the porch waiting for him. Drake was seldom bothered by anything, but something had gotten him worried. He may have sensed all the spirits entering the world or perhaps he was worried about Jacob or maybe both. Jacob stopped the car in the front yard rather than the garage a bit to the side. He got out and walked around to the passenger door.

"Jacob, are you alright?" his father called and ran down the steps. He had put on his black suit, complete with the tie and the hat. "There was an incredible disturbance."

"I know, Dad; can you help me really quick?"

"Two Shadows attempted to make it through the barrier around the house. What's going on?" Drake asked.

"I don't know what happened." Jacob explained, "But they came after me, too—six Shadows and a Wraith." Jacob leaned into the truck and eased Emily into a sitting position before he tried to pick her up.

"Are you okay?" Drake asked. "Are you hurt? You're bleeding." He stepped beside him. He saw Emily and paused.

"I'm fine; she's alright. She just fainted." Jacob put one arm behind her head and one arm under her knees and slid her out.

"What happened out there?" His father inquired; his steel eyes collected the moonlight vibrated with concern. "Who's she?"

Jacob eased away from the door, "I'll explain after we get her inside."

"Is this Emily?" Drake asked. He shut the door to the car and ran ahead of Jacob to open the front door.

"Yes," Jacob replied, "We had just left when the fog rolled in. I tried to get her home, but they showed up before I could get her to a safe place."

Drake got out of the way and went ahead of him to the couch and made a space to lay her down. "Should I wake Lucile?" Drake asked.

"I thought she would still be awake," Jacob answered. "That is why I brought her here. No, don't wake up Mom. Emily will be fine."

"Oh, I'm already up," his mother stated as she entered the room.

She looked down at Emily and then up at Jacob. She wasn't worried, more like approving, "Emily?"

Jacob nodded, "I was attacked while I was trying to take her home. She fainted."

"She just needs rest. I'll get a blanket." Lucile turned and went back to her bedroom.

Jacob tucked her hair behind her ears and situated the flower again. It wouldn't stay put, so he just took it and placed the stem in her hand and laid it across her chest.

"You said a Wraith found you?" Drake asked as he brought a pan of warm water and a towel.

"Aye, and six Shadows," Jacob answered looking up and taking the water.

Drake knelt down beside him and examined Emily, "How did you manage that many?"

Jacob unsheathed the Light Shard and handed it to his father. "It's from Mom's side of the family." He watched as Drake's face contorted with fear and hesitation. "But it's a holy weapon. It shines in the darkness, and it made the spirits weak."

Drake looked it over, "Where did you get this?" He asked marveling at the craftsmanship.

"I made it," Jacob said and dabbed the moist towel against Emily's forehead. His hand left red stains on the towel, and he remembered he had his own wounds to tend to.

Lucile came back into the room with two blankets and stopped when she saw the blade Drake held. "Jacob, is that what I think it is?"

"I made it last week," Jacob smiled but did not turn his focus from Emily.

"What is it?" Drake asked.

"Drake, that is a Light Shard." Lucile answered. "It's a legendary weapon. It has been said that the only ones in existence were owned by the Fallen and brought to Earth when they were cast from heaven."

Drake eyed it with curiosity and then handed the blade back to Jacob. "I like it." That was the first time he had ever liked anything that was used to fight from his mother's family.

"Is she going to be alright?" Jacob asked his mother.

"Oh, she'll be fine," She replied, "She just needs to sleep." Then she looked at the towel, "I'll bring you a fresh towel and a bandage for that hand."

Drake stood up and placed a reassuring hand on his shoulder, "I'd say she was in good hands tonight." He said and looked up at Lucile. She nodded in agreement.

Jacob wasn't sure what to say, so he didn't say anything. He dropped the towel beside the bowl and grabbed one of the blankets with his clean hand and spread it over her.

"We'll make sure she is comfortable." Drake said.

"Thanks. I'm going to stay here until she wakes up." Jacob replied.

"She'll be alright, son," His mother replied.

"She was so scared when she passed out, and the last thing she saw was me fighting a Wraith." Jacob explained. "I want to be here when she wakes up so she knows everything is alright."

His mother smiled, "I understand." Then she nodded to Drake. "I think he can take care of her. There's not much else to be done until she wakes."

His parents left the room, and he sat down in the chair across from the sofa and watched Emily as she slept. It was only a moment before Lucile returned with a clean towel for Emily and a wrap for Jacob's palm. As soon as he was tended to, the house was quiet again. He wanted to ask his father about the Wraith and the words it had spoken. But he decided he would wait until later.

Jacob sat by her and applied the cold towel to her head. What a shame it was; he had just decided he liked her and then this. Two hours went by. The chair had moved to the side of the couch, and Jacob was holding her hand. She was still asleep. He had moved the end table over and had two glasses of water, one for him and the other for Emily when she woke up. Thinking two hours was a long time to be asleep from fainting, he took the Vitality from Emily's delicate grasp and waved the petals under her nose. *Perhaps it will give her good dreams*, he thought.

Emily drew a deep breath and exhaled slowly as the aroma filled her and soothed her in her slumber. She inhaled once more, and her eyes fluttered open; she held her breath and looked about the room. Before she had time to process what had happened or where she was, she sat up. Even in the unfamiliar room, seeing Jacob holding her hand, she relaxed. Emily met his eyes, still not quite sure what was happening. "Where . . ." No, that wasn't what she wanted to asked, "What . . . happened?"

Jacob smiled, "You're okay. We're fine."

"Jacob, it's real," Emily gasped.

"You're okay," Jacob reassured her, "This is my father's house. You are safe; they can't hurt you here."

She leaned forward into him and wrapped her arms around his shoulders and started to cry. "I'm so scared."

"Emily I'll never let them hurt you." Jacob promised, "Ever."

Emily needed to cry. It's what any sane person would do if they had just seen what she had. Jacob just held her. "Would you like something to drink?" he asked.

Emily nodded, and he handed her the water.

She sipped it first and then gulped half the glass. She would have finished the glass, but a sob broke the flow, and she handed the glass back. The back of her hand wiped the moisture from her lips, and she sat back against the couch trying to absorb what had happened. Jacob took the flower and stood up, "Would you like something warm?" he asked. "I can make a very good tea from this. It will calm you down and help you sleep tonight."

Emily nodded and sank down in the couch and curled up in a ball. She pulled the blanket over her while Jacob started the water boiling.

The petals and seeds of the flower were crushed in a mixing bowl; one of the things he had learned from Ellen's research was how to make a healing elixir. He tossed the mix into the pot as the water heated, and then for better flavor, he added a few cinnamon sticks and some dried orange peel and other cider spices. He returned and sat beside Emily while the water boiled. Neither of them said anything; Jacob just held her hand.

Soon the water was done. Jacob moved the pot off the stove to cool and prepared a strainer to remove the bits and pieces of the Vitality and the other spices. The water had turned a faint red from the flower, and it smelled of herbs and cinnamon and orange. Carefully, he leveled out two small cups and placed them on saucers.

He brought them over and took the water glasses away. When he returned, he helped Emily sit up and handed her the elixir. "It's hot," he warned.

She smelled the liquid and then smiled, "Thanks." She blew on it gently and took a small sip. It soothed immediately, and she took another. Her tears dried and the color came back into her smile, and the shine returned to her eyes. Jacob sat down beside her and only took a few sips, watching as Emily took in the healing tonic. When she finished he took the cup from her and set it aside, "Rest; I'll take you home in the morning."

Worry crossed her face at the thought, "My parents will be so worried. What am I going to tell them?"

"That's up to you. We'll talk about it in the morning," Jacob answered. "Just rest."

Emily laid down again, resting her head in Jacob's lap. Jacob propped his feet on the chair he had moved. "Jacob?" She whispered.

"Yes?"

"Don't leave, okay?" she asked.

"I'll be right here," he assured her.

"Never? Please don't leave me. Promise?" she whispered, nearly asleep.

Jacob grabbed her hand and gave it a squeeze, "Never."

Emily drifted into a slumber induced by the elixir he had made. It was a rejuvenating slumber that healed the body and mind. Jacob finished his tea and then rolled his head back and drifted into the same slumber. It was peaceful.

Six o' clock came early. Lucile was up and preparing breakfast when Jacob woke. He looked around to see if anyone else was up, but it was just his mother. The smell of fresh bacon was in the air. Every morning his mother cooked breakfast. On Saturdays, she made bacon and a casserole. He nudged Emily gently, and she woke.

"Hey," he smiled. "Breakfast is almost done. Are you hungry?"

Emily thought through the fog of everything still settling in her mind and then smiled, "I'm starving."

"Oh good; you're awake." Lucile said and turned from the stove to see her. She walked over and gave a warm smile to Emily. "I'm Lucile, Jacob's mother."

"I'm Emily."

"It's nice to meet you, child," she replied. "And it's good to see you're healthy after that escapade; most don't walk away from an encounter like that, much less a first. But I suppose my Jacob knows a bit more than I reckoned. I don't recall teaching him those tricks he used. You were in good hands."

"What happened?" Emily asked as she sat up. "Those things just started appearing; they were horrible. And Jacob . . . You . . . but how? What were they? That man in the road—what happened?"

"The smaller ones were Shadows. Remember how I told you the differences, and the man was a Wraith. You couldn't see it for what it was until I dissolved the evil surrounding it," Jacob explained.

"But you . . . was it real?" Emily asked. It was normal to not want to believe it. Jacob held her hand, "Yes it was real, is real. This is my life."

"I have to get home!" Emily suddenly remembered.

"Of course," Lucile replied. "But first you must be fed." She returned to the kitchen, "What would your parents think of us if we kept you all night and sent you home without breakfast?"

"Oh, but they must be worried." Emily ran her hand through her hair and held it there, the only thing keeping her from bursting into tears was the lingering effects of the tea. Frustration crossed her face, and that familiar smile washed away.

"Emily, they will be fine." Jacob assured.

"Drake has already spoken to them," Lucile added. "Now the best thing for you to do is move slowly and make sure you get a good breakfast."

"How?" Jacob asked. "What did he say?"

"Well, he called them to tell them what happened. It's not that hard to find a phone number," Lucile replied. "No sense in keeping them in the dark." She opened the oven, "Perfect. Jacob go get Sarah and Dom. Emily, you can come have a seat over here. Breakfast is finished."

Jacob stood up and helped Emily stand. "Please eat first," He insisted, "We'll leave straight after." She held onto the blanket and wrapped it around her so that it draped about her feet when she stood.

"It will be alright," Jacob said and turned to go wake his brother and sister.

Jacob returned and found the table set, a glass of orange juice with each plate, and each plate with three thick pieces of bacon and a generous serving of his mother's breakfast casserole. Saturday mornings had to be his favorite. He didn't get to sleep in like normal people, but this breakfast made up for it a hundred times over.

"So, Jacob, Roth called a council meeting for tomorrow." Lucile said casually.

"Mom, I don't think this is the time to discuss that," Sarah said quickly and nodded at Emily.

"She knows," Jacob said. "She's okay."

Emily nodded, "Jacob told me many things, but I didn't know it was all real, just like he said." Her expression was still slightly disconnected.

"You were not expecting my adventures to be this real?" Jacob asked; he knew she hadn't until last night.

"Not quite," she answered and took a strip of the bacon.

"So this meeting . . . it's early." Lucile replied.

"I assume it is because I have a gift for the old man," he asserted.

"No, Jacob, the Light Shard?" His mother asked.

Jacob looked up, "Not mine; I intend to create another one today to present to him."

"Is that wise?" Lucile asked.

"Jacob made a Light Shard?" Dom exclaimed.

"Why didn't you tell me?" his sister demanded.

Jacob pushed his seat back and gestured for the questions to slow down. "Yes I made a Light Shard. I didn't tell anyone because it is the most powerful weapon I've ever held. And yes, I believe Roth should have one." His mother glared at him; he understood why. Power often got abused in their family. "I'm not giving him the technology, just a gift."

Lucile took a forkful of the casserole, chewed, and swallowed before answering, "You are the Chosen. I suppose you know what you're doing."

"Please don't talk like that," Jacob said, "I don't like that title, it's so . . . cumbersome. Just because Roth said it doesn't make it true."

"I know, son. I'm proud of you no matter what you do, but Roth only gives this title to those he thinks to be the wisest and most able."

"But it makes everyone expect so much from me," Jacob protested.

"Jacob, I understand what you mean, but listen to me when I say you are the most qualified in our very long history. You should take pride that Roth sees that in you," Lucile explained.

"I just want to be normal sometimes, you know?" Jacob replied.

"I know," Emily said. All the eyes around the table fixed on her, "Kind of how I want to be like you sometimes." She looked around, "But it's not always as great as it seems, I guess. Sometimes, maybe the lives we have are better than we give them credit for."

Jacob thought for a moment. That was a very insightful comment—perhaps he was better off as he was. But he would never know that until he had been normal for a day. Just like Emily thought his life was so much better until she caught a glimpse of it firsthand.

To be normal—he would not have to endure all this torment he had been cursed with or the burden of so many souls. But in reality, his life meant something; to be normal would be to forfeit the meaning his life had. Where he was going now, down the hard road, would make a difference. If he were normal, he'd die and be forgotten and erased by the sands of time.

"I suppose that's right," Jacob answered. "Maybe I should start thinking about it a little differently."

His mother looked at Emily, "But he won't listen when I tell him." She smiled and then returned her attention to her home-cooked meal.

Emily calmed down a bit on the way back to her house. The reality had some time to sink in now, and the shock had worn off a little. Her parents were not thrilled about the story.

Emily backing up the story didn't exactly help their disbelief; it was tough stuff to swallow. They really didn't like the idea of Jacob being around, what parents would? Emily was stuck in the middle. Part of her craved the adventure, but the side of her mind that had awakened to just how real it was told her to recoil to her drawing room and shut out the world.

After a lot of talk that got nowhere, Emily took over the situation and made her parents stop talking. She showed Jacob out and said that she would calm down her parents, and they could see each other Monday after she convinced them she wasn't hurt. "They just need some time," she had told him.

Jacob wasn't exactly eager to leave and would have forgone the urgent business he had preparing for tomorrow's meeting to stay with her and make sure she was all right. But Emily insisted it would be better for him to come back later. "They will take it better if they hear it from me."

So Jacob tried to focus; he had an assignment. He had promised a gift for Roth at the meeting, and his deadline was approaching. However, it was hard to concentrate on the delicate work—he was worried about Emily. What would she be like on Monday after this sank in? She would probably reconsider his advice on keeping her distance. She had said she would work it out, though, and there was nothing else he could do but just trust her. It just wasn't fair; as soon as he decided he genuinely liked her, his life, the very thing that captured her interest, showed up and ran her off.

As he settled into the forge, Rain wanted to watch the crafting process, but Jacob had told her he needed to be alone. Perhaps the company would have helped; she knew something was wrong again. Rain didn't miss things like that. Two centuries of wisdom and her thriving intuition made it impossible to lie around her. You might as well just tell her truthfully that you don't want to talk about something than try to tell her nothing is wrong. At least then she might not pry it out anyway.

Today she had decided to leave it alone. But she had a way of finding out, and Jacob figured she'd start prying later. It wasn't like he really needed to keep it secret; he just didn't want to talk right now. Part of him remembered the last time they had talked—she was still keeping something from him. Did she really deserve to know what was going on in his life? Maybe she already knew.

This new Light Shard was progressing on time despite his broken concentration and lack of desire to perform the task. He was making a double-edged long sword. The new blade was much greater than the dagger he had forged last week but, given the power contained in it, Jacob doubted that size and shape had any bearing on the weapon. As he worked the metal of the blade, he wondered if he could forge *any* weapon into a Light Shard like a Morning Star mace or a spear.

The thought of a spear that had that power seemed grand; it would be like a bolt of lightning like Zeus casting thunderbolts from Olympus. The fact was a lot of his ancient relatives were tyrants and had claimed status as gods among the people they ruled. Many of them were worshiped by ancient civilizations for centuries after they died. So the likelihood that Zeus, and all the other gods of Olympus, were also his old dead relatives wasn't exactly out of the realm of possibilities.

That would be something he would never know for sure. What he did know was that where the lines between history and man's imagination crossed and blurred and twisted facts, his family was often there at the middle of it. Maybe they were not mentioned in their exact appearance and often exaggerated, but they accounted for a good portion of legends and myths.

When the shadows grew long, Jacob was applying the finishing touches on the blade. He joined the blade and the handle, and the light that he had seen the first time filled the room. It was beautiful. The sword was ready. Jacob took his creation and ascended to the upper level. He wanted to show Rain, but he couldn't let too many people know what he had done. Anyone in the facility would be curious because they would have sensed the power, and Jacob didn't actually want the word to get out.

He entered the library and saw Rain sitting at a table, reading by lamplight. Her hair hung down around her head as she read deep into the book in front of her and hid her face with faint blues and streaks of white-blond. "Have you done it?" she asked without even glancing up. She knew that he had made the weapon last time—this was not new.

"I have; would you like to see it?" Jacob asked. He had no sheath for it, and it was wrapped in a towel. He placed it on the table and unwrapped it.

Rain looked up and studied it for a moment. She touched it gently and ran her fingers down the edge of the blade to the marvelously crafted hilt. She twisted her fingers around it and lifted it off the table. Her ever-young stare followed the blade as it lifted from the table, and her hair fell away from her face. Its tint melded from blue to strawberry-blond, but not completely. In the folds of silk, there were still traces of the blue where the light had been trapped and lingered in her locks. Again Jacob found himself desiring her eternal youth, to be as young and beautiful for centuries was something most would covet.

"Spectacular, Jacob," she said as she lowered her stare from the blade to his eyes, "What do you call it?" Her face had almost no expression; her golden eyes were focused and serious.

"It's a Light Shard," Jacob said.

Rain sliced the air with the blade and twirled it about, making it whistle. "A blade this fine must have a name, Jacob." She said and looked at him again.

"A name?" Jacob repeated.

"Yes, do you intend to give Roth a blade with no name?" she asked and gently ran her had up and down the smooth side of the blade.

"I'll call it . . ." He thought for a moment trying to think of a good name, one that would define its purpose. "Judgment," he whispered.

Rain squinted as she quickly thought it over, "A fine name." She opened her eyes and laid Judgment back on the table and rewrapped it. "You are very skilled, Jacob. There is nothing you can't do."

The serious expression she had moments ago was gone, and her eyes appreciated him. "I try," Jacob said. "Will you keep it until I come for it in the morning?" Jacob asked gesturing at the sword.

Rain nodded at the request, "I'll take care of it in your absence."

"Thank you," Jacob replied, "Does Roth know what to expect?"

"I only told him you had a gift as you instructed." Rain answered. "Roth will be very pleased when he sees this. He will be very pleased with you." She hesitated as if she meant to say something more, "I am pleased with you."

He wanted people to approve of him, right? This was a good thing. Then why did it only make him feel worse, more weight and more nervous? Jacob suddenly felt the fatigue of his restless night and long day of work, and worry hit him. He sighed heavily, "Thank you, Rain. I've had a long day. I think I'll go rest now."

Rain gave him a look, almost an inquisition, but it was like she already had the answer, "What's wrong?"

There it was, Jacob knew she would start prying at some point. "Just stuff. I'll be fine; I'm just tired."

"Of course, your task must take so much from you." Rain said it more as a question for him to explain. "You mustn't wear yourself too thin, Jacob."

"It is very tiring," Jacob said and then stepped back toward the door. "I'll be here in the morning to pick up the gift."

CHAPTER 12

Again, morning came too early. Jacob had not rested well—his mind was still full of worry, and he was anxious to know what was happening with Emily. But she had told him to wait until Monday. He trusted her judgment, but he still wanted to see her and didn't like waiting. He thought about sending Roth's gift with his mother and skipping the meeting to see Emily, but that would be highly frowned upon. Perhaps it would be best to lay low for a while anyway. Emily needed to process what had happened. He wouldn't doubt her if she never wanted to speak to him again.

The air was still crisp, and the sun was barely above the snowy hills when he arrived at the library. Rain was waiting for him with the sword still wrapped in the towels. "Good morning." Her salutation hung on the icy breeze and mingled with the rays of the morning sun. She stood facing east in the gateway to the courtyard, the farthest she was allowed to go by the magic of the castle. The air was brisk and chilly, but she did not seem to be affected by it. In the morning light, she was stunningly beautiful and almost terrifying.

Jacob had worn thick clothes and a heavy coat, but all Rain was wearing was that dress of otherworldly weave, which appeared bright blue with illusive steaks of gold in the wind-tossed folds. The winter wind blew strands of her hair about her face and caused her dress to flutter around her feet. Her hair was white-hot blond in the sunlight and danced about her like snow in the wind. Jacob saw the sunrise in her eyes, and she seemed to be the only thing in the world that had warmth as if she had stolen the energy of the sun and caused it to be so cold.

"Good morning, Rain," Jacob said and stopped in front of her. "Aren't you cold?"

Rain lifted her arms to catch the first rays of the morning sun as they bathed her. "The sun will warm and sustain all. Nature sustains me, and the sun is a gift for my eternal youth."

Jacob didn't understand what she meant. "You shall have to teach me that someday," he said and held out his hand for the blade.

"The secrets of immortality I may show you." Rain replied and dropped her arms to her side, "But the price is great for those that seek long life."

Now he was worried she might actually show him. Would he be like her? Eternally young? Everlasting youth didn't sound so bad, but the fervent solitude of being immortal and alone was just as inviting as the blast of cold air ripping at his legs. Then he remembered that she felt that aloneness and lived that solitude every day. If there was a way to share that kind life, Jacob would take the chance. But he would rather die young while he still had friends and family than live alone for centuries after all his kin had died.

"May I have Judgment?" Jacob asked.

Rain shut her eyes and inhaled the sun, "If it is what you wish; it belongs to you." She opened her eyes and stared into his and took his hand with hers. It was warm. Impossible, how was she not freezing? She then placed the blade in his palm and withdrew from him.

Jacob followed her into to the courtyard and noticed she was barefoot in the snow. Her hair and dress trailed behind her until they entered the castle. Out of the wind, her hair fell about her shoulders and warmed to show faint steaks of red in the bright blond. The dress she wore imitated her hair, though not as subtle, and slowly melded into a light pink.

In the lower levels of the library, he would find a portal that would take him to Stirling where all meetings were held. Rain stood aside at the passage and nodded down the hall. "I wish you the best, Jacob, I have other things to tend to. We may talk later."

"Thank you," Jacob nodded. "I will be here often in the next few weeks; there will be a lot of time for talk."

Then he turned down the dark tunnel. Torches illuminated it just enough to see the width of the passage. Jacob knew the way and had grown used to the maze of dim lights. He passed a few corridors that went to places he did not know about. Perhaps a project for the time he was away from school would be to explore more of the castle. On his left, one passage let in a cold wind and the light of day. That was the Oasis, one of the few places in the grounds that was outside. Perhaps he would figure out what was under the Oasis's east gate. He had been told not to bother, and so far he had not asked questions. But he was on the council, and he was the Chosen, so he should deserve to know. He would ask Roth today to permit him unlimited access to the grounds and try to appoint Rain as a guide for him. He knew she could tell him a few of the ancient secrets.

He kept walking until he came to a place where the hall turned right. Walking to the wall, he knocked until he heard a hollow sound. He then removed the ring Henry had given him so long ago and placed it on his finger. Just a whisper and the bricks restacked and formed a door. He passed through, and they clattered back into place.

The room he stood in was huge with a vaulted ceiling. It was lighted by torches that had been enchanted to never extinguish. This was the newest megalith known.

It was built in secret by Roth's father. Jacob stepped toward the middle and mumbled to the ring, and a white orb appeared in the center. He stepped in. The next moment he was in Stirling. The transfer no longer jarred him; he had become used to it, and the feelings of vertigo were a thing of the past. But what did take him by surprise was the sheer number of people in the room. The council was only two families and only three members from each, along with Roth. There were at least two-dozen people here.

He stepped back and noticed snow was falling through the hole in the ceiling. The council normally sat together so that any one speaking to them could address them all at once. But the members were scattered about in the stone ring. Jacob looked around and spotted Roth. Roth nodded and raised a hand for silence. He spoke in Latin and announced Jacob's arrival and called the meeting to order. Jacob thought nothing of it. Tradition was to do so, and with such a large crowd, it would be done.

"May I conduct the first order of business?" Jacob asked.

A man made a remark in a language he did not understand.

Roth raised his hand again and waved him away and again spoke in Latin, "He was not aware that others were here, Ress. The boy was not informed this was a joint council meeting."

Jacob looked at the man who had made the remark; he was a tall black man with tribal tattoos all over his bare chest. He was bald and carried an ornate war spear. Jacob nodded in his direction and said, "I apologize, Ress. May I conduct the first order of business?" he repeated in Latin. Many of the members in the family knew many languages, but it would be impossible to have all clans speak the same language. They were on every continent, and there were over twenty different native languages among the scattered people. The only way to ensure that they all could communicate was if they all spoke one language. So all council members of each clan were to learn Latin. That way clans from Africa could communicate with clans in Europe, and clans in Asia could talk to clans in South America.

Ress smiled and nodded.

"Proceed," Roth said.

Jacob turned to him, "For you, I have a gift."

"I was told you would have something," Roth replied.

Jacob walked to him. "I think you will be pleased, sir, with what I have for you."

Roth sat straight and prepared to see what he had.

Jacob took the sword out from under his coat and held it up for the council to see. "Judgment, the blade of the sun. I crafted this as a gift to the man who rules the clans of the Fallen." He kneeled and presented it to Roth still wrapped in the shoddy towels.

Roth took it and laid it in his lap and unwrapped it curiously. When he saw the delicate craftsmanship and the glorious beauty of it, he knew what it was. "Jacob, is this real?" he asked, his old dry voice had a bit more power to it.

"It is real, my lord."

A murmur ran through the council as they strained to see what it was. But Roth did not show it to the other members. Lucile was the only one not surprised, and she smiled at her son's handiwork.

"It is a Light Shard," Roth whispered, covering it back in the towels. The archaic dusty tone he usually spoke with seemed less dead. "Our Chosen has forged with the angels," Roth remarked to the crowed. He stood up and held the blade backward in a gesture to return it, "My son, I cannot take this from you, such a fine workmanship belongs in the hands of the Chosen."

"It is a gift for the man who is worthy to wield it and only proper that the ruler of us holds it," Jacob replied. "With your permission, I will craft my own. But Judgment, my lord, belongs to you."

Roth withdrew the blade, he looked at it curiously as if he were afraid of it. He lowered his voice to a whisper, "Jacob, the Chosen has the right to our weapons, and you have discovered this technology. You may create what you wish. But exercise caution with whom you present these things; this is power, and there are many here who should not see such things." He sat back in his seat. "I accept your gift," he declared.

"Thank you." Jacob stood up and found a seat between a Chinese monk and a man who looked to be from Russia.

"This meeting has been ordered to present the interest of all the clans in the one I have named the Chosen." Roth said as Jacob sat down. "The people in this room are chosen from the clans far and wide, one from every ruling family as their representatives to you. Some are revered on their councils, and some are assigned to the task. They are the wisest and the strongest among the clans. They are here to represent their clans before you."

"What does this mean?" Jacob asked.

"They will communicate with you and let you know what is happening in their homes. They will report problems within the clans to you, so you may know what to do." Roth replied.

Jacob didn't understand at first. But he stood up as if to give a speech. He paused as the Latin was lost for a moment and then began, "Thank you all. I'm sure among you are volunteers and elected, but I want to let you know that you are appreciated. I asked for your help because I do not know what to do. Does anyone among you know what I must do?"

No response came from the crowd.

"Can you forgive sin?" he asked to the Russian looking man on his left.

"No," he replied.

"Neither can I. I am not Jesus Christ. So why should I be the only one to carry this? I need your help. I am damned, you are damned, and we cannot commune with God. How will we fix this?"

The man did not have an answer. "How will we fix this?" He asked a woman who looked to be from India. She gave no response.

"How will we fix this?" he repeated to the entire room. He waited a few moments and then continued. "Roth you don't understand. I don't know what to do. These people can no more help me than I can redeem my own damned soul." Jacob turned to look at the old man. "I cannot ask for their help if I don't know what needs to be done. Tell me first what I am to do. You pass this burden off to me, so you don't have to be judged, but you will still stand to be judged with or without a Chosen. Therefore, it wouldn't hurt to do something to help."

Jacob sat back down, and a long silence ensued. The faces of all the strange people were confused; some were disappointed, others contemplative, a few were sympathetic, but most were shocked. They had all heard Jacob was the Chosen, but they had never stopped to think about how he felt about the whole thing and now they knew. And now they would go home to their clans and tell them what he was like.

"Jacob the Chosen will know what to do when the time arises. It's not going to be something you know how to do. You will just do it." Roth finally told him the truth—there was no plan. There was no plan for salvation, just a random shot-in-the-dark guess that he would have a revelation and be shown the direction he should go.

"So what good was it to bring them all here?" Jacob asked. "None of the other clans know what needs to be done."

"They are here to let you know when there are issues within their clans that need your attention."

"Such as?" Jacob asked looking around the room. He was not sure he liked where this was going; he could barely handle his own family, and he was not excited about getting involved in the problems of people he didn't know.

"You will make sure they stay in check and do not advance our debt of sin."

For two hours the meeting continued; Jacob learned that he had only placed more of a burden on himself. He was disappointed but not surprised; all the council had really ever done to him was make him responsible for others. It was one thing to be responsible as a leader, but this was getting out of control. He might as well be in Roth's position as the leader of the clans.

A few clans were unruly and needed to be dealt with. He would have to speak with the councils and set them straight. The consensus was that the clans that did not fall in line would be subject to the punishment of the Chosen, which meant Jacob and his aids would have to dispatch and replace the council. He was basically assigned to be the law.

Again, it should not be his responsibility.

Not only was it one more responsibility, it was dirty work. Jacob didn't like the idea, but it wasn't that different from what he normally did. His family was half-breed demons. The ones who surfaced in history tended to be more corrupt, such as Dracula and Nero. Evil exuded from them, and they had to be removed. He would of course use every resource possible before he resorted to aggressive tactics. Had it not been his own family, he might not be so careful. Had it not been his own family he would not be involved.

He did get Roth to grant him unlimited access to the library. But he decided against asking for a guide. Rain would probably do it, anyway, but he didn't want to seem too needy. The next few months, as the clans came together, would be interesting.

His council also gained a new burden of sorting everything and keeping all the information from the other clans together. Jacob obviously could not do it and had asked that the home council keep up with it so that they could come to him with the problems, and if he needed to attend to them, he would go where he was needed. Though, as he would have guessed, most issues were petty, and either dismissed or handled by William and Henry. Jacob knew he would only seldom hear anything important come from the other clans.

As soon as he returned from Stirling, he wanted to visit Emily and tell her about it. The good news that he finally had help, the not-so-good news that he was expected to police his family if they got out of line. Maybe she would have something to say. Or would she even want to hear it anymore? First thing in the morning—part of him was tempted to wait until midnight so it would be Monday, but he decided that was a little too literal. Emily said Monday, so he would give her until Monday. He just hoped that he hadn't caused so much damage that she would stop talking to him.

He decided to spend the rest of the day translating and went to the library to find Rain. The familiar smell of old dust brought him some comfort, and it had grown on him enough that it had begun to stimulate his mind when the scent was strong. He had almost completed retranslating the *Book of Anzel*, and he had begun retranslating the parts of Denomoi that had been previously deciphered and was getting ready to start looking at the parts that had yet to be translated. For practice, he had also begun to retranslate and attempt to finish the translation of Arteminus, *The Book of the Heart*. From the parts that were understood, it was written by one of the fallen angels thought to be a female and went into great detail about the distinctions between human thoughts and emotions and angels'. It glorified the human heart for its unbound ability to love and hate. But it was also full of questions as to why humans could not comprehend God so fully as an angel. Arteminus wondered if she had been deceived to rebel and be cast down. How then could a human who does not know, as well as she does, the true glory of God ever come to salvation?

Parts of the book where the translation was lost seemed to explain that comprehension and emotion were two parts of God's mind. The angels had lesser emotions because they lived in God's presence. Humans were made to live on Earth and were given greater emotions, so they could better experience God through them. Understanding this might help him in some ways. At the very least, it would prove a good read and a challenging exercise. Today he stuck to the retranslation of Anzel, though. He had nearly finished it, and he was getting a very accurate translation now and almost understood the language enough to read it fluently.

He sighed and closed the book, three thousand, four hundred six pages down—and only two hundred thirty-nine to go. He closed the translated version and placed it on top and then folded up his translation and placed it on top of that one. He hefted the heavy books and carried them back to Rain's desk.

She was not there to receive them. He wanted to tell her what had happened. They had not had a chance to speak, but she was not here, so he left the books and the comforting smell of knowledge on the stone table and returned home.

CHAPTER 13

Many more late nights and early mornings like this, and he would have to quit. But today it didn't matter if he was tired. He had worried about Emily the entire weekend, and now he could finally go see how she was—or rather how her parents were doing, she had seemed very clam and actually took it a lot better than most people would have.

When he arrived, her father opened the door and wasn't thrilled to see him, to put it nicely. Fortunately, Emily arrived in a hurry and diffused the situation. Even though he knew she had been alright, he was instantly relieved to see she was still okay. The last time he was here, her parents didn't care what she had to say, and he couldn't blame them. But today Emily had them calmed down, though they still refused to believe Jacob was everything she had said he was. They assumed her hyper imagination had cooked up this world, and he had tried to make himself part of it. In reality, his world existed first, and she imagined it later and tried to make herself part of it.

She knew better now. She understood she had to be more careful. Jacob had a long talk, apology mostly, with Emily and her parents before they accepted the story. He promised numerous times that he would never hurt Emily or let her get hurt. And finally the air cleared and the glares and condescending tones dropped off. Jacob wasn't going to call Emily's parents "friends" yet, but they were not prepared to kill him anymore, and he took that as a good sign. Once everything was understood, it was in the middle of the lunch hour. Emily's mother got up to prepare lunch. He had been invited to stay for lunch but hesitated to accept until Emily insisted. After the conversation, he just felt disruptive and out of place, but he stayed. He expected this would be the last time he saw Emily outside of school anyway.

The room was really quiet. Jacob had asked if he could help but was answered, only if he could make the water boil faster. He actually could, but he didn't think it would be a good idea so he just stayed silent.

"Well as exciting as it is sitting here," Emily started after the silence had endured too long. "I would like to show you something."

Jacob looked up at her and saw the familiar light that he could not place had come back into her eyes.

Her father looked at her curiously as she stood up. "Would you excuse us?" she said kindly. "Come on," she said to Jacob.

She took him down a hall and came to a door bearing a sign that said Drawing Room. She used a key to open it and turned the knob. She hesitated before she opened the door. "Nobody has ever been in here," she said and looked at him smiling. Her green eyes were sparkling with anticipation. She reached up and brushed her hair back, not really accomplishing anything; the reaction was more from nervousness.

"Is this where you keep your pictures?" Jacob asked.

Emily nodded.

"Are you showing them to me?" He was rather surprised; the way things had gone, he was certain this friendship was crushed.

"Do you want to see them?" she replied.

"I'd love to," Jacob answered.

"But you promised you wouldn't laugh," Emily reminded him.

Jacob smiled, "I'm sure there is nothing to laugh at."

"Okay." She gently pushed the door open and walked through.

Jacob entered after her and beheld a room not terribly big, but all the space was used. The room smelt of fresh paper, used erasers, pencil shavings, and wet ink. It was a not-so-different smell from the dark halls of the library where he spent so much time, and it rendered the same enthusiasm and creativity in his mind as the old books did. Small shreds of paper were strewn about in the floor along with broken pencil nubs and ground bits of charcoal. There was a huge drawing table in the middle of the room and the two far corners each had large easels with half-finished pictures on them. The floor around the table and in front of the easels was dotted with ink stains. Rolled up scrolls leaned on the walls that were either clean sheets or completed works; Jacob could not tell. On either side of the door were chests that held supplies and possibly more completed pictures. And on the walls, in relief style, were murals of a man fighting monsters.

"Are these?" he asked pointing around the room.

Emily walked to the left wall and spread both hands out in a presentation. "I call this one 'A Hero,'" she stated.

Jacob looked; it had three panels showing a story in three parts. It was just like the first story he had told her about the time when his dad got hurt. The first panel depicted him pulling the spirit out of the girl, and the second was him locking blades with a grotesque monster. The third was skewed a bit from the actual story as he stood with his father leaning on his shoulder while he cast the spell to remove the Wraith.

"You drew this? How long did it take?" Jacob asked.

"I can do one panel in a day if I put my mind to it."

"Incredible," Jacob gasped.

"Do you like it?" Emily asked. "I enjoyed your stories so much I wanted to sketch them. They were always so fascinating." She paused and then added quietly, "I never imagined they could be real."

Jacob tore his eyes from the lifelike detail and looked at her, "It's amazing. You should take some of these to a gallery; they're incredible."

"Sometimes I think I could," she replied, "But mostly I draw for pleasure. I'd never sell anything. Then it would seem more like work, I guess."

"Well, if you ever changed your mind, you are an amazing artist," Jacob encouraged.

"You mean that?" Emily noted, trying to hide a smile that indicated she took more pride in her skill than she let on.

"Absolutely," he said as he stepped to the next wall to his right, "What do you call this one?" Only two panels had been filled in, the first was Jacob sitting in a ring with some other people. It was just as he had described the council to her, almost exactly how it really looked. The second was him at a chess board and a girl across from him. Even the pieces were detailed so that they looked real.

"I usually don't name my works until I finish them." Emily said as she walked to the middle panel. She brushed the figure of the girl as if she were moving a strand of hair from her face and then stepped back to appraise the sketch, "But I'm leaning toward 'The Chosen.'"

Jacob sighed and smiled.

"I know how you feel about that name, but it's what you've been given." Emily smiled, "I could call it 'Jacob' or something."

"No, that's fine," Jacob stopped her. "It's beautiful. You made it, and you can call it whatever you want. And you're right, I should stop running from my name." It was who he was, but he was slowly learning that it wasn't defined. He was still free to make his life and the choices he made shape him, not the name his family forced on him. The name did not define Jacob, but rather Jacob defined "The Chosen."

He looked at the next wall on the right and saw only one panel filled. It was a depiction of the last time they had seen each other. The single panel was divided into two pictures. At the top was a picture of him holding Emily with his Light Shard held high to ward off the evil spirits that surrounded them. This image was shaded heavily, capturing that moment in the darkness just as the Light Shard began to shine. The detail was stunningly accurate. Emily had caught the image of the spirits so perfectly, it scared him. But then another line parallel to the first separated it from the bottom picture.

The last picture was in Jacob's living room: Emily asleep in his lap.

"You did all this in just two days?" he asked and knelt to look at the last depiction.

She nodded, "I can work fast when I'm focused, and sometimes when I get something stuck in my mind, the only way to get it out is to just sketch it out." Emily paused and placed her hand on Jacob's shoulder, "I couldn't stop thinking about that night, everything that happened, those creatures . . . and you. I'm still not sure how to process all of it."

"I couldn't stop worrying, either," Jacob said as he looked up at her. It was odd to have someone worry about him—odd but nice in a way.

"I don't know what I want to call the story yet, but I named the panel." Emily replied and knelt down next to him. She brushed some shreds of paper away as she more or less sat down.

"Oh?" Jacob asked. "Do all the panels have names?"

"No," Emily replied, "Just this one so far."

Jacob touched the image of him holding Emily's hand in the bottom picture. It seemed so real he could almost feel the detail. "I see, what do you call this one then?" He looked up and saw her smile next to him; her green eyes were like diamonds, and her hair dangled about her shoulders.

"I call it," she began. Her eyes went from his to the mural and then to the floor where splotches of spilt ink, bits of paper, and pencil shavings littered the ground. She looked back up and finished in a whisper, "Falling in Love." She smiled as if not sure of herself.

Jacob smiled, and he saw the look in Emily's face that it wasn't just a name she made up, she called it that for a reason. He had thought he would lose his only real friend today, that Emily would realize the gravity of his life and flee. But she hadn't. He knew he had begun to feel things for her, but he was almost certain anything she might have felt for him was destroyed by the haunting event she had endured. And yet, it was that specific moment that she deemed the origin of her emotions.

Something inside him clicked. It had been there the entire time, but he didn't really know what it was until just now. It had been subtle. It wasn't something he planned, but it had happened. To hear Emily admit it made him comfortable, and he didn't really know how to interpret it, but he liked it. It felt good but also strange, like walking into a really large and ornate room for the first time and getting disoriented under the grandeur of it. But it was also familiar. The feeling perplexed him; he knew so much about so many things, but this was way out of his expertise.

Just like stepping into that grand hall for the first time there was a sense of fear, or was it excitement? He was so jittery he couldn't tell. Emily looked as if she felt the same. That smile of hers didn't know whether it wanted to hide or break free across her face. Her eyes still held that familiar glow, but they were full of energy and excitement. Jacob reached—it felt natural like something he had wanted to do for a long time, something he should do. He placed his hand behind her ear. She closed her eyes, and the smile decided it wanted to show itself, but it was not too sure of itself yet and did not fully appear. He gently pulled her close and leaned in.

Jacob was reacting on something deeper than his thoughts, something instinctive, because his mind had still not caught up to what was happening. As his brain struggled to process all the emotion and the impulses, their lips met. He had never even been close enough to a girl to kiss her before, and he was not expecting it to happen any time soon, much less today. They pulled away slowly, and they stared at one another until their brains caught up with the moment. The smile Jacob was looking for exploded into view, and Emily's jade-green eyes crackled with laughter that she had held in. Jacob felt like he should say something, but he was afraid to ruin the moment. He just smiled, took her hand, and stood up. He hugged her tight as she stood up also. "Thanks for showing me this," he whispered. "I know it means a lot to you, and I'm glad you showed it to me because you mean a lot to me."

"It does mean a lot." Emily replied, "But you are worth sharing it with." She gently pushed away. "I have more if you want to see them."

Jacob looked around. There were a few on the table, and he guessed there were layers behind the easels, "Those scrolls?" He asked.

"They don't tell stories, but they are other pictures I drew. They used to hang on the wall, but I took them down to start this story," she answered, waving her hands around at the mural.

She picked up one of the scrolls and flattened it out on the table; it depicted a man fishing under a willow tree. It was in ink with heavy brush strokes, not in relief style that the mural was, but the details were incredible, much better than he could hope to do with a brush.

"This one is called 'Tranquility,'" she explained. "I used ink for this one because I like the way water looks when it's painted." Jacob looked at the pond in the picture and noticed the ripples and how it really looked like water if he stepped back and looked at the black and white as a whole. She showed him a few more ink pictures and then started flipping through some sketches she had done on the easel. Most were incomplete, but all were stunning.

Jacob was thoroughly impressed with just how life-like they were. She had a talent.

After about fifteen minutes of looking through pictures, there was a knock on the door. "Lunch is ready," her father called with a rap on the door.

Emily opened the door just enough to peek her head out and make sure her father had his back turned. Then she opened it wider so Jacob could get out, and then she shut the door and locked it.

"But you won't let me see?" Her father asked.

Emily just smiled. Her own parents had never even been in that room, at least not since they gave her a key for it. Not that they couldn't open the door if they wanted, but Jacob thought the way they respected her privacy was interesting.

CHAPTER 14

Jacob had enjoyed the break for the month of December, being able to study late and spend more time with Emily. But it was almost over. He was in the library with Sarah and Dom, working on the Nimba. Dom had just completed Bolor, and Sarah had made her way through several volumes. Her chief interest was spell casting, tapping into the powers that flowed in her veins. Dom had not made up his mind yet as to what he liked to study, but he had a strong desire to learn hunting and took lessons in archery. The Nimba was especially interesting to Sarah because it focused on incantations, charms, and spells. There were many things in the book that were way over Jacob's head, but he was pleased with the way the three of them could work together to figure out some of the harder parts. Even Dom was helping almost as much as Jacob was.

In the middle of the lesson, Rain came to him a bit worried, "I'm sorry to interrupt." She began, "Something has happened, and Roth must speak to you."

Jacob gave curious look. "Where?"

"There's a chamber for such times; this is not a matter to be discussed here." She stepped back, "It's urgent."

"Roth is here?" he asked, "What happened?"

Rain cast her golden stare on him, insistent and ominous, "I cannot discuss this. Come, I will take you to Roth."

Jacob looked at Sarah and Dom, "It looks like that is all for today."

They wanted to go with him; he could see it on their faces, but they had learned not to ask.

Rain took him down a secret tunnel and showed him a chamber where Roth and his mother stood. "Jacob," Roth said as he entered. Jacob entered and looked at them both, wondering why they were here. Rain followed behind him.

"I told you as soon as I found out. You were the first to know, Roth," she said.

"First to know about what?" Jacob asked.

The room was silent. "Have you meddled with the Game?" Roth asked.

Jacob thought for a moment; something was wrong, "If I have, I swear to you I did so without knowing."

"You would know; it's not something you do by accident!" Roth insisted, "Perhaps you may mettle out of ignorance but never without knowing it."

Jacob paused and thought of anything he might have done. It bothered him that he wasn't sure what they were asking him. "What is it that has been meddled with?"

"Someone has challenged you, son." Lucile explained.

Jacob looked at her as if she was about to explain, but she stopped.

"This is a serious business, Jacob, and very dangerous." Roth began, "This Game has claimed lives, fought wars, and told futures. When the Game makes a challenge, it is held in the most reverent respect."

Jacob held up his hand to stop the conversation, "Explain first what this Game is, and tell me why it is dangerous. I wish to know these things first before we discuss this challenge."

"Long ago a Game was created by my father. It was a living Game on which wars were waged. It is a game of chess, which may decide the fate of nations."

"Why did he make this?" Jacob asked.

Roth cast a glance at Rain, "The board is a prison. My father placed something terrible inside it." His eyes fell on Rain as if to pity her and then he snapped them back to Jacob with callousness, "But he was not content to just trap his adversary in this game. Over time he sought to abuse the great power he had sealed away; he wanted to defeat nations on this board, to be able to wage against his enemies without the shedding of blood." Jacob looked puzzled, and Roth continued; "The board draws the mind of the player into it during the game. When a challenge is played, the board will grant a wish of the victor."

"So it's like playing a game in the Courtyard?" Jacob asked.

"Our games in the Courtyard were taken after the style that this board plays by," Roth sighed, as if remembering something long forgotten. "But it has its own rules and if you lose you are bound to what the victor requests. My father built it to deceive nations. He used it to save nations and also for destructive vengeance."

"How does the board have this power?" Jacob inquired as he tried to follow the legend. "What did your father trap there?"

Roth again looked over at Rain as if he felt sorry for her, "My father sealed the spirit of Aries in the board. They knew each other in the early years of the earth, and their rivalry ended when my father trapped him in this game."

"So I have been challenged on this board?" Jacob asked. "This demon wants me?"

"No, son," His mother answered, "Another has issued the challenge. Aries may or may not influence the game."

"Aye," Roth sighed, "It is not to be taken lightly, and you may decline. Remember, if you should lose, your opponent can have you do anything with the authority of the god of war. Whether they want a favor or blood, you will be bound to it."

"Who did this?" Jacob asked.

"We don't know," Rain replied. "The way it works, you must enter into the board to find out. The challenge is for you, and you are the only one who can enter the board."

"So I must play?" Jacob replied.

"It is a huge risk," Roth answered, "You don't have to."

"What sort of things can this board demand?" Jacob asked, "Has anyone played on it?"

Roth nodded, "Aye, I have a score settled with it, and Rain was challenged a long time ago." He drew a breath before he continued, "Your mother was also challenged."

"What happened?" Jacob asked.

"Perhaps your mother was the wisest of us; she declined. I was challenged when I established leadership of my clan, and the board wished to test me. I was victorious, and I demanded that I live until I see the one who will redeem our race." Roth explained. "For a hundred years I was young, and I grew impatient. I stepped up and challenged it. I wanted to be the redeemer, and I wanted it to make me the savior.

"But I lost that game. The demon could not go back on the promise it had made me the first time, it could not remove my immortality from me. But it took my youth, my fire, it destroyed my passion, and I became old." The tremor in his voice told that he had been old and on the doorstep of death for far longer than he had ever wanted.

Jacob looked at Rain, "Same story with you?"

She shook her head, "My youth comes from other magic; the board challenged me long ago and I lost, but it took nothing from me."

"Why?"

"I don't know," Rain said in a way that seemed like she really did, "Perhaps Aries had mercy on me because I had nothing to give up."

There was a long silence while Jacob thought. It was a dangerous game, but the part of him that was curiosity was taking over, "Show me this game." Jacob said.

Roth nodded, "Show it to him. Don't take it lightly, son; you are not bound to it yet."

"I shall consider my options before I make a commitment," Jacob replied.

"Be wise, Jacob," Lucile warned.

They all took him to the Oasis and into the secret chamber beneath. The passage split two ways: one door was locked and bolted, and the other stood agape. He assumed the game was down that way. Both the open passage and the closed one had large double doors that stood about twelve feet tall, neither appeared as if they were meant to be opened. The one that remained closed had a large, radiant depiction of a golden sun against the dark iron plates. "What is behind the other door?" he asked.

"Do not be bothered with that," she replied. "It is a deep magic from the sun people. No one gets to see it."

Jacob wondered still. Everything else he had been warned about he was getting to see. Perhaps sometime he would get to find out what was back there. The tunnel seemed to go on far too long, but they finally came to a large room. In the center was a large board that was raised five feet over the stone floor and over twenty feet wide. This was a mammoth chessboard. The board was carved from granite with stair steps leading up to the tiles.

The white pieces were made of quartz, and the black were cast iron. All the pawns were roughly equal to his height. He looked at the sets all ready for battle. Some of the pieces were worn and missing parts, and others were like new. The squares of the board were black and white marble, and in the center of each was an engraving. In the center of the black tiles there was a silver sun, and in the center of the white tiles was a golden oak leaf.

He looked and saw that the pawns had the corresponding symbols on their shields. The rooks were fashioned like executioners rather than the traditional castles and also had the symbols on their chests. The knights had the symbols on their steeds, and the bishops had the marks sewn into their cloaks. The kings and queens oddly had no markings.

And then he noticed that each corner of the board had a large construction. On the black side stood two towers made of onyx. They loomed over the board like two great shadows; one had suffered time poorly and was missing most of the left side. The other was unblemished. On the white side, two silver oak trees rose above the field. Around one, a golden snake wound. Beneath the other was the image of a woman carved from ivory. She was wearing no cloths, holding a golden bow, and was poised to kill. Around her neck was a silver chain with weighted balls on the ends, but the sands of time had claimed her head, and it now lay beside her feet.

Jacob made a move to step up on the tiles. Rain caught his hand, "Be careful," she warned, "Once you step on it, you accept the challenge and cannot go back."

Jacob relaxed and looked into her for wisdom. Her golden eyes were worried as if words could not describe the fear she had for that game. "Let me give you something."

"What?" Jacob asked.

"I see you are not going to back down so let me give you something that might help," she urged. There was confliction in her voice, almost as if she had just chosen a side between two friends. It was almost as if she felt guilt. Rain pulled him down so that he was kneeling, and she stood one step below him so that they were eye to eye. She touched her forehead to his, and Jacob felt her trying to connect with his mind. He had grown uncomfortable with this, but she had something she wanted to give him. Gifts in this family rarely came free, and Rain wanted to give him a key to this game. He let her in and saw the board in his mind; he felt the terror and the thrill of the game. It lived and thrived on the emotions of the players. The rules were different, and will and determination played as much a part of the game as knowledge and skill.

He understood her pain, real pain, when a piece fell from the board, and he felt her bloodlust when she struck down pieces. The information flooded into his mind, and there was no metaphor. It was straight and simple, from her mind to his. There was more that she did not show him, a deeper truth was still hidden from him. But he understood now; this was more than just chess. The images of the board and the game dulled and passed away and as the link was severed, he caught another glimpse of the void inside her. It was only for a moment, but it was still there and it still called him. He had not been in a link long enough to figure out if it was from her mind or his, and he wanted to inspect this metaphor. But he was also afraid, and Rain was also still cautious of the oddness between them.

She withdrew and stepped down and backed away from the board, "Be careful," she whispered.

Jacob nodded and turned to face the tiles. He stepped on the board and felt it pull him in. The only way out now was to play the game. First his feelings and consciousness slipped out of his body and absorbed partially into each of the white pieces. He felt them all, and he felt as if he were in all sixteen places at once. Then his body melted into the board, and the game began. He could see everything on the board. He felt his pieces, and he felt the black pieces weighing down on the board. Everything on the board was in view, but he was not there. He was there, but he was away; he was in the pieces but knew was standing behind them observing. He was in the board with the pieces crushing him, but he was in the air above looking down.

He sensed his opponent. The feeling was curious as if he was standing in front of the person, but also separated as if they were worlds apart. "Shall we begin?" he spoke. No sound was made, but he felt the will of his opponent answer, "Let us test each other."

At that moment something dormant clicked in Jacob. He felt a power that he owned and feared, something he had only used twice. But this time he had not channeled the power from his sleeping demon. Could it have been awakened by the presence of this true demon? He suddenly feared that he had pushed it too hard and caused it to rouse. Jacob thought for a moment; he was still collected and still in control, but he knew something had changed. His senses pricked, the sensations excited him, but he had to check himself. This odd experience wasn't from within him; it was part of the game. Rain had given him an understanding of this game; his emotions could make or break him. It all depended on balancing his mind with his heart better than his opponent.

Jacob reached out and touched the king's pawn. He felt it, but he was not touching it. He felt the pawn on his hand, and he felt his hand on his back. It was almost as though he was the pawn but at the same time still himself. It was stubborn and did not move, it was much too heavy. With his mind, he willed it to move. Jacob became the pawn, and its face took his likeness. It stepped and proceeded with its shield raised high and its blade pointed forward. Two clumsy steps and it stood on the edge of the next square. The experience was quite unique, but the glimpse of the game Rain had offered to him made some part of it seem familiar. Marveling at the magic and the way it interfaced, Jacob lost his train of thought and disconnected with the pawn.

He willed himself back into it and finished the move, attempting to cross the first square. But the pawn hit an invisible wall at the edge of the square. He fought with it for a moment. Then he realized this board was ancient, it was governed by early rules in which the pawns were not allowed to move two spaces. He released the pawn and withdrew. He saw and felt the opponent move a knight from the back row. The black rider trotted between the pawns and situated itself, poised to strike anything that came too close. This was a problem because the knight now attacked the next square he intended to move the pawn to.

With the pawns' movement restricted, it would take some time to build momentum in this game. But that was probably a good thing. It would give him more time to think. It would give his opponent more time as well; either way he still had to out-think this person.

So Jacob moved the pawn in front of the knight on the queen's side forward. Technically, his opponent had a better position since their knight was attacking the center of the board, but Jacob needed to mobilize his bishops. He worked well with them. He crossed his fingers and hoped his opponent had not played by the old rules before. Jacob had never played by the old rules, but he had studied them and noticed that pawn structure was critical. It was much easier to advance major pieces too soon and walk into traps. So that would be his strategy: work on his pawns first so he could have support for his major pieces.

This opponent liked knights and brought out the second one. Jacob moved his king side bishop across the diagonal and placed it in position to attack the knight. The bishop walked elegantly down the row of white squares carrying a war spear in hand and stood meditating in front of the knight. In return the opponent moved the rook's pawn to attack the bishop.

Jacob considered trading his bishop to take a knight and put a flaw in his opponent's pawn structure, a wise investment so he willed the bishop into the square that the knight occupied. What he failed to remember was that this was not normal chess. The move was not complete. The bishop readied his spear but did not attack. Before Jacob could will it to end the knight, his opponent reacted. The knight fought back. The horse reared back and came down striking the bishop in the head. Jacob felt the kick throb and rock his skull as if he had been kicked as well.

As he scrambled to his feet he felt a hot sensation in his back—a sword. He could not turn his head to see the horseman stabbing him in the back, but in his mind he saw the black-clad knight had killed his bishop. Jacob faded out of the bishop, and it became white quartz and then shattered, leaving bits of debris on the surrounding squares.

Jacob stood up with the throbbing pain in his back and the splitting ringing in his head. He felt the bishop's pain as real as if it were his own. This was a grave disadvantage. But with these new rules, he might be able to turn the game around, he was very skilled in combat. It appeared it was still his turn. Jacob thought about this as he tried to shake the pain off. Perhaps you could sacrifice a turn when you were attacked to defend your square.

Jacob moved his remaining bishop into position to attack the other knight. The black army advanced the queen pawn one space, and it was his turn again. Normally he would have been more patient and developed his pawns a little better. But he was curious about these new rules. He willed the bishop to attack the knight. This time he crossed the entire board to assault the black knight. The warrior-priest ran with the long spear ready. The knight reeled when the bishop entered its square. It tried the same maneuver the first had, but Jacob thrust the spear into it, and it rolled back and landed on the rider. The spear shattered under the force.

Jacob did not hesitate—the rider was still alive and struggled to get out from under the horse. With the broken spear, he rushed over and plunged the splintered end into the knight. It wounded him, but it did not finish him. The pain his opponent felt was so great that Jacob heard the screams. This was the part of the game where emotions came in. This was a real war, except that it was played by the rules of chess. Jacob stood for a moment, the bishop was not there; it was him standing over the knight. The screams ate at his nerves. He thought it best to torture his opponent to make them regret the game and try to break their mind.

But his heart held too much compassion. He stomped the knight's sword out of his hand and used it to severe the knight's head. The screams ended. The knight morphed into cast iron as his severed head rolled about clattering across the tiles, and then he shattered as the bishop had and again left bits across the surrounding area. Jacob understood that this would become very treacherous once the killing really started.

His opponent had used their turn to defend and had lost. It was his turn again. He focused on his pawns and moved the king's pawn forward one more square.

The black army elected the knight's pawn to advance and attack his bishop. He readied and defended. The long spear had returned to normal after the end of the last battle. He leveled it and stabbed at the pawn's uncovered head. The black shield with the white sun insignia moved up and pushed the strike out of the way. The iron pawn thrust forward with his sword hand. The bishop stepped out of the way and tried to sweep the sword arm away with the butt end of the spear. A hard thud knocked him off. The shield had come around and hit him. The bishop rolled out of the square of combat and the pawn came after him. Could they fight on the entire board for that one square? Jacob ran. The other pieces on the board were quartz and iron and not animated, thus oblivious. The entire board was the arena, and this battle was for one square. He gained some distance and turned to swing the spear, the pawn stopped and watched the spearhead pass a safe sixteen inches from its face.

Jacob pulled it around, and as it swung back around, he released his grip a little and allowed it to slide almost two feet further. This caught the opponent off guard, and the tip of the spear split through its helmet and shattered his skull. The piece exploded as the others had, and before Jacob knew what was happening, the king's pawn was moving into the square his bishop had come from. It was attacking, but the bishop was not there. Jacob threw the spear across the board to defend his ground. It lodged into the pawn's shield, and he ran to meet with it in combat. The pawn rushed also. They met and the pawn lashed out with its sword. The weight of the spear in its shield threw it off, and it missed.

Jacob seized the spear and pulled hard to get it dislodged. He jerked the pawn to the ground with the motion and quickly took advantage of the situation and stabbed it in the chest. It too exploded, and the spear shattered in his hand. The next instant he looked up and saw the black queen upon him. He grabbed the pawn's sword and prepared to meet the attack. The queen rushed at him with passion and blood lust. She was much taller than the bishop and wielded two long swords. The black-clad queen raced to meet him like a juggernaut. Jacob suddenly regretted using his turn to defend.

The queen lashed out with fury and vengeance. He blocked it but had to step back. The queen began a second assault. Jacob blocked the first strike with a skilled parry, but the second made its mark. It struck him in the chest and ran through until it pierced through his back. He stumbled back, but the queen followed, pressing the blade harder into his chest. Crimson stains spilt on his white robes where the blade entered and exited his body. He dropped his sword and stumbled back until he reached the edge of the board. It was like he had hit a wall. Unable to move further, he was pinned. The pain was fierce, but he tried not to think about it. He felt it fully but it was not him; it was the bishop being stabbed.

After struggling for a moment, Jacob knew he had to let go. The game was drawing him in, and he was getting tunnel vision on his one piece. He had become emotionally attached to it. That could cost him the game. They were just pieces. Though he could feel them, move them, and be in them, they were not really part of him. He had to let go before he lost his mind. The bishop suddenly was not Jacob anymore. He still felt the hot pain in his chest, but it was no longer his chest where the blade was lodged. The queen twisted the blade, and the bishop fell to his knees. Then the second blade came. It ripped at him, slicing his side and cutting him open across his abdomen. And Jacob still felt the scars in his own flesh.

Red scars formed where the blade cut him, ruining the pure white of his robes with red blood. Jacob felt each blow—it was toying with him by not delivering the kill stroke. He regretted not making that knight suffer now. He felt the blood pooling around him. His right side burned from a stroke across his ribs, and his stomach felt like it was ripped apart. Then a searing pain ripped through his left thigh as the blade ripped his flesh open. He grabbed the blade that was in his chest and mustered all his strength. He pushed himself off the blade, cutting his hands in the process. Once the blade was removed from the wound, the blood gushed out. The bishop slumped over now, finally able to bleed out. It rolled backward and became still. Then like all the pieces so far, it broke and scattered across the board.

The queen crossed her bloody blades across her chest and marched back to the square that she had just brutalized Jacob's bishop for. Jacob no longer had any of his bishops, which was a considerable loss for him. He was most offensive with bishops so he would have to play this game defensively. The problem with that was if he always played defense, he would only have half the moves his opponent did. It was still black's turn.

The opponent moved the king-side bishop to back up his queen; he now had a straight shot at his rook. In a normal game, his opponent would have no reservations in capturing it with his queen right now, but in this game the rook, or executioner, could defend himself. Nevertheless, he wanted as many pieces between his rook and that queen as possible, so he moved the queen's knight to block the diagonal.

It was a secure move; his knight was guarding his kings pawn, which was now boldly in the open, but it was also guarded by the queen's pawn. If he was going to play defensively, he had to start working strategically, and he had to make up for the time he lost while he made mistakes trying to learn the rules.

CHAPTER 15

This game fought to take his mind. His opponent made every effort to demoralize him in combat. He gave into his feelings once and repaid the brutal torture with brutality that was buried in some part of him that barely seemed human. It was instantly apparent that this is what his opponent wanted. In moments, the battle turned and before he knew it, he was largely disadvantaged. He had to remember to keep his emotions in check. It seemed harder for some reason, like every feeling he had was exaggerated. There was no way he could afford to lose that much ground again; he had to think clearly. It was tricky to fight with his emotions and know when to release all the passion and when to forfeit a battle. And entering a battle with no emotion was suicide.

Throughout the game he sensed that the board was influencing his thoughts. His opponent was trying to get into his mind, and the board was making it hard to resist. He wondered if the board was playing mental warfare with the other player as well. The presence of the board was subtle at first, but now it was driving him, daring him to reach for the satisfaction he could have if he gave in to his feelings. When he entered into a battle, it urged him to demoralize the foe and have his vengeance. When he was merciful and dealt with his foe swiftly, it nagged him and whispered curses that he was not strong and he would break. Jacob had managed to block out the noise and hold in his desire well enough to recover and now had a kill stroke on his opponent's queen. He had her attacked by three pieces, a pawn, a knight, and his own queen.

Any wise person would send the pawn first, but this game was different. Jacob knew he had to strike, or his next turn would be defending against the offender's queen. But which piece first? The pawn stood no chance. If he sent in his knight and lost, he would sustain a large disadvantage, having only rooks left. He surely could not afford to waste his queen, one of the other pieces had to go first. He decided on the knight. It was stronger. Maybe if he was quick, he could weaken the queen, and the pawn could finish her. The knight vaulted the pawn and landed in the square to face the queen. Pieces of iron and quartz scattered under the horse's powerful hooves.

The queen defended and attacked. Jacob deflected the blows and backed up to gain space. The queen stood ready but did not advance. She was taller than the horse and her head reached the mounted knight's shoulder. This would be a hard fought battle. But Jacob had an idea. It was a long shot, but earlier when he killed the black knight, he had killed both the horse and the rider separately. He rushed with the knight and as he neared the opponent, he separated the horse from rider. The knight stood on the horse's back and leaped through the air over the queen. She turned to cleave him in two but was caught off guard by the hooves of the beast in her back. It had worked!

She stumbled forward. Jacob scrambled among the shattered remains of the fallen pieces to gain his footing and the knight rushed in to deliver the kill stroke. He was deflected by a mighty blow and swept aside. The knight was knocked to the floor and rolled over chunks of the debris. Jacob backed up for a moment—he controlled the horse and rider independently as two pieces. With vigor the horse reared and prepared to charge while the dismounted rider readied his blade. The beautiful white horse charged with all the passion Jacob could muster and the rider drew his secondary short sword with his left hand. The queen turned one blade at each foe, and the horse fell on her blade first. Jacob willed it to struggle through the pain. It pushed her back.

She staggered under the weight of the beast and swung at the knight with her other blade as the horse's struggling body forced her to kneel on the marred black marble. The knight deflected the blow with his main weapon, the long sword, and drove forward and planted the short blade in her chest. The queen stood up as the cold steel burned through her. She dropped both of her weapons, the one in her right hand clattered to the floor and the one in her left was wrenched from her grasp by the flailing steed. The knight's short sword was but a small dagger to her, but it had found purchase and pierced her heart.

The horse collapsed and shook the ground, sending rattles through the loose pieces of the fallen warriors. The queen staggered back as a bold crimson streak oozed out of her breastplate. She looked down at the smaller knight. Clad in black and her face hidden, Jacob sensed all of her emotions, fear, anger, and passionate rage, which were focusing on him. He had made it personal for his opponent; he would exploit that as his foe had tried to do to him in the beginning. He had caught his opponent off guard with that last move. He had out maneuvered his foe and used the game to his advantage.

Blood trickled from her black plate mail, and she fell forward to her knees and became eye-level with the knight. She clenched the hilt of the blade and pulled it out of her chest. She held it as if to examine it and then dropped it and fell backward. As she hit the ground she broke into chunks of iron, and her remains scattered about the board.

Jacob was pleased that he was able to do what he had done, but there was no time to celebrate—it was time to end this. All his opponent had left that had range was a single bishop and one knight. It was time to put the choke on the king. With the way this game had gone, Jacob was not assuming the standard checkmate applied. He would have to kill the king. Jacob had a strategic advantage. Building his pawns up earlier had proved useful. All of his pawns were directly in front of his enemy's pawns and therefore stopping them from advancing. He no longer had to worry about his back row and his opponent resurrecting his queen. He had a queen, a rook, and a horseless knight. The black side had only their last knight and a bishop.

He positioned the knight so that his next move would put the king in check. Oddly, it still moved in the L-shaped pattern a normal knight would, even though it was dismounted. The black counter move was to place the bishop on the square he would have to attack next. Jacob did not worry about that yet; rather, he positioned his rook behind the knight so that when he moved the knight, whether or not he succeeded in besting the bishop, he would still have a shot at the king. Then the black knight moved closer to the fight. Jacob positioned his queen to attack the king. He had the upper hand; his pride welled up and all the anger of the battle swelled in him. He wanted his opponent to pay. This person had tormented him, ripped his pieces apart, and brutalized his army. Not any more.

Jacob checked himself. If he became overzealous now, he could still suffer defeat. His revenge would be best taken off the board; he could not afford his emotions to cloud his judgment now. The board whispered to him as his rage subsided and tried to bring back his temper. He was justified in his feelings. No man should have to suffer a death like his army had; he knew their pain—he had felt them. No! They were not people. Yes, he felt them. No, they were not part of him. It was the other way around. He was part of them. He risked their lives when he set foot on the table. Their suffering was as much his doing as it was his opponent. The feeling he had was meant to confuse him; it was meant to make this fight personal, and that is what this could not become: personal.

The black knight positioned beside its king, between him and Jacob's queen. Jacob's horseless knight still moved like a knight. He slid it over and attacked the bishop. He had a grand upper hand. His next move would be to attack the king. If he won this scuffle, he would have two chances because his opponent would spend their moves defending and not moving. The knight approached the bishop with his swords drawn, the long blade in his right hand and the short blade in the left. The only emotion Jacob allowed in his mind was determination. All around him were limbs and heads and pieces of cast iron and white quartz; one of these two pieces would soon join the graveyard. Would it be the dark priest or Jacob's white knight?

The bishop swung the spear as Jacob had done in the beginning, but he knew what that tactic was. The first swing passed by, and the second extended to where he was standing. He jumped forward rather than back and braced both blades at the incoming shaft. The spear splintered against the knight's steel, and the force nearly knocked the knight over. Jacob recovered quickly from the anticipated blow and charged as he shrugged it off. The bishop stood there, accepting its fate. This was the first time his opponent had surrendered after being defeated during the entire game. His foe had learned to let go.

Jacob remembered how drastically his perception had changed when he learned that and wondered just how his opponent's new mindset would change his task—or if this was planned. With the victory nearly clenched, he wondered if it was too late for his opponent to apply this lesson. The knight stabbed the bishop in the abdomen, and the bishop fell to its knees. "Make him suffer," Jacob heard the board whisper to him for real this time. It wasn't just in his head, it wasn't just trying to influence him, the demon was speaking to him, or was it something buried inside him? At first, Jacob was sure it was part of the game, but now he questioned if it was the dormant spirit inside him attempting to call him to fulfill his own desires. He knew he wanted to. So did his demon if it had awakened, and so did Aries. He wasn't sure what was trying to influence him, but either way, it wasn't trying to help.

Jacob contemplated the thought as the bishop gasped for air. Should he make it suffer? It was exactly what he wanted to do, but that was wrong. Jacob lifted the short sword and made a swift end of the foe before him. With the base of the sword against the bishop's neck, he dragged the entire length of the blade across the opponent's flesh. He laid him down with respect, and the bishop disintegrated, his pieces scattering explosively across the tiles.

He wasn't sure what was urging him to give in to his impulses, but Jacob stood up with honor and faced the king. It was his turn again, and he had two angles on the king, something he never had encountered before in a game of chess. He chose the knight first. Like the queen, the king stood tall above the other pieces. He wielded a massive sword that was almost three meters long. The knight approached the king, defying his stature and sovereignty. The king brought his great sword high, and it raced downward at the knight. The knight rolled among the debris of his fallen comrades and the massive blade clanged against the marble, creating sparks. As the king recovered from the failed stroke, Jacob rushed forward to make the kill. The king lashed out with is massive armor-clad fist and repelled the knight. The white armor of Jacob's knight cracked across the chest. Jacob felt the wind knocked out of him as the knight collided with the ground. His not-so-graceful slide ended when he contacted an iron pawn that stood face to face with one of Jacob's white pawns.

The pawns stared into each other's expressionless faces oblivious to the battle happening before them. They were not aware—they remained iron and quartz and kept silent as the stone they stood on.

He stumbled to his feet as the king marched mercilessly toward him. Jacob imagined that there was no feeling, no regret, nor any emotion behind the plate mail of the king's helm.

With fury, the massive blade came down again. Jacob reached up and deflected the stroke with both of the knight's blades. The goliath sword slid off and thundered to the ground between the two pawns. The board shook from the blow, and the pieces of rock and metal scattered about the arena made clattering sounds as they vibrated. Jacob wasted no time. The knight could not best the king. He knew that. He hefted the short sword as he struggled to force the king's blade down with his long sword. He hurled the short sword with as much skill as he could muster. The blade found purchase and lodged in the king's shoulder. It had wounded him, but it would not be a fatal wound.

Reeling from the hit, the king jerked his great sword and slung the knight into the iron pawn. The knight slid down at the pawn's feet. His arm had been shattered when he hit the piece. With his good hand, he tried to pull himself up. Before he could lift himself, Jacob looked up and saw the mighty blade raised to strike him. He gave in. There was nothing more he could do for the white rider. He had been valiant and had lost his horse, and now he would meet the same fate. His opponent still believed in demoralizing him. The king severed the knight's legs first. Then he lifted him up high and held him in a choke until Jacob was ready to pass out. Just before the black closed in around him, the king tossed him up and brought the grand blade to the knight's chest with so much force that he hacked through the black pawn, and smashed him against the white pawn; destroying both pieces.

There was an explosion of white quartz and wrought iron, and his knight was no more. The horse also crystallized and shattered, and their pieces joined the fallen. With a cold satisfaction the king returned to his square, and Jacob stared in amazement that he had just lost two pieces in a single move. Jacob commanded his rook, the hooded executioner, to proceed. The white robes and armor seemed to contrast his duty. He readied his silver axe and marched as commanded. The executioner was taller than the knight but still fell short of the king's stature.

It was custom in the old days that no man's head should be higher than the king's, and this board was no exception. The rook lumbered forward like a tree. His powerful steps were like a slow-rolling thunder, and the end of the axe dragged across the marble with an ominous grinding noise as he approached. Normally, the object to be beheaded would be locked in the stocks, but this time the victim was poised, ready to strike back. The king struck first, dropping the gigantic blade from high. The white robed hand of death raised his axe with both hands and let the king's stroke glance off the shaft. Then with skill and precision Jacob hefted the axe horizontal. The king stepped back, but his cape was caught in the stroke, and it ripped from his shoulders.

The axe head continued around in a circle, and the king tried to cleave Jacob's head while he was off balance. But the heavy axe head came back around, and Jacob connected with the king's blow. They stood for a moment, locked in conflict. Pushing with all his might, Jacob threw the king off balance, and he was forced to step back. In that instant, Jacob brought the axe down and sliced open the armor of the king's thigh. The king stepped back as if he had not been affected, but Jacob knew he had made contact when he saw red blood ooze from under the metal. Enraged, the king lashed out. Jacob blocked the blow but was slung to the ground. A thud and a clatter as the executioner and his axe rolled through black and white metal and stone. The king marched over and reached up to split Jacob in two.

The blade fell, and Jacob locked it again, but the axe shaft failed and shattered. He fell back and stared up at the black king towering over him. The king bent down to get closer to the disarmed rook. He grasped him by his cloak and pulled him closer. Jacob reached for the sword that was still lodged in the king's shoulder. But he could not reach it. The king gripped Jacob's neck and slowly applied pressure to asphyxiate him. With his one hand, he continued to reach in vain for the blade of the knight. And with his other he searched the ground for anything he could grab to pull himself away.

His hand found something—a rock: part of a fallen warrior. He grasped it and mustered as much strength as he had left and smashed it into the side of the king's helmet. Jacob fell on his back as the king released him and stood up. His vision blurred and his throat swelled. Breathing was impossible. Through his blurred vision, he saw the king looming over him and then his chest exploded as the blade crushed his bones. It was still Jacob's turn. He tried to focus over the throbbing pain, Jacob didn't know how much more he could take. The wounded king sat once again on the square he had so valiantly defended.

Jacob's last warrior was his queen, and between his queen and the black king stood one last black knight. If he killed the knight, he would move his most powerful piece to strike the black king. If his queen failed, each of them would only be left with pawns. Jacob's white queen marched with swords drawn to the horse and rider. The knight did not hesitate, and it charged to meet her. Jacob knelt low and swung at the beast's legs but his opponent was a skilled rider and had the horse jump over the attack. The black knight turned around to face the queen and charged again. Jacob waited until the last moment and raised his strong hand to block the strike as the horse sped passed his queen. He plunged the second blade into the knight's chest, and it ran through him completely.

Before the knight hit the ground, he was in pieces. The horse stumbled and fell as it's legs turned to iron in midstride; the knight was not dependent on his horse, but the horse was dependent on the rider. It was still his turn. The white queen faced the black king. Jacob had not willed the move yet. He could buy some time and make sure he secured his victory. But he wanted this to end. He could not stand any more suffering. Each of his pieces that had been destroyed took a part of him with them. This game was eating his mind and driving him to be like his brutal opponent. He wanted to leave.

The king was very strong; if his queen failed, the tide of this war could turn on him and he might lose. For an instant he thought he might deal with the loss, but then he remembered the pact he had made by stepping on the board. The loser was forced to yield to the victor's demands, and he still did not know who this was or what was wanted of him. His queen drew back and stood behind one of the pairs of pawns. Jacob released his turn.

Fear exuded from his opponent. The incessant nagging of the board stopped, and it whispered to him with irritation, a wise choice. The buzzing in his ear to demoralize his opponent and fight with brute force dissipated, and a hush floated over the board. For the moment, the game was quiet. Whether Aries had seen his wisdom, or his demon had tested him, the voice was silent. The black king looked around and stepped one space closer to his nearest pawn. Jacob walked with his white queen into the square of the black pawn and did not defend. His opponent knew the battle would be in vain and could not afford to waste the move trying to win the fight.

The queen stood behind the pawn in execution fashion and cleaved the pawn's head from its shoulders. The black king took one more step toward the pawn. Jacob was unsure if the standard rules applied that the king could not move into a square being attacked so rather than back up his pawn he moved into position to attack the pawn that the black king meant to rescue. One more step; Jacob pushed his pawn. Two more moves and he would have a second queen and more confidence in his victory.

The black king stood beside Jacob's white pawn now. Jacob pushed closer to the back row. The black king moved on the frail pawn. Jacob gave it up. The little pawn landed on the back row of his opponent, and he promoted it to a queen. His opponent moved beside his pawn to attempt to protect it. Jacob moved his new queen to attack the pawn in such a way that it could not move without revealing the king.

The black king stepped back in front of his pawn. Jacob took his first queen and charged at the pawn. His opponent did not give it up this time; it was a desperate move for a pawn to stand its ground to a queen. The pawn raised its sword and shield to defend, and the queen towered over it. With one powerful stroke, she clashed a blade against its shield and thunder rang out in the hall. The pawn was spun around by the blow; his shield cracked and clattered on the tiles, and Jacob had a clear view of its unprotected back. It was not difficult to chop straight through his spine. Then he faced the king. Rather than attack, he moved the second queen beside the first.

The white queens stood side by side with the black king before them. By normal rules this would be the end. But this was not a normal game. The king had to move; he had to attack but that forced him into a square that was under attack. It had to be done. Unable to retreat, the king moved against the first queen. He lifted his huge blade and swung wide at her. She parried the blow with both blades and then lunged forward to strike. The king turned sideways to avoid being stabbed, and the queen pulled the blades back dragging one of them across the king's back. The king did not allow the wound to stop the momentum of the blade and continued to pull it around and lifted it up to strike down at her.

Jacob blocked the blow and guided the heavy sword to the stone tile. Once again, the floor shook. Jacob swung one blade at the king's neck, but the king ducked under the strike and hefted the huge sword off of the floor and tossed the queen aside. She rolled through the remains of the pawns that had stood there just moments before, and her fine white dress ripped on the sharp stones and jagged metal shards. Jacob recovered quickly and saw the king had wasted no time. The king was on him and in midstrike. Jacob rolled forward under the blow but was not fast enough. The butt of the weapon below the king's grip smashed into the queen's back, and she fell on her face before the king. Jacob rolled over to see the king with his sword raised and ready to run her through. He was poised to stab all the way through the marble floor.

Jacob rolled out of the way, and the sword clanged into the ground. Chips of black marble flew from the impact and left a small crater. The king rolled the blade and swung down at the queen as she rolled to her back again. Jacob used all his strength and braced against the blow. The force behind the impact shook Jacobs chest when the king's strike connected with the queen's crossed blades. His arms went numb from the shock, but he resisted. They locked blades. Jacob stared straight up at the king as he grinded down upon him. He had to be quick.

With all the strength he could spare, Jacob slid the bottom blade out and around the queen's head, slicing across both of the king's thighs. Then she reached up and plunged the sword into his abdomen. It was a good stroke but not the kill stroke. Her arms were weak, and she could not hold on to the sword as the king wrenched away. The sword fell out and clattered across the board. Jacob stood with his one sword and faced the wounded king. He was bleeding, but Jacob hardly had the strength to lift the queen's sword. The king raised his blade once more, slower this time. Jacob had substantially weakened him. It came down climactically, and Jacob barely had the dexterity to raise the queen's sword to block it. He did not have the strength to withstand it, and the queen buckled under the blow, and the queen fell to her knees as her blade flew from her grasp and danced across the tiles.

The king drew the blade back and hurled it horizontally. Jacob was too tired to move, and he watched the razor edge of death race to his neck. It was still black's turn. The first queen had fallen and now lay across the board in chunks of pure white quartz. But that is why Jacob had acquired a second. He was very wise not to underestimate this king. His knight, rook, and queen had fallen by his hand, but each of them had done their damage. The black king lumbered into the queen's space; he had no other choice. This would be over soon.

The white queen stepped up to challenge the foe. This queen was fresh and not tired, and her adversary was bleeding and battle weary. She lunged and launched a flourish of attacks at the king. He backed away, blocking a few and trying to avoid most of them all together. When Jacob paused, the black king swung overhead again. The white queen stepped aside and let the blade thunder to the ground. She stepped close and severed the king's left wrist from his arm with one swift motion. The king dropped his mighty sword and backed away, holding on to the bleeding appendage. The sword collided with the tiles, bounced, and then clattered to a rest among the rubble of the fallen warriors.

The queen stepped forward over the bastard sword that had caused so much damage as the opponent backed away. The black king drew the short sword that had been lodged in his chest and tried to make a last stand. The old short sword of the knight appeared to be reduced to a steak knife in the king's enormous hands. Jacob struck it down with a quick flick, and the black king was defenseless. As Jacob stepped closer to finish the battle and end this cursed game, the black king fell to his knees and bowed. Jacob paused. Did he have to kill the king or could he accept the surrender?

"Kill," the board whispered again. Was it the board? Jacob held both blades at his opponent's neck. "Surrender!" he bellowed. The voice came from nowhere and everywhere. It rang out from the queen's lungs like the clap of thunder. It held authority and demanded respect. The voice shook the board, and Jacob feared its power. Was that his inner demon bellowing, or was that his voice just perceived differently within the game?

"Kill!" The voice continued to urge. He felt Aries breathing on him as if the Demon was standing beside him. At the command, he tensed to sever the King's head. He stopped; that wasn't right.

"Jacob, kill him!"

The voice wasn't in his head; it was beside him. He felt the Demon imposing on him, he could feel its breath, and the cold, calculating god of war urged him to kill. He knew that this was not from him. He resisted the urge to give in to the voice, and his emotions became rage and anger. He wanted to kill and he focused on something else, the only other thing was Aries. His next impulse was to turn to the Demon and face him. He quelled his mind, he could not defeat a full-fledged demon; he couldn't even attack it in this realm. It was trapped in the board. Jacob closed his eyes and pushed out the influence of the board; he felt something strong come between them. He searched his heart for his emotions and drove out those of the demon. When he opened his eyes, he was in control—this game was over!

Jacob stepped closer more threatening and demanded again, "Surrender your crown!"

The black king lowered his head. With one hand and a bloody wrist, he removed the crown on his head and handed it to Jacob's white queen. She placed it on her head, and then the board warped. All the pieces were back as they were, and Jacob stood holding one of the queen's swords pointing it at his opponent: Julie.

CHAPTER 16

A few moments of volatile awkwardness passed, and Jacob caught his breath, "You just want to talk?" Jacob asked, still holding a sword to her throat. "Play a game of chess? What was the purpose of this?" His blood boiled that he had for even an instant let himself think she had been sincere when they talked in the courtyard. The energy of his Fallen blood still raged in him, and his blood had not yet cooled. He wasn't concerned with the surge of power in his body; he was angry. Julie looked up; she was still drained from the battle. The game was extremely mentally challenging, and it even took a physical toll on one's body. "I needed to test you." She said as she looked up at the blade. Though her voice was steady and confident, she was on the verge of collapsing.

"For what purpose!" Jacob yelled. He wasn't sure if it was fatigue or anger that made the room warble in front of him. "What do you want from me?" His rage welled up so great that his vision blurred, and the blade he held at her throat trembled. Out of reflex, he poised to attack her.

"Drop your sword!" Malcolm yelled from across the room.

Jacob, irritated, looked around; Malcolm, Lucile, and Roth were now here. Realizing the position he was in, he stepped back and dropped the blade. It merged with the marble floor and vanished back into the board.

"What did you wish to take from me?" Jacob repeated, still angry, but much more composed. His voice carried a strong, smooth tone of justified fury that he did not know he had. He took a deep breath and the red fazed out of his vision.

"I needed to know if you were strong enough," Julie replied.

Jacob scowled at her, "Was this Malcolm's idea? You needed to see if I was fit for this position? If you could do it better?"

Julie looked at her father, lost for words. "No, I needed to know. They said it so often, I had to know if it was true." Julie stood up shaking, "I wanted to be you, Jacob. I wanted the clans to look at me as the hero, and I needed to know if I could do it."

"Treason against the Chosen!" Lucile exclaimed.

Jacob turned to face the audience. Roth held his face in his hand, "This must be dealt with. Malcolm, you know that the code demands traitors to be executed."

"I'll kill you before you touch her," Malcolm replied distastefully in the patented tone of his family's arrogance. His right hand grabbed the hilt of his sword, and he held his left hand up high, sparks dancing around his fingers.

Lucile stepped between them, facing Malcolm; as she did Jacob saw a terrifying side of his mother that he had never seen before. Her mild manner and naturally calm expression vanished. Her eyes became hard, and her face filled with malice. Her features became stone cold like he had seen years ago when he was indoctrinated.

"Don't make it a double trial, son!" Roth demanded. His voice carried a superior authority that vibrated through the air in the room, and suddenly his age seemed to fade and an ancient fire burned in his eyes as the powers he held for so long kindled for the fight.

Rain backed up and got out of the way as her eyes filled with determination and her hair flushed white as centuries of refined magic pulsed through her.

"Shut up, all of you!" Jacob yelled. "This is why we never get anywhere. Why start another feud? Look at yourselves—ready and willing to kill your own family. For what?"

"Jacob, she just tried to murder you," His mother replied. Her voice was the voice she reserved for council business: hard and cutting. Did he sound like that right now?

Something welled up in him; recently he had raised his voice to his own grandfather, he had told off the entire council, and he was about to establish his voice. Jacob moved to step down from the board. If there was going to be a fight here he would be the one in the middle of it. He opened his mouth to speak and was frightened by the power of the words that ripped through the stone walls of the chamber. They were not his.

"Today the Chosen has faced the trials! An old promise has been fulfilled, and the right of command to the victor shall be given." The board was speaking. Aries's voice filled the room with a deep resounding bass.

It stopped the fight and brought everyone's attention to the board. Jacob's insides pounded with the pulsing sound. After a few moments of terrified shock, he continued toward the crowd and tried to run off the board, but he found some kind of barrier holding him back. "I have no desire to make a request. The game is over, let me down!" he replied forcefully. Jacob was upset; he knew there was something important about this moment, he knew this was going to be the moment he truly became a member of the council and this stupid game was in the way. The tone he took was bold and angry; he had found his voice, it was powerful, angry and justified, but the Demon's was much greater.

"The pact of the game is final! The defeated is subject to the victor's willing," the board bellowed.

As the floor beneath him rumbled Jacob understood that there was no way to argue with this thing. He had to demand something from his cousin. But what did he want that she could give him? The only thing he wanted was for someone to step up and help him; and that's what he'd get.

Turning, Jacob marched to Julie, "You want to be like me?" he challenged; the wheels in his head were spinning rapidly as he stepped back to her position. His voice had surfaced, and he wondered if he looked cold like his mother. He remembered how cold her hand was that day he was brought to Stirling, and he felt his own, only half aware that he did so. It wasn't cold like his mother's; it was blazing hot.

She stepped back afraid of what he might demand.

"You are now bound to me," he commanded hot and angry, his voice now carried authority, "Your words are my words, when you speak I have spoken. All you say is from my authority; if anyone questions you, they question me. You will dedicate your life to serving the Chosen, and your firstborn will inherit this responsibility until the day of reconciliation. And on that day you and your line will stand with the line of the Chosen to be judged as one. My pain is your pain, my work is your work, and we are bound by this pact to find the path for the salvation of our people."

Jacob stepped back, "You have been given what you wished for. You have been cursed with a blood curse that your children must suffer, and you must now shoulder the weight of the world as I do. If you should be found in contempt of this pact you will be blotted out and cast down for your double treachery." This isn't exactly the help he had been asking for, but it was probably the best help he could get. Despite the council, he had what he had asked for. Julie would not have been his first choice because of their family's history, but this way she could not stab him in the back.

"This pact is made and in stone is laid," Aries bellowed.

Jacob stepped down and walked up to the group that was ready to clash. He stepped straight up to Malcolm and stood nose to nose with his uncle, "Nobody is being executed. You now have what you want. Julie is Chosen just as I am. We'll see who is more worthy." If Aries had not been part of the conversation, Jacob might have found his tone imposing. His blood still raced with his oversurge of power from his dormant demon.

They all remained speechless. He knew they could sense his brimming power, too. Did they know it was as unstable as he did? He smirked to himself: *they fear me*.

Jacob stood for a moment, staring into Malcolm's eyes. He never would know why that man hated him so. Convinced he had nothing to say, he pushed past Malcolm, purposefully bumping into him and walked toward the door. Julie stepped off the board as he walked out. As soon as her feet had made it back to the floor, the board bellowed again.

"Another trial I wish. Sir Jacob, I shall test." Jacob turned around slowly and looked at the massive table. The booming voice of the Demon caused Julie to misplace her steps, and she fell forward as if she had been shoved.

Had it not been enough for Julie to test him? Not only did he never want to set foot on that board again, he could not possibly endure another round. A long pause ensued before Jacob did the unthinkable. For reason that defied his own will he stepped *toward* the board.

"Jacob, do not act now!" Rain pleaded and grabbed his arms. "You are not able to defeat it now. Come back after resting and make your decision to fight or decline."

"And why should I not just decline now?" Jacob asked, knowing that just a moment ago that thought had not crossed his mind.

Rain shook her head. "I know you have felt it." She began, "The sense of the challenge becomes addictive. You don't want to decline, do you? Many things could be possible, but you must first take time to weigh your risk."

Nobody else made a statement.

Jacob thought about it, as much as he never wanted to play on the board again, it did call to him. The challenge, the thrill, the danger, the pain, and the vengeance— everything that drove him to hate the game also made him desire it more. Unsure why he felt this way, he stepped back and left the chamber without saying anything.

He reached the Oasis and noticed that the sun that had been at its highest when he descended was now about to set. He breathed deep and exhaled. As he did so, his adrenaline and the power surge left him, and he felt the weight of his battle press down on him. The game had taken a lot more time than he had realized. With that realization, he became fatigued; he still felt sore in the places he had been wounded in battle.

Given how many times he had been stabbed, thrown, and choked, his entire body ached. He hurried home and lay down early. His mind and body had been tormented, and his energy was gone. Within minutes he was fast asleep, reliving the game in his nightmares.

Waking to an all too familiar feeling, Jacob wished he were still in his nightmare. Diligently he readied his things and prepared to march out into the night. His body still ached from the small war he had fought with Julie. His head still throbbed, and he still felt every cut, bruise, and scar as if they were real. Once he finished preparing, he walked out of his room. Normally his father was right behind him or right in front of him, but the bedroom door was still closed tonight. Jacob thought it was odd but didn't wish to wait. He knew where the creature was, and he could take care of it himself. Funny, not even a year ago he would have been completely lost without Drake, and now he was considering leaving him.

He shook off the pain, and placed the imaginary wounds out of his mind as he stepped down the hall to leave. He heard a door jam open and turned, not to see his father but Sarah. She was fully dressed with a set of leather armor, adorned with runes and other symbols of protection and power. It looked like something she had made for practicing her Seracata. There was a small dagger similar to Jade on her hip, and she wore gauntlets she had received in Serecata classes. The left gauntlet went all the way to her shoulder and had a small shield on the forearm. The right side only extended to her elbow but had a razor sharp spike that extended further.

"What are you doing?" Jacob asked, knowing full well what answer he would get: he had awakened her while he was getting ready, and she dressed out to come with him.

"I heard you getting ready." She replied, "They're out there again, aren't they?"

Jacob sighed, "No."

"Then why are you dressed at three in the morning?" she demanded in a whisper.

"No, you cannot come with me."

"And why not?"

"I've told you before." Jacob started, "This is not something you want to do. I get it; you want to help me, but please do not get involved in things you don't understand."

Sarah crossed her arms in defiance, "Then teach me so I can help; I want to understand and so does Dom."

"Look, you are very close to me, and I do what I do because I have to because I have to protect people and because I have to protect my family. Now what good does it do to have you right there in the middle of it? I want you, especially, as far away from it as possible." Jacob repeated the old lecture; he felt that each time it was less effective.

"You asked the council for help, and they didn't give it to you—why won't you let me help when I want to?" Sarah asked exasperated.

"You are my sister; I can't put you in danger like that." Jacob stated, "And, this is totally different. If you have any advice for what to do about Mom's side of the family, I'll gladly take it, but for your own good and my peace of mind, do not press this issue."

"It is the same issue. You are Chosen, not by Roth or the clans, but much higher powers chose you. Both families need salvation, and you are both families now. I'm your sister. I'm also both families."

Jacob walked over to Sarah and placed his hands on her shoulders, "Please, go back to bed." She relaxed and unfolded her arms. Jacob hugged her gently and then turned to go.

The night was cold, and the wind bit at him malevolently. In the biting cold, he could feel his phantom wounds smoldering and aching. The door handle of the truck was cold when he grabbed it. Jacob paused for a moment. It felt wrong for some reason to leave alone.

But he had to do it someday.

As he turned, the thought over in his mind he heard the door open. His father walked through the doorway and down the stairs of the porch.

"It's a cold night," he remarked as he approached. "You weren't trying to go out alone were you?"

Jacob opened the door and reached for the ignition. The cold engine turned over and rumbled to life, "No, just warming the truck."

"Good," Drake replied. "It's been a while since we had a chance to talk."

Jacob stepped aside and walked to the other side of the truck. He wasn't sure this was exactly a good time to talk. But he was glad his father had made it; the stress his body had endured earlier was made much more apparent in the bitter cold. He always hated the cold.

They got in the truck and began toward the source of the disturbance, "Your mother told me about what happened today," Drake started.

Jacob palmed his forehead, "Julie is such a fool."

His father looked over, "Perhaps," he agreed, "but even so, you know not to act out of anger."

Jacob looked out the window into the night and sighed. As he did so, the glass fogged up. "I know; I already regret that." He replied, "It was just so much, all at once. Everyone wants me to be something, and I don't even know what that is. Julie, the demon . . .," Jacob paused, "Even the demon said I was the Chosen."

Drake reached over and placed his hand on his son's shoulder, "Jacob, you are Chosen, but not by any power of man. I can't say I would have done anything differently in your place."

Jacob just shook his head; he had created a mess and he needed to clean things up.

"I'm just glad you're alright." Drake continued, "To stand that close to a demon, even one that is bound, is very dangerous." There was a moment of silence; then Drake spoke again, "But that's not what I wanted to talk about. I wanted to discuss what we do."

Not quite sure what his father wanted to talk about he turned to him and began, "You know . . .," he started, "I could handle it by myself." He didn't mean to sound like he wanted to be independent; he didn't want that at all. He just couldn't properly express that he had the same concerns for his father as Drake did for him.

"Of course you could, son." Drake replied. "You're very skilled, but you know it worries me that the weapons you use are . . ."

Jacob stopped him, "You don't understand the power of that blade. It's different from the other weapons."

"I know where the power comes from," Drake answered.

"I never told you what spell I used to get it to work, did I?"

"It wouldn't make a difference," His father said.

"It's not like the other ones, forged by demons in dark places; it uses divine light." Jacob explained, "It paralyzes the evil."

"I wish I could believe it was that simple," Drake sighed.

Jacob paused before he continued. "The spell I used was John chapter one."

His father was silent in contemplation for a moment, and Jacob continued. "It really is a holy blade. It responds to Scripture, and it repels the darkness. Just wait until you see what it does; then you'll understand; I have a great advantage now."

Drake frowned, "Then perhaps that is why the attacks suddenly got worse. Maybe they are trying to put out your new light."

"Then the game has been changed," Jacob replied, "Our job has just become more dangerous." Rain's word echoed through his memory, *"You are always being watched. What you have done is only a proof of the threat that you pose to the Powers of the Air. They will move against you for this; already they plot from the darkness."*

"That's one of the things I'd like to talk about, Jacob," Drake said as they turned onto the main road.

Jacob remained silent.

"It won't be our job much longer, son. Soon you'll be on your own," Drake continued.

"Dad, I really don't like to think about it."

Drake looked at him curiously, "Which part? You on your own or me not being here?"

"The latter," Jacob replied, "I'm sure I can take care of myself. I've got a better . . . leverage. But I worry about you getting hurt out there."

"Well, Jacob, I'm getting older. If these things don't get me soon, I might retire in a couple years. But I'd be the first in my line to do so."

"So why don't you retire?" Jacob asked.

Drake sighed, "You already understand; it's something you have to do." He paused for a moment. "Why should I explain it to you when you just explained it to your little sister?" Jacob knew this was true; he had just never thought about it that way. "I believe you'll take care of yourself fine. I was only sixteen when my father died, and I had to go it alone. I think part of the reason I'm still in this business is because you've got a knack for it. It's like you were born to do this, even if you hadn't been cursed like me."

"You taught me everything. I should be the best," Jacob answered.

Drake gave a slight chuckle, "Aye that is true, son. I taught you well, I suppose, perhaps I will get to see retirement."

A few moments of silence passed, and Jacob's mind went to Sarah's repeated attempts to accompany them. She had always wanted to be just like him, part of being the big brother. But she was getting more urgent and demanding about it.

"Dad," Jacob began, "Could you talk to Sarah in the morning?"

"I heard you two talking while I was getting ready. I must be getting really slow if Sarah can get dressed before me." Drake said it with a smile and a light laugh.

Jacob did not find it as funny.

"She does have the same blood as you, remember that. The blood of angels naturally seeks to vanquish evil," Drake replied.

"Then why did you never take her with us?"

"It's not her place." Drake answered.

Jacob didn't understand why he could not deny her for the same reason his father had. "But that's what I tell her."

"Your mother's side of the family has a very rare strength, especially in your generation," Drake replied. "I was not sure I liked it until I saw how you used it; your sister just wants to do the same. Otherwise, what else are her powers and knowledge good for? It would certainly be better to have her help than find destructive ways to use her abilities."

"So you want me to start letting her tag along?" Jacob asked.

"It's not her responsibility; for her it is a choice. But you are the bearer of the curse now; it is your decision," Drake answered. "It's no longer my call. I don't know if you have realized, son, but you are leading this outfit now. You get to call the shots from now on. If you think it's wise, then let her help, you of all people know that there is so much more to fighting demons than confrontation."

He briefly recalled confronting Aries. Jacob quickly shut that thought out; now was not the time to be thinking about that game. It had battled him all day and dominated his dreams until the spirit woke him by ripping through the barrier. He did not want it on his mind; his body was still aching from the experience. Jacob noted what his father had said, pondered it for a moment, and then decided he would try to unravel the words later. Sarah had a choice, but he had to decide —it was something not meant to be understood at this time.

He was sure he would figure it out, but his concentration was meant for other things at the moment—they were getting close. He had still not asked his father about the Wraith he had killed the last time. Now might not be a good time to ask questions, though. The words were bold in his memory: *Will you kill your own fathers? How can you save a soul by destroying it?* If it was trying to plead with the side of him that was half demon, it was a lost cause. His life had been dedicated to revoking his Fallen ancestry; he was not his fathers of old. But that left the last bit about saving a soul. Jacob was not trying to save the Wraith; the opposite was true. So what did it mean by that?

The truck stopped. The creature was in a graveyard. Jacob sensed a Wraith. Normally, he would be terrified, but he remembered the Light Shard and the holy power it commanded. With his father here now, he had nothing to worry about. Even with his aches, he was actually a little excited to try his Light Shard again; especially now that he had some idea of what it could do. They got out of the truck; the rest of the way would be a walk.

The graveyard was large, and the headstones were massive. Many stone crosses were standing upright. It was a curious paradox that a spirit would choose such a hallowed spot to reside. Then again there were many things Jacob did not yet understand about the nature of Hell and the creatures in it. Drake opened the iron gate, and it swung open with a creepy grinding sound. Jacob stepped and felt the eyes of evil pierce him. Drake followed and then closed the gate and used an ancient spell to seal it. The Wraith was now unable to escape—Drake had confined it to the perimeter within the gate. As long as no one opened the gate, the spell would remain intact.

Jacob stepped forward into the darkness, crunching through the undisturbed snow. In the middle of the graveyard was a large tree with boughs weighed low with snow, and beneath it was the shadowy figure. The sight of the creature caused his phantom injuries of the day to hurt worse. Drake reached down and ignited his ball of incense and readied his charm. The thing only stood there, giving no indication that it had a reason or purpose for arriving tonight. It could have gone completely unnoticed, which meant this meeting was intended. This Wraith had called them here.

"Stop," Jacob urged. That thing had called them here, but he did not sense a trap as he moved forward. He removed his coat and laid it on a headstone. The winter cold ripped at him, but he did not feel it; his blood was hot with anticipation and his adrenaline surged. "I'll handle this; it came for me," Jacob said. Something about the adrenaline numbed the pain of his nonexistent injuries and blocked out the cold that he hated so much.

He thought he heard movement to his left but did not turn his focus from the Wraith. "Watch my back," Jacob trudged forward until he stood under the shadow of the tree. He could hear the Wraith breathing under its mask. He reached down and grabbed his ball of incense and started it burning. The ball dangled by the chain at his thigh, and the sweet smoke escaped through the holes.

"Be gone!" Jacob commanded, "This is a hallowed place; the ground you stand on is holy!" He tried to use the voice he had discovered just this afternoon, but he couldn't get it right. It only hissed and drew its weapons from beneath the black cloak of fog that shrouded him. This was the first Wraith Jacob had seen that carried two of the ghostly blades. The swords screamed as they violently slid out of the sheaths and raked across each other in a taunting gesture. Jacob drew his weapons and assumed a challenging stance. The Wraith lunged at him. Jacob stepped to meet the attack and tapped into his own power from the Fallen to match its strength. He blocked both blades and locked up with the Wraith.

"I command you back to the pit where you came from!" Jacob screamed. This was not at all how his father had taught him to fight such a powerful opponent, but Jacob had changed the rules. He felt the surge of power flow from his demo, and the world slowed down.

The Wraith wailed and exerted his strength against Jacob, causing him to stumble backward. Jacob raised Jade to block the attack and once again locked up, "In the beginning God created the heavens and the earth." Jacob smiled as the passage began to flow from his lips; his voice was back. "The earth was formless and empty and darkness covered the surface of the watery depths, and the Spirit of God was hovering over the surface of the waters. Then God said, 'Let there be light!'" The Light Shard began to glow in his left hand as he spoke and a bright light began to repel the dark shadow that surrounded the Wraith. "And so there was Light!" Jacob yelled defiantly in his new voice of hot anger.

"God saw that the light was good and God separated the light from the darkness." The weapon beamed, and light crackled between them. The Wraith stumbled, driven back by the light, and his shroud of evil aura was blasted away like fog before a gust of wind. The creature had a massive hole in his helm, and beneath it Jacob could see bone and something metallic. A burning red glow emitted from the head wound and the stench of death hung in the air near the Wraith. Jacob went on the offensive, releasing a flourish of attacks against the creature. The snow around them melted and shimmered in the illumination of the dagger.

The Wraith blocked skillfully with passion and hate. The blades howled through the air as they raced to meet, and they clanged and screeched as they slid off one another. It had a rhythmic chime to it. The light filled the graveyard and illuminated all the snow-covered stones, and the place was white. Drake stood in awe at the beauty of the light contrasted by the evil projected from the Wraith his son was fighting. He tucked the spells back into his coat, satisfied he would not need them and stepped closer.

The Wraith locked one of his blades against the Light Shard and used his leverage to throw Jacob's back into the tree. It swung with its other blade, and Jacob blocked it. "The Fallen cannot rise, my son." It growled at him in the Fallen language. "Why do you hope to ascend to the heavens when you know you will fall to Hell?" Jacob felt the evil pressing on him, and he smelled fire.

He pushed back, but the Wraith did not budge. Why had they suddenly taken an interest in talking to him? "My resting place is to be determined by God," Jacob replied. "Dominion and awe belong to God; He establishes order in the heights of heaven! Can his forces be numbered? On whom does his light not rise?" The energy emitting from his Light Shard focused on the Wraith, and the armor covering its face began to boil. Jacob pushed back again, summoning the strength of his Fallen side, and the Wraith's strength gave in. Power coursed through his body; it was more than he had experienced before. It was almost like he wasn't controlling his powers; rather, he was just a channel for them.

Jacob released another round of attacks and caught the Wraith in the thigh. It collapsed and kneeled; he then took the Light Shard and raised it up above his head and dropped the blade into the Wraith's skull. Fire spat from the splintered helmet rather than blood. A roar of hate resounded from within the hollow helmet and the armor crumpled as the body beneath it contorted and burned. Jacob had to step back from the heat that emitted from the burning armor. Red-hot ash spewed from the joints in the armor as flames from beneath burned through the metal plates.

Water began to drip from the frozen branches of the tree they had battled under, and the snow around the collapsed armor was melted and vaporized. The armor now lay in a heap, incinerating rapidly as the burning ash lifted into the air and dispersed in the wind. Within moments, nothing was left but a circle of charred ground, the only blemish in the white snow.

Jacob turned and saw Drake standing abreast of him with his hand blocking the light from the dagger from blinding him as he beheld the smoldering remains of the Wraith. Jacob stared at the heap as it disintegrated. That had been too easy. Drawing on his hidden power had been far too easy.

"I saw my father once kill a Wraith," he said, "I never found the strength, so I always sent them back to Hell, never really solving the problem. You made it look so simple."

"Did you hear what it said?" Jacob asked.

Drake gave a curious look, "Was it speaking? I could not tell the difference, sounded like demonic muttering to me."

Jacob sheathed the Light Shard, and the graveyard darkened. A few moments passed while Jacob's eyes adjusted, and the place glowed slightly in the moonlight. "It was the language of the Fallen," he explained, "I think they have been speaking to us from the beginning, but we just didn't understand."

"You know this language?" his father asked.

"I've been studying it in the library," Jacob nodded.

"Do you know what it said?" Drake continued with an enthused interest. Jacob could not tell if he was curious or frightened.

"It told me that the Fallen cannot rise," Jacob replied. "It asked me why I hoped to ascend to heaven when I know I'm bound to Hell."

Drake thought about it for a moment, "You think they have been talking to us the whole time?"

Jacob was silent for a second, "I meant to ask you if you had ever heard one talk to you."

"No, never."

"The one that attacked me that night when I brought Emily to the house said things to me, also," Jacob said. Now would be a good time to bring it up. "The language is hard to decipher, but I understood its words clearly, I just don't know what to make of it."

"What did it tell you?"

Jacob shrugged, "More riddles. It asked why I would kill my fathers and then asked how I would save a soul by killing it."

"Kill your fathers . . .," Drake repeated.

Silence ensued as they stood in the cold and pondered. Jacob crunched through the snow to where he left his coat. Now that the rush had ended, he was feeling the extreme cold. "One more thing," he added, "The first one asked why I was killing my fathers, and this one called me 'son.'"

Drake turned to walk toward him, "I'll think it over and see what I can come up with." He sighed and trudged to the gate. "I'm not sure what to make of it."

"You think it could be the line that Mom belongs to?"

"I don't know, son." Drake replied reflectively as if he were contemplating a much simpler meaning. He turned around and paced back to the truck.

Jacob walked after him, "I mean the Demon that fathered Mom's line. Could this be his domain?" Then he realized his father had not read the same books he had. "Each of the Fallen has a domain, and the Wraiths and Shadows we fight are all commanded by the same the Demon that is like a general. Do you know the name of the Demon that resides here? I can check the archives and find out if it's a match."

Drake paused and looked back over his shoulder, "What good will that do?"

Jacob shrugged. It would solve nothing really—he was just curious. "I guess you're right; it's more of a personal curiosity."

He trudged back to the truck and got in. The engine was still warm. It was a good thing, too, because Jacob's adrenaline had kicked out, and he was starting to feel the cold biting all around him.

"You know, Dad, on second thought, maybe we ought to find that name." Jacob said. "Names are a powerful thing to a demon, you of all people know that. Isn't it easier to command a demon if you know its name?"

"Well, son, in theory yes, but there's not a man I've ever met that faced a demon and lived to tell about it," he sighed. "There aren't many that mange to walk free on the earth; I've never seen one. But my grandfather died taking one back to Hell, and that's the only one I've ever heard of."

"It's just a thought," Jacob suggested.

"Well, thinking is your strong point; I'll leave that to you."

CHAPTER 17

J acob couldn't go back to sleep. It was becoming more frequent. It bothered him when he was younger, gave him nightmares that kept him awake, but those wore off eventually. Recently he was finding it harder to rest after these hunts. Tonight was especially difficult because he still felt bruised and battered after his game of chess with Julie. It wasn't fear that kept him awake. Anticipation? Contemplation? Reflection? Maybe all the adrenalin wasn't quite out of his blood.

For whatever reason, he couldn't sleep after these things anymore. He had only been home for about half an hour. It was nearly five, and he knew he would not get back to sleep before dawn came. Being restless wasn't something he was good at, so he made a sandwich from a leftover pork chop from dinner and went to the library. The cold was bitter in the early morning before the dawn. He was glad he had magic rings and amulets that could transport him there. He stepped out the front door and down the porch, and then two steps later, he was in front of the castle. To an outsider, it looked like a ruin with nothing impressive to hide. But he knew where the secret passage was that led to the castle beneath the castle, and even in the dark without a torch to see by, he pressed his hand against the stone wall and opened an invisible door.

It was too early for anyone to be out. Rain was in her chamber, still asleep, and Naff would be down here somewhere. There was nothing to really protect, the only things of any substantial importance were hidden in the secret passages. As Jacob entered the secret chambers, he heard the demon of the chessboard whispering to him. Was he just imagining it, or was it really calling? He closed his eyes, and he felt the pain and the rush of the battle all over again. A chill ran down his spine and he shook it off. That thing was trying to communicate with him, and he wasn't sure what was best.

He found Naff in the study. Naff was not surprised to see him; he was the only person who obsessed over his research and the only person that would be in the library before sunrise or after sundown, for that matter.

"Welcome, young master. How may I be of assistance on this very bright morning?" Naff greeted.

"I think I'll start with Arteminus today," Jacob replied.

"Then you have completed the retranslation of Anzel?" Naff asked.

"I'm close, Naff, but I think I will give it a rest until the weekend."

Naff turned to walk down the long hall of books and stopped short. He turned to a small shelf and grabbed a large book and handed it to him, "I had a hunch you wanted this one today. So I got it while I was looking for my own study book."

Jacob was surprised. Naff wasn't as good at such things as Rain was, but he was getting much better. He had only been the keeper for five years, so it wasn't like he would be an expert compared to Rain who had been the librarian for one hundred and eighty-three years in this place.

"Thanks, Naff." Jacob said as he accepted the book, "Am I that predictable or are you getting that instinct that comes from spending too much time here?"

"I'm afraid you're just predictable. I still haven't got the foggiest idea when the magic of this place will start giving me insight," Naff replied. "It will take more than my lifetime to acquire the skills Rain has; the magic here works slowly, and the magic that defies time goes to the librarian only. Keepers are not so fortunate."

Jacob gave a slight laugh, "Fortunate?" He sighed, "Is she really that fortunate to be young forever?"

Naff looked at him curiously; his brow wrinkled as he squinted. The way Naff looked at Jacob made him see his age. Suddenly the elfish-looking man looked like his grandfather. But then the look and wrinkles faded with Naff's inquisitiveness, "Of course, she is. Wouldn't you desire to live for a thousand years and remain young?"

Jacob looked around the room, "Trapped in this place alone? Can you imagine how lonely she gets?"

Naff sighed, "When you are my age, you will think differently. Once your youth starts to fade, you'll do anything to keep it."

"I'm not sure I would want to," Jacob answered. "In my line of work I could use an early retirement."

Naff smiled slightly, "Well, you had best get to studying."

Jacob nodded and went to the lower study to begin. He enjoyed the open air of the upper study; the view of the snow-covered ruins and the white rolling hills was a breathtaking sight, but the bitter cold this time of year discouraged anyone from sitting among the rows of chessboards. The chessboards—after yesterday he never wanted to see another chessboard in his life. But it had challenged him, and he had not yet answered it. The sudden urge came over him to put the book back and march to the Oasis and accept the challenge. His better judgment snuffed out that spark of a thought. Why did he desire to play the game? His last experience was not pleasant at all, and the risk if he should lose was immense. So why did he *want* to play?

Jacob pushed the thought and the question out of his mind—he still felt the bruises from the last time. It was odd, there was nothing physically wrong, but when he thought about the game, he felt the cuts and all the broken bones not yet mended, and a desire to shed blood welled up in him. Anything with that kind of power should be avoided like a plague. If Jacob ever worked up the courage to walk back into that chamber, it would be to decline the request.

He found his place among all the empty tables of the lower study. Nobody was ever here this early. Later his sister and his brother would be here; sometimes he saw Julie, but there were few others that were here often. Mostly people came here when they needed help; there were very few who actually came to study.

In reflection, that was probably the reason so much had been forgotten. Only a small group of people tried to remember the lost secrets. Jacob couldn't understand why, though. He was so fascinated by everything in this place, and to think there was a library like this for each clan. What could he learn from the others? Perhaps he would study with some of the other clans. Maybe he would work on some of the Books of the Fallen that were not in the collection here.

But for now he was working on *The Book of the Heart*, and he was quite glad this particular book was in this library's collection. Jacob opened the book, and the smell wafted to his nostrils and stimulated his creativity and enthused him to read. He had come to a chapter that had no accepted translation yesterday, and he continued on it now. Translating was tricky, but he was understanding most of it quite well. The passage he was working on dealt with the notions of love and hate. Arteminus was comparing and contrasting her understanding of the two notions to the human understandings. After writing everything down literally and then rewriting it so that it made some sense and then rewriting it after examining the subtle clues for hidden words, he came up with a very insightful thought. Suddenly he realized how similar the two emotions were; both were very powerful and both had their proper places. Had he ever really understood what they were? Arteminus seemed fascinated that the human mind could house both of these "notions" at the same time, whereas angels, fallen or otherwise, could only feel one or the other.

The text suggested that even some of those who had fallen didn't understand or feel hate, and there were many who never gained a comprehension of love. It was a bit muggy, but it seemed to distinguish between four emotions based on the notions of love and hate: righteous hate, holy love, burning hate, and tainted love. It seemed these notions each had a constructive and destructive form, and Arteminus argued that the human mind, in its struggle to comprehend both simultaneously, was only capable of understanding two of the four emotions at one time. Therefore, mankind only had a half understanding of the notions of love and hate.

This book had proved to be very interesting because it was written from the vantage point of someone who could not feel like human. It was different to think about such things this way because to humans it was normal and part of life. But to a higher being, these things and the distinction between them were so great, it really was a wonder how they could both reside in the heart at one time. Jacob rolled this around in his mind for a while until a gentle touch brought him out of his cloud of wonderment. "We didn't get a chance to speak to you last night." Sarah said. "You went straight to bed, and this morning before you left I didn't get to ask you, either. I wanted to ask you when you woke last night."

Jacob looked up and saw Sarah beside him and Dom walking toward him. "Good morning."

"I meant to ask if you were alright after everything that happened yesterday." Sarah continued, "You must be incredibly tired."

"I am," Jacob nodded.

"You didn't go back to sleep last night." She continued not hiding her concern. "Are you alright?"

Jacob sighed trying to hide his fatigue, "It will pass; I just have to sort it all out in my mind."

Sarah shrugged and looked down at a massive old book that she carried, "If you're too tired, we understand. I brought the Nimba."

"If you don't feel like studying, I don't blame you." Dom said and slapped his brother on the shoulder. "I hear you had had a rough day; I wish I could have been there."

"Actually," Jacob replied, "a good study might take my mind off of it."

"Then let's get to it!" Dom said with enthusiasm.

"Well then, I suppose it is time to get started." Jacob said and folded his papers into Arteminus's *Book of the Heart*.

"You're sure?" Sarah asked, "Next week is just as good, I know you need to rest."

"I'll rest after the lesson," Jacob replied, "It might help settle my mind."

Sarah sat down across from him, "Before we get started today, I had a question about what we studied the last time."

"Well it's new to me, too, so I'm not sure I can answer it now, but ask me so I can be thinking on it," Jacob replied.

"I was wondering: last time we studied energy transfers and how to put essences of objects into different objects. In the books I've been studying by Croff, it was talking about cloning essences of spells. Would it be possible to share a spell like a charm or curse between two objects or two people?"

Jacob stared for a moment, wondering how that had welled up in her mind; then again charms and forgery was his trait, and Sarah was much better with real magic. Of course she would have thought about that. "Why would you want to?"

"I suppose the reasons are limited, but it might apply to some of the things you do," she continued.

"Like what?" Jacob was now curious.

"Like all the different weapons you make. You could clone the essence of the Light Shard and infuse anything with that power. Then you could do just about anything with it." Sarah said.

"Well I suppose it could be possible, but you are actually much better at those kind of things than I am, so I would not be surprised if you figured it out," Jacob answered. "If you do manage to get that working, I would be thrilled. I don't think I've ever heard of that before though, so it might be a first."

The lesson from the Nimba that day was a continuation of what they had studied the day before. There was no answer to Sarah's question yet. Sarah was really keen on using spells and such, and she soaked up all the information better than Jacob. Dom was still learning, but he was following pretty well. He furrowed his brow and scrutinized the text with his steely eyes the same way their father would read his Bible. He seldom said anything, but he soaked up every word and piece of information like a sponge. There was still much to learn from the Nimba, and Jacob wasn't sure Dom could keep up—he wasn't sure he could keep up. He excelled at things with puzzles such as crafting and language. He could perform these spells, but a lot of the subject matter was taking spells out of their original context; cutting, mixing, splicing, and augmenting natural magic to change its purpose. He had not figured out what Dom's talent was yet, but it was clear that Sarah was way beyond her brothers in this field.

On the one hand, Jacob was a little jealous that it came so easy to her, but on the other he was really just proud. Sarah could conjure spells far beyond many of the mages he had seen, and she was only seventeen. He was the same way with languages two years ago when he was seventeen, and Sarah was just starting to go to the library. It was a good thing.

After the lesson from the Nimba, Sarah had a class in Serecata. She was doing extremely well in that, also. The fighting technique of the angels was difficult to master, but she could not only perform the movements, but could perform the advanced techniques that involved the use of her powers. Dom had decided if he were ever to get in a fight, he would rather keep a comfortable distance and so he had taken up hunting. The practice was not as heavily involved in magic as the upper levels of Serecata, but his brother had become quite skilled with a bow and arrow. The magic that was applied would help him read nature, camouflage himself, and walk through crowds unnoticed. Dom had really enjoyed practicing the latter at school recently. It was surprising to Jacob; his brother could quite easily sneak up on him, and that was a task most people found impossible.

They were all so different, but Jacob liked that. If they were all gifted in the same area, it wouldn't be much fun studying things together. He got up to take the *Book of the Heart* and the Nimba to Rain. The board was still heavy on his mind— so much was heavy on his mind. demons speaking to him, his cousin trying to kill him, the board challenging him; he had done a good job of keeping it off his mind until Dom and Sarah left the lesson.

Now, walking in the dimly lit halls alone, recent memories filled his head. He wanted someone to talk to. Emily appeared in his mind, but how could she help? Then his thoughts went to Julie. How could she try something like that? Their families didn't get along, but to risk a crime that demanded death just to test Jacob wasn't worth it.

When he arrived at the desk, Rain could tell that he was bothered. She brushed her white-blond hair back, and blues and reds streaked through it for an instant as it moved. "Are you well?" she asked, paying no attention the books he placed on her desk. Jacob shrugged, he didn't really know what to think; he hadn't had time to think. No sleep and so much stress, he had not realized it, but his emotions had been suppressed since he walked away from that board. His mind had stopped processing fear, anger, pity—he just felt empty.

"Jacob if something is bothering you, if there is anything I can do, please let me help." She reached as if to connect with him, to share his thoughts and to know his feelings. She held out her hand and her golden eyes latched onto him, expecting him to accept the gesture. There was nothing to read; it was clear on his face. Her hand hesitated before it touched his cheek. Maybe she was uncertain she really wanted to know. Or perhaps the weirdness that happened when they connected had her worried. Jacob couldn't ever read her face, not completely; she could become completely void of outward emotion if she put her mind to it. Even when she didn't, it was hard to tell.

Recently the connections had been acting up, but in the past Jacob had learned a lot about her through them. Her inner person was much different than what she expressed. Jacob reached up and stopped her. He pushed her hand aside, and then gently lowered it to her side. He really wanted to let her in; she might be able to fix the problem. But right now wasn't a good time. He needed to better understand himself first. Right now, he just felt disconnected.

"I'll be alright."

Rain's eyes flooded with sympathy, and she allowed him to see it, her golden gaze that was often fiery and daunting was cool and sad. It made Jacob feel relaxed. It was a very subtle difference. Jacob could only tell because he had known her so long and taken the time to learn who she was. Most of the time her emotional responses were minute and often missed, but every once in a while she would let emotion slip out of her that was crystal clear. This was rare, and even the slightest sign of emotion on her face revealed that there were oceans of feeling behind those golden eyes.

He started to pick her hand up to let her in his mind but then he stopped.

"Jacob, it's okay," Rain whispered. "The things that happen on that board change something in you—I know."

Was that what was happening, was he changing? It had been an ordeal, but he didn't think it was that bad that it could change who he was.

"I'm not different," Jacob said and then sat on the desk. *Or am I?* Something *had* changed, but he wasn't sure if it was the game, or if it was something else that had caused it. He knew his demon was waking up now, and he needed to learn to understand it before it took over. But he was afraid—afraid of the power he held and afraid to let anyone know what was happening.

"What happened last night changed who Julie will be," Rain replied, "Who she is and who you will make her will in turn change you. Sometimes the change is internal, and sometimes the change is from your choices. The board changes you." She locked her golden eyes of wisdom into his; she knew. Jacob knew everyone had felt his outburst of power. No one in that room would have been blind, and they all now knew that he was on the verge of unleashing something dark and dangerous. But that wasn't something Aries had done. Perhaps it was a catalyst, but that had already been buried in him.

Jacob looked up into her eyes, they were neither approving or condemning of his choice, just sympathetic of his struggle against himself and his own decisions. "Does anything good ever come from it?" he asked.

Rain sighed and sat down beside him; the books lay between them, "I have lived a long time and I have many more years to come, but I have only seen one battle on that board.

"I still hear him calling to me sometimes. Sometimes when I close my eyes, I can feel it. It knows you now; the only way to get it out of your head is to accept or reject its challenge," Rain said. "The longer you wait, the louder the voice will get. It will be harder to resist."

"Should I go there now?" Jacob asked.

Rain placed her hand on his shoulder and looked him in the eyes, "Go when you are ready, but don't wait too long. The board does not like to be kept waiting."

"How long do I have?"

"Until he gets angry."

That wasn't the best answer he had ever received, but it told him a lot. And at the same time it told him nothing. If it got angry, he would walk away. How difficult could that be? He already didn't want to walk away, though. Would he be able to if the board really started pulling on him?

"I should go," Jacob sighed, "I can't think in here; that thing gets in my head when it's quiet."

"Aries is dangerous." Rain said, "Please be careful, Jacob. Don't do something you're not prepared for."

Her hand slid off his shoulder as he stood up and fell on the books. Jacob looked at her and saw something she could not hide behind her mask, something she wasn't allowing to be seen rather she couldn't stop it: concern, caring, and worry. Jacob knew she had these feelings, but he had never seen her unable to repress them. Even if Rain didn't have an answer or even if she couldn't help, it was nice to know that under all of her flawless features and stoic posture, she really cared about him. In his business, friends were few and far between, Rain was a good friend to have.

"Thank you," Jacob whispered. "The vision you gave me saved my life."

"It was nothing, Jacob," Rain said as she also stood up. She turned away, "Even when you are in the shadow of Hell's fury, I will protect you."

Jacob cocked his head at her remark, "Rain . . ."

She did not turn to look at him, "Jacob, you do not know the depths of my power or the things that I do. One day your power will overshadow many demons."

"Is that prophecy or your speculation?" Jacob asked.

"It is the truth," Rain replied, "Until you come into your full power, I have intervened on your behalf."

Jacob took half a step forward, "I never asked for you to do this."

"If I had not, you would have been destroyed," Rain said quietly.

Jacob began to fear; what could possibly be out there that was worse than the things he had already dealt with? "What's out there?" he asked, "Who is that?"

Rain was silent for a moment, and then she began to walk away, "Someone very close to my heart."

Jacob stood in the room alone, wondering what Rain meant. If she had wished for him to understand, she would not have been so vague. After a few moments he turned to leave to get some much needed rest. Once he was in the dim halls he began to hear the board calling him again. Aries wanted to talk. Before Jacob realized it he was standing in front of the board. He could feel the presence of the demon bearing down on him. It was curious; Aries could not harm him, and Jacob felt no fear in his presence. He almost felt like he belonged. That could have been because he almost did belong. Being half a demon, sometimes places like this felt right.

Normally his powers didn't move on their own; he had to summon them when he wanted, but right now he could feel his blood turn hot. He subdued the ancient blood that pulsed through him. Aries was calling him; the god of war was speaking to a part of Jacob's soul that belonged in a greater world. The urge to fight this thing suddenly grew. The desire to fight was immense. Then Jacob realized that Aries wasn't calling Jacob's demon—it was calling his flesh. His inner demon had risen up to protect him. The distinction was sharp now. Then why was his demon growing enraged? Was it the mere presence of Arise that agitated it?

Jacob now feared. Aries could not harm him that was not what he feared. His demon blood, the very thing that made him dangerous, was the only part of him that was resisting the call of the board. It was coming between his flesh and the battlefield, holding him back from Aries's call. He normally kept it subdued, but it had overpowered him and totally confused his understanding of the slumbering spirit. Jacob had heard of terrible things happening to clan members who gave into to their demonic wishes. He could not lose control over his. Completely aware of what was happening and completely terrified, he stepped closer. Jacob didn't want to, but he could not resist the subtle whisper.

His inner demon screamed to be released. He could not focus on both; he either had to give in and face Aries or he had to let his demon blood seize him. Neither choice was desirable, and right now Aries was winning. Aries was far too strong for him to face; the risk, should he lose the game, could be tragic. Then again if he gave into his demonic powers, he might never get them back under control. But it did seem that his inner spirit also feared Aries. Not many people ever had this issue, only the ones who had strong wills. Most coped with it and kept the Demon subdued; a few fell into their desires and destroyed their lives and dragged the world around them down with them. His had never given him any resistance until just now. But his had tried to protect him—was this different, or was his blood trying to make an excuse?

He had taken two more steps toward the board now. Jacob lost control over his impulses. "No!" he yelled at the air around him. His blood flushed hot, and his powers welled up, not like they normally did when he called them. They were forceful and blurred Jacob's reason. He felt the same surge as he had last night against the Wraith. His powers were unchecked; he tried to restrain part of them, but he couldn't. He either had to let them flow, or he had to completely quench them. Right now he didn't have a choice.

A hiss ripped through the room, Aries had heard him. Jacob hissed back and bolted for the door. He could hear his heart beat boiling in his ears, and it blotted out the cold whisper of the Demon and broke the trance that the board had put on him. Jacob ran; as soon as he left the room he felt the Demon part of him ease up. He didn't fight it though; he just let it run. It was odd, letting his powers control him. Now he understood why people might fall into this folly. But his powers did not desire control; they were not fighting him. They wished to be subdued again.

Satisfied that the danger was gone, Jacob relaxed; he took a deep breath and closed his eyes. The pulsing power of his demon blood subsided, and he felt a cold wind rush past him. He was in the courtyard where Julie had first sat down and played chess with him. The upper study was desolate and frozen. It was cold. The morning rays of sun did not warm the place. He looked out the east wall; the sky was golden, and the ground was white. In the west, the sky was still dark blue above a silver blanket of powder. He wasn't sure what urged him here; nobody came up here to be in the cold.

He relished the cold for a moment and allowed his blood to cool. On an average day he hated the cold, but right now he needed to calm down. He had to figure out what that was inside him before it fully woke up and consumed him. The power he gained from it was useful, but all the fibers of his body were afraid of it. It had been more active since he had stepped on that chessboard, and Jacob worried it had awakened—as if he didn't have enough to worry about. At first it had been all right, he was in control, but what had happened on that board had done something to him. It altered his demon in some way. He needed that power to do what he did, but he could no longer risk using it if the demon had become this volatile. He began to sit down at one of the boards to think and then he noticed a figure at his favorite table. Sitting still as a stone statue and wrapped in layers of thick fur coats was Julie. She had moved one piece forward and was awaiting a challenge. She looked cold. And she was staring at the board, either oblivious to Jacob or not caring that he was there.

Jacob stepped over and sat down on the black side of the board. "Can I play?" he asked.

"There is nothing I have to wager against you," Julie replied. Her features were locked to the table and stray snowflakes had frozen to her jet-black hair and covered it in a thin sheet of ice. How long had she been out here? The last snowfall was seven hours ago, and this place was sheltered.

Jacob pushed a pawn forward, "I don't want to bet. I just want to play." His blood cooled down, and he began to feel the bite of the cold. But right now he needed to talk to his cousin, so he would have to endure it.

Julie sat up and pushed another pawn forward with cold fingers, "Okay."

A few moves were made in silence, and Jacob had to break it, "Yesterday." He began, "Why would you go through all that to test me?"

Julie captured one of his bishops with a knight and set it to the side, "I needed to know who was better."

"You don't want this job." Jacob replied, "It isn't all that great."

Julie sighed, "Well I got what I wanted now, I guess."

Jacob looked down at the board. He moved a rook to take the knight she had just used to capture his bishop. "I was angry at the time," he admitted as he blew in to his hand and folded his arms to warm his fingers. "I'm still angry. But what I really need is a little help." He looked up at her. She had not moved her eyes from the board the entire time as if she had been frozen to the table. "I can't do it alone so, please, help me."

Julie moved a pawn forward to attack Jacob's other bishop. "Do I have a choice?" she asked.

"I'm sorry you played the game. You know what it makes you feel." Jacob replied, "Please, as your friend, as your family, I'm asking for your help."

She sat in silence and waited for his next move. Jacob pondered for a moment and then retreated his bishop. "I didn't intend to place a curse on you, but I did, and I really would rather us help each other. There is a lot you can teach me, and I have a few things you ought to know, as well. I don't want this to burden you as much as it has me, okay?"

Julie finally looked up, "It can't be undone, can it?" Her words were quiet in the cold air.

"I'm not familiar with the functions of the board," Jacob answered. "I don't know."

She spoke softly as if she might break the table if she made too much sound, "Jacob, I'll help you, but I want my children to be released from this curse. If there is a way, I don't want them to partake of this."

The cold grabbed Jacob by his spine. He understood exactly what she meant. For him there was no escape; his children would be cursed. But did it have to be that way for her? Well yes, they would be Fallen children, but did they have to share the same fate as the Chosen? What had he done? He tried to help people to take away their share of torment, and he had done the opposite. He was only trying to get a little help in this job. Maybe it was a sign that he was supposed to be alone in this.

Jacob was beginning to understand now, his job, all the responsibility that had been given to him—he wasn't supposed to be a grand warrior, he was supposed to serve. Isn't that what Christ did? But his task was still impossible. How would one man living a good life bring reconciliation to an entire race of damned half-demons? If he was supposed to be perfect, he had already failed. The only thing he had left was to just hope his best would be good enough.

"I'll look into it," Jacob said after a moment, "I was angry when I said those things; I didn't think. I know what you feel, my children will be cursed, and I cannot change that so I understand. I'm sorry, I didn't mean for that to happen, but if there is a way to lift the curse on yours, I will find it."

"Could we ask the board?" She asked timidly.

Jacob's blood turned to ice when she mentioned that. "I don't know. I would make that a last resort. I don't want to face it." He hesitated to tell her, did she know what had happened to him? Had the same thing happened to her?

Julie nodded and looked back to the board in front of her. She leaned forward and pushed a knight into a better position.

As Jacob studied the board, he saw two drops of water splash on Julie's back row. He stared at the tears as they froze. Then he stood up. "We can finish this later," he said. "It's too cold out here for this."

He helped his cousin out of her chair. She was stiff, whether it was from her sadness or the cold, Jacob wasn't sure. But he had only been out here for fifteen minutes, and he had already had more than enough, Julie could have been out here for hours, and it was past time for her to go inside.

Jacob walked her down to the lower study and made her sit beside the furnace. "I'll do what I can to help you, Julie."

She gave a weak smile as the ice in her hair began to melt. "Thank you, Jacob. I will not forget it." She replied, "When you need my help, I will be there."

Jacob nodded, "I'll ask around. I'm sure someone will know what to do."

And then he walked away. He would normally spend the day here, but it was getting close to the time for him to go back to classes, and he only had a few days left to be free from school. He wanted to spend more time with Emily. Even though going back to school meant he'd get to see her every day, it wasn't the same as making time to see her. He had a lot to tell her from yesterday, and this place was starting to get strange.

First he had to go home and get a car, but home was just two steps away with his magic ring.

Before he left, he told his mother about Julie, hoping she had a remedy, but she didn't. When the board had challenged her, she had declined, and now he had more experience in that field than she did. He expected as much; he would have to ask a few books and that could take time. He would have to learn to be more careful. These kinds of things would become normal, and he would become responsible for the people around him. His choice had put his cousin in a rather bad situation, and there may not be any way to undo it. Just being associated with him was dangerous; who else might get hurt? He shuddered at the thought of something happening to Emily.

When he arrived at Emily's house, he found her in the yard rolling snowballs for a snowman as if she were a kid. She had rolled a great base about a meter wide and made the second only slightly smaller. She appeared to be having a hard time lifting it on top of the first. She had it about halfway rolled up the side of the base when she saw Jacob. She let it go and ran to greet him. It fell and cracked in half, but she didn't seem to care.

Jacob stepped out of the truck and had to catch her as she sprang for him. She got her feet back under her and then hugged him as tight as she could, "I'm so glad you came over today!" she exclaimed and then stepped back to look up at him.

Jacob nodded to the cracked snowball, "I see you could use some help."

She smiled wide like always, and her green eyes sparkled against the white backdrop of the lawn. "I don't need any help." She said smartly, "I'm just glad to see you." Jacob had given up on figuring out why her eyes seemed so familiar, but it always triggered something in the back of his mind when he saw her.

Jacob smiled and then hugged her again, "After the day and night I had the only thing I want to do today was see you." He didn't care why, but just looking in her eyes made his worries melt away like the snow when winter ends.

"Do you want to talk about it?" she asked, always excited to hear about his latest adventures. Though now she knew they were real and she didn't want to tag along any more, she still liked to hear about them.

"Oh it's one to end up on your wall, I'm sure." Jacob replied, "But not right now; there are more important things to do."

"Like what?" Emily asked.

Jacob looked across the yard, "Like getting the poor snowman on his feet." He laughed and then started for it with a slight jog, "Come on. Let's get him fixed; it'll be the best snow man ever."

Emily followed him back to the project she had started.

Jacob picked up half of the broken snowball and it crumbled into several smaller pieces. "I guess we start by rerolling this one."

Emily bunched up the pieces and started forming a lump to roll around. Jacob stopped her, "No, I mean this one." He said patting the huge base she had made.

"Why? Is it too big?" She asked.

"It's not big enough." Jacob replied. "This is going to be the best snowman ever, remember?"

"But I can't move it anymore; it won't roll." Emily said.

"Well then, I'll help you." The ball was already waist high, and it did not want to roll. But Jacob and Emily got on the same side and pushed it across the yard until it was almost to their shoulders.

"Alright," Jacob said after they had finished rolling the base. "I'll work on the middle; you make the head."

"How are we going to get them staked up there?" Emily asked.

Jacob looked at the mass of snow that was almost as tall as he was, "We'll figure something out."

Emily skipped off and started rolling the lump that would be the top piece and Jacob began to work on the midsection. Emily finished her smaller piece first and carried it to the soon-to-be snowman and went to help Jacob roll up the middle. Once the mass was large enough, Jacob rolled it back to the base and stood up, "I don't think I can lift it," he said.

"I told you," Emily complained.

Jacob squatted down and placed his hands under the large snowball, "Help me out with this."

Emily got on the other side and prepared to pick up the giant mass of snow. "Are you ready?" Jacob asked.

Emily nodded, "On three."

Then Jacob counted, "One . . . Two . . . Three!"

They strained against the heavy weight of the mass. The ice was heavy, and they had packed it tight. But they did it. They lifted the ball above their heads; Jacob was honestly surprised it held together. They set it on top of the base and situated it securely so it would not roll off.

"Now how are you going to put the top on?" Emily asked, "I can't reach that high."

"Are you sure?" Jacob replied, the middle was above his head as well. "Can you pick up that part?" He said pointing to the ball she had rolled to make the head.

"Yes, I carried it over here," she answered and picked it up off the ground.

"Good; sit on my shoulders." Jacob said and got low next to the snowman.

Emily looked at him, "Is that a good idea?" she asked.

Jacob shrugged, "We have to get that up there somehow, unless you have a ladder."

"I think we have one." Emily started.

"Just do it," Jacob urged.

Emily sat on his shoulders, "If you drop me . . ."

"I won't," Jacob assured, "Just don't let go of that snow ball."

She got situated, and then Jacob grabbed her legs to steady her and stood up slowly. Now she was just tall enough to place the mass of snow on top. "It worked," she remarked.

"Great, now we need to give him a face and a hat." Jacob said and let her back down.

"Oh I wish we had done that before I put it up there," Emily said.

"Do you have the stuff for that?" Jacob asked.

Emily nodded, "I put them on the porch."

"Then I'll just hold you while you put his face on."

Emily smiled, "Okay, I'll be right back." She trotted through the snow up to the front door and stooped down to pick up the carrot for his nose and the top hat and the two pieces of coal and the scarf—all the traditional necessities for a snowman. She carried them all back, and Jacob took them from her.

"You get on my shoulders again, and I'll hand you what you need."

And so she got back on his shoulders, and he stood up so she was level with her work, "What do you need first?" he asked.

"Give me the carrot," she said.

Jacob handed up the carrot, and then Emily asked for the coal. Jacob handed her both and then he handed her the top hat, which was a bit small for the giant snowman. Last came the scarf. Jacob had to walk a circle around the snowman so Emily could get the scarf around him. He got back to the front and stood there while she tied the scarf to secure it.

Once she was finished, he let her down.

"We did it," he said as he stepped back to look at it.

Emily leaned against him, "It is the best snowman ever," she commented.

"You know, I haven't built a snowman in years," Jacob said. "This was fun."

"Me, neither." Emily said and took a small step away, "It's been since I was a kid."

Jacob kept looking up at the Goliath they had made, "I think it must have been seven or eight years the last time I played in the snow."

"You want to know what else I haven't done since I was a kid?" Emily asked.

Jacob turned to ask what and caught a face full of white frozen powder. He stood there stunned for a minute before he reacted. He calmly brushed the snow from his face and tried his best to hold in the laughter for just a little longer, "You know . . . my mother told me to never hit a girl," he said as he brushed himself clean, "But . . ." He squatted and grabbed a double handful of snow, "She never said anything about snowballs."

Emily turned to run, but Jacob hit her in the shoulder. The loosely packed snow exploded into confetti and returned to the ground. Emily stopped and created a projectile to return fire. Jacob never stood up. He made one more, and when Emily turned around to throw hers at him, he had already reloaded. As she reared back to throw, another snowball hit her in the knee. She stomped her foot in frustration, but the expression on her face was pure bliss. She threw the snowball at Jacob, and he tried to roll over to avoid it but did not succeed, and it pelted him in the chest. He scrambled to form another and didn't bother standing up.

Emily formed one more, and this time ran closer. Jacob tossed his first but missed on purpose, and Emily stood over him and nailed him in the head from a close range. Jacob flopped over and feigned as if he had been knocked out. Emily ducked to make another. Jacob opened his eyes and saw her standing above him ready to pelt him again. He threw his hands up to cover his face, "I surrender!" he yelled.

Emily paused for a moment and then Jacob let his hands down. Then she pelted him in the chest anyway.

"I said I surrender," he repeated, "What was that for?"

Emily shrugged, "To get rid of the last snowball."

Jacob held up his hand for Emily to help him up. She took it, and he pulled her down with him. She squealed and flopped in the snow beside him and laughed, "What was that for?"

Jacob stood up, "It was a cheap shot to win the war. Since we're playing by your rules."

Emily grabbed a handful of snow and flung it at him. She had not meant to hit him, she had not aimed or packed the snow and it just spread out as it flew through the air.

Jacob leaned forward to help her up, she took his hand and tried to pull him down, but he resisted. When she gave up, he pulled her to her feet, "Let's go warm up a little. I can't feel my feet."

It was nearly noon by the time they had finished with the snowman and gone inside to warm up. Emily's mother was preparing lunch when they finally came in, and was surprised to see Jacob. Hot cider was already brewing. They took the cups and Emily took him back to the drawing room where all of her pictures were. The smell of art was thick in the air, pencils and ink, rubber erasers and paper. The place was still messy; disposed paper clippings and broken pencils littered the ground. Dried ink was smeared on the table and dripped on the carpet—all signs of work. The greatest of these signs, though, was the grand murals she had shown him the last time.

Jacob explained all about the game of chess and about the cursed board and what he had done to Julie; the challenge the board had issued and how he wanted to undo the curse he had put on his cousin, not to mention last night he had killed another Wraith. So much had happened, and it had only been two days since he had seen her.

Emily listened intently and sympathized with his feelings of regret for cursing Julie, "I guess she got what she wanted, didn't she," Emily asked.

Jacob sighed, "I suppose she deserved it. But I wasn't thinking very clearly when I spoke; her children don't deserve it, and so I must do what I can to undo it."

"Is the board the only way?" Emily asked.

"I don't know," Jacob shuddered at the thought of stepping back on those tiles, "I hope there are other ways around it."

Emily pause for a moment, "If that was the only way, would you do it?"

Jacob had to think about it, "I would have to."

"You don't have to go back there," Emily insisted, "Would you?"

"I would have to, Emily. I'm the Chosen, the one that is supposed to redeem my entire race. How can I do that if I can't save one life?" Jacob answered, "It's my job."

"I'm glad you finally realized that," Emily said. "When you first told me these things, when I thought it was all just a story, I thought you knew already. I imagined you were the hero of this world you created and were acting the part of being lost. Then when I found out it wasn't a story, I knew you hadn't figured it out yet."

"I guess I realized that this morning, the reason I have been given this responsibility is because I'll do what it takes."

Emily smiled, "That's why it's your job, Jacob, because you're not selfish, and you'll do it. Just don't get hurt. I don't want anything to happen to you."

That comment warmed him more than the cider ever could. He felt proud that Emily though so highly of him, especially after what had happened recently. And he was glad that she cared about him enough to worry. "I won't."

Emily stood up on her toes and kissed him. "Good."

He set the cup down on the table and sighed, "I'm not worried about getting hurt; I never have been. I guess I get more worried about other people."

Emily smiled, "Because you're such a nice person. You're always thinking of other people, and I like that about you."

"I mean I worry about people getting hurt because of me, people like Julie." Jacob said, "I'm dangerous—I'm a half-demon and sometimes I do more harm than good."

"Oh that's not true; there are some things you can't help." Emily replied and gave him a hug. "You do your best, and everything will be fine."

"I just don't want to hurt anyone else," Jacob held her close, "If I ever let anything happened to you, I don't know what I'd do."

She laughed lightly, "Jacob, I'll be fine. I'm not sensitive to those things, remember? And you would never intentionally hurt anything."

"That doesn't mean you're safe from evil; it just means your salvation is already complete." Jacob said, "I told you I was dangerous to be around; why didn't you listen?"

"I understand you now; I can't leave you in the dark alone." Emily smiled, "I know what I'm doing. I won't get hurt."

Jacob hugged her tighter, "I hope so."

"I won't," she assured him, "You won't let me."

Jacob held her, he was glad to have her. He didn't worry anymore about not being able to defend his friends and family, about protecting Emily from the darkness around him; he knew he could protect them from the darkness of the world. But who would protect them from him if he lost control?

CHAPTER 18

It was nearing the end of winter by the time the next council meeting was held. Snow was still on the ground in the places that did not get much light. But for the most part, it was melted. There were patches of dried brown grass that seemed would never be green again though it would only be a few more weeks before the lush green blanket caused everyone to forget all about the white blanket of snow that had just been there. School was back in session, and now Jacob was looking forward to long summer days. He sighed as he entered the dark council chamber and feared he would spend more time here than he cared to over the summer. It was like having a job that you didn't get paid for.

It wasn't like the task he had inherited from his father; he recently found out it paid the bills. His father had given him a note from the Church of England, stating that he would be given a generous salary for his services. His father never really talked about where the money came from to support the family, and they always lived a modest life, but Jacob had found out their family was well taken care of.

But this council didn't hold any benefit for Jacob. Sometimes he just felt used. He hated it, but was this a righteous hate of a flawed system or a burning hate of the duties it bestowed upon him? What was the difference? He hardly felt that either was constructive. Jacob was surprised that Roth had not called a meeting about the old chessboard coming to life. He was sure to hear about it, though. The voice of Aries still nagged him. He wondered how long it would be before it got impatient.

The stale air of the chamber was still and quiet. In the center was a ring of torches that the council sat in front of, one torch for each member who was expected to be present. Jacob took his seat and waited for Roth to call the council to order. There were a few people missing, Henry, Julie, and one other torch burned which meant someone from a different clan was expected to be here. Jacob waited in the stale darkness without speaking. Nobody spoke; nobody had anything to say to their cousins that wasn't official business. He looked at the faces of the other members—all stoic. Except for Roth; his face was tired. It was always old, always wrinkled, but today it was tired.

Julie was the first to enter the chamber, she took the seat immediately to Jacob's right. This was odd since she would have normally saved that seat for Henry and taken the seat beside her grandfather. But this action was a sign that some social barrier between these families had finally been broken. The next arrival was the mystery guest. Jacob wasn't thrilled that this meeting would be in Latin again, but he knew this man; it was Ress. Ress sat beside Julie and the only seat left was between him and William, which meant Henry would have to sit next to his brother. Jacob still didn't know why, but it was pretty obvious that they didn't like each other. Finally, Henry walked in. He stopped upon entering the circle and noted that the seating arrangement had been altered. Henry wasn't particularly pleased but didn't protest and took his seat.

Roth called the council to order in the universal language of Latin. "The first order of business will be the waking of Aries." His voice was always dry, but today it seemed to lack its ancient fervor.

Ress looked curiously at Jacob. Apparently news did not travel, and this was the first he had heard of the board being awakened.

"Julie has awakened the great board and issued a challenge to Jacob." Roth continued, "This is not a matter to be taken lightly. Do either of you have anything to say?"

"Only what I said in the chamber. I needed to test him." Julie replied.

Roth nodded. "And it has come with a great price for you," he said dryly. "It is not the behavior expected of our council members to mettle with such things."

"I have a question to ask the council," Jacob spoke before Roth could get too far into a lecture about it. He felt his reaction had adequately punished his cousin already. The council remained quiet and Roth nodded indicating he had the floor. "Is there a way among any of the knowledge in this room that I may undo the curse I put on Julie's children?"

The chamber was silent for a moment, and then Roth answered him, "As far as my knowledge goes, there is no way to revoke your claim. Pacts made on that board are not meant to be undone. I warned you before you stepped on that field." Roth's voice was meant to chastise, but it was frail.

"I was angry when I found out who it was that had tested me, and I spoke in rage. Julie shall have what she desires and she shall share my burden, but I realize it was wrong to place the curse on her children as well." Jacob explained.

"You have set that in stone," Roth assured him.

"My children will be born cursed. I understand that feeling, and it is not something I would wish to place on anyone else."

"But you did wish it on your cousin," Roth replied.

Jacob nodded, "If I may petition that between now and the next meeting the council might inquire of other clans to try to find an alternative."

Roth sighed, "As the leader before all clans I may petition one to aid another, but it is not likely for the clans to oblige one another in matters of sharing wisdom and skill. And I personally know all the living individuals who have been on that board, and I doubt they, much less anyone else, would have an answer for you."

Roth struggled a deep breath, "Also, on this topic I would like to know if you intend to accept the challenge that Aries has offered you," Roth continued.

Jacob was silent for a moment as he thought; he didn't want to, but something in him drew him to it. He was afraid of the Demon in the board, but at the same time he felt he needed it to get answers and perhaps find a way to remove the curse he had placed on Julie. It was too much for him to just decide, but then again he had been deciding for nearly six weeks. "I'm not sure yet," Jacob answered, "Could Aries undo the curse?"

Roth frowned and stroked his grey beard with a wrinkled hand, "I don't know. Would you risk your life for Julie?"

Jacob had already answered that; he had promised Julie he would do whatever it took. "What else would the Chosen be expected to do? If I cannot save her, then what hope is there for the rest of you?"

Roth eyed Henry and William, "Your grandchildren understand this family better than either of you."

"How do you say that when they go about cursing each other?" William objected.

"The boy admits he is wrong when no such accusation has been brought forward, and he has offered to rectify the situation," Roth replied, "If I ever saw one of you do that, I would think the end of the world had come and gone."

The old man paused and drew a weary breath, "I'm glad that I lived to see the Chosen begin to mend this feud before I died. It means a great deal to me."

The council brimmed with curiosity. Nobody asked, but they all had the same question. "Jacob is the Chosen," Roth assured them, "When I conquered Aries, the pact was that I should live to see the Chosen, and since Jacob has stepped on the board, my health has begun to fail."

Jacob's gut turned into knots, *why me?* Is that why Aries wanted to test him? Could Julie have been the Chosen and everyone had it backward? Now he really wanted to accept the challenge. Maybe Julie never really challenged him; maybe it was Aries the entire time.

"I must make arrangements to name a successor." Roth continued, "That is the next order of business. I will accept nominations from the prominent clans, and we will have a meeting of the Council Elders to decide." The Council Elders were members who had been on the council for twenty-five years or more. He was not going to be in this decision, and it bothered him.

"Are there any among you that believe you know someone or that you yourself may be capable of carrying this mantle?" Roth asked.

A discomforting silence settled on the council. Roth had been the head of the clans for longer than the records extended. Before he took the position, this happened regularly, but no one in the family even knew when the last change of power was. They had all accepted that Roth was their immortal leader.

"I will cast my name before the Elders," William spoke after the quiet had grown stale.

The quiet resettled as everyone thought of this. Jacob didn't want William to be the head, but he decided it would be best not to worry about it. There would hopefully be others. But his opinion didn't matter in this decision.

Julie stood up, "I am not allowed to vote, but am I allowed to make nominations?"

Roth half closed his eyes while he decided. Typically, she was not allowed to make a nomination if she was not an Elder, but he was the head of the clans for longer than her family name had been around. Nobody knew the rules; he could change them if he felt so inclined.

He sighed weakly and nodded, "You may."

She looked at her grandfather who had nominated himself, "I want to nominate Jacob."

At first all Jacob heard was the sound of everyone thinking. And then he realized what she had just said. Why? He could refuse. He didn't have to refuse; he wasn't old enough to vote so he wasn't able to be in that position.

"Jacob is a fine leader, and he is our savior, but he is not old enough to take this position," Roth replied after the shock wore off.

"That's just it." Julie said, "He is the Chosen. You said he was; Aries said he was. If he is, then he should be the one we follow, not William."

William prepared to make a rebuttal, he was outraged that his own granddaughter would choose not only someone from the other side of the family, but someone who was far too young for the job anyway.

Jacob stood up before William had a chance to say anything, "I nominate Julie."

Silence ensued once more.

Roth, Henry, and William all laughed with no humor. Julie turned to him and glared, "I was serious, Jacob. You're the Chosen; it is your right."

"One shall come from the stars as you have but shall bear not Hell and walk among the Fallen of this world and raise them up," Jacob replied, looking at his cousin. "One, Julie, it didn't say who. Aries promised Roth would live to see the Chosen. He assumes it is me, but Aries never said I was the Chosen; you played that game, too. I won, I cursed you to be everything that the Chosen is." He paused and looked around the room, "You could be the Chosen. If that is so, then by your own words I must follow you. What if I made you the Chosen that day? What if that curse was the fulfillment of the prophecy?"

Julie blinked at the argument trying to think, "Jacob, you're different. You have powers that none of us will ever hold." She said, "You defeat the darkness."

"That is a different curse." Jacob replied, "I have been dealt two damned bloods, and I can only reclaim one."

"I don't believe that!" Julie argued, "I have tested you on the board; you are different. You said it was your job as the chosen to reclaim the souls of my children from the curse you made. You wouldn't have said that if you didn't believe in yourself."

Jacob sat back down, "By the pact we made before Aries, you are my right hand. Everything I am, you are also. If I have the right to be made head of the clans, then you do as well."

"These nominations have been taken into consideration." Roth said before anyone had time to add more remarks. "Are there any other requests?"

William stood up, "You cannot be serious, Roth."

"Sit down, William. I have not asked for your objections, only your nominations," Roth dismissed him.

"But Roth."

"Sit down!" Roth ordered. "No decisions have been made, your opinion will be asked for when the Elders convene. I'm sure you will have objections to many of the nominations that the other clans shall put forward."

William sat down slowly and crossed his arms and scowled at the grandchildren.

"The next order of business is from Ress, regarding Jacob." Roth announced. "My friend from the Valley of the Nile, you may speak."

"Jacob, I am here to make a petition of your strength." Ress's Latin was thick with his native accent.

"My clan has a spirit that we cannot drive from our midst. I understand that you hold the powers to fight these, and we need your help," Ress explained. "I am like you, I hunt for these creatures, and I banish them, but I cannot banish this one. Will you help us?"

Jacob was caught off guard by the request. As Roth had just said, it was not common for clans to assist each other and therefore they did not often ask things from other clans. But just as Jacob had used his status a moment ago to inquire about Aries, here was a member of a separate clan, seeking him because of his status. Strange requests were made often, but he seldom even heard about them. Henry and William either handled or dismissed most of them. But this seemed serious. If he expected cooperation on his requests, how could he refuse when the other clans came to him? Jacob nodded, "I will go with you to your clan, and I will see to it that this spirit is banished."

Ress seemed stunned, "Many Chosen have refused to help my clan," he continued, "But you have made it your priority."

"What do you mean 'many Chosen'?"

"This spirit has been with us for five generations. It plagues us in our homes, and it haunts our land."

"Tomorrow you will meet me in the library. You will show me the way to your clan, and I will study this spirit," Jacob replied.

Ress smiled, "Thank you."

"Does anyone have anything to bring forward?" Roth asked.

No one replied, "Very well. All matters have been tended to." Roth continued. "I have other business to attend to with other clans. Jacob, I will inquire what may be done about this curse you have made. All nominations for my successor have been noted, the Elders of all clans will vote between all nominated persons at a later time. Motion to adjourn."

"Second," Jacob said. He always seconded that motion before anyone could bring up another topic.

"This meeting of the council is concluded."

Jacob arrived at the library early to meet Ress. Once he knew the way to the clan, he could come and go freely, but his first trip had to be escorted by someone who knew the way. The air was crisp in the twilight before the dawn. Here it was dark still, and winter was making one last effort to hold on with its icy fingers before spring ran it out. But where he was going, it would be nearly noon in the heat of summer. The chance to travel to another clan piqued his interest almost as much as this request. Perhaps he could periodically study with them. Though he could never hope to learn everything in his own clan's library, he desired to study in the halls of other cultures. Though they were all of one bloodline, the many branches had developed with drastic differences. Some of these differences were cultural and some clans had found different powers. Jacob, aside from his genuine curiosity, felt that as the Chosen before all the Fallen, he ought to get a better understanding of some of the more prominent clans.

As Jacob turned into the halls he again heard Aries calling, he had learned to ignore it. But it still nagged him. It made him want to avoid this place. Soon he would have to face it and make a decision to deny the challenge or risk untold dangers and play. Why was it such a hard choice? He was afraid of what he could lose, but was there anything he wanted to gain? He didn't want power—he had that. He didn't want anything that involved a pact with a demon. If he did step up to that board again he would do it for his cousin Julie.

He hoped that there would be another answer, but after a month of searching, he had not found one. His last hope was that someone on the council might know. But if Roth did not know, there was probably no chance for a different remedy. He would give Roth some time to ask around, but he wasn't going to wait much longer. Roth's health was failing now and finding his replacement was more urgent than Jacob's problem.

Jacob made his way down the dim corridors until he came to the central chamber where the portal was located. Ress was waiting for him there. He wore a tribal outfit that consisted of a loincloth about his waist and a leopard skin draped over his shoulders. The skin was fastened like a cape, the front paws dangled over his chest and the head of the leopard rested on his right shoulder while the rest of the pelt dangled behind him. He had a spear, not the ceremonial spear he had carried to the council meetings; this was a war spear. Across his back he carried a bow and arrows, and by his side was a bone knife.

Ress was intimidating; tall, bare-chested and barefoot; he wasn't the kind of person you wanted to pick a fight with. Looking at him, Jacob got the uneasy feeling he had no idea what he had agreed to. Ress seemed to be prepared for a war. Julie was standing beside him. He had not asked for Julie to be here; did she intend to go with him? Rain was there, too. Jacob held up his right hand to Ress as a greeting. He stepped to Julie and looked at her; she was ready to fight, she had a sword similar to Jade at her side, and her outfit was something he would picture an assassin wearing: a suit of light leather armor, covered by a long, thick cloak.

"Do you plan on going as well?" Jacob asked.

She looked at him boldly, "My words are your words, my authority is your authority, and my work is your work," She reminded him. "By the pact I must do as you ask."

"Julie, this is different; this is not a clan thing," Jacob replied.

"Yes, it is," Julie answered, "This matter concerns the clans, and it has concerned the Chosen. Where you go I must go. I said when you needed my help, I would be there."

"You did, Julie," Jacob searched for the right words. "This is dangerous; you have not been trained for things like this."

She stared back at him and sparks of defiance flew from her eyes. "If I'm not ready then you must teach me."

"Some other time," Jacob protested.

Julie did not let him finish, "Jacob there is no other time; if you want my help, you have to take it."

"She has a point," Rain said. "If she is to ever assist you in your work, you need to take her with you."

Jacob had to concede, if he wasn't going to use Julie then why had he placed that curse on her? "I just wish there was a better time."

"Is there ever a good time to face a demon?" Rain asked. Jacob understood that it was a more direct question. She knew he needed help, and she was trying to break his pride and help him.

Jacob nodded and hummed reflectively, maybe she had something to offer, but at the moment he needed to focus on what Julie was about to experience. He remembered his first hunt; it was a little more structured. They were not after a spirit on his first night. His father took him out in the middle of the night and showed him some of the weapons and how to use them. It was probably two months after his training started before he got to watch his father in a real fight. And it was another two months before he could fight beside him.

"Don't get in over your head," he said to Julie. "You can come, but I don't want you getting into any trouble you can't handle. Understand? Stay close, but not too close. Watch only."

"Okay," she replied.

"Are we ready?" Jacob asked in Latin, remembering that Ress had not understood anything they had said.

Ress nodded and motioned them to the center of the port.

167

"Jacob, this is a great thing you are doing." Rain said as they walked past her. "Take care of yourself. This thing is very strong." Nobody else could pick up the slight and subtle inflections in her voice that indicated she was worried about him.

Jacob sighed, "So am I." He knew he was strong, but there were things he knew were beyond his scope. Rain had said his power would one day overshadow demons. He hoped he was at that point now.

"I know you are," Rain replied. Her words made him feel stronger, the way she said it with utmost confidence. She never doubted him. Even though he often questioned himself, in her eyes he could do no wrong. At least there was one person who would support him no matter what. Well, two really, there was Emily. He remembered he had not had a chance to speak to her about this yet. If anything happened, she would be upset he hadn't mentioned this.

Jacob locked on to Ress's signal, and they launched through the portal before he could reply.

The very first thing he noticed was that prick at the back of his neck that told him there was a spirit near. It was strong, almost as if it were in the room with him, but a quick look around told him otherwise. The air here was hot, not like the cool air of the library in Scotland. He looked around and saw that the chamber was a natural formation. There were no torches lit, but there was still a bright red glow illuminating the room. Jacob looked around to see where the source of the light was and noticed a cliff about fifty meters away from the edge of the portal. Out of curiosity, he walked over to the edge and looked down. At the bottom was a viscous pool of molten lava. That accounted for the heat and the red light that filled the room.

They must be in or near a volcano. He turned to Ress and noticed Julie was standing right beside him, looking over the edge in a trance. "Where are we?" he asked.

Ress smiled with his bright, white teeth, "We are far from my home; this is the Grand Chamber. We are inside Mount Nyamuragira, an active volcano in Congo.

"You should see the lake of fire at the top. Perhaps there will be time later, it is one of the few volcanoes that has an active lake. Nyiragongo to the south is very impressive, much larger and more active." Jacob looked back to the pool and wondered how it stayed down there and never boiled over into the chamber to destroy the portal.

"The library is on the other side of the mountain. My home is to the east in Kenya, but the spirit we seek is on this mountain."

Then he motioned to a hole in the wall, "Let me show you around."

Jacob had to force himself to stop marveling at the construction of the room and follow Ress. This was impressive. Then he realized the clothes he wore were not for this climate. He removed his coat and a few layers of clothing and left them by the portal. Julie threw her robe down beside Jacob's things. Jacob took two orbs of water and two stakes out of the coat, he gave one orb and one stake to Julie, and he kept the others. They proceeded as Ress directed.

They were led through a series of tunnels that Ress assured them they would become familiar with over time. It wasn't laid out like the secret passages of the castle; these were old tunnels left by dormant lava flows. There was no pattern to them, there were intersections where one might split or where a new one may have joined with an older one. And then there was a smaller network of man-made tunnels that connected dead ends to the next empty tube or led to a dead end to discourage people from exploration.

It was a maze. It reminded him of the caves he explored in his childhood, though much bigger and more disturbing.

After wandering in the dark labyrinth for some time, they came to fresh air. It was hot outside. Jacob now only wore his undershirt and black slacks; the button-up shirt and the jacket had been left behind. The only gear he carried was Jade across his back and the Light Shard at his side. He had left his other tools in the coat he had removed—there was no other way to carry them. He wasn't planning on doing any real fighting today anyway. If this thing was as dangerous as he was told, he would need to study it first.

In the meantime, he would get a set of clothes that better suited the environment that would allow him to carry his things. Julie's assassin's suit seemed like it breathed well, but that black leather had to be warm. He was sure he would not see her wear that again.

The passages led them out to a steep rock face. It overlooked a second lower crater that at one point had contained a pool of lava. Jacob looked to the top and noted the steam and other gasses that were emitting from the lake at the top. He had never seen one before and would like to make a trip up there. Ress guided them along a path that led them to the south side of the mountain. It was different than mountains he knew; the sun didn't show on the south sides of the mountains here like it didn't shine on the north faces of mountains where he was from. That didn't do much to make it cooler.

The other mountain Ress had mentioned, Nyiragongo, loomed on the horizon. It was such a beautiful site, the volcanic mountain range stretched off into the distance behind Nyiragongo. Most people marveled at the destructive powers of volcanoes, but Jacob was being entranced by what they had created. The set-up of this place was different than he was used to. In his home, the portal and the library were quite close. But here they had to walk almost an hour to the opposite side of the mountain before they came to the secret tunnel. Jacob knew it was there before Ress showed him. A seemingly ambiguous mark revealed that it was there. Ress tapped a rune that had been painted on it, and a door appeared leading back down into the mountain.

When they entered, the prick on his neck rushed down his spine and filled his body. Something was different about this one. He looked back at Julie, wondering if it really was best to bring her along. The power from this beast was strong enough that she could obviously feel it. It wasn't just a Shadow or Wraith; this was thick with evil. To Jacob's surprise, fear was not present on Julie's face. There was apprehension across her brow, a tinge of excitement in her cheeks, a morbid curiosity in her eyes, and a healthy caution to her posture. She was aware of what lay beneath the mountain.

Jacob rested his hand on the sling he had made for the Light Shard, relaxed, but prepared to draw the weapon at a moment's notice. The spirit was also recognizing their presence.

Ress led them down the dim passage. It reminded him of his library except the passages under Dunnottar were smooth and purposeful. The passages here were crude, half natural, half hewn, with hand tools. It looked ominous. There were stairs that were odd and uneven and the turns were not angular, but rounded. The deeper they went, the more Jacob felt the spirit. For the moment it was curious, but Jacob understood that it felt threatened by his presence. They began to arrive at chambers for study and a bit further they came to the source of the problem: the Forge. Ress pointed down the hall, "The demon mostly remains in there." Jacob stepped forward to inspect the room.

Ress placed a hand on his shoulder, "I have tried many times to drive it out."

"You have faced this thing?" Jacob asked.

"I am a Shaman of my people. I have tried many spells; some have done nothing, and others only angered the demon."

"It's not a demon," Jacob said. "If a full-fledged demon resided here, nobody would be in this room."

"It is pure evil; it is a demon."

"Look, there are different types of spirits," Jacob began.

Ress held up his hand to stop him, "There are degrees, I know, soul minions and undead. But this is a champion among demons."

Jacob paused for a moment, "Do you know its name?"

"It won't speak to me in any tongue I understand."

Jacob nodded and then proceeded into the room. There wasn't as much equipment around as there was at Dunnottar. There was no furnace; instead there were holes in the ground where lava bubbled up.

For some reason, this is where the spirit was strongest. Jacob felt it prodding at him, not sure why he was here. The thing knew Jacob could sense him, and it pushed at his mind aggressively. Jacob stood for a moment processing what was happening. Fear began to creep up his spine. The creature had decided it wasn't happy that Jacob was in the room. Jacob's feelings were mutual. If this was a weaker spirit, he could force it to appear. But Ress had said it was a champion, and if Ress was correct and this was a real demon, the act would only insult it and make it angry.

"Have you been able to see this spirit?" Jacob asked. He stood in the center of the room with his hands slightly out from his side, not in an aggressive position but not too far from his weapons, either. Jacob could feel its breath on his face, and his fear intensified. Then he felt a surge as his demon blood curled in response, and every muscle in his body tensed for a fight. Some part of him defied this thing and overrode his body's fear. He was glad for it, but he didn't ask for this strength, and it made him nervous. Jacob felt the subtle heating of his blood, his natural draw on the power of his dormant spirit. He was afraid though, he still didn't understand his own power, or know how to control this force, and now it was moving on its own.

"I've called it forth from time to time," Ress responded as he stepped next to him.

Julie followed, entering the chamber last, "How do you do that?"

Ress frowned and looked at Jacob seriously. "It speaks through others," he said.

"You mean you coax it to possess an individual so you can interrogate it?" Jacob confirmed.

"Yes," Ress answered. "It is quite dangerous."

"Is there another way?" Jacob asked trying to suppress his own power surge. After what had happened that last time, he wasn't sure he wanted anything to do with his sleeping demon.

"Many generations have tried to call it forth; it only speaks through a body," Ress explained.

"I'm not comfortable with that," Jacob said, "There has to be a better way."

"He makes the rules, not us," Ress replied.

Jacob scowled at him. "It is not his place to make rules," he said in his hot anger that had started to become his council voice. Then he turned his gaze to a particular spot in the room where he felt the prying eyes most intense. "He came from Hell; this is not his domain. Can you fight this thing?"

"I do not wish to anger it."

"It's already angry," Jacob replied as he felt his own blood begin to boil as his inner power surged. It was not a proactive sensation; it was reactive. This demon did not like his presence or the fact that he was asking questions about it. A brief thought crossed Jacob's mind that his spirit had reacted without him even tapping it, but with the imposing evil surrounding him now, the feeling of his powers brimming offered a veil of comfort to the situation.

"Why else would it be here?" Julie added.

Ress was silent for a moment. "I have seen him do terrible things."

Jacob stepped forward, "Can you fight it?"

There was a pause where Jacob could hear his own heart beating as the adrenaline began to spike. For a moment he thought he heard the demon whisper to him, but he was not sure. He unleashed his demonic powers, and his blood burned and raced in his veins. The pulse in his heart was similar to the energy that permeated the air, but there was also an intense distinction. The aura wafting off of the Demon's presence was like the stench of death to Jacob once his own energy was released.

"If that is what it takes," Ress replied.

Jacob nodded and focused on the spot where the power was strongest, "Julie, stay out of the way." The voice of anger he had learned rang through the chamber. Then he stepped toward it and took out a small leather book like the one his father used; it had several spells written in it, not as many as his father had, but there was one that might call the spirit forward. As he opened it, he also ignited the incense ball on the chain. He began by taking the orb of water and tracing a cross in the air. Then he read an inscription from his book, and at the end, he threw the orb down and it shattered. The result was not what Jacob had hoped for.

Typically, the spirit should have appeared above the puddle, but there was nothing. A cold wind passed by him. Jacob felt a tingling sensation all about him. He had made it angry.

"You want to be difficult?" Jacob asked, "There's more than one way to pull you out and I'm not leaving until I get answers."

He flipped through his book and was about to begin reading another passage when he heard an old language fill the chamber. It spoke the language of the Fallen, and it was behind him.

"Leave!" the voice demanded.

His blood chilled as if the hiss had drained his veins. Jacob turned around to see where the voice had come from. He only saw Julie pointing at him, angrily. Her face was blank and had no emotion, and her eyes were wide and dilated.

"Julie?" Jacob asked.

"Leave my house!" It wasn't her voice that came from her lips, and it wasn't a language she could speak.

Jacob was frightened; he wasn't prepared for this. He knew it wasn't a good idea to bring her. So this really was a real demon; avoiding an all-out confrontation was paramount. His blood flushed uncontrollably hot, and he felt powers well up in him that he could not fathom. Summoning all the courage he could, Jacob stepped forward and replied in the same language, "I will not leave until I have answers." His voice was forceful, but his hands shook with the combination of adrenalin and fear. He had to be in control, but he was truthfully scared out of his mind. His own powers were the problem, though.

"You speak his tongue?" Ress asked, also trembling. Jacob ignored him; he had to focus on the Demon.

"I will not answer questions," the voice erupted from his cousin.

"Then I will not leave!" Jacob defied.

Julie convulsed and sprang at him, "My house!"

She threw Jacob to the floor with inhuman force. Jacob tried to roll away, but her grip was sure. He looked into her eyes and saw only a dark void. A low growl that vibrated the ground under him came from somewhere inside her.

Jacob summoned his demonic strength and hurled the girl off of him. She scrambled to her feet and lunged back at him. Jacob was quick though. He drew Jade and stabbed her.

She stopped suddenly as the blade ran through her. The darkness left her eyes, but there was still no expression on her face. Jacob drew the Light Shard with his other hand and held it to her face.

"Release her!" he yelled in the language of the Fallen. The small blade glowed and then flashed with beautiful white light that made the air crackle with heat. She shut her eyes against the light and screamed as her flesh began to bake.

Julie fell back, sliding off the blade. There was a thick translucent liquid clinging to the blade where it entered her flesh. As the blade finally came out of her, the liquid formed into the shape of a disfigured man contorting in pain, and it darkened and became solid. Julie collapsed on the ground, and there was no wound where the blade had been thrust into her.

"Ress, get Julie and go!" Jacob demanded.

"Will you need help?"

Jacob scowled at the figure on the other end of his blade, "None that you can give me." He answered in his council voice.

Ress did as Jacob commanded.

Jacob twisted Jade in the Demon's stomach and forced the sharp end of the Light Shard into its jaw. He could not see its full features, only murky darkness. It reeked of death, and he could feel it's hot breath on his face and arms. As long as he kept Jade in its chest and held on to his end, he would be fine. But there was no way to kill it, and if the creature got off the blade or if Jacob let go, he would be in trouble.

Jacob yelled as he summoned the depths of his demonic powers. He had given in to the demon that slumbered in him; he had to. He pushed against the demon and forced it to back into a wall. "I need answers!" He demanded in the language of the Fallen. Somehow he understood more of the language than before.

"I'll break you," the demon hissed back.

Jacob jammed the Light Shard into the darkness and felt it scream out in pain. "What is your name?" he yelled.

"You will not know," the demon bellowed back.

"I command you to reveal your name!" Jacob twisted Jade again and then ripped the Light Shard out and plunged it into the demon's chest.

"Fallen!" it growled.

"That is the state of your existence; I want your name!" Jacob insisted. He jammed the Light Shard into the creature's ribs and then grabbed it by the face and brought its vile gaze to meet his own. "Your name!"

The dark form hissed and its phantom flesh sizzled where Jacob gripped its jaw, "Be warned, my child, I am King of Fires!"

A title was all he would get from the demon. But that was fine; he knew a few books on demonology, and he could match the title the demon gave him to its proper name. It might take some time and research, but he had what he needed.

"Adramelech!" Jacob yelled in authoritative fury. "I know your name, demon!" He didn't know that. Perhaps the demon that slumbered in him already knew his name. For all the fear Jacob had of his own power, he had to admit it was very useful; and that's what scared him. It reeled with disgust at the words. Jacob had all he could gain now. Unfortunately, that was the simple part; the hard part was getting out alive. To his knowledge, there was only one way to send a full-fledged demon back to Hell. He would need specialized help for this one.

He could not face the demon alone—he knew that. The options for help were limited, and the process wasn't pleasant. Perhaps he and Drake could bind it until they found a better way to deport it. For now, he had to run. Jacob muttered a hex that would hold Adramelech for a moment. It would only last a moment, and he had to run and hope that Ress didn't hesitate to get Julie out. He finished the hex and yanked Jade out of the monster. Then he twisted the Light Shard and pulled it out also. The beast fell to the floor and convulsed, trying to escape the spell. Jacob did not waste time. The spell was meant to bind Shadows; there was no telling how long it would hold a real demon.

The dim hall seemed a lot longer now than it did on the way down. Perhaps that was because he was going uphill or maybe it was the rush of danger. He could feel the anger erupting form Adramelech clinging to him and trying to hold him back. His demonic blood rose up like it had the other day in front of Aries. The demon in him fought the pull and spurred him to run faster. Up the crooked stairs he ran, skipping two or three at a time—never looking back. He made it to the top of a staircase and slipped. Jade clattered across the floor as he fell. Reflexively he jumped back up and grabbed his blade. His knee was bleeding, but he didn't notice; he just ran like Hell was after him.

As he rounded the corner he saw Ress with Julie in his arms making his way to the exit, they were not far, but he was really hoping they were already out.

"Move!" Jacob yelled. He forgot that Ress didn't speak English.

Ress didn't need to understand the language to know what Jacob wanted. The urgency was all over his face. He upped his pace but was burdened by Julie's unconscious body. Jacob met him and slowed down to try to help.

A deafening crack ripped through the caves and a shriek of malice vibrated the stone walls. The hex had been broken. Jacob could hear the thunder of the Demon rumbling through the corridors. He took Julie from Ress and bolted, "Come on!" He urged again in English.

Though Ress was larger, Jacob had more strength because he could tap deeper into hidden energy than Ress could. Julie was a burden to Ress, but to Jacob she was nothing. Jacob ran unhindered by Julie's weight, and Ress was right behind him. Up a few more stairs, and Jacob could see the light at the end of the tunnel. The rumble of impending doom got closer and louder. It sounded like the mountain was falling down on them. Just when Jacob thought they were not going to make it, he burst through the cave.

He didn't stop; he kept running. The area outside was steep, but he hugged the cliffs and kept running. Ress fell behind once they got out of the cave. He had to be more careful around the steep edges, but Jacob's blood pumped with adrenaline and flooded with demonic aura, and his perception and reflexes were sharpened. Even with Julie in his arms, he had no issues negotiating the terrain. He stopped running after a few minutes and laid Julie down against an upright stone. The rage of Adramelech still pulsed through the mountain as if it were erupting. Jacob breathed a sigh of relief that he had survived an encounter with a demon.

He waited for a few moments until Ress caught up. By the time Ress arrived Jacob had nearly passed out, his body was drained. Ress was breathing hard, and his eyes were wide, "What happened?" He gasped once he reached Jacob.

"I pulled a name out of him." Jacob replied he was still winded from bolting out of the caves and highly fatigued from pulling that much power form his demon.

"His name?" Ress exclaimed. "Is that why he was so angry?"

Jacob nodded, "He is the Arch demon, Adramelech. I don't know why he is here, but it's not going to be good."

"Arch demon?" Ress repeated, "What can be done?"

Jacob lowered his head and paused to steady his breathing, "I don't know. There is only one method to deport known to my family, and it's not a good one. Perhaps my father knows a way to bind it until we can figure it out."

"Your father knows demons?"

"He's the reason I know demons. His fathers before him were bound to Satan, and one of them rejected the mark of the servant. Now we bear the mark of the defiant. It is a curse that Hell will always come for us to return what it owns," Jacob explained.

"Your father is not Fallen?" Ress asked.

Jacob shook his head, "Not like us, but fallen from grace because of the sins of his fathers."

Ress crossed his arms and steadied his own breathing, "I see. Does he know what to do?"

Jacob stood up and looked at Julie, "He taught me everything I know. If anyone knows what to do, it is him."

"How did you face him?" Ress asked. "I have never seen a man match the strength of a demon."

"He was more than a match for me," Jacob replied and left it at that.

They rested for a moment before they picked up Julie and began to make their way back to the portal.

CHAPTER 19

Jacob returned to Scotland where the ground was still splotched in patches of white. Though it was afternoon when he left the library in Africa, here it was not noon yet. The first thing he did was to take Julie to Rain. All the times he had done to others what he had just done to her, and he never stuck around to see how they recovered. She should be fine, but he was still worried. Rain brought some dried Vitality petals with some other medicinal herbs and burned them in a bowl. She wafted the smoke in Julie's face, and she woke up. Her eyes opened slowly and she looked around as if she were dreaming. Then suddenly she jumped. She stood up tense and ready to fight not knowing where she was or what had happened.

"Woah, Julie. It's okay; we're back," Jacob said. "It's okay."

"When . . . what . . . happ . . . ened?" She stammered confused, as she should be.

"Julie, the Demon tried to use you to attack me. You won't remember what happened," Jacob explained.

"Julie, how do you feel?" Rain asked.

"I . . . hurt," Her face twisted in discomfort, "like I was stabbed in the stomach."

"Julie," Jacob stood up, "I drove the Demon out of you." He said and placed his hand on Jade to indicate what had happened.

Confusion wrinkled across her face, and she touched her stomach where the phantom pain was. "You stabbed me? There's no wound, just pain."

"It is a magic I created." Jacob began, "It is used for people who are possessed. It stabs the spirit, but it doesn't injure the person."

She pressed against the spot where there should have been a hole and tried to process what had happened. "Jacob, what happened?" she exclaimed, "I don't remember. Are you hurt? Ress? How—what happened down there?"

"Slow down," Rain insisted. She stood up and placed a hand on Julie's back and guided her to a seat. "You are still waking up."

Then she looked at Jacob, "Why don't you explain what happened?"

Jacob sat down. "When I tried to make the demon appear, it got angry, and it took your body," he began. "It warned me to leave, but I refused. When I refused, it became angry, and you attacked me. I used my technique to bring it back out of you, and you became unconscious. I had Ress take you out while I forced the demon to tell me his name.

"After I got it out of him, I placed a hex on him to temporarily bind him while we ran. It was close." He left out the part about his demon taking over.

"Did I hurt you?" Julie asked cautiously.

Jacob shook his head, "I'm fine, Julie. Are you alright?"

She nodded, "Yeah, I'm alright. Do we have to go back?"

"The job isn't done; it won't be easy. You don't have to go with me next time," Jacob answered.

"No, I'm going with you. It's my job now, too," Julie replied.

Jacob had spent most of his life wishing for a way out of this. There had never been a way out for Jacob, even though he always did the job. But Julie wanted to be a part of this; she wasn't as capable, but her desire was greater. Maybe it would take the two of them to do this right.

After he made sure Julie was alright, he went back home. He needed to talk to his father and see what could be done. Jacob had become a great demon hunter and his powers from his mother's side of the family were strong, but his father had much more wisdom to share, and Jacob hoped that Drake had an answer.

"Adramelech?" Drake asked with wide eyes, "You faced an Arch demon alone?"

"I didn't fight it, really I just got its name and bolted out of there," Jacob replied, leaning against the table in the kitchen.

"Are you sure it was really a demon and not a higher Wraith?" Drake asked, scratching his head.

Jacob nodded, "It wasn't a Wraith."

Drake was silent for a moment. He crossed his arms and stroked the red stubble that already threatened to take over his face as his mind worked out the issue. "This is a problem."

"I know it's not in your area, Dad, but I need help with this. I need to get rid of it, but I don't know how." Jacob explained.

"The only way to get it out is by dragging it to Hell," Drake replied, "Finding a soul to do the job is hard." That wasn't the answer Jacob wanted to hear.

Neither of them spoke for a minute. Drake stared at the wall with his steel eyes puzzling out the issue.

"I suppose we all have to die sometime," Drake finally said.

Jacob looked up curiously, "What do you mean?"

"We have to get rid of it, son. I'm considered old by my fathers. You're a strong young man that I'm proud of. I've lived my life, and this is the work I have been given to do. This is my mission in life, and I must not fail it."

Jacob couldn't believe what he was hearing, "No, there has to be another way."

"I really wish there were, son," Drake said.

"No, Dad, I can't let you do this. You would send yourself to Hell?" Jacob protested as he stood up straight.

Drake unfolded his arms, "I'm going anyway, Jacob. I might as well take some of the evil back with me."

"You can't," Jacob repeated.

Drake placed a hand on his son's shoulder, "I don't have a choice; my fathers are already there! Our final place will be in Heaven. I have every confidence that you will succeed."

"I know there is another way," Jacob insisted, "We can bind it, trap it, until we figure it out."

Drake nodded, "We'll see. I will take some time to prepare. Once you are out of school, we shall face this King of Fires."

Jacob shrugged; he knew his father, and he knew he wasn't going to look into any other option. There were a few months before he would be out of school. Perhaps in that time he could find another method to deal with this demon. It would be much easier if he were full human, or not cursed to always be at odds with evil, but Jacob didn't have either of those options. He was only half human, and he was also cursed to be at war with Hell. Sometimes it irritated him that the very things that made him strong were his weaknesses. The things in his blood that allowed him to do his duties were the same things that made it difficult.

Drake turned and left. Jacob had learned that his father was stubborn; once he made a decision he didn't talk about it; he just did it. And he knew he had the same trait. This was one of the rare times Jacob had made a decision opposite of his father's wishes.

Normally, Drake always had his way by virtue of being the father, and most of the time Jacob ended up seeing the good in his father's decision as opposed to his own. But this time was different—there was no good in it. And he didn't have to yield to his father's desires this time, either; he was capable of taking things into his own hands, and he would find a way to save his father. Drake had said last time that he was in charge. It was his decision now. And he had decided that his father was going to live.

After Drake disappeared into his study, Jacob returned to the library. Since his father didn't have an answer he liked, he would find one—make one if he had to. He walked into the lower study and called for Rain. As the sound of his voice vibrated off the cold stone walls and died in the darkness, he heard the light sound of feet against the granite floor. Rain appeared a moment later. She peered at him, and her eyes flickered like candles. It was her way of asking questions. Her hair flickered with blue and lavender as it swayed around her neck and shoulders. "Jacob? What has brought you back?" she asked, sensing something was out of place.

"I need your help," Jacob replied.

Rain stepped closer and stood before him, the flicker in her eyes calmed, and the golden fires of her gaze dimmed to embers as her fey locks settled to a cool shade of silver blue as if struck by moonlight. She didn't speak, but Jacob could tell by the slight changes in her eyes the she was concerned and attentive.

"Rain, I need to fight this monster, but I don't know how," Jacob continued.

Rain offered a rare expression of compassion; she took one more step and embraced him. She understood him; she knew how alone he felt, and if anyone would help he knew she would. He felt the surge as she connected with his mind to fully grasp his problems. Jacob did not resist and gave his feeling and fears over to her as she had done with her memories of Aries. In a moment she understood all things about him that he wasn't aware of: fear of loss, fear of failure, fear of Adramelech, fear of the demon waking inside him and what it might do to the people he held close, and the fear of facing the world alone. She understood what must be done as well as he did; she knew the sacrifice that it would cost, and she shared his feelings concerning his father. As long as she was in his mind, they were one.

Having Rain bring all of his thoughts and concerns to the surface and sift through all of his deepest feelings made him feel like crying. He swallowed them and tried not to dwell on his own thoughts, but it was difficult with Rain prodding them, sympathizing and empathizing with him.

Jacob pushed gently into Rain's mind and saw himself. The image immediately became blurred, and his features became hidden. Was Rain trying to shut that out? Or could this be himself from her perspective? Something was different in him, and it was redefining who he was. Could this be a metaphor for his own confusion? He kept looking and saw another figure standing beside him. But the image was so distorted and dim he could not see who it was or what was happening. He tried to grab it, but it vanished. It was a metaphor, but was the blurring and breaking the metaphor or was the blurring and breaking hiding it from him? Jacob lashed out in frustration, trying to interpret this transfer of knowledge.

The image dissolved to black, and he felt the void again. There was something wrong. He had seen this metaphor before, but was it his or Rain's? Was there just something she would not let him see, and she portrayed it as a void? No, the void clung to him; it didn't hide from him. It sought him. Then was it his metaphor? It was like something was missing inside one of them, but he could not tell who. Was this void the darkness growing in Jacob? He didn't think so; he knew it was there and so did Rain, so why was the metaphor so complex? He searched it, and it felt like Rain, like it was part of her.

Then he felt the link dissolving. Rain's cool, liquid presence was retreating from his mind. Suddenly the walls of the study snapped back into focus. They were still standing, and Rain still held on to Jacob consolingly resting her chin on his shoulder. "I don't know any way to help you," She whispered. She had delved into his feelings so far that her face betrayed his agony, sorrow, and fear.

"Is there only one way?" Jacob asked. "In all of the books of demons and demigods, is there only one way?"

She pushed away gently. Rain blinked off the feelings she had absorbed from Jacob and gained her composure—her face appeared as still as ever, like nothing had happened. The fire lit back into her eyes. "We will search them," she said.

"And if there is no way?" Jacob continued.

Rain looked down at the grey floor.

"Can a way be made?"

"I don't know," Rain whispered, "The magic must be strong, and it must be old—as old as the demon—and Adramelech is very old."

"Will you help me? Can you show me where to find this magic?" Jacob asked.

"I will do what I can."

"Thank you," Jacob whispered and hugged her again. He was very glad to have her as a friend.

"But what of the other?" she asked.

Jacob stepped back; he knew she had figured it out before she had linked with him just now, but it wasn't something he wanted to discuss. He turned away as if he could avoid the question and hesitated before he replied, "I fight my own demons." He finally said, "That thing is inside me, and I will deal with it. Right now my concern is to save my father. Can you help me?"

Rain stepped forward and took his hand. She nodded, understanding his resolve, and guided him toward the long rows of old books, "Let us first see what you're up against," she insisted.

She led him to the section all about demons. Then she selected one that read, "demonology," and rubbed the dust off of its cover. "This will tell us about the demon and perhaps give us insights on where to turn for specific information." She cracked open the book and began to flip through pages, "If we are going to craft a spell for him, we must know his past, even before his fall."

Rain was very strong with magic, but she wasn't a spell inventor and neither was he. His sister might be able to help, though. This was beyond any one person's scope, however. Rain knew how to find and apply magic, Sarah was good at inventing it, and Jacob could modify almost anything. But he hated to get her involved in his work. Would it be worth it to save their father? Yes. Drake had told him to call the shots from now on. This was the first difficult call of his new command.

Jacob sighed and closed the book. It was late. Rain had stayed here with him the entire time, researching and helping him take notes. They each had a blank set of pages that they had begun jotting down anything they thought might help. There were scattered parchments in haphazardous stacks according to topic—it was an unorganized mess.

"Rain, I think we should call it a night."

She looked up at him, "It is getting late, isn't it?"

Jacob closed a reference book he had been using and stacked it on top of the other, "Thanks, Rain, for everything. You're a good friend to me."

She smiled and folded her books as well and began to shuffle the scattered, unorganized papers into a neat, unorganized stack. Jacob helped her clean the table and then stacked the books. "I'm going to see if Sarah can help us," he said, "She is good at inventing spells."

Rain placed a hand on his shoulder, "There is time yet; go home and rest. Don't think about this tonight."

Jacob nodded, "I'll try. Good night, Rain."

A lot had happened today, and it would be hard not to think of it: his first encounter with a demon, trying to save his father, everything he had learned. He was tired and ready to collapse. His eyes ached from reading all day long and his stomach, which had been ignored until now, was knotted up and empty.

When he got home, he was too exhausted to eat; he was hungry, but his mind and body were eager to shut down. He got to his room and laid Jade and the Light Shard in their places and collapsed on his bed—asleep before his head hit the pillow.

To Jacob's disappointment, there was little rest in his sleep. His thoughts repeatedly came back to Arize and Adramelech. Startled, he woke into the silence of his room. It was dark. For a moment he thought he had sensed a spirit, but he quickly realized it was only his nightmares or his own beating heart; they were so similar now. The silence was discomforting. He could hear his own excited heart beating in his chest. He didn't feel rested at all; he felt like he had been running for a long time. His heart was racing, and he was sticky with sweat.

Jacob closed his eyes and tried to sleep again, but every time he shut them, he saw these demons. There were so many things on his mind. Even in the silence, he couldn't hear his own thoughts. He'd rather not hear any thoughts and just go back to sleep. Silver rays of light danced on the floor under his window. The moonlight wasn't helping his rest. It was too early to get up for school. Jacob thought about going back to the library, but if he did that he knew he wouldn't go to school. It wasn't so much his classes that he worried about; even though he had missed them yesterday, he was still way ahead. He just didn't want to miss Emily again. Perhaps that would be best, though.

But he also really wanted to work on saving his father. He had looked forward to the end of school, but now it was a deadline, one he dreaded, a date to turn in a final project, and he didn't have enough time to finish it. When classes were over, he and Drake would go study the demon and eventually try to deport it. Jacob didn't understand how his father was so willing to do this. Yesterday he had gone to him for help, and now he wished he hadn't. He felt like whatever happened to his father, he would be responsible. And he was determined not to let anything happen. He was also determined to sleep, but that was not going to be a reality for him. Four o'clock seemed to laugh at him as well as five, and then six came around and it was time to wake up. Though he was still very hungry, he just didn't feel like eating. It was as if eating meant he had to start the day, and it was a day he didn't really want to begin. He pushed himself out of his bed and made himself ready to get started. Today he was a little slower than usual. When he got to the breakfast table, the toast was already prepared, and his siblings were already up.

"I thought I was going to have to come wake you," Sarah said as he sat down.

"I thought you were, too," Jacob replied. He reached for the bottle of orange juice and poured some into the glass in front of his plate.

"You seemed a little worried yesterday, and you came home late." Sarah was always to the point. "Did something happen?"

"I don't want to talk about it at the table," Jacob answered, "But I do want to talk to you—both of you, actually." He added, casting a glance at Dom.

"What's wrong?" Dom asked giving him a weird look.

Jacob sipped his juice and sighed, "Can you meet me in the library after school?"

Sarah looked up, "Sure."

"I guess," Dom said and returned to eating.

Jacob's food didn't seem to have a taste. His appetite left him, but he ate anyway; he knew he needed it. When he finished, he got up from the table, washed his dishes, and prepared to leave.

The morning was dark, and the sky promised a cold rain before the sun would show, just like his life—dark and getting worse. But the sun has to come out some time, if it didn't, everything would die. With that bleak thought, Jacob trudged out to his truck and departed for school. It wasn't as cold as it had been, but winter wasn't going to give up without a fight, and this morning it was as if the battle was raging. Cold bursts of wind ripped at the children as they approached the school, and the clouds snuffed out the light of dawn.

Jacob strode forward from the parking lot unaffected by the weather, there was too much on his mind for him to notice. He got to his locker and retrieved the books for his first class. When he closed it, he saw Emily's face on the other side of the door.

"Jacob!" She exclaimed with a smile that put the sun to shame. At least someone had gotten up to brighten the day.

She hugged him, "Are you okay? You weren't here yesterday, I was worried."

Her hair smelled of her art room, and he found the scent of the paper and ink comforting this morning. "I'm fine," Jacob replied, "I had some things to do."

Emily let him go, the faint smell of art lingered in the air between them. "I'm sure it was important; you look tired."

Jacob sighed, "I'm not, okay . . . A lot of things happened yesterday. It's a long story. I think I might be in trouble."

"Oh?" Emily frowned, "That's the first time you've ever said that. What's wrong?"

Jacob hesitated, "It's my dad. Something happened and he's counting his days."

"I'm sorry, Jacob. What's the matter with him?" Emily said with concern and sympathy.

"It's me; it's something I did. He's fine right now, but I don't know how much longer I have before what I did . . . I think I'm losing it."

Emily wrinkled her brow inquisitively, "Jacob, what happened?"

"Yesterday I went to the library in Africa with a member of that clan. His clan was having issues with a spirit that had been with them for several generations."

Jacob explained, "I went to investigate it; its name is Adramelech. He is an Arch demon, a pure demon."

"How does that impact your father?"

"There is only one way, only one known way, to deport a demon." Jacob continued, "You have to attach it to a willing soul, and then you must throw that soul into Hell."

"So your father?" Emily started, "he has to be the willing soul?"

Jacob hung his head and pressed his palm into his forehead, "I didn't ask him to, but he won't have it any other way. He said once school is over, we are going to go together and see that it gets done. It will take a few days to set up the ritual once we get there . . ."

"Jacob, that's horrible." Emily gasped, "You have to do that to your own father? I don't think you need to be at school today." Looking into her green eyes made it seem a little better; they gave him hope and courage, as if things had to get better around the bend.

"I don't have to, yet." Jacob said and looked up, "I swear I will find a better way, I have two months to find a better way in the old books. I will not sentence him to Hell for this."

"I hope you can," she replied and gave him a kiss.

"I will," Jacob said firmly. As long as he could look in her eyes, he didn't need the sun to rise or the rain to go away.

"So were you doing more sketches this morning?" Jacob asked to change the subject to something about her. He liked that she cared about what was happening in his life, but sometimes he just wanted to forget about himself, especially when Emily was around.

Emily smiled, "How did you know?"

"The faint smell of dried ink and old paper and pencil shavings followed you to school," he replied with a smile.

"Oh, I didn't notice," Emily said as she pulled a lock of her hair to her nose and sniffed to see if it was true. "I fell asleep in the drawing room. I guess I got used to the smell," she said as if she thought something were wrong.

Jacob stopped her, "It's a very nice smell. It reminds me so much of that first day you showed me your art gallery."

"That's sweet," Emily commented and let her hair fall back to her shoulder, no longer worried about the scent.

The school day seemed to drag on. Whether it was from his lack of sleep or the things that he could be doing instead, it just seemed like it was never going to end. The rain had finally come—if you could call the cold drizzle a rain.

By lunch time, the sky was still dark and the steady drizzle made it so the outside area couldn't be used. Jacob found Emily before they got in the line, "I wish the weather was better," he remarked as he approached her, "I like sitting outside much better."

"I do too, but I like the rain also," Emily smiled and walked with him to the back of the line.

"I wouldn't call that a rain." Jacob commented, "It's just a cold mist—the dying breath of winter."

"It will rain," Emily assured him. "I always like the rain because of the way everything looks when the sun comes back out."

Jacob stopped for a moment and stared into space. For the longest time he had wondered what made her seem so familiar and now he knew. "That's exactly what I see when I look in your eyes," he whispered accidentally.

Emily smiled and blushed a little, "Really?"

Jacob laughed slightly, a little at his epiphany, and a little because he hadn't meant to say it. "Yes, they always seemed like something familiar, but I never connected the images." Jacob replied, "Every time I looked in your eyes, it seemed like no matter what was wrong at the moment it would get better. No matter how dark it was, the sun would always come out. And just like how beautiful the sun is when everything is damp, dark and grey, that's what I see in your eyes. It's hope that I see in you. Until now the metaphor escaped me."

"That's so sweet," Emily said, "No one has ever said anything that beautiful about me before."

Jacob smiled and hugged her, "Well, I'm honored to be the first."

Lunch in the dining hall was loud, and the rest of the day was long. The weather continued to be depressing, and the thoughts pressing on Jacob's mind were getting heavy. In spite of it all, Jacob's heart felt light after he had talked with Emily. They were leaving now; she was going home, and Jacob was returning to the library. He had wanted to make plans for tomorrow, but the business of saving his father was still too heavy on his mind. Also, he wasn't comfortable to have Emily near him when he could not control something that lived in him.

The dreary weather wasn't isolated to Jacob's home—it seemed to blanket all of Scotland. Jacob went straight to the study to retrieve the books and begin researching. He found the books had not been put away; they were still on Rain's desk. One was open as if someone had been looking in it.

He picked up the book he was reading last night and fumbled through some of the papers he had made notes on until he found the ones that went with the book he had picked. Then he found a table and sat down to study. A few minutes later, Rain entered the chamber.

"I left the books out; I figured we would need them," she said. She didn't offer a greeting as if not putting the book back meant they had never said goodbye.

"I asked Sarah and Dom to meet me here this evening."

"They are very young for this work," Rain replied.

Jacob looked up. "I'm very young for the work I do," he said matter-of-factly.

"It must run in your family." Rain said and gave him an appraising glare. She picked up the book that had been open and continued to hold eye contact with Jacob. She carried it over to Jacob's table and sat down beside him, "I often forget how young you are, Jacob. Time has passed me by, and I have learned to judge the age of a person by their mind and not their years."

"I suppose I grew up too fast," Jacob replied.

"As did I," Rain sighed, "I was your age when time stopped for me. I suppose I'm still your age, two centuries later." Then she looked up and smiled, "But we are still young, time might have escaped us, but life has not."

She gestured to the book she had picked up, "I've been reading throughout the day." Her hair was a white-blond with tinges of red and blue, and her golden eyes had a serious auburn, huge underlying her golden gaze.

"This is something new, Jacob." She remarked as she moved a strand of her silver hair behind her ear. It seemed to turn red when she touched it, and once it was settled in its place, it shifted to the slightest shade of blue. It was like a very light watercolor, the blues were places the light hit and the reds were places of shadow.

"I really appreciate you helping me," Jacob said as he tried to distinguish the pattern of colors in her hair.

"I don't know if we can do this, Jacob," Rain said trying not to break his frail hope, "But I'm here for you and with you for whatever end. I'm helping because you matter to me."

Jacob wasn't entirely sure how Rain meant that, but he knew she always meant what she said. He questioned the wisdom of spending this much time involving her in his studies. But right now he needed her help.

She looked toward her book and began to thumb through the pages yet to be turned, "There is a lot of work to be done. This is the sort of labor that only the wisest sorcerers of old dreamed of."

Jacob's attention shifted to the doorway, "And that is why we must have the very best assisting us."

Rain turned to the direction he was looking and saw Sarah and Dom entering the study, "Even so," she replied looking back into Jacob's eyes, "It will be far more difficult than either of us imagined."

"So be it," Jacob said, "It will not alter my choice; I have to do this."

"Do what?" Sarah asked as she approached the table and took a seat opposite Jacob.

"First let me tell you what I found yesterday when I went with Ress," Jacob answered and motioned for Dom to take a seat.

"The spirit that rests in the library of Africa is a full-fledged demon, a chief of his kind. His name is Adramelech," Jacob began, "It is my job to see that it is deported. Father has taken interest in the work, seeing as he is the demon hunter.

"There is only one known way to deport a pure Demon." Jacob paused as if he might think of another method before the words came out, "That is by sacrificing a willing soul into the flames of Hell. Sarah, I need your knack for creating spells. I knew you could not keep a secret from Dom, so Dom, I'll need you to help us find the information we need." He gestured at the stack of books he hoped would not slowly become a mountain.

"So how are you going to do this?" Sarah asked, "And what can we do to help?"

"Father has elected to be the sacrifice. I won't stand for that." Sarah and Dom's faces changed with the morbid news. "I need to find another way. Father said we would do this once I am out of school, but I intend to use all of that time to search for a different means of deporting the Demon. It's a hard job and there will be a lot that I can't understand alone. Rain has helped me get started, but I need more help, I need people who I know can break codes and who I trust not to speak of this project." He looked at them trying to hide the fear that was trapped inside him.

Sarah jumped up and slammed her palms on the table, "I'm in. Where do I start?"

"It is a complicated process." Jacob explained. "First we have to learn a spell or make one if needed. Then we must learn and apply knowledge of the demon we wish to deport. Rain is fantastic at studying and references, I can build and modify nearly anything, but you will have to be the person who synthesizes all the spells and creates the catalysts; you're good at that. Dom, I need you to help me research. You're good with history and legends. And we need to get organized."

Jacob pointed to the papers on Rain's desk, "We made that clutter by ourselves last night. I can only imagine how much worse it will be with two more hands."

Sarah scratched her head, "It seems like an odd spell to find. We might have better luck if we go straight for creating a new spell."

"That," Rain interjected, "is far more complex."

"If you have never heard of any such spell in all of your years sequestered in this library, I doubt we will find one." Sarah replied, "I'm good at inventing spells, and I'm sure you know how. I think it would be best for us to begin working on it. Between your knowledge and my ingenuity, I think we could manage."

"She has a good point," Dom agreed, "Rain knows a lot about the old magic. If she has never heard of any other method, it probably doesn't exist—yet."

Jacob smiled at the optimism his brother and sister had. It would be that kind of attitude that would make this succeed.

Again the night ran late. The time passed a lot quicker this time, though. There was more energy, they had a direction, and they had a drive for their work. Even so, it would take every day to prepare this incantation by the end of the school year. Jacob looked up at his brother who was intently reading the *Book of Enoch*, trying to gain any possible reference to Adramelech's nature or his story. Jacob had been trying to decipher the Scripts of Adramelech, a few tattered parchments that were all that remained of the book he had written. It was one thing when he was translating for his own purpose, but now he was putting his knowledge of languages to the test with his father's life on the line.

"Dom, I think we'd better call it a night. We have school in the morning." Jacob told him. Dom nodded and took the notes he had been keeping, sticking them in the book as a marker. Jacob did the same, and they stood up and walked to Rain's desk where Rain and Sarah were studying arcane magic. Jacob looked curiously at the books; Rain had the translated copy of the *Book of the Flies*, considered to be

Beelzebub's handiwork of dark spells. His sister was reading a guide of advanced catalysts written by Blaze, the first Archon of Light. The depth of this task was massive. Just now Jacob realized that they would need a mastery of light magic as well as an intimate understanding of dark magic, and they would need a rare set of catalysts to tie the two together. He and Dom were working on the background information needed to make the spell work specifically for the intended target, and Rain and Sarah were working on the actual spell. At least they were organized now.

"Hey Sarah, it's late. I think we should go."

Sarah looked up and blinked as if she had been in a deep sleep, "Right, I suppose we should," she replied and rubbed her face with both hands. She sat up straight and ran one hand over the top of her head through her red hair.

"I'm going to leave these books out so that any of you can pick them up whenever you want," Rain said as she tore her eyes from the pages in front of her. "They will be on the return shelf, but I won't take them back; we will be using them often."

"Thanks again, Rain. Good night." Jacob placed the book down on the desk and turned to leave. Sarah and Dom followed him, and he went back home to another restless night.

All day, the miserable cold mist had drizzled down, slowly soaking everything in a shivering wetness. The sky was now starless, and the rain had finally begun to fall. Lightening periodically lit up the sky only to reveal the dark clouds that loomed overhead. As Jacob tried to sleep, he could hear the sound of the drops getting larger and heavier as they fell against the roof. The pace quickened, and the bottom fell out of the sky at last. Rolling thunder lit up the world outside his window and rumbled through the house. The storm had been brewing all day, and now it had broken.

CHAPTER 20

If Jacob was going to get this spell created, he was going to have to get some rest sometime. He was so tired, but the things on his mind just wouldn't let him sleep. One would think that living real nightmares would make him callous to things that happened in his dreams, but Jacob was repeatedly awakened by strange nightmares and the whispering voice of Aries. It seemed to call to that part of him that he was afraid of, enticing it to wake up. The two spirits seemed to whisper to each other when Jacob was asleep or when he entered the library.

The storm didn't bother him any; he was so tired he could have slept right through it if only his restless mind would let him remain in slumber. Sometime around four, he managed to find sleep amidst the pounding rain and the flashing, booming lightening. He was still none too happy when the alarm woke him two hours later—time for school. He sat up and looked wearily out the window. All that was left of the snow was now gone, washed away by the storm. The yard was wet, and puddles were scattered everywhere, sparkling in the early light of dawn.

Various shades of blue filled the sky between the thin, white remnants of the storm clouds. As he stared out the window, half trying to wake up and half wondering how the land could look so beautiful and peaceful after such a great storm, the sun broke over the horizon victoriously. The storm may have hidden it the day before, but it outlasted the rain. Jacob smiled as if he were looking into Emily's eyes and pulled himself out of bed. Something about the scene gave him hope, and that hope gave him the energy to get on his feet. How far that would carry him was still to be determined.

It was almost the weekend now. That didn't mean much for Jacob anymore; he worked so hard that it was almost like being at school—being near Emily during the week—was his time off. He always looked forward to spending time with her on the weekends, but for the next few months he would be sequestered in a dark chamber, feverishly working on creating a new spell. Perhaps that was a good thing; he was becoming more dangerous the longer he was near Aries.

Normally he would be ecstatic about a task that put him to the test like this, but the weight of his success or failure dampened his enthusiasm. He hated not being certain of himself, and more and more that fear made him want to avoid the only thing that seemed good in his life at the moment. Part of him wanted to take Emily with him; surely she could brighten the dim halls, but it was restricted to anyone outside of the bloodline. At least the sun was shining today, and it shined all day.

After school, Jacob took Emily to a small café to finish their homework over some desperately needed coffee. They remained there for some time and talked until it was time for dinner. Even though all of his energy was drained, he wished the day had been longer. They lingered at the café for a little while after dinner and then parted, Emily to her home and Jacob back to the library. Jacob felt so much more at peace when he was near Emily that he could not bring himself to warn her of what was brewing inside him. She needed to know; she would want to know. But Jacob didn't yet have the courage to push her away even for her own safety. There was nothing she could do to help him, and if he told her she would try; she was just that kind of person.

Jacob entered the study to see not only more books added to the stack, but Rain, Sarah, and Dom studying them intently. He could not have asked them to be this diligent in the trial, but he was very glad they were doing this for him—no, not for him—for their father. This wasn't just his problem; it was a family matter. Rain wasn't part of his family, though, but she was a very close friend, close enough to care just as much as Jacob. He picked up his books and sat down without saying anything. For a moment, he indulged in the old smell of the musty paper and ink; the scent made him comfortable. The familiar aroma jarred his brain into a studying mood, and he began his work, falling into a deep concentration.

A few moments later a gentle hand rested on his shoulder. He looked up and saw Julie standing beside him. "Hi," she whispered as if something was weighing on her mind.

"Julie, what's wrong?" Jacob didn't mean to be so forward, but his subtlety escaped him.

"I heard that you were preparing to fight the demon," she said, "That . . . you plan on going back there."

"I have to," Jacob replied. "I don't expect you to, and I won't ask you to."

Julie sat down in the chair on the left side of the table and sighed.

"I'm sorry about the last time, but now you understand what I do. I can't let that . . . or worse happen to anyone else again."

"I know, it's your father. He's going to help you isn't he?" Julie asked.

Jacob nodded; he knew she understood what that meant.

"I want to help you," Julie said.

"Why?" Jacob insisted, "You don't owe me anything. I won't ask you to do this."

Julie looked as if she was going to cry, "He's in my dreams." She whispered though half chocked words. "Part of that demon is still in me. I can feel it." She stopped and took a breath to keep from breaking down and crying, "I have to face it now. I have to be there with you when it's done. I can't sleep; he won't let me. I haven't slept since."

Jacob felt like the weight of the world was pressing down on him again. For a while it seemed to let up, but now so much hinged on this one deed. None of this would have happened if he had not placed that curse on Julie. How much more could he mess things up?

"I know," Jacob replied, "The voice that whispers in your dreams. Even now Aries's voice buzzes in my head. He beckons me when I am here, and when I lay down I see visions of Adramelech."

Julie squinted and wiped a run-away tear from her face, "We have to stop this— both of them. I'm sorry I got you involved with Aries. This is my fault. I did it to myself, and that is why I have to help you."

That seemed true, but Jacob couldn't place the blame on his cousin; she had stepped into a world she had no idea about.

"No, I shouldn't have been so rash when I faced you in front of Aries. You can't have all the blame for this."

"Jacob, you're too kind," she sniffed and drew a quivering breath trying to steady her nerves.

Jacob sighed; he knew how heavy this was. He reached up and placed a reassuring hand on Julie's shoulder, "Remember when you said I was different? Because I defeat the darkness? And that was what made me the Chosen?" Julie looked at him with her saddened eyes, and he continued, "One of us is the Chosen." Jacob said, "Whether it's me or you—one of us will defeat this darkness."

"We will do this," Jacob assured, "Both of us have our share of the blame, but these spirits won't be the end of us. We will fix this." For his own sake he prayed that was the truth.

"How can I help?" Julie asked.

Jacob looked at the stack of books at Rain's desk and shook his head, there was no way they could read, understand, and apply all of that information in the allotted time. "We need intimate knowledge of the information in those books before the summer." Jacob said, "I don't know what your strong points are, but you can go pick up whatever suits you. Sarah and Rain know more of what we're doing, so you might want to talk to them about what you need to look for."

Julie nodded and stood up. She sniffed again and wiped under her eyes and then walked over to the desk and began looking in the pile of books for something she might be able to help with. Every time she tried to help him, it made him feel worse about what he had done to her. Soon he would have to step on that board and fight to undo what he had done.

Jacob redirected his attention back to his book, hoping to learn something of this monster that could be useful. The book he now delved into was Rikeen's *Account of the Order*. It wasn't so much a book as it was a set of rules that more or less governed Hell. Rikeen was one of the lesser-known agents of Darkness. Though he was ambiguous, he was very influential in setting up the hierarchy of the Fallen.

Before the Fall, Rikeen was the second scribe in Heaven. The records indicate he brought forth order among the Fallen. This book contained information as to how he did so and the characteristics of the members that composed the Order. Somewhere among the clans the *Book of Times* was locked away, untranslated and collecting dust. Jacob couldn't help but wonder if it would help. But he didn't have the time to translate another book at the moment. He was still working on one and not yet finished retranslating the *Book of Anzel.*

Adramelech was made the head of the Order of Anarchy once Rikeen had formed it. The demons within this Order were given areas to "govern" on Earth. Some demons remained locked in Hades by Satan due to various reasons. There were some records of demons that were too powerful and then some seemed to be just useless to the cause and were therefore not allowed to venture out. The text was unclear as to why Satan himself did not host this Order or why he did not divide a section of the Earth for himself or where exactly he was. Some instances seemed to imply he was lost or wandering. It was as if he had abandoned the Fallen and had gone in search of his own purpose or plot and the Order of Anarchy had been set up in rejection of his rule. That was all good information to know, but Jacob didn't think that would help him. He needed to find something that might detail some of the rituals used in Adramelech's "rule" or even better what he might have done in Heaven before the Great War of Hosts.

His mind wandered, and he felt very tired. His vision blurred as his eyes tried to close, but he forced them open—he had to study. Hours passed by as if only a few minutes, and Jacob found the scent of the old books lulling him to sleep. The voice of Aries was like a loud buzzing in his mind, and it was driving him mad. Part of him wanted to go silence the board and just reject the challenge. But he knew that he would have to face it again to make things right; he was just waiting for a good time.

There would never be a good time, and every day he delayed made it worse. Julie needed him to act now, and he need to act on both of their behalves. The subtle buzz kept nagging him, and it kept pricking the interest of his waking demon. He was afraid to step back on that board because it might fully awaken his demon. But he knew if he waited too long, it would wake anyway. Jacob stood up at his table, suddenly on fire with determination. He slammed the book shut, sending a strong signal to everyone in the room. He knew what he needed to do, partly as a resolution and partly out of annoyance and frustration.

"Jacob, what's the matter?" Rain asked and stood up ready to rush to him if he needed.

"I have a job to do," he replied, "I have waited long enough, and I can't wait any longer."

"What are you talking about?" Rain asked.

"I have to meet Aries," Jacob said firmly. "I cannot fight two demons at once; one must be dealt with. Julie, I'm sorry for what I did, and it's time I made it right."

"Jacob, not tonight. You are very tired. It can wait," Julie urged.

"No, I've been waiting. You know what it's like to have that buzzing in your head. Every day I wait, it gets worse. Every day I wait, it will get harder." Jacob turned to look at her, "This part ends tonight!"

Everyone stood up and closed their books. Jacob turned and walked with a hastened sense of purpose out of the chamber. Dom was the first to hurry after him, "Come on; he's going to need us there, too."

Jacob stood in front of the board for a long time. Nobody said anything; they understood his decision and the weight it carried. Many people had battled on the board for personal glory, but Jacob was the first who would to step on the enchanted tiles for the sake of another. The tension in the air was so thick, it was smothering and heavy. There was no sound in the chamber except the dull buzz of Aries in Jacob's mind. Jacob was strained by the gravity of the choice he was making. He finally took a step forward, and the small group of onlookers took a deep breath as if they were moving forward with him.

Jacob's heart pounded, and the demon in him protested as the drumming sound of Aries quickened. Whatever was in him was already awake, and it feared this game more than Jacob did. He quenched the surge of powers that urged him to run—he owned them, not the other way around. He stepped onto the shiny tiles of the grand board. All the pieces of the last battle were as if they had never been broken; the cracks and scars in the black marble and white quartz had vanished and appeared as if no one had ever set foot on their surface. The silver suns glowed in the white tiles, and the golden oak leaves shined against the jet-black marble.

Jacob walked into the middle of the board, and as he did, the incessant whispering died. His inner demon became still and time all but stopped. He took a long deep breath; he felt strong, not intimidated like he thought he might. Then he took the last step, "Aries of War!" he announced loudly. He found his voice and commanded an audience with the demon, "I have come to answer the challenge you have decreed to me! Come forth that we may settle this matter; I accept your challenge."

As custom the challenger, in this case Aries was the black pieces. Instantly Jacob felt the pull, and he was sucked into the board. This time he knew what was happening, and the odd feeling of being all of the pieces and none of the pieces did not surprise him. He surveyed the board and noticed some differences that did surprise him.

When Jacob had played Julie, the pieces were all generic. But this time they were each different. The white king was in Jacob's likeness; the black was in the form of Adramelech. The black demon-king appeared as a man with the legs of a mule. He wore no armor, instead a robe of peacock feathers draped around him. It was a vain attempt to reclaim the beauty that he had lost. A dark aura exuded from him, hate was in his dead-blue eyes, and his face was twisted by malice and suffering. This scared him a bit to think this could be foreshadowing his upcoming fight with the demon.

192

He looked to his left to see if the other pieces had changed. The white queen was a familiar face, one he did not want involved in this: Emily. Still shocked, he looked further down the row and saw the queen's bishop was his father. Aries knew what he valued most and was trying to play games with his mind. The knight on the queen's side was Dom, and the rook was Roth. He looked down his right side and saw that his bishop was Rain, his knight was his sister, and the rook was Julie. Why would Aries show him this? Then he looked across the board and saw the black queen was Aries, and each of the other pieces were different ranked Wraiths.

Aries stood in the Queen's place. He was tall and thin, and his skin was charred black and dried. He had no hair; it had been singed from his scalp. His ears were just holes in his head, they too had been taken by the flames as well as his nose and most of the features of his face. His eyes glowed red, and malice flowed from them. His lips were mostly burnt away and revealed broken, jagged, yellowed teeth. In his right hand, he held a dark blade, and it was on fire. In his left hand, he carried a large shield that had been made in the shape of a skull at the top that bore a large crack that spread to the right eye socket, a battle scar from millennia of fighting.

The bishops held two swords and the knights rode black horses and carried massive maces. Both of the rooks wore heavy armor and wielded long halberds. They all exuded evil and the hairs on the back of Jacob's neck stood up just as they did when he faced the things for real. All of the black pawns were Shadows, and then he notices all of his pawns were just normal people. His pawns had the same swords and shields as the first time, but the others had different weapons. Emily had the charm and the flower he had given her and carried an elegant blade that Jacob recognized as Jade.

Rain, on his right, held a book of high-level spells that was attached to her waist by a thin chain and by her side was a small dagger. The other bishop, Drake, held a Bible and his normal tools for hunting spirits. Both of his siblings were the knights and carried different weapons. Sarah had been thoroughly trained in Seracata, and because of her powers could use advanced techniques that few ever learned. She sat upon a white horse in silver armor with only a short sword; her real power was in her hand-to-hand combat. Dom also sat on a white horse with a bow and arrow, as he had diligently studied archery and was an esteemed marksman. Roth stood ready; holding in his hand, Judgment, the Light Shard Jacob had given him. And Julie waited on the opposite side of the board outfitted with the gifts she had received in her trials. These were not so different from the tools Jacob had been given.

Even though everyone was outfitted in their best and ready to fight, the thought of pitting his friends and family against the forces of Hell discomforted him. That's exactly what Aries wanted him to see. This was the reality of what he had done. However, they were not the people they looked like; they were just pieces. Jacob swallowed and sent Dom forward as his first move. "Gladly," he replied. He didn't have to think as much about controlling the piece this time as if they could think on their own. What was happening? These pieces made no sound at all the last time, no shrieks of pain, nothing. How could they speak now?

A black pawn paced forward. Jacob moved the pawn in front of him forward, as well. Unsure just how real the people on the board were, Jacob tried to play as defensively as possible. He worked on setting up angles and tried to construct traps for his opponent. However, Aries was a master of war and far better at setting up offenses that Jacob was at setting up defenses. The pressure of the game was real; it felt as if the lives of the people that these pieces represented were in his hands and that he controlled their fate. Until this point, only pawns had been exchanged, but now the game was well developed, and it was time major pieces began to fall off the board. The cage Jacob tried to construct around his friends was now a trap, and he had to face the demons and Wraiths that marched forward mercilessly. The power inside him was fighting hard to get out, and Jacob was fighting it just as hard as he was fighting Aries.

One of the rooks had moved in a position to attack his brother, and Jacob was nervous about that so he positioned Rain between them where he could back her up. This did not intimidate Aries in the least. The juggernaut Wraith rushed forward with the halberd in full swing. Jacob jumped into Rain to defend. Suddenly he felt more of Rain's feeling and understood more of her than he ever had. It had to be a trick, something to distract him from the game. It was weird and alien. He could smell the scent of the old books on her, and he could feel inner conflict within her. It was as he had guessed; she was very alone, and somewhere in the dark places of silence she wept.

He moved out of the way and let the halberd crush the tile where she had been standing. Rain backed away, and Jacob fumbled through the book of spells. Half of his mind had fallen into the trap already, and his thoughts were slow. He foolishly explored the new ocean of emotion behind Rain. There was something bothering him, that void he felt when he touched her, perhaps he could figure out what it was. He stretched into her mind as he tried to locate a spell. He found it. The black part of her heart, the shadow she would not let him see had been sealed off and hidden from him, but now the way was open.

Jacob had to move again as the Wraith brought another heavy blow down. He stepped into the shadows and felt the surge of emotion that Rain never showed. The dark was her feelings, not all of them, just toward him. Suddenly Jacob understood so much. She didn't just respect him for what he was; it was something deeper. Somehow to her, Jacob dispelled the loneliness she dealt with in the dark years. Rain would never let it show, but her desire to be close to someone was overpowering. Jacob stepped back, shocked at the revelation of how deep her feelings were for him. As he did, he heard her whisper. She wanted him to stay, but he had to let go. If he was going to survive, if she was going to survive, he had to get out of her head and focus on saving her life.

The Wraith was already charging again. Jacob needed to buy some time to search the spell book. Rain rushed forward and plunged the dagger into its belly, and she dodged a third strike. That would certainly be a minor blow, but it might just slow it down enough to locate a spell. Now Jacob understood how much he meant to Rain and just what he represented to her—the light in her dark world. Was it real or a mind game? He found a spell, a repulsion technique that was immensely powerful. Channeling rippling energy through Rain's arm, he ejected a bolt of blue light that raced through the air like a cool liquid. It struck the Wraith and flung it across the board. It landed in the rubble of two pawns that had been broken earlier and stood up as if unharmed. The monster picked up a chunk of the wrought iron remains of a ruined black pawn and hurled it at Rain.

Jacob knew this spell and reflexively held up both hands dropping the book and letting it hang by the tether. The small boulder deflected and glanced off an invisible shield. Then the Wraith picked up another piece of the fallen pawn and hurled it again. Jacob guided Rain again to deflect the projectile. Then the beast hefted the head of the white pawn that had fallen beside the black one and launched it across the field. Jacob focused and stopped it, it was much too heavy for him to lift, but with the spell he could leave it suspended in air. He then used a push spell and hurled it back at the creature. The effect wasn't what he had hoped for. With an irritated and enraged sweep of his hand, the Wraith knocked the white quartz out of the air. It then picked up its halberd and rushed forward.

Jacob ran. He had to keep the distance between the Wraith and Rain. Rain had spells, and as long as she could stay away from the halberd, she had a chance. He picked up the book and flipped it open to the first spell—lightening. He turned and stood defiantly in the Wraith's path and unleashed a mighty bolt. The spell was extremely strong but very inaccurate. Sparks flew from Rain's fingers, and the bolt struck the ground in front of the Wraith. A loud crack like a dynamite blast in a rock quarry ripped through the halls and left a large hole in the white tile. The Wraith stepped in the hole and fell forward with all his force. The ground shook when he hit the tile and the halberd clattered forward. Had he done it?

He turned the next page and found a spell to freeze an opponent so thoroughly that the soul would not move. An icy chill rippled through the air, and frost began to form on all the inactive pieces. A faint glow danced around Rain's fingers, and then a jagged icicle shot from her hand and pierced through the Wraith's armor. At first the fire inside it died, and then it turned blue as frost began to envelope it. Even as the frost enveloped the Wraith, a chill ran down Jacob's spine. All the warmth seemed to be sucked out of everything, and patches of ices formed all over the board.

As it reached forward to grab the halberd, it froze and ceased to move. Rain walked to the body with the cool composure she always had and knelt to pick up the massive halberd. Even for a weapon in its class it was huge. She struggled to lift it and slowly stood above the fallen foe. Standing with her feet apart for better balance, she hefted the massive tool above her head and brought it down on the frozen body. It crashed into the cold iron and broke through the frozen and brittle metal. The Wraith exploded into rubble as all the pieces did and sent Rain backward. Jacob felt the shock in his chest and he stood up slowly and trudged back to the square he had guarded. He had succeeded in protecting Rain.

What he didn't realize was that he had left Julie stranded when he moved Rain to guard Dom. Somehow Aries had manipulated him into letting his guard down. The black queen, embodied by Aries, walked malevolently down the diagonal toward his cousin. Jacob looked at the situation. If he did nothing, the score would be even, and he could use his next turn to move Roth against one of the black knights. Jacob debated quickly in his mind which course of action was best. Even for a strategic advantage, he could not sacrifice his cousin so quickly. Maybe he couldn't win this fight, but he had to try. That's what this entire fight was about: Julie. If he could not keep her piece alive, how could he hope to win this game?

He sacrificed his next turn and his chance to maintain the advantage and willed Julie to defend against the demon. Jacob stepped into her and felt her mind. How come he didn't feel this connection when he had moved the pieces earlier? Was this just an illusion from Aries to keep him distracted? Julie was cold, frightened, and felt so small. Jacob felt all her regrets for what she had done. It seemed impossible, but she felt more gravity for what had happened than he did. This time he had to remain focused if he was to stand a chance. He did not delve into Julie's mind, but that didn't stop her emotions from wrapping themselves around his thoughts. She had all but given up; Jacob was her last hope to undo what she had done. Julie needed him. Again he was the last light in someone's darkness—the only faint glimmer of hope in her despair. That wasn't fair. He knew how much rested on his shoulders. Did it have to go to a personal level with every single member in the clans?

Aries twirled the flaming sword and slashed at his cousin. Jacob rolled out of the way and stood with the elegant enchanted blade ready to make his stand against the monster. Julie was about half the size of the Demon-queen and hopelessly overpowered. Jacob mustered all the skill he had so diligently studied and lunged to cross blades with the Demon. The two blades met with fiery sparks. Hot discharges like molten rock spattered on to the tiles and left black burn scars on the decorative suns and oak leaves. The patches of ice that had formed from Rain's last spell melted away and curled off the tiles in thick vapors.

Julie could not match Aries's strength and was pushed back. Jacob stumbled back and fell against a black pawn. The demon slashed again, and he ducked out of the way. There was a splitting sound as the flaming blade severed the pawn's right arm clean off. Jacob hid behind the pawn, trying to keep some kind of barrier between them. Surely the Demon wasn't going to demolish its own piece to get at Julie. It was a good plan. However, Aries kicked the pawn over, and it tipped over in Jacob's direction. He jumped back as the pawn thundered to the ground. The floor shook, and Julie stumbled as broken pieces scattered at her feet. The only thing he could do was run. Julie jumped over pieces that had not yet come to complete stops and then tried to vault over a larger piece.

The twisted chunk rocked under her weight, and she slipped and collapsed on the marble. Before Jacob could look up the demon was upon her. He raised Julie's sword to block the inferno, but it was wrenched from her hands by the blow. All he could do now was watch as the fiery blade rose one last time and came crashing down on his cousin. In that one moment, he felt so much racing through Julie's mind: her complete despair and his utter failure. She wasn't the one who had failed, he had. His failure had extinguished the last ray of hope in her mind and now, on death's doorstep, she was completely lost in the darkness.

"No!" Jacob yelled out. He could understand that he failed, but he could not endure the knowledge of the sheer depth of the darkness Julie was being sentenced to. The blade slashed through her, and Jacob felt the searing hot pain in his chest. Julie turned back to white quartz and burst into pieces that scattered across the board. Jacob didn't know this could feel so real. Something else inside him cried out in pain also. He wasn't physically here, but he could feel the tears running down his cheeks—mostly from the frustration of being helpless. He was angry with himself for what had happened to Julie, he was angry with himself because he couldn't fix it, and he felt like she had just died for real.

Then he realized the depth of his folly. Going all the way back to placing Rain between the rook and his brother. Now Aries had a clear shot across the horizontal at Rain, and he was marching. Jacob quickly processed the odds, and they were not good. Rain would most likely stand less of a chance. If he let the demon have her spot, he would be able to attack her on the next turn, but he couldn't let her die like that. Even as his elder, she looked up to him; she loved him. He had not sorted out all the ramifications that entailed, but he had to make a stand.

Jacob jumped back into Rain and hoped that Aries would attack him personally if he bested Rain. The spirit inside Jacob protested and tried to draw him back, but Jacob ignored it and took control of Rain's statue. He summoned the repulsion spell he had before. The liquid blue light arched at the demon. Aries stepped back and braced against the impact, absorbing it with his shield. He grounded his feet in the tile and created huge claw marks as he slid back, but the blast did not manage to throw him as it had with the Wraith. He recovered effortlessly from the blow and trudged forward with the flaming sword burning the air around him. Jacob fumbled the spell book and located a spell called, Victory Lance. If this did not stop Aries, then Rain would be lost.

It took a few moments to conjure and Aries crossed the board rapidly. The demon raised its blade to dispatch Rain just as Jacob completed the spell. A bolt of golden light shot like a cannon from the pages of the book into the heart of the demon. It stumbled back several steps but did not fall. It stood straight and arrogant, ignoring that there was massive hole in its chest and made one quick, ruthless strike, detaching Rain's head from her shoulders. Jacob felt her pain and agony. He felt all the sorrow she had inside her. Though he had failed her, he still felt her esteem and admiration of him, and he felt the insecure aloneness of her life become complete. Jacob grabbed his throat and wailed in pain and from the trauma and surge of feeling. He cursed Aries for this. The thin, charred beast glared at him with red piercing eyes as if it were staring at his soul. The hole where his heart should be burned and ash fell out of it. Flesh grew over and sealed the wound and then turned black and brittle. The monster stood for a moment to taunt Jacob.

He wanted the queen to attack him; she was only one square away, but it was her turn. He wanted revenge, but she had to move on him. Why shouldn't Aries attack him? He could end the game here. However, Aries wasn't playing this game to win, he was playing to get under Jacob's skin.

CHAPTER 21

J acob ached from the blows he had taken, and the inner pain from losing two people so close to him seemed so real he wanted to vomit. He burned with anger against the demon, and he wanted to kill. But the queen passed him by and turned down the vertical toward Dom.

"Coward!" Jacob yelled, "Face me!" His anger erupted, and he lost control over the monster he had been suppressing.

He knew Dom didn't have a chance just like Julie, just like Rain. If he let the queen take Dom, he could still move Roth against one of the knights, but he could not bring himself to leave his brother defenseless. Passion and hate welled up in him, Aries was ruthless and cruel, and Jacob had no way of stopping him. He seized control of Dom's character even as his inner demon protested and aimed the enchanted bow at the demon. The first arrow flew, and the demon took it in the chest and continued trudging forward as if the arrow had been a bug. The arrow lit on fire, burned away, and fell on the tile. Jacob froze in denial. He could feel Dom's fear; his little brother wasn't prepared for this. The demon of his heart chastised him for not listening to his council. There had to be something he could do, but he couldn't think. The only thing on his mind was the panic racing through Dom's body. He was shaking, and Jacob could not control it. He raised the bow one more time and tried to shoot, but Dom's nerves could not aim and he missed.

Aries took slow intimidating steps, thundering forward as if to the beat of a war drum. He stood before the white knight and cleaved the rider and horse in half. White quartz blasted into the surrounding squares, and his brother was gone. Jacob felt his skull split, and then he felt a void in his heart at the loss of his brother. *This isn't real!* He assured himself. It felt real; the demon in him was getting agitated like it was real. Was it? The figure of Jacob's king was on his knees, face in palms weeping, just what Jacob felt like doing. His family and friends were getting ripped apart, and all he could do was watch. His feeling of helplessness began to give way to fear. He was lost now; he was losing this game, and he was losing control.

Finally, Aries was out of moves. The demon-queen was not an immediate threat to any more of his friends. His next move was to take the knight Roth was threatening and place it safely out of the way. Jacob had taken a huge disadvantage, and he had become emotionally involved in the game. The last time he had avoided that error against Julie, but Aries knew his buttons. Jacob didn't know what to do next. He had to play with the utmost care if he wanted to turn this game around. Right now he was too emotionally compromised to think clearly. He pondered and contemplated as he tried to suppress the awakened spirit in him. There was no way to discern the passage of time inside this game, and he had no idea how long it had been since the game began.

Jacob decided the best thing he could do was to secure the rest of his pieces, his friends and family, and wait for Aries to make a mistake. He took Emily, his queen, and placed her in a trio of pawns where Sarah was nearby. Aries moved the black king, Adramelech, forward, sensing the fear in Jacob. Jacob took Drake and tucked him away also, being careful to leave enough room so that he would not trap any of his pieces in the fortress he was constructing. He had barricaded the right center portion of the board fairly well, and if he could move himself over there, he might be able to stand against his foes. Roth was still outside, and Aries moved one of his dark bishops to block him from joining the group, cutting him off from the safe place. Jacob drew him back to himself rather than attempt to take the bishop. They were both out of the circle he had made, but if he played right, he could get them both over there safely.

The board urged the king to step forward again, driving the black lord toward Jacob's stronghold. Jacob moved Roth so as to make his way to the cluster, but he couldn't let him go too far because they were guarding each other. Aries didn't try to stop him; instead he moved his knight near the area and prepared for the soon-to-come battle. Jacob saw that his father could take a clear shot at the knight and debated taking the chance. There was nothing backing up the knight, and this was what his father specialized in. Why could he not bring himself to attack? The power in him was pounding and trying to escape and pushing him to attack, but he was afraid. Why? He was almost certain he could win. Was it because the piece he had to attack with was his father, or was he really that fearful of the board?

Dragging out his decision only made it worse. Jacob decided not to chance it. He moved Roth closer to the stronghold.

The next series of moves consisted of Jacob and Roth crossing the board while Aries encircled the camp. Once Jacob arrived in his fort, he positioned himself to best defend the group. He knew that he was the strongest among them. Not only on the board, but in actuality, he was the only one who could face the black demons. He was the only one who could save them. But what would he be like once he was done? That thing inside him grew more powerful with every fight, and soon it would be totally out of his control.

Adramelech pushed into the edge of his keep and dashed away a pawn effortlessly. Jacob did not try to stop him; he didn't want that demon to have the chance to move any closer without being able to react. Jacob moved Emily closer to him, as far away from the danger as possible. Above all else he had to keep her safe.

This wasn't her battle; she did not have any stake in this. Why should she suffer any pain? Why should he lose her, too? *Because you brought her into* this *world.* Jacob heard a menacing whisper curl around the back of his neck.

One of the knight-Wraiths vaulted his barrier and positioned himself to attack Roth or Sarah on his next move. Now Jacob had to make a choice. He had to let one die. He should have seen it coming. He should have thought about it on his last move instead of bringing Emily closer. Roth held a lot of respect from Jacob; he was something Jacob aspired to be, but Sarah was his sister. He had already lost his brother; he didn't know if he could stand to lose Sarah.

"It's not real," Jacob tried to convince himself and thought about the decision tactically. Roth was more powerful and might stand a chance against the knight. Then again, he could attack the knight with Sarah since she was also a knight. But that would leave her in the path of Adramelech. If Aries decided not to defend and took his next turn, he could kill her. If Aries defended and Jacob won, he could move her into a better position. Jacob swallowed hard; if he didn't risk it now, he could very well seal his fate. This could be the one chance he would have to make a stand, and for once, the energy welling in him agreed.

He took control of his sister, and regretted it the moment he set her in motion. He could hear her voice, "I'm so glad you finally let me help you." She didn't have any weapons that she could use effectively on horseback. Her real power was in her hands. Elite training of arts that had fallen from Heaven resided in her. Sarah was keen in the ways of fighting that the angels used and would know how to fight this Wraith. Her powers were his powers, and though he had not trained in them, he could use them as long as he controlled her statue. Jacob hoped she was strong enough. As the horse built up speed and began to dash toward the black knight, Sarah stood up on its back in a ready fighting position. The horse would not help her in this fight. The last time Jacob had learned that the knight didn't need the horse. This time he would use that to his advantage.

The white steed raced to the dark knight, and Sarah jumped off and propelled herself at the Wraith with a war yell like a banshee. She hit the Wraith, planting her right hand in his face and tipping the dark rider off of his horse. They fell to the ground. Sarah slammed the Wraith's head into the marble so hard that his helmet split. She did not release her grip and with her free hand, she punched him in the chest with a special technique that only the most expert users of Seracata could perform. Dust from the tiles crumbling beneath the Wraith exploded out from around his body. He withered and died and crumbled into pieces of wrought iron.

Aries had not resisted. He had freely given his knight to lure Sarah out. Jacob cursed him. The king, Adramelech, turned to face Sarah. If he didn't defend, he could possibly use Roth to lure him close enough for Jacob to kill him. But that would be another gamble, and it would require him to sacrifice two of his few remaining pieces. For such a small chance of success, he could not allow his sister to die. The chance of her winning this fight was remote, but at least he would have a chance to fight. Sarah stood with her horse beside her and waited until the

Demon-king entered her square. She readied to defend. Jacob's demon screamed at him for standing his ground, and Jacob nearly withdrew, but he remained firm.

Adramelech was massive; he was ferocious and foul, and death was concealed under his regal robes of peacock feathers. Unclean claws protruded from his angry hands, and his hooves scraped the tiles as he stomped forward. He raised one hand and brandished a flowing blade of molten rock. Sarah used her hidden powers and blocked the first strike by catching the blade. It took immense amounts of energy to stop the devilishly strong attack. Jacob felt Sarah's arms both go numb from the hit, and he felt the energy jump out of his body as if it had pulled from him. Sarah lunged forward and struck the demon with the same technique that had obliterated the Wraith. The blow sent the king back, grinding his hooves into the tile. His chest should have cracked and collapsed, but the king shrugged it off and gave a low growl as if it were amused.

Otherwise unaffected, Adramelech stood straight up and pushed out his chest. He flexed, and the robe of feathers fanned out making a wide mane behind him. The feathers that had covered the front of his body turned to the sides and stood on end, hovering parallel to the floor just above his shoulders. With an intimidating yell, he swung his great sword again. Sarah stepped back, unable to muster the strength to block another attack. As the blade hit the ground, it changed form into a whip and raced forward slashing though her armor and burning her body. From the left thigh all the way to the right cheek, Jacob felt the searing pain. Before Sarah could recover, the whip had come back for another strike. It grabbed her around the neck and burned into her flesh. Jacob felt the suffocating heat on his face, and he struggled to get away. The spirit he had trapped inside him wriggled, trying to break free, but Jacob managed to hold on just barely.

The demon jerked the whip back and sent Sarah tumbling through the air. She came to a crumpling halt when she impacted the stone-cold white king. Jacob watched in horror as she writhed from the burns and broken bones at his feet. There was nothing he could do to ease her suffering, nothing he could do to protect her. He could not move—it was not his turn. Blood oozed from her armor and stained the white tile at the king's feet with crimson as she died. She turned white and burst into fragments, but the blood remained pooled at his feet. Jacob's heart wrenched from what he had seen. The demon in him only burned hotter. It would have been enough just to witness it, but he had felt her every step of the way. The pain and the fear she had to endure in her last moments lingered in his mind, and he cried. Both of his siblings and Rain and Julie were dead; he had intimate understanding of their last moments, and he regretted stepping on this board.

Adramelech stepped closer to him. There was now one square between them. Adramelech stopped and folded his feathers back around his body; his turn was over. Emily was right beside Jacob so he moved Emily diagonally behind him to protect her. Aries moved closer and threatened to attack Drake. Jacob did not hesitate, and he moved Drake out of the way, opening a direct line for Aries to attack him. He did this partly to get his father away from danger and partly as a challenge to the black queen. Since this was not a normal game of chess, there were no rules prohibiting the king from exposing himself.

The black queen did not take the bait. Instead, Aries stepped into a position to attack either Drake or Roth. The square he occupied was in the direct path of both pieces, but Jacob shuddered to think what that demon could do to his father or the old man if he attacked her. Roth had more power, but if he lost the fight, Aries would be able to attack Emily next if he chose. It was another no-win situation for him. He felt bad about his choice, but his father came before Roth.

Once Drake was in a secure place, the demon trudged to Roth, and the next fight began. The awakened spirit in Jacob urged him to leave him be, but Jacob insisted Roth defend against the foul beast. Judgment flared, and fire glinted off of the silver blade as Roth unsheathed it. Jacob could feel the old man's heart. He was full of wisdom and power, but his body was frail from a curse that Aries placed on him long ago. The red flaming sword that Aries wielded burst to life, and the epic blades clashed with thunder. The demon and the ancient warrior collided in the square. For an old man, Roth was strong. He shoved the demon and pushed him back. Jacob could feel Roth's emotions, old feelings of bitterness he harbored toward this demon, not from what Arise had done to him but something far older than that. He wanted to know more, but that had caused him to falter earlier, so he refrained from exploring Roth's mind.

Jacob attacked again and tried to keep pushing the creature back. But Aries was skilled and parried and blocked the flurry of blows that Roth threw at him. The duel went on; the pair was evenly matched in skill, but Roth could not withstand much more, his body was weakening quickly. One wrong move and he would be destroyed. They pushed through the rubble of the pieces that had fallen before them and danced across the cracked tiles until Jacob made the tiniest error. He kicked a loose stone and shifted his attention from his opponent to the stone. For less than a second his concentration was broken, but it might as well have been an hour.

Roth moved to block the blow, but his tired hands were beginning to slow. It was a fumbling move, and Judgment slipped from his hands. Jacob wanted to scream at the simple mistake, Roth stumbled back and tripped over the same rock and nearly fell. Judgment clattered to the ground an arm's length away from his grasp. Jacob looked at the blade as if he could will it back into Roth's hand. Then he felt the hot pain in his chest as Aries's sword plunged into Roth's heart. The burnt savage yanked the sword out, and as Roth struggled to stay on his feet, he took his massive skull-shaped shield and bashed it into the old man. Roth went limp and crumpled as he went sprawling across the cold marble.

Jacob felt sick when Roth joined the thick graveyard of broken quartz. So much failure—he was hopelessly outnumbered now. He might have been able to do something if he had not been so protective, but that time was come and gone. Now he knew he had lost this game, and once Aries had dealt with him, he would be able to demand anything he wished. This was too much, and the power inside him was burning to get out. Jacob's mind began running through all the horrible things the demon might make him do. Aries stepped into the newly claimed square and prepared for his next move. Jacob felt his empty eyes appraising his queen. He feared the demon would try to attack her. With the power given to her rank, Emily could probably take him, but he didn't want to find out; he cared for her too much to put her in harm's way.

You cannot both keep her close and out of the reach of the darkness, the whisper sneered again. The demon knew what was in his heart. If he got any ideas he could turn Jacob against her if he lost. He would kill himself before letting that happen. Jacob scowled at the demon, and his anger and rage boiled as Aries continued to contemplate his next move. All of his feeling welled up, and he felt the demon in him come to life and energy ripple through the board. This caught Aries's attention, and he took his sight off the queen and examined the air curiously as if trying to figure out where the pulse of energy originated.

Snapping back into focus, Aries set up to attack his father again. Jacob detested his persistence. There was nowhere safe to move his father; he was trapped on a diagonal that forced him to face the queen. Against most of the pieces he would have a fair chance, possibly even an upper hand, but no man could go toe-to-toe with a demon. Jacob swallowed nervously and trembled as he took his father and marched against Aries. He might as well end it now. If he ran the demon's next move would just be to catch him. Jacob's demon reeled from his choice, and Jacob was made physically sick.

Aries watched as Drake approached him. The flames of his eyes were shadowed by cold malice that repelled Jacob's courage and incited fear in his heart. He focused, concentrating hard. There was only one known way to get rid of a demon. This wasn't real though; this thing could be beaten. He just needed to find a way. He flipped through his old tattered notebook, looking for something that would help him. Drake mumbled words that would open a one-way portal to Hell. Lesser spirits would be caught in it, but for stronger ones he would have to push them in. Jacob had an idea.

Drake walked forward slowly and continued to mutter the incantation. When he stepped into Aries's square, the demon lunged at him with hellish force. Drake finished the inscription, and the portal exploded between them. Aries froze and did not complete his attack, staying his hand just inches away from the surface of the fiery vortex. The air between them crackled with heat and energy that crossed the barriers between the two places. Looking through Drake's eyes, he could see the distorted figure of the demon through the reddish glowing film of rippling energy. Aries curled back what was left of his lips and snarled though his nasty teeth and his open nasal cavity. He moved around the swirling portal, and Drake backed up.

He tried another spell that might push him backward into the inferno, but it didn't work. The demon raised its blade, and it came down violently. Drake threw up his arms in vain as the blade descended. He turned to quartz and broke, and the portal he had summoned withered and died. The pain in Jacob's heart was much greater than the pain from the blow. He stumbled to the ground and felt as if he could sink into the tiles and give up. What was the point anymore? He had lost everything in this one game. The raging demon in his heart refused to let him. It was not angry or vengeful, but it forced him off the tiles and muted his feelings so that he could see the game, so he could fight this war.

Aries's next move was to step into a position that attacked Jacob in such a way that if he moved it would expose Emily. Jacob contemplated his options. He summoned enough courage to step toward the queen instead of away from her. Then Aries moved the king a step closer. Jacob had two squares to go before he would be at the black queen. He pushed one more. Adramelech took another step; he was only one step away from Emily. Jacob had one chance. He could make one more move and defeat the black queen or he could turn back and try to rescue Emily. There was nowhere safe to move Emily, and if he took the time to take her away Aries would also slip away. This is exactly what the demon wanted.

Strategically, it was an even trade, but there was nothing Jacob would ever trade for Emily, and his deficit was so great at this point it didn't matter. This wasn't real. Then why did he feel like it was so real? He felt connections to each character like he felt to the real people. In his mind he knew they were just stone, but his heart did not understand the difference. Jacob could not bring himself to let go. He turned and began to walk back to his queen. The demon, the very same one that had picked him up a moment ago, let out a frustrated moan that Jacob felt shake his soul.

The black king took the next step and closed the gap between them. Suddenly Jacob felt stupid for not moving Emily to his side on his last turn. He might have bought some time if he had thought of that. However, his mind had been so one-tracked on saving her and getting to her side, he never thought of moving her to his. He took his last step and stood beside her. Now Emily was between the two kings. In a normal game this would have been a good position for the white pieces. But this wasn't a normal game.

Adramelech was not intimidated by Jacob in the least, and he stepped into Emily's square without hesitation. With slow deliberation Emily pulled Jade from her sheath. Her hands did not possess skill, but Jacob knew very well how to handle the blade. Emily was in his hands, and so that meant Jade was also. He could feel the terror in the girl's heart, but she wasn't panicking. Emily was confident simply because Jacob was beside her. In real life that would mean something, but here there was nothing he could really do to help her. He knew it was lost and his demon begged him to withdraw, but he could not let her die.

Jacob was more afraid than she was. He wanted to step between them and fight for her, but his feet were carved stone. In the moments of a fight, he could feel the characters' true feelings, and right now he was being overwhelmed by Emily's emotions. Her heart quickened and adrenaline flared as she came face-to-face with things she used to believe were only fairy tales. Though she had always wanted to believe in angels and demons, her mind was struggling on accepting that it was this real. Through all her confusion Jacob could distinctly read her emotions. She loved him. She trusted him completely. Even in the face of the Arch demon, Adramelech, she did not doubt him. He hoped he would not disappoint her.

As the flowing red blade of the demon ripped to life, Jacob's heart screamed. There was nothing he could do to protect his queen. In a normal game, she would be the first and last line of defense, but here in this game Jacob would have given the victory just to ensure she wasn't harmed. Adramelech fanned out his imperial robe of feathers in his war display and began the fight. Jacob gripped Jade tightly with Emily's delicate hands and moved to block. The enchanted sword met with the molten blade, and fire spewed from the point that the two collided. Jacob pushed against the blade of the demon and slid down, taking a desperate swing at his legs.

With a little luck, he managed to catch the demon's leg. The wound was minor, grazing the flesh just above the hoof.

Adramelech stomped in anger, and Jacob moved Emily back from the explosive wrath. This had been the same mistake he had made with Sarah. The demon lashed out, and the molten sword extended into a whip and wrapped around Emily's sword hand. She struggled as the blade scorched and seared her arm and then she dropped the magic blade. Jacob felt the intense pain rip though his arm as if he had been in Emily's place. Then he felt the jerk as Adramelech pulled Emily back to him. The force popped her shoulder out of its socket, and Jacob felt his own muscles rip. Emily sprawled on the floor and slid to the feet of the demon. The red-hot whip recoiled and reformed into a sword, and the demon executed her as she curled into a ball and clung to her burning arm.

Flames ripped through Jacob's body. The pain caused by this evil blade tore him apart. And to think Emily had felt that pain. His heart wrenched as she turned into quartz and cracked into pieces. He had failed her, too. Jacob wanted to cry—he was crying. The king, made in his likeness, was weeping.

Then Jacob realized he was in motion, Adramelech was moving against him. He looked at Aries and saw the black queen still stone silent and the realized the dark king was attacking him personally.

He moved. He only held the Light Shard, and it was not enough to face the demon. He scrambled out of the way of the first blow and then rolled as the whip cracked beside his face. There wasn't much time to think. He wasn't thinking clearly; the last image of Emily being executed tortured him with grief and filled him with burning, blinding rage. Out of the rage, his demon emerged with full force, and the tiles beneath Jacob grew hot and glowed red.

Jacob found the place Jade had fallen and picked her up. Now it was time to stand. As he turned to face the foe, he felt the heat of the whip. By the time he could see it, he was already on his back. He couldn't breathe—his lungs would not inflate. His leg felt as though it had been ripped off, but he could still feel it burning. He rolled over and tried to push himself up. His strength was now limitless, all he had to do was stand and face the demon. His inner spirit called to him, for each move he had made that it disagreed with, it now urged him to fight with confidence. That dangerous part of him was certain he could win this fight.

He looked up for one moment and saw the head of one of the white statues lying in front of him. It was the head of the white queen, in the exact likeness of Emily. Her eyes, though only stone, shot through his soul, and his strength was sapped by his grief. He dropped Jade and reached out to touch the face. His inner demon screamed to regain his attention, but it could not get through Jacob's emotions. The smell of the paper and ink surrounded him, and he drew the broken image to him and collapsed on it and began to cry. The demon tried to bring him back, but Jacob's emotions were so strong, the spirit could not overcome them.

This game was over. It didn't matter anymore; he had lost and there was no hope. Jacob just clung to the head of his queen in the last moments before the hot pain pierced his back. Flames shot down his spine, and he felt like he had just been thrown into a pit of fire. He yelled in agony. The scream of pain faded and died as his flesh became quartz. Then, as all the pieces before him, Jacob broke, and his body was scattered over the tiles.

CHAPTER 22

J acob returned to reality, he was sprawled in the center of the board wriggling from phantom pains and a broken heart. Everyone he cared about had just been destroyed. It didn't matter if it wasn't real; it was real to him. His blood boiled and he desired revenge. As he struggled to his feet, the booming voice of Aries cracked through the room. "The first test is over, but another I wish you to endure." The demon inside Jacob wanted to rip Aries's head from his shoulders, but another game would not accomplish that, he wanted to bring him out of the board and make him wish he had never been loosed from Hell.

"Curse you!" He yelled from behind his rage and tears. "What do you want from me? I played your game, and now you want another! Why should I enter another? Am I not already in your debt? Curse you!"

"One to whom my heart is attached has interceded on your behalf. Because she is the last thing that remains of me, I have obliged her. I, the war god, offer my mercy at her request; you will be given one chance at redemption at the risk of a greater debt. Double or nothing. If I win, you shall take my place as the master of this board, and I shall go free, for you are a male of the blood that has banished me." The voice was not as loud, almost as if he was trying whisper, trying to entice him.

"Why would she intercede for me?" Jacob asked confused.

"It is not my place to inquire," the demon snorted.

Jacob paused; his anger and rage wanted to fight, but he now had an awful fear of what could happen if he played again. If he refused the new challenge, he might get something as severe as Aries's retribution. But if he gave into his anger, he might have a chance not only at revenge, but to clean the slate. If lost, he would be double in debt to the demon and that could be a fate worse than death.

"Why this?" Jacob asked weakly.

"Because my mercy can be earned, but my forgiveness was poured out on my sons," Aries replied bitterly.

"And if I refuse?"

"Then I shall demand you to bring me what I desired from your mother," the demon said flatly.

Jacob remembered his mother had denied the challenge that Aries had offered her and had no idea what he could have wanted from her. "And what is that?" he asked.

"Blood!" Aries sneered. "The blood that was used to bind me here is close to her. The same that banished my shadow, in a female, may also bring back the angel who perished at the hands of my children."

He didn't understand the last part about the angel who perished, but he understood what Aries wanted from him. There was no chance he was going to harm his mother. Even if it meant he could end up trapped in the board, he knew this would haunt him forever if he stepped down now.

"Why her? I have the same blood." Jacob hadn't meant to offer himself in her place, but that didn't seem to add up.

"You cannot resurrect the angel! But if I claim victory, I shall have you both!"

His demon had fled from the board before, but now it drove him to fight. He weighed the risk, double or nothing. He wanted to flee, but he knew that there was no escaping the arm of Aries. He either had to accept his defeat now or reclaim his honor. Somehow his family had dealt with this thing before. He was somehow significant to this demon, and so was his mother. He flinched in anger; he would never sacrifice a life to save his own, especially not family. However, if he played this game he gambled both of their lives. But, he had no choice.

"I'll rip you apart!" Jacob screamed, "You will rue the day you were summoned to Earth, I swear it!"

"I already do, young Jacob," the demon replied almost remorseful.

As the words vibrated off the walls of the cavern, Jacob fell back into the board. A single white pawn had been pushed forward. Had he made a move already? No, he could feel it was still his turn. He looked to his left and saw a black queen standing beside him. It was Rain. Then Jacob realized that he was the black pieces. He quickly looked at the white pieces and noted that they were the same creatures that the black pieces had been the game before.

His pieces were different than the last time. Rain was the queen, and his grandfather and William were the bishops. Jacob didn't understand why the pieces had been changed or why Aries had chosen this set. The last set was pretty apparent after the first opening moves, but this one was different. Lucile and Malcolm were the black knights. Jacob was curiously surprised to find his rooks were dark men, Wraiths, clad in black armor and clutching massive claymore swords that had a phantom-like appearance. This game would be much different, and he didn't understand the setup.

Already he could feel the thoughts of the characters. They did not wait for him to act; they pressed in on him, and he could hear the voices in his mind. To his right, Rain whispered visions of his future, things he didn't understand: the dark things he had seen stretched out before him in blackness, and he felt urged to wander down the path. His curiosity piqued, but he remembered what he had found in her mind the last time and his drive to gain revenge was greater. He silenced the voice and focused; this was his game. The demon he carried with him became excited, and this time Jacob gave into it. He paid dearly for ignoring it the last time.

Further to his right, his mother and his grandfather heaped the weight of the world on his shoulders, the Chosen one, that's what he was—bred to be great, the first born of a line that had been orchestrated for great things. He had always wondered if the blood had been set up that way. Was this the truth or was Aries playing with his mind? Here, there was nothing to be certain of; it didn't matter anyway. The gravity of the things they had placed on him pressed in on him; things he had accepted and tried to forget burdened his mind. The detailed scrutiny he had been under all his life and all the expectations crushed him. Not one of them had the slightest doubt that he was the perfect Chosen one.

On the left side, Malcolm and William whispered behind his back of feelings of discontent, resentment, and anger so strong Jacob could smell it like a pungent dead marsh. They had been slighted, or at least they thought they had. Jacob was the fulfillment of that to them, the heir of a favored son. That wasn't fair; it wasn't Jacob's fault though he didn't ask for this. Now things began to become clear, he understood now why there was a divide in his family. He understood the past of these people as if he had been there with them now. So many memories flooded into his mind as if they were his own: the feeling of pride carried down from his grandfather to his mother and the feeling of rejection that permeated his twin brother's family.

Jacob sympathized with them; he had been given the full responsibility and honor that William and Malcolm had wished for Julie. She was to be the polished jewel that regained the family's equality to Henry and his clan, and Jacob had placed a curse on her, tainting their treasure. They hated him for the things his parents had done and for the things he had done. But wasn't this a testament to his character? He had come here today to free Julie. He had failed already, but he would not be here if he had not been fighting for his cousin. He had sacrificed some part of himself to this demon in vain to help her, and they still shunned him.

The Wraiths were hollow and empty. Only fire was inside them, they were golems at his disposal. They didn't expect things from him—they didn't care. To them, it wasn't a matter of his merit; they didn't think about his authority, where it came from, or his failures. They just followed orders. Jacob would have rather had more pieces like them instead of having so many people he knew surround him and to know their honest opinions and to have to listen to their evaluations of his life. He tried to shove it all out of his mind and ordered Malcolm over the pawn in front of him. The knight moved, but not without resentment.

The opposite white knight copied the move. All the voices flipped a switch inside Jacob, and he became callous to everyone's feelings. The demon inside him sensed this and drove a stake into the heart of Jacob's emotions that enabled him to quit feeling. Rain's pull on his mind was severed, the words of praise became empty to his ears, and he became indifferent to the opinions of those who hated him. This was his game to win, and he didn't care what division was between him, his pieces, or anyone else. It didn't matter anymore. He might not be able to force the families to cooperate outside, but here these pieces answered to him. He pushed his pawn forward.

On the other side, a white bishop stepped into the field under the protection of the knight. Aries was following his aggressive style. Jacob moved William in a similar fashion, but he did not have the support of a knight like Aries had set up. That didn't matter; support in this game was overcome by firepower, and all of his pieces were battle ready. The white pawn that had been pushed forward to begin with stepped forward again. No games this time, Jacob was going for business. He pushed Rain out into the board to meet the Wraith mocking the white garb of a bishop. Aries pushed his queen to back up the bishop.

Jacob held off on the capture; he worked several moves to secure the center portion of the board. Aries worked the same. Jacob could sense the demon had recognized the change in Jacob's mind. Aries understood the mind games no longer affected him, and they settled in for what would be a quick, climactic, and decisive ending to a very slow-starting game. It must have taken hours, but Jacob had all of his pieces out. He had placed his two rooks together, most of the pawns were gone, William and Lucile had been sacrificed for a bishop and a rook from the opposing side, so Jacob had a slight advantage.

Now it was time for the real war. It was Aries's turn, and Jacob could feel that the demon had reached the same conclusion. The last white rook, the white Wraith with a long halberd stepped up to Henry. Jacob seized his bishop, not out of respect and love for his grandfather but in cold anger; he was going to rip Aries apart. His newfound strength from the demon flooded into the bishop with him. The rook came down on him with the great axe, and Henry pulled out a blue sword Jacob had never seen before. It sparked with light and the air tingled with electric pulses.

The halberd clashed on the blade, and arcs of electricity danced around them. Henry slid the blade down, turned and spun around, allowing the great halberd to clash on the tiles. He brought the blade around and slashed the Wraith across the chest. Burns from the electric charge marred the white armor, and fire spat from the wound. It wasn't a kill stroke; it was meant to inflict pain. Jacob guided it, and his demon demanded it. The Wraith choked up on the handle of his weapon and began to wield it like a staff with a blade on one end. He struck with the blunt end, and it was blocked with ease. Then the bladed end came for a low blow, also blocked, but this created a hole in Henry's defense that the Wraith exploited.

The Wraith agreed with the force Henry applied to guide the heavy-bladed end down and brought the blunt end straight down on Henry. The man staggered back but recovered. Jacob felt the pain, but it gave him a dark satisfaction. He lunged in, and the Wraith blocked by raising the staff. Henry slipped under the shaft of the weapon and kicked the monster in the knee, breaking the bones beneath the armor. The Wraith came down to the ground from the pain inflicted. Before he killed him, he circled the fallen Wraith. He moved in a circle with a taunting posture as if he wanted the Wraith to rise up and continue the fight. Satisfied he was not getting any more fight from him, he stepped around behind him and jammed the sword into the creature's back just below his neck. He ran it through, and it pierced through the monster's chest. Electric blue sparks mingled with the bleeding flames shot from both wounds.

It was still Aries's turn, and he moved a knight to attack Malcolm. The two horsemen erupted into battle. Jacob's demon wanted to abstain from this fight, but Jacob flung himself into the knight. Both held two blades, and they charged at one another. The blades danced off each other, and so they charged again. Jacob stopped his charge at the last moment and caused the horse to rear back on his haunches. The rider urged the horse down, and the beast kicked the Wraith and knocked him from his mount. Jacob waited for him to stand and then charged to attack him. The Wraith recovered quickly and ducked underneath the attack, cutting the legs out from under Malcolm's horse.

The horse landed hard and flipped, breaking its neck and throwing the rider across the cold hard floor. Malcolm stood up and ran to meet the foe. The cold steel clanged together with a rhythm that the warriors danced to. Rubble of pawns littered the floor around them, and each step they made had to be perfect: one counter to the opponent's step and another to avoid the stepping on rubble, one blade to block and the other to thrust. Jacob let the rhythm of the fight soak into him and meld with the anger he had. His demon had been reluctant to join this fight, but it swayed to the beat of the swords clashing as if it was lulled by war. The fight had become a dance to the methodical beat of a war drum. Jacob added an extra beat to the music and slashed the Wraith's thigh. Then he stepped back and waited for the Wraith to come back at him.

The dark creature in white armor lunged as if the wound had not bothered him, and the rhythm resumed. Jacob twisted it, and made it his own. He commanded the fight and stabbed the Wraith in the shoulder. He did not finish the kill but stepped back. This was his game. He had made it so, and he would cut this Wraith down one small piece at a time, Aries wouldn't dare cross paths with him again after this. The Wraith began again, and Jacob jumped back into the rhythm. He found that place where there was room for something else and pushed both of the Wraith's blades out of the way, thrusting with both of his swords at the creature and grazing both of his sides. The Wraith had prepared for a counter, however.

Jacob was caught off guard when the creature repelled both of his blades outward. The Wraith had anticipated this; no, he had led him into this position. Jacob had not been directing the music; he had been playing the tune. The white Wraith stepped forward and crossed his blades under Malcolm's chin and scissored his neck between them. Jacob felt the dizzying effect of the blood rushing out of his brain as Malcolm collapsed and his scattered pieces joined the graveyard. It took a moment for Jacob to realize what had happened. He realized his mistake. He had passed up two opportunities to kill the Wraith just because he wanted to inflict pain. How had he fallen into that trap? In this game, pain did not matter. What mattered was the king—here on this board the king was the only piece that mattered; all of the other pieces were pawns. His strategy was still intact. Aries had won that fight, but it had not done any real damage to his plan.

Aries's Wraith-knight now stood in the line of his two rooks, which was perfectly fine with him. On the other side of the knight was the demon-queen, and he was itching to bring Aries to his knees in a fight. The knight also had the opportunity to attack Henry and finish what the last opponent failed. It didn't matter what the demon chose; Jacob had his plan worked out. Aries willed the knight against Henry; the horse walked back to its rider, and he remounted it. Jacob thought about defending. He had a good chance of winning, but if he didn't defend, he would have the opportunity to bring down the queen, and he desired that so much more. The demon in him agreed, and for once Jacob yielded the fight. Henry bowed to the opponent and knelt down. The white knight paused to give Jacob one last chance to rethink his decision, and then he trotted up next to him and executed him.

Jacob wasted no time, it was his turn now, and Aries had set it up for him. He charged the queen with the first of his Wraiths, and the energy of his own demon spurred him on. Aries drew his flaming sword and readied his cracked shield; the Wraith gripped the phantom blade and thundered into battle. Aries stepped back and let the evil blade of the Wraith clatter against his shield. Then he dropped the shield and thrust his fiery sword at Jacob. Jacob sidestepped the blow and attacked again. They exchanged a flurry of blows, and Jacob found his opening. He lunged in and stabbed the demon in the abdomen. It was not fatal, but it would hurt. Jacob had to be careful not to slip back into the mindset of vengeance and pain, but that was the only way to win against a queen on this board.

Before he had attacked, he was counting on losing this rook. And even if the second one succeeded, he was still counting on losing him because Aries was only one square away from Adramelech. Without flinching, Aries pounded the Wraith with his large shield and sent him stumbling back. Jacob almost lost his sword as he struggled to keep his balance. By the time he looked up, the massive skull-shaped shield smacked him again and was quickly followed by the flaming blade in his other hand. It cut and burned through his armor and left a smoldering scar where it sliced his flesh. The Wraith toppled backward and thundered to the ground. The helmet that had hid the Wraith's features rolled off and revealed a human face—his father's.

Jacob was confused, but he didn't have time to think. He had blocked out Aries's mind games, and the surprise could not set in. Aries raised his foul sword to impale his father. Jacob didn't try to stop it, he reached up and stabbed the demon in the shoulder of his shield arm with the phantom sword just as the fiery blade punctured his heart.

Jacob felt the blow, and his chest burned, but it did not affect him anymore. With his new power surging in his blood, he had become accustomed to the pain and callous to the emotions. The Wraith with his father's face crumbled and broke and without hesitation. Jacob marched the second rook straight for Aries. As the second Wraith neared Aries, raised his shield, and readied to defend, it was clear that Jacob had wounded the beast. His movements were slowed just a little, and he could tell that the shield was becoming a burden to the creature. Perfect.

He hastened the second Wraith and sprinted with his sword raised at the enemy. The power of the demon housed in his body pulsed as his adrenaline spiked. Just before he got in striking distance, he kicked his legs out from under himself and slid on the tiles beside the white Demon. Aries dropped his sword against the tiles, barely missing the Wraith's neck. As Jacob slid past, he dragged the phantom blade over Aries's thigh and severed the muscles that allowed him to stand. The Demon fell to his knees. In one motion, Jacob stopped abruptly and raised himself to his feet, turned, and brought the sword down to execute the fallen Demondemon. Aries fell forward from the blow, and as he collapsed on the tiles he cracked and scattered.

It was still Jacob's turn. He looked at Adramelech, contemplating if he should try it. He was itching to get at the Demon's throat, but what he really wanted was to personally destroy him. It would be best to wait and let both of the kings fight to determine the game. Jacob left the rook beside the white king and took Rain. There were a few things he wanted to take care of first. He guided Rain to the first order of business: the last white bishop. He set her beside him and then yielded the board to his opponent. Aries took the king and turned to the rook. Jacob debated quickly whether or not to fight. If he really wanted to fight, he would have attacked on his previous turn. He let it slide. This time his demon urged him to defend, but Jacob wanted to bring down the Demon himself.

Adramelech flared his royal feathers. Even with his white armor on and his robe of peacock feathers, he still looked menacingly evil. He strode to the Wraith and drew the whip. He lashed out angrily and wrapped the flaming chain around the Wraith's neck. Jacob could feel the burn, but he didn't resist. Then Adramelech yanked the cord and brought the Wraith to his feet. Before he killed the creature, he picked it up with his free hand and removed its helmet to show Jacob who was underneath the mask. It was Sarah. Jacob didn't know if this was supposed to symbolize something or if it was more mind games, but he tried not to think about it. The whip returned to the form of a blade and jabbed through Sarah's sternum, engulfing her torso in flames. The demon dropped her, and her pieces scattered as she crashed to the floor.

Jacob shrugged it off and turned Rain toward the bishop. He summoned the repulsion spell he had used in the previous game. Rain's powers were much more powerful as his queen than as his bishop. The blueish liquid-like energy arched from her fingers and impacted the bishop. There was the sound of a large muffled explosion and a large shock wave and the white bishop lifted and flew across the field as if it were nothing. The Wraith smashed into an invisible barrier at the edge of the board and exploded.

As the chunks of white quartz rained down, Aries took one of his knights and positioned it to attack one of Jacob's pawns. Jacob studied the board for a moment and then formulated a plan. His king was already in the center of the board, so he pushed him forward. He was coming for Adramelech. The pawn vanished, and he pushed his king forward again. There was one square between them. The knight moved to attack Rain. Jacob moved next to the white king. Aries pulled Adramelech away, the first nonaggressive thing Jacob had seen him do. Jacob's demon rejoiced.

He followed, and the demon moved away again. Then he brought Rain down the board to help convince him. He put her in a spot where, on the next move, he could place her between the two kings. Aries picked up his second knight and placed him in the square that Jacob intended to occupy. Undaunted, Jacob moved Rain against the knight. He was surprised that Aries decided to fight this time. His demon was brimming with laughter. The Wraith charged out to meet Rain. Jacob flipped through the book of spells and found the spell to cast ice. The air around the board snapped to a cold chill and a bolt of ice hurled at the knight and froze both knight and steed. With a loud, progressive crackling sound, a thick frost raced across the floor causing small fissures in the quartz and marble. The horse and rider toppled over, and their frigid, brittle bodies were dashed against frozen the marble.

It was still Jacob's turn. Aries had planned it that way, letting his queen defeat the knight so that Jacob would have to attack Adramelech. But Jacob didn't want to. He stood for a moment and noticed the breath of Rain's statue was thick in the frosty air. The only piece he wanted to pit against that demon was himself. So instead of sending Rain, he moved a pawn. Aries's next move was to challenge Rain. There was a good chance he could fight and even win, but if he lost, Adramelech could run away again. He had him right where he wanted right now and so he did not defend against the attack.

Adramelech stood in front of Rain and waited. Aries was hesitating, not convinced Jacob had forfeited his chance to defend. Once Aries was sure he had handed over this fight, Jacob felt the board shutter from the demon's rage. The god of war was not happy that he had been lured into such a trap. The demon, Adramelech, pulled out the fiery whip and cracked it malevolently with the explosive rage Aries now fostered. Then he slung it with expert skill and precise aim. Rain was still a wrought iron statue and the whip severed the metal splitting the image in half laterally. The two halves screeched together as they slid apart and then crumbled as they fell to the ground.

Adramelech now stood before Jacob. Jacob could feel the wrath of Aries's burning gaze from all around him, but he didn't care. His own burning power flared, and his demon empowered him to fight. All this time that demon had played mind games with him, trying to govern how he played. Now he was insulted that Jacob had managed to do the same to him. It may have been late in the game, but Jacob had finally learned how to play this game, and he was about to win. Jacob stepped forward, and Adramelech flared his feathers in his war display. This time Jacob held Jade and the Light Shard. He stood before the demon-king and initiated the fight. The molten sword flared out to stop his attacks, but Jacob was pushing the beast back.

Jacob brought a heavy overhead blow at his opponent, and the demon blocked it and locked blades with him. Jacob could feel the intense heat form the sword burning the air around him. Adramelech turned quickly and fanned Jacob with his wide spread robe of bright colored feathers. Once Jacob could see again the flaming whip was already on its way. He lifted his left hand and let the whip wrap around it. The Light Shard was thrown from his grip. It burned his arm and his entire body. Jacob fell to his knees from the pain. He had failed again. *No!* The demon in him yelled.

Anger welled up in him, anger at the demon and himself. And fear—how long would he wait in silence? What would stop Aries from taking the blood he desired? So much raced through his mind so fast he could not even think about the battle at hand. Then suddenly he felt the strength of his inner demon erupt with all the fury of Hell. All other thoughts were snuffed out, and he stood up and cast off the pain and the fear. The expression on Adramelech's face was of pure surprise, and he tried to pull the whip away to try again. But Jacob caught the whip. It seared his palm but he held on tight. Aries tried to jerk him, but the demon strength Jacob now had didn't budge.

Jacob wrapped the whip around his arm further and stepped forward to make slack. He could smell his flesh burning and the searing pain was immense, but his demon blood gave him the strength to push through it. Adramelech kept trying to toss him and jerk the whip free, but Jacob refused to release it. Jacob repeated this motion and wound the whip around his arm until he was close enough to the Demon to strike. He plunged Jade into the creature's chest and twisted the blade while the demon bellowed in pain. Then he ripped it out and raised the enchanted blade high and chopped off the arm that held the whip. The arm became quartz and smashed against the tile. Now without a weapon, the great Demon stepped back.

Jacob grabbed the handle of the whip, and it uncoiled from his arm as if he had commanded it to. With a glare of satisfaction, Jacob lashed out with the whip and struck the monster on the side of his torso, burning his pure white armor and throwing him to the ground. Jacob snapped the whip back and walked coolly over to the Demon. The glowing whip trailed behind him as he approached. Jacob stood over the body; the white armor and royal robe of feathers were now singed and stained with red blood. The whip formed into a blade, and Jacob crossed it over Jade and placed the "v" under the demon's chin. He paused for just a moment to let his satisfaction set in and to let Aries grasp the concept of defeat and then he ended the game.

The glowing red sword faded and vanished, and the crumbled pieces rose and reformed. But they did not form in the shapes they had been during the game; instead they became the normal shapes they had been originally. Jacob looked about as the veil around the board was lifted and saw Rain and Lucile and Sarah and Dom and Julie standing beside the board, all with marveling expressions across their faces. Even while all the debris was still floating through the air and reconstructing the broken statues, Jacob turned to walk toward them. He picked up his leg and suddenly felt all the fatigue set in. He collapsed on the cold tile. His mind was numb, and his body was riddled with the phantom pains of dozens of mortal wounds and the stress of long hours of fighting. The strength that his demon had given him flushed from his blood, and he felt cold. The air above him was alive with the swirling chunks of pawns and fallen warriors.

His mother and Rain jumped up the stairs, and as they stepped on the board Aries voice boomed forth, "Jacob!" The board bellowed. "The trials are both complete; you have achieved victory after defeat." Rain froze as the intimidating voice rolled through the cavern, but Lucile darted to his side.

Jacob pushed himself up to his knees, "Trials?" he echoed, his lips were heavily parched and the words barely made it out of his dry throat. "What was this for?"

"I have tested your heart. Truly you are worthy of your status," Aries answered.

Sarah and Dom cautiously stepped up to the board behind Rain. Rain stepped closer warily and then assured herself there was no danger. She hurried underneath the flying quartz and wrought iron chunks to Jacob. She reached his side and helped Lucile get him to his feet.

"I have forfeit my demand of you, but still I ask, one champion to another, that you guard the life of the one who interceded for you," Aries said softer, his rage subsided. "My protection has been withdrawn, but my heart still feels for my child."

"What does that mean?" Jacob yelled. He waited a moment and did not receive a response, "What does that mean!" Again only silence met his call. Rain tugged on him, urging that he move. Jacob wrenched free from her grip and nearly collapsed again. All of his extremities were like numb weights holding him down, and he lacked the strength to command them. "Answer me!" he shouted with dry words as he rolled to his back.

"Are you the one to release the Fallen from their fathers?" Aries demanded, "Would you seize my children from my hand?"

Anger surged in Jacob's blood as he staggered to his feet, "Not even the god of war can stand between me and my kin!" he spat back.

The remains of the pieces came to rest, and the reconstruction of the board was complete. Then Aries's voice rumbled like thunder over the board, "So shall it be, Jacob, the Chosen."

"Explain these things!" Jacob commanded as best he could.

"Our score is even; I will not yield for I am not beaten!" Aries yelled back.

Rain grabbed Jacob's arm again as he began to falter, and Lucile secured his other side and they forced him to stand. "Jacob, you need to rest; you've been without food or drink over two days." His mother urged. Then Rain turned her golden eyes back to where she had come from, "Julie, go get some water!"

"Two days?" Jacob gasped, going completely limp on the shoulders of his mother and Rain.

"Yes, Jacob," Rain answered, "It was just past midnight Saturday when you walked up there, and it's Monday now. The sun has been up for six hours."

"Sun up?" Jacob asked, "School?"

"No, Jacob! Don't even think about it," Lucile insisted, "You're not going today. It's half way over anyway. You won't be going tomorrow, either; you need to rest."

Jacob was too tired to argue, and that meant she was right. He felt all the bruises and broken bones, the stab wounds, and the burn scars still throbbing in his body. He was famished and thirsty and too weak to stand on his own.

"Did you see?" he murmured as he looked up with his tired expression and dim eyes at Rain, "The pieces on the board, they were like you."

"We could not see the game as you saw it. The tricks Aries plays are illusions."

They more or less carried him down the steps. Jacob looked up as they reached the bottom and saw Julie coming back with a clay pitcher of water. She handed a small wooden cup to Rain and then filled it with the pitcher herself. Rain offered it to Jacob, and he took it and drank. Sarah held him up as he turned the cup back to get all the water out of it. His throat was so dry that the water burned at first as it went down. As his throat became wet again, it glided down smooth, and he gulped the rest of the cup. Finished, he tried to extend the cup for a refill, but he dropped it. He ignored the cup clattering on the ground and reached for the pitcher. Julie gently offered it to him but did not let go of the clay jar.

Jacob turned it up and drank some of the water; most of it went around his mouth and splashed on his shoulders, but he really didn't care—he was just tired and thirsty. The water was warm, but to a dry body it was the sweetest taste he had ever experienced. He paused to gasp for air and then continued to drink until there was no water in the pitcher. He pushed the jar away, and Julie took it back.

"Let him sit down a minute." Dom said, "He's been standing for days."

Sarah nodded and guided Jacob down to the stair he had just stepped down from. Jacob found it not only comfortable, but the feeling of the cold stone relaxed him.

"Son, don't exert yourself. Where does it hurt?"

He drew a few breaths; his mouth still felt dry. "More water," he said and slumped back against the stair behind him. It hurt everywhere. He couldn't even talk about it; it hurt so bad.

Julie hurried away to refill the pitcher, and Jacob didn't remember much else.

CHAPTER 23

J acob woke up late that night still in the library; a bed had been made for him in the lower study. His fatigue was less, but his body still ached. The room seemed to spin as he looked around trying to determine if he was really awake or still dreaming. Rain was sitting at her desk, studying the old books. She looked up when she saw him stir, "How do you feel?" she asked in a genuine, caring way and rose from her seat.

Jacob, still in a daze, scanned the room. His throat wasn't dry anymore, but he still felt like he had been hit by a train. "Better, I suppose," he replied, "I'm terribly hungry."

Rain walked to where the furnace was, "Sarah fixed some soup before she left; it is quite good."

"Where did she go?" Jacob asked.

"Sarah and Dom left just an hour ago; they all needed rest," she answered as she ladled some of the soup into a bowl. "We thought it best not to move you far so we put you here, and we've been waiting for you to recover."

"How long was I out?" Jacob mumbled and rubbed his palm against the side of his head, "and why am I still here?"

"Your mother did not wish to move you. We have all the ingredients for remedies here. You were out a long time, Jacob. It's late at night now," Rain replied.

With slow, achy movements, he sat up and tested his feet against the ground. Satisfied he would be able to walk, he stood up and ventured to the nearest table with shaky steps. "We all stayed here with you. None of us have slept since your game started. I told the children to go rest and I would watch you. Had I known you were about to wake, I would have let them stay."

Jacob thought "children" was an odd word to choose; he wasn't far from it, and to Rain, everyone was a child. She walked over with the soup, placed it before him, and then took the seat beside him.

"Thanks," Jacob said and took the spoon and stirred it around. He looked up at Rain; she didn't look tired at all; her golden eyes still burned with vigor, and her white-blond hair was tinged with the faintest highlights of sky blue and copper

219

that you could barely notice. But he knew that even Rain had to become tired eventually; somewhere under that youthful, ever-young gaze, there was a person just a frail as any other. "I think I'll be okay now; you should probably get some sleep also."

She smiled, "My energy comes from other means. Sleep is something I do to pass time in the dark hours of the day."

Jacob nodded, remembering the day he had seen her standing barefoot in the snow outside the castle, "Right, the Sun People magic," he remarked and then tested the soup. It wasn't too hot, so he ate. If he hadn't known any different, he would have guessed Lucile had made it. Everything she cooked was amazing. He didn't know that Sarah had acquired the same skills. He would not have cared at the moment, his body had been starved and beat, and it ached for the nourishment. It was thick and heavy with vegetables and spiced meat. He was so hungry he didn't really focus on what was in the soup and ate it quickly.

"Would you like more?" Rain asked as he set his spoon down.

Jacob nodded, "Please."

Rain took the bowl and walked back to the furnace. As she was up, Lucile entered the room. Jacob smiled to see his mother, and she quickly noticed he was awake.

"Jacob, are you alright?" she said and hurried to his table.

"A little sore," Jacob answered.

"You're so pale," she remarked and hugged him, "How do you feel?"

Jacob returned her embrace with tired weak arms, "Tired, beaten, and hungry," he replied.

Rain placed the bowl back on the table, "Then eat more."

Lucile let him go and smiled at Rain, "We must have pulled out every remedy we could think of."

"Indeed we did." Rain replied, "It has been a long time since we worked together. Working with Jacob has been just as much of a privilege."

Jacob remembered what he had learned about her during the game. He wondered if that was real, whether she really did feel that way about him or if Aries had put that there just to play games with him. Could it have been Aries manifesting some hidden desire within him? No, he was pretty sure the idea didn't come from him. That left the first two options: it was either just as real as the girl standing in front of him or Aries just wanted to mess with his mind.

"He is quite special." Lucile remarked, "He's so strong for a lad his age, and I'm very proud of him. He is the first one in our line for nine generations to have only one parent from the fallen lineage, and he still has powers beyond what most of us only hope for." She smiled at him and placed a hand on his shoulder, "And you've got the heart of your father, chasing demons around like that. Dom said you fought him for two days?"

For some reason, he just didn't like it when anyone talked big about him. He just nodded and ate the soup.

"It was longer than that," Rain said, "Nearly sixty hours. I do believe that is the longest time any one person has ever fought the board."

"It had to be done," Jacob said as if it were no big deal. "I had to try, Julie was counting on me." He placed the spoon down in the half empty bowl and looked up at his mother, "She needed me, and I failed."

"No, Jacob, you had a choice and a chance. You risked your life to do something for her. The demon isn't a simple foe; it's not your fault," Lucile tried to explain.

Jacob shook his head, "No, it is my fault. Had I not been so angry at her when she challenged me, I might not have cursed her." He turned his gaze down and flexed his left hand. It still felt burnt and flaky from the flaming whip. "If I had not cursed her, there would have been no need to go back."

Rain took the seat beside him and picked up his hand. At first, it felt sensitive like it would if it were really burned, but then her touch began to make it feel restored. "Jacob, I know the voice in your head. You would have found a reason to go back. Aries wanted you, and he would never stop calling you. He would have pursued you to the point of death to convince you to give in."

Jacob's hand felt better; all the pain in his arm melted away. He wanted to connect with her and see if the feeling would cover his entire body, and maybe poke around in the darkness to see if what he had found during the game was true or if there was something different in the depths of her mind. But if she delved into his recent memories, she might find that as well. Then whether or not it was the truth, she could infer the wrong message.

"I still failed," Jacob muttered, "What happened was my fault, and I couldn't fix it."

"Okay, son, don't beat yourself up," Lucile said, "Aries has done enough of that for you, I'm sure. You tried, and you tried for the right reasons. I tell you not one person in Julie's family would have done the same for you. And I can't say I would have attempted what you did, either. They didn't deserve it, but you gave them a chance."

"Do you know what it's like to have a demon in your head?" Jacob asked, "To hear it whisper in the silence and to see it in your dreams?"

Lucile blinked and her face grew sad. She shook her head "no." Rain squeezed his hand, and he felt the prick to merge their minds; she wanted to understand, the way he had let her understand his fear of Adramelech and for his father. But Jacob had things inside him now that he didn't want her to see. He gently pushed away with his mind and then recoiled his hand.

"I know what it's like," Jacob continued, "Julie has that thing in her head now, and it would not be this way if I had not made her authority equal to mine. I've had the itching in my ear, and Aries has haunted my dreams. Adramelech, too. And now Julie hears the voice. It's an incessant buzzing: a whisper, a call that taunts you. It pricks at your fear and eats slowly at your soul. I can't let her endure that."

Lucile straightened her posture. "Drake has told me what is to become of this demon." She began, "It would seem that destroying him would free Julie. I'm sure you will succeed; just be patient."

"I don't want Dad to go." Jacob said, "There must be a better way."

"Jacob, it is already cleared for him to use our gateways to get to the site. You are to guide him through. He has no reservation and no regrets. I knew this day would come when I married him, and I knew this would be his fate." Lucile replied, "It will be alright; this is what he was born to do. I'll miss him as much as you, but I have long known this day would come."

Jacob didn't understand how she could be so at peace. "I know I can make a better way."

Lucile smiled and touched her hand to his cheek, "There is only one way. I have looked a long time for another means since I met your father; no such means exists." She walked around him and took the seat on his other side.

"Why does this have to be my limit?" Jacob asked, "I've been chosen to redeem our race, Mom. Shouldn't I be able to do this if I really am supposed to be the savior of our people?"

Lucile paused for a moment looking for something to say. Her lips quivered as she thought of Drake surviving and then living to be old with her. She almost came to tears from the fantasy, but she shoved them down, "I wish it were so, Jacob." Then she got up and gently pulled his arm, "Come home and rest. You shouldn't be burdened by these things after what you've just been through."

Pain riddled his body as he stood. The last time, it had taken weeks for the phantom wounds to heal. He hoped it wouldn't be so long this time, but he was doubtful.

Rain stood up also, "Yes, you should get more rest."

"I certainly feel like it," Jacob replied, "Thanks, Rain."

Rain hugged him gently, being careful not to agitate any of the pains in his body, "I hope you feel better soon."

It was good that Jacob could teleport because he couldn't possibly travel the distance. When he got home, he went straight to bed. Even though he had already slept the last twelve hours, his body was eager to rest again. He couldn't remember the last time he slept without dreaming of Aries. It was nice to be done with him. But in the back of his mind, he was still dealing with the deaths of his family and Emily. He knew it was just a game the demon had played with him, but it just felt too real. Even though he had seen most of the people who had been in the game, he still wasn't going to be at ease until he saw Emily. No, he would not be at ease until he knew she was safe, and he was beginning to fear that meant until she was far, far away from him. He had unleashed something when he faced Aries, something extremely powerful. It was not brimming in his blood right now, but he could feel its presence, poised and waiting. It was strong enough to defeat Aries at his own game, and that frightened Jacob.

Tossing and turning with new nightmares Jacob began to fear he'd never really be done with the demon. He might have defeated him, but the scars were still on his mind. The morning came, and Jacob rose against the protests of the aches and pains. He ate breakfast like it was his last meal. His body was still drained, and he needed to eat. Against the advice of his mother and siblings, he readied himself and went to school. He might be beat, but the world wouldn't stop turning just for him. He needed to go. None of your teachers really care if you miss a day here or there when you've got the highest grade in the class, so there was never any question about why he was absent.

The first thing he did was find Emily. The last time he missed a day, she had been worried about him, and he wanted to make sure she was all right. Images still flashed in his mind of her reeling in pain under Adramelech's cape of feathers. He knew it was only an image created to play with his mind, but it had worked. That trick went deep into his heart. He found her just about to go to her first class, and he stopped her. Emily turned around and smiled when she saw him. Jacob hugged her tight, still unable to get over how he had seen her die. It was horrible to have seen that, and he wanted to never let anything dangerous ever happen to her, real or fiction.

She hugged him just as tight, "Welcome back." The embrace made his phantom bruises and cracked ribs scream, but he ignored the pain—it was just letting him know Emily was here.

"It's so good to see you," Jacob whispered.

"I missed you yesterday," Emily said, "Are you all right?"

Jacob squeezed her tighter, "I'm scared and scarred, but I'll live."

The memory began to melt away. It was still there and probably would always be there, but now he knew it was only a figment of his imagination. Emily was here with him, and she was safe. It settled his mind just to hold her and to hear her voice. He let her go and stepped back so he could look in her green eyes; he could see clear skies and green fields after a long storm, and he knew she was okay.

"What happened?" Emily asked concerned.

"The last two days I fought with a demon on a chess board." Jacob replied, "It tore my mind and beat my body, but that doesn't matter. I'm here, and you're here now; you're okay."

Emily lowered her voice, "You went back to Aries? Did you go back for Julie?"

Jacob nodded, "I had to try." He was so glad she cared. It was obvious she really cared because she remembered names of people she had never met, and she remembered things he had done.

"Did it work?" Emily asked.

Jacob dropped his gaze from her pretty eyes and sighed, "I failed."

Emily hugged him sympathetically, "What did it ask you to do?"

"He wanted two games." Jacob said, "When I lost the first, it gave me a choice to walk away with a curse or try to even the score, a double or nothing. It wanted to know something about me, I think. I won the second game, but I think he still got part of what he wanted, and I got nothing."

"I'm glad you're safe." Emily said, "I can't imagine what that thing might have done to you."

Emily looked as if she were about to cry just thinking about it. "I'm safe now, and you are, too." Jacob assured her, "But . . ." He hesitated, "There's something I need to talk to you about. Something happened and you should know; it's been happening. Something's been changing, and what happened made it worse."

"Okay," Emily let him go, "After school then?" She said and stared into his eyes, looking for something to tell her what had happened.

"Yes," he nodded and smiled. "That would be best." Emily smiled back and then turned to go to her class. Jacob watched for a moment as if to make sure she made it down the hall safely before he also turned to go his way.

Sometimes Jacob wondered if she really understood what was going on in his life. It didn't really matter how much she understood; the main thing was, she cared. There were too many people who understood perfectly and didn't care in his family. They just looked to him as the savior. But Emily saw him as something he had just about given up on: ever being: human. Even the people who did care—Sarah and Dom, his mother, and Rain—all saw him as something better, something he had learned to accept, but truthfully was never completely comfortable being.

In the short time he had known her, she had become his greatest support. She didn't seem to care about any personal danger she might be faced with; if he needed someone to talk to, she was there. And it was more than that, she just made him happy, and she always seemed happy. Jacob just liked talking to her about anything, especially things other than what he did. Emily respected that. As much as she was fascinated by what he did she knew he didn't want to spend any more time discussing it, and so once she heard the story, she would move the conversation.

After school, Jacob met Emily in the school library where they often studied together. She sat down with him at one of the tables; only the most studious students, the few who did not procrastinate, remained, working on final projects,. "So you had something to say?" she asked, "Is everything alright?" She moved her hand to pick up his, concerned because she knew the honest answer was, "no."

Jacob looked at her and tried to force a smile. "Run away while you still can," he whispered.

Emily's face wrinkled with confusion, "What? Jacob, tell me what's happening."

"I don't know," Jacob admitted. "Something inside me has changed."

"What do you mean?" Emily asked.

Jacob struggled with the words for a moment, "I'm different now. I'm not the same person I was. I'm *more dangerous* now."

"Jacob, just tell me. You're strong enough to deal with this, and don't forget I'm here to help if you need me," Emily said, shaking her head.

"Nobody can help; I'm falling apart," he replied. The words hurt him just as much coming out as they hurt Emily to hear.

She moved her chair closer and pulled his arm to her chest, "Jacob you are strong, I will not get hurt from being near you. You can protect me, and you can protect your family. I've seen you do it, and I believe in you."

He leaned forward and gently kissed her, "I know, but who will protect you from me?" he whispered as if he were going to cry.

"You would never raise your hand against me. Even if you wanted to, you would never," she replied. "What happened?"

Jacob drew a deep breath; he had to let her know. He didn't want to, but he had to. "I disturbed something," he began, "There is a power in me, a sort of demon. It is the source of my powers, and it was supposed to remain in slumber, but it woke up."

"Okay, so what does that mean?" Emily asked, trying to understand his concern.

"It means that I'm becoming stronger, but it also means that this demon is becoming stronger," he explained. "Because my powers are from an ancient blood-line, the demons stay dormant in most of my family, and only a few of us can leech their power. I think when I fought Aries, I might have nudged it a bit, and it woke up."

Emily frowned, "What happens when it wakes up?"

"If it's not subdued, then it will consume me," Jacob answered, "Every time I draw on its power, it will draw from my soul, and eventually we will become one."

"Can it be subdued?" she asked.

Jacob found the words hard to say, "Nobody has ever learned to control their demons once they wake. Mine has not fully awakened and bent me to its will yet, but I cannot control it, and every time I fight something, it grows more conscious and stronger."

Emily smiled and still clutched his hand, "You are stronger, Jacob. You are smarter; you can overcome this."

"You don't understand," Jacob protested, "I cannot control this. I don't know when it might wake up and drag me to Hell, and I don't want anyone to be around when it does, especially you. I'm trying to protect you from me."

"But who will protect you from you?" she asked, just as serious as he was. "Jacob, worry about yourself for once; you can't save people if you're going insane alone. I know what's dangerous. I believe you. Jacob, I'm not scared."

Jacob looked down, "I just can't see how you could help. I want you to, really, but I can't put you in harm's way; I love you."

"Give me a chance," Emily requested, "I have listened to you. I have learned who you are. Now let me use that knowledge. I would walk through fire for you, Jacob; I love you."

"If anyone is walking through fire, it will be me," Jacob replied, "I already have, and I would never see anyone do it for me."

"Can I have a choice in this, Jacob? It's not just me that needs protecting; you are in much more danger from this thing than I am," Emily pointed out. "I'm not going to get hurt; I'll stand here with you."

Jacob stared for a moment at her lovely green eyes, completely baffled by her desire to help him shoulder his hardships. Then he smiled, "Promise me?"

Emily smiled, "You once promised me that you wouldn't leave. How could I not?"

"I meant the part about not getting hurt," Jacob replied, "I know you would stand with me."

She pulled herself toward him and gave him a kiss, "I promise."

Of course, she would not break her promise, but Jacob still worried he might do something he regretted. He hoped he could learn to control this thing that had awakened in him or send it back to sleep. He had so much to do, and he really needed to find a way to cope with his newly awakened other self. But he only had a few more weeks before school would be over, and that was the deadline to have this new spell completed. He went to the library.

When he arrived, he found Rain diligently working, reading the old texts. They had gathered a lot of information, and she and Sarah had gotten together and started laying out the framework for the actual spell. They had some of the basics down, and now they could see what they needed to look for. It would make the research a little bit simpler, but it was still a daunting task. He smiled as he walked in because Rain put more work into this project than any of them. She had the least interest as far as personal gain, but it was still important to her.

Jacob sat down across from her and took one of the books form the stack. She looked up, "We thought you weren't coming today." She said, "I thought you would have rested. I suppose you're just a lot stronger than we think you are."

Jacob caught a glance of her ageless golden eyes. "I don't know," he sighed and rubbed one of his many aches. "Strong maybe, but perhaps there's just no rest of the weary."

"The others were here this afternoon," Rain said, "We've made some good progress."

Jacob cracked the book open and then let the pages close again. "Show me," he said curiously. His level of understanding about the mechanics of the spell was far less than Rain's or his sister's, but he wanted to know just how complex it was going to be.

Rain pulled out a small black book with no markings on it. She unfolded it and turned to the first half-dozen pages. They had been inscribed front and back with instructions and diagrams and symbols from the language of the Fallen and other languages that had sprouted from bits of their language. It looked like a mess. As Rain explained some of the organization, Jacob began to see the layout. The entire thing was all prep-work; the actual spell had not even been started yet. Most times the preparatory pages were about half as complex and one-eighth the length of the actual spell. If a given spell had one page of preparatory work, then that usually meant the actual spell would be eight pages long. It wasn't a strict rule; it varied a lot, but it was a good way to get a ballpark guess of the level of a spell you were trying to learn.

Of course only the most complex spells required one whole page of preparatory inscription. Even a lot of stronger spells would only be half a page, and a lot of simple spells didn't require any preparatory work. Jacob wasn't thrilled to learn that the six or seven double-sided pages were only the beginning. If they had calculated it correctly, the little book of one hundred pages would be nearly completely full with just prep-work before it was finished. That meant that the actual spell would be about the size of a thick novel. The good news was, it seemed to be possible. The bad news was it would take a lot longer than the six-week deadline they had.

Rain spent several hours explaining some of the intricate parts of constructing new magic to Jacob. He had good base knowledge, but what they were doing was far out of his realm of knowledge. That's why Rain was in charge of that, and why Sarah was helping; she wasn't on the same level as Rain, but she was brilliant and had a knack for spells. When Rain had finished explaining the theory of how spells work, it was late. Jacob had not taken the time yet to fully recover from his battle with Aries, and he could feel the strain still pulling on him.

"So much to do in such a short time," Jacob complained as he sat back in his chair and slumped down.

Rain glanced up at him, "You have not rested well?" she asked tuning her gold eyes upon him.

"Aries is no longer on my mind, but what he has shown me is still heavy in my thoughts," Jacob replied as he pressed his fingers against his temples.

"What did he show you?" Rain asked curiously as if she had an inkling.

Jacob looked up, "You have faced him before. You understand what he does to your mind."

Rain nodded, "Yes, for the life time of a mortal, his tricks plagued my mind. But he tests each person differently, and he uses your own mind against you. He pulls the things you love and makes you feel the loss."

Jacob was silent; he knew some of the things he had seen did not come from his own mind, but he could not separate the tricks from what was real.

"I think I should try to sleep. I still have to wake up early." Jacob said and slid his chair back as he stood up.

As he was sitting in his bed, trying to let go of his thoughts just long enough to close his eyes, memories of a time not so heavy drifted through his mind. There was a time when he was very young—it seemed so far away now—a time when the weight of the world wasn't pressing on him. Now he feared going to sleep because he might wake up under the power of his inner demon. He had learned that the expectations of him did not define who he was. For a while, that had lifted some of the burden. But now he was beginning to realize that his expectations were higher than those of his family. If he failed, he was only failing himself.

This is who he was becoming; he wasn't sure if he was becoming the Chosen or if he was already the Chosen. He struggled with the definition; was he defining the role or was the role defining him? Part of him was entertained by the idea that he defined who he was and what being the Chosen meant. But then he wanted a clear direction and his path to be laid out before him. There was a time when he believed he could make his own path, but now there was so much pressing in on him, he felt like he couldn't move.

He was grown up now, and there was no more wiggle room between that rock and hard place he had been born into. It was getting harder and harder to deal with the different issues that rested on his shoulders. The situation with his father was particularly delicate because it involved the problems from both sides of his family. In his world, where he could no longer turn around freely, he dreaded to face the two problems at once. Exasperated and frustrated by being unable to sleep even though his body needed rest so badly, he threw on his pants and coat and went outside for some fresh air. He hoped it would clear his mind and let him get to sleep.

The air was crisp and cold with the last lingering fingers of winter gripping on to the early spring nights. The sky was clear and bright with stars. Jacob wished he could see his future so clearly.

He stood on the porch, leaning against the rail of the stairs for nearly an hour and then he heard the door shift and ease open. His mother stepped out into the night air and leaned against the opposite rail.

"What are you doing up?" Jacob asked.

Lucile sighed and looked out at the host of stars, "I woke. I saw you standing out here, so I put on my coat to come sit with you a while."

Jacob folded his arms and looked down at his feet, "There's so much going on right now," he started, "I can't sleep. I'm just so tired, but there's so much to do—it's overwhelming, you know?" She still didn't know about his problem with the caged demon waking up.

"Jacob, you're strong; this won't break you," Lucile replied.

"Do you really believe I can't do anything?" Jacob asked.

Lucile looked from the open sky to the door, "About your father?" She adjusted her coat around her and shrugged her shoulders underneath it as the chilly breeze tickled her neck. "Jacob, I tried for years before you were born. He never wanted me to; he wanted to have a family. That was more important to him than growing old. He invested his time in family, caring for me, and raising you and your siblings. He always believed he had such a short time, and he simply wanted to love and be loved.

"I still tried to find a way for him to escape this fate. When I look back and see the way he cared for his family, loved me, and raised our children, I realize that I should have simply enjoyed the time we were given rather than try to prolong the inevitable. After you came along, I didn't have the time to research it anymore, and I began to see things as I should have in the beginning." She looked at her son, "I can't say it's impossible, Jacob, but it's not what he would want. Have you talked to him about it?"

Jacob looked up to meet his mother's gaze, "He's pretty settled with his decision."

"Then it may be best to respect it." Lucile replied unconvincingly.

Jacob shook his head, "I've never, not once, gone against anything he has told me. But this is different. I am old enough to make my own decisions, and I'm not going to let him do this."

"So Rain is helping you?" she asked and looked back to the stars as if she had asked the question to the sky. He knew nobody had talked to her about his project. But his mother was very smart; she knew he was going to try. All the extra time he was spending in the library also seemed sort of obvious. She knew he wasn't going to be able to do it alone, but how had she figured Rain?

"And Sarah and Dom. Julie, too." Jacob replied, and looked up also.

"Mmhh . . . I wasn't going to bother, but something about you makes me believe," Lucile muttered.

"Believe what?" Jacob asked curiously and looked back at her.

She smiled still looking out at the stars, "In you." She sighed, "I wasn't going to tell you, but I stored all the research I had done when I met your father. I was so intrigued. I began to study all the facets of his job; I suppose I wanted to help him to understand him.

"Intrigue became interest, and interest became love. And then I began to worry. I wasn't helping him anymore. I was just afraid to lose him . . ." She continued reminiscently, "I spent long hours searching for answers that might save him from his fate, but eventually he convinced me to give up and enjoy our time.

"I thought I had learned to accept it, but I guess I'm still afraid—or else I wouldn't be telling you this."

Jacob got off the rail and stepped beside Lucile.

"I was so close, Jacob. Tell Rain to get my old scripts out. I think they could help you. She never knew what I was working on . . . I . . . intended to compile my findings into a book. It was a grand challenge, one I never finished.

"I think you can finish it. You may very well have the other half of the information already." She added with a smile that was forced and devoid of hope.

Jacob was somewhat surprised his mother had never mentioned this before. She was brilliant and had so much knowledge and skill, but he never would have thought she could spend that much time holed up in the library.

"Thanks," Jacob said and slid one arm around her to give her a comforting hug, "I'll ask Rain about it tomorrow."

Lucile smiled as she wrapped one arm around her son, "She's a very strong woman and smart, too. But I would be cautious of any relationship with her."

Jacob gave a curious look, "Relationship?" He asked not quite sure what his mother was insinuating.

Lucile sighed, "You are very wise for a young man of your age. I should expect no less from my own son. But there are still things you don't see, things you don't know about the power that encircles certain members of this lineage. I trust you'll do the right thing when the situation presents itself."

"What situation?"

"It's not to worry about. There is no way to determine the right choice until it is time to choose." His mother smiled, "It's so cold out here. You should rest."

"What is rest?" Jacob sighed, "Sleep is useless, and waking is futile." He turned and frowned wearily at his mother, "In my sleep, I am tormented, and when I wake, I must toil."

Lucile went into the house, and Jacob was left only further confused by what she had said. He came out here to clear his thoughts. What did his mother mean by *relationship?* What *situation* was approaching? And why didn't he have a clue? Better yet, what secrets were his mother keeping from him?

Choices . . . First, Rain and now his mother; were they talking about the same choice?

CHAPTER 24

I f only school didn't consume so much time. If he didn't have to attend classes, he could spend the required time in the library to complete his project. He had gotten his teachers to allow him to take his exams a week early since the last week was to be for study only, and they all agreed he didn't need to study. But that wasn't helping him out now. He had hardly seen Emily all week. He had just been so busy and she understood why, but she was still worried about their last talk. Jacob was worried, too, but it would have to be something he resolved later. He hated to do that, but perhaps it would give him a chance to get some control over whatever he had unleashed. If he could cope with this new entity, he might feel more comfortable being around normal mortals that he cared about. Until then, he thought it would be best if he stayed around people who were not completely defenseless.

The information his mother had given him helped a lot. They still had miles to go before they would see the end. Though Jacob was dreading the deadline, the day could not come quick enough. Julie was getting worse by the day. She didn't sleep; this week alone she had only gotten two hours of sleep, and that was after passing out from a fit of terror. She was dutifully studying right now, but she was falling apart faster than Jacob was. Time was something they both needed more of and could not afford.

Though it seemed like they were making progress Jacob was beginning to realize that setting up this spell would take a very long time. Once Drake got over there, he would have no time to set it up. Fortunately, Jacob was out of school a week early, he could sneak over there and set up the detailed, tedious prep work before his father arrived. But they would have to be done by then, and he would not have the benefit of having anyone to help him. Sarah and Dom would still be in school, and Rain could not leave the castle grounds. He tried to be optimistic; he had to. Again it was after midnight; he needed rest, but rest wasn't something he did anymore. He folded his book and began to walk out. "I'm done for the night," he said as he walked to the door. He was totally exhausted, but he knew he wasn't going to rest when he got home.

"I'll be right behind you." Dom said, "I'm going to finish up this last bit."

"You guys go on ahead." Sarah said, "Rain and I are going to stay here a bit longer. I think we might be getting somewhere."

Jacob smiled weakly, "I hope so. Goodnight. I will see you all tomorrow."

Recently, Jacob had begun to define rest as the time his eyes were closed. He would be fortunate to get two solid hours of sleep in a night. That was a lot more than Julie who had become completely insomniac after what had happened a few weeks ago. But still he needed rest, real rest. Nothing helped; sleep aids only gave rise to nightmares, and he would wake more tired that he was when he lay down. The only solution was to remove the whispers in his head, the ones from Adramelech. His demon was mostly quiet, but he still felt uneasy to turn his back on it.

He wrestled with sleep for a few hours and found that he was unable to subdue it. He was tired of struggling against his nightmares constantly. Frustrated and fatigued, he rose before the sun and returned to the library unrested. Walking out the door, he wondered if it had been worth leaving only to return so soon and still tired.

When he returned, he found Sarah had not yet left, and she and Rain were still deep in study. "Sarah, have you slept any?" Jacob asked.

"Not yet; I think we're making some progress, though," she replied without looking up, just as if only ten minutes had passed since they last spoke.

Jacob bent over her shoulder to see the tangled mess of symbols she and Rain had been concocting. "It's almost morning; you should get some rest," Jacob insisted.

Sarah slowly looked up at him and held his stare for a moment before she responded, "And you left only a few hours ago; how much rest have you had?"

He knew she was right; he needed rest more than anybody, but that was something that escaped him at the moment. "I have not slept," he admitted and slumped down in a chair beside them.

Sarah nodded and turned her attention back to the book she was studying. "You cannot wear yourself out, Jacob; you will need your full strength to face this challenge."

Jacob did not offer a reply. He picked up the thick stack of dusty books and shortly became entranced by the familiar dry smell of knowledge. Hours passed, maybe days—it was hard to keep track of the time under the castle. It was hard to keep track of the days when you didn't sleep. Jacob paused from his study, trying to remember the last meal he had eaten, perhaps to remember what day it was. No, it couldn't possibly be that long. He hadn't been to school yet; it was still the weekend. Sarah had gone already, finally. Dom had slept late; maybe, Jacob didn't remember what time it was when he arrived. Come to think of it, now that he looked around, he didn't remember what time Dom had left.

Then he realized he was alone in the study. He thought back to remember when his companions had left, but he could not recall. Jacob rose slowly, the air was far too still; it seemed stale, heavy, frozen, and dead. He wandered through the dim halls without making a sound, and he heard nothing, not even his own footsteps or heartbeat or breathing. Jacob strained against the silence, trying to listen for any sign of life. The air seemed to have died in the dusty old corridors.

Even the light of the torches seemed stale and crusty, and the small fires made no sound or smoke. Where had everyone gone? There were far too many passages that he had not yet explored for him to just wander aimlessly, but it took him nearly half an hour to cover the halls he had grown familiar with. The forge was empty: cold, void. The Oasis seemed abandoned, and the carefully tended plants appeared fake and lifeless.

Jacob ventured to the upper study and still didn't find a soul. It did give him an idea of the time of day, though: late evening, about one hour of daylight remained. The sun was not as bright as Jacob thought it should be. Somehow the view from the upper study seemed to lack color as if someone had watered it down. He listened and could not hear a single sound, not a breeze or even a bird. It was as if God had pressed the mute button on the world. He descended back to the dark halls and meandered his way to the portal that lay beneath the castle. Typically, he used the one in the courtyard when he arrived and departed from the castle, but this one was better constructed for longer distances, and it was a different magic that was not sensitive to specific blood lines. This would be the one his father would have to depart from. As Jacob neared the chamber, he felt the stale air become uncomfortably warm and thick. He stepped into the dim room and noticed a figure standing in the middle of the portal.

Jacob strained to see through the rusty torchlight and identify this lone figure. Then it took notice of him. It looked at him, but Jacob could not tell his features, "You're late, son," it spoke.

The voice startled him. It sounded like his father, but it seemed so callous and distant Jacob wasn't convinced. He hesitated to answer, wondering if this was some kind of manifestation of his waking demon or perhaps something concocted by Aries. "Late for what?" The only time he should have seen his father here was right before they left to fight Adramelech. He was not supposed to be in the secret parts of the Castle; special permission had been granted for Jacob to take him through the portal only once, and it was not yet time.

Jacob's voice seemed to cut the silence, but at the same time he could not muster anything more than a whisper. It was getting difficult to breathe. The figure stepped forward and a pale amber beam from the dying torchlight illuminated his face just enough for Jacob to tell it was Drake. "Jacob, have you lost track of the time?" he asked, "Did you forget what we must do?"

It could have just been his overwhelming fatigue, but Jacob could barely make out the words.

"No, it is not time yet," Jacob protested, "It can't be; school isn't over. I can't go away that long." His voice was weak, and the silence ate it up and seemed to smother it.

"But Jacob, there is no time left," the figure of his father urged, "We must hurry before it's too late."

"I don't understand," Jacob replied.

"Your cousin needs your help," Drake insisted, "The demon grows strong over her."

Then Jacob heard a weak sob and noticed a hunched figure he had not noticed before, sitting slumped against one of the outer pillars of the portal. It stood up, and Jacob instantly knew it was Julie.

"She is weak," Drake said sternly, "The demon is strong. You must help me defeat her."

Jacob wasn't sure what his father was talking about, "Her?" he asked.

"She is taken, Jacob." As the words struggled through the muggy dead air, they seemed to fade out of existence. Julie stepped forward, and the complete silence resumed. Around her the air pricked with red embers and then flames erupted in her footsteps. She grew taller, and her eyes burned. It was not Julie.

The flames caught up to her and danced around her feet and grew until they brushed her shoulders. Her eyes were like fire, and her hair blew wildly, growing much longer and tangling into knots. She reached into one of the tongues and pulled a sword from the flames. This sword Jacob had seen before, it was red and flowing and shifted to the wielder's will. It was the sword of the Arch demon Adramelech.

Wielding this sword, Julie stepped closer and closer to Drake who stood with his back turned. Jacob could see his father's mouth moving, but he could hear nothing. His arm began to throb as he recalled that sword transforming into a red-hot whip and ensnaring him. The closer Julie got, the more she resembled the demon that haunted her body. Jacob tried to run to rescue his father from the danger, but he couldn't. He ran, but it seemed like the distance between them would never close. It seemed like they got further apart.

Jacob tried to scream, but he only felt his voice vibrating in his chest as the words were snuffed in his throat. The air was fighting against him, trapping his breath and words. He reached for his weapons; Jade he clasped with his right hand and with his left grasped the Light Shard. The phantom of his cousin raised the red blade of magma and thrust it through his father's back. Drake showed no reaction other than the glowing tip of the molten sword pushing through his chest.

He sank to his knees, and the demon pulled the blade out. As he fell forward, Jacob finally made it to him in time to catch him. Reaching under both his father's arms, he knelt to support his weight while he continued to hold tight to his weapons. He could see his father trying to tell him something, but the sound was not coming out. Though his lips were moving, his eyes were dead, and his face was pale even in this dim light.

Then Drake made the motions of coughing and his blood splattered on Jacob's shoulder. Drake saw the red splotches and his mouth stopped moving. He looked up at his son in horror, and for once the silence seemed too loud. Jacob wanted to say something, but his words were muted by the stale hot air pressing them into his chest. His father lost his grip and slumped against him. Jacob looked up at his cousin, who he now could not recognize. It still looked human, like a woman, but it was unearthly and wielded the sword. It wore the cape of regal peacock feathers that belonged to the King of Fires. "Jacob . . ." it whispered, half as a taunting challenge for him to rise, yet part of it was Julie trapped inside pleading for help. Though he could barely hear the whisper, it shook the ground. Jacob's blood boiled in him, and his temper flared like the sword in her hand.

"Jacob . . ." it repeated.

The Light Shard in his hand flickered to life, and everything to his left side was blurred out by the white brilliance. His demon flared as well, and Jacob stood, dropping his father's limp body to the side as he screamed. His voice rumbled through the silence; he could hear nothing, but the walls and floor vibrated violently with the thunderous force he created in the suppressing air.

"Jacob!" A new voice rang out. It stopped him in his fit of rage and cooled his blood. The demon before him evaporated, the room stopped shaking, and the light was not so dim. He drew a sudden breath as if he had been suffocating—the air was fresh. Rain clasped his shoulder. "Jacob?" she asked, her golden eyes searching his.

He blinked and found that he was still sitting at his desk. "Yes," Jacob stammered. His throat was dry.

"I hate to wake you, but perhaps you would be more comfortable if you rested by the furnace," she suggested.

Jacob squinted at her, puzzled. "Wake me?" he asked.

"You fell asleep a few hours ago," she explained. "At first we decided you needed the rest, and we let you be, but if you continue to slumber over your books like that, you will regret it when you wake."

"How long was I out?" Jacob sat up straight and clasped the back of his neck with his hand.

"I noticed you had passed out before supper. It's been six hours at least, and it's getting late," Rain said. "I know you're used to being late, but I think you need to take this one home."

Jacob gave a half-laugh at the suggestion, and then he stopped himself; it was very true. "I'm already as rested as I'll ever be. I ought to stay. I'll only be awake if I go home, and if I'm awake I'll end up here anyway."

"If you say so," Rain said as if she didn't approve. She shook her head, the reds and blues danced though the white-blond of her hair. Under the light of the torches, the reds were more dominant, and her hair appeared to be a washed and shiny auburn. "I have taken a considerable break from the tedious business of tracking the spell, and I'm ready to get back to work myself."

"Is it possible?" Jacob asked himself out loud.

Rain took the seat beside him, "I believe it is; you have the drive that makes anything possible."

Jacob thought about his upcoming battle, and his mind went straight back to the dream he had just awakened from. There was something about that dream that he could not ignore. He couldn't help but wonder if there had been some kind of meaning in it. If so, could he change it? He would change it. Then a feeling of despair encircled him. This took so much of his time and energy, and he was so scared. How could he ever hope to really be the Chosen and save his people? If a simple family issue could paralyze his world, would he be able to stand before the others? There was nothing simple about his family. How could he stand up to the demons in his family if he was falling to the one he carried?

Rain apparently saw the change in his demeanor. "What is wrong Jacob?"

He thought about how to answer for a moment and then he just sighed, "Everything."

She made the motion with her eyes for him to let her in his mind. Jacob shook his head, "You already know," he said, "I know you saw it. You saw it the first time I stepped off the board, didn't you? Before you even touched me, you saw it in my eyes. The same way I can see through yours."

Rain nodded, "I'm sorry." She whispered, "I should have warned you; the others didn't want to sway your decision by telling you the true risk. A battle on that board may risk waking that which slumbers in some of us."

Jacob looked up, trying to see her expression. Today her stoic mask was perfect, but he could guess what was turning behind her eyes. "And yours?" he asked, cautious of the answer she might give.

"Intuitive," she remarked, then sighed, "Mine—My father taught me to rule it." She hesitated. "Aries tried to unleash it, but I kept it safe. It cost me the game, but the demon didn't want anything else."

Jacob remembered the glimpse of the game that she had given him before his first battle and recalled the pain that he felt from the board. Then he realized the pain was felt by his demon, he was not physically there. Aries was not fighting him when he stepped on the board, just trying to prod his demon to wake, and he had done it, too.

"What can I do?" Jacob asked. "Can you teach me to rule this thing as you have done?"

Rain just lowered her stare. "It is part of you now," she replied hesitantly. "It should have slept a little while longer, until you were ready to wake it. But, now it has already been unbound."

Jacob frowned, "I can't have that— *'One shall come from the stars as you have but shall bear not Hell and walk among the Fallen of this world and raise them up.'* Bear not Hell," he stated, "I must rule it."

Rain shook her head, "I know. Just be careful; be strong like you already are. There's no way to stop it once it is unbound."

"Isn't that what we are trying to do here?" Jacob asked, "Stopping that which is unbound?"

236

Rain stared at him and nearly faltered from her statuesque expression, "That we are."

"Then why should I not be able to quell him?" Jacob replied.

"Because he is you," Rain explained, "It's not just part of you; it's your very nature, the core of who you are. You are the demon."

Suddenly, everything Jacob had feared solidified in his stomach. He was terrified to meet his true nature, and he was more afraid to become it. The answer hit like a stone wall collapsing on him; there was nothing he could do. He could not get out from under this. For so long he had felt the weight of the world crushing him, and now it seemed it would finally be the death of him. But something else solidified in his stomach: resolve. He had responsibilities he had to fulfill and he could not let anything, not even himself, get in the way. "Then I'm a demon," he muttered, "What of it? It won't stop me from carrying out my duties. My strength shall be my weakness. So be it." Now he understood his greatest power was doomed to be his downfall. With his powers unleashed, nothing could stop him except the powers themselves. His curse was his blessing, and his blessing was his death sentence, and he would carry it all boldly against the darkness. Perhaps it should be him and not his father marching to death and glory at the end of school.

Jacob rolled the thought about his head and somehow he knew that this demon, Adramelech, would be his demise, not his own soul.

"And this is why I love you," Rain mused. "Be strong like you already are," she repeated.

CHAPTER 23

The weeks seemed to go by like hours and at the same time it seemed like years. It seemed like the hard work they had all put in was about to pay off. Jacob was in the study with Sarah, Dom, Rain, and Julie critiquing their work. This was not his field of expertise, but it looked like solid work to him. He had a good enough understanding to apply it, but if he had been left to develop this technique alone, it would have taken him years.

He had spent most of the time recently, practicing how to set this thing up; it was going to be complex, and he needed to be perfect. His part in the actual gathering of information was over, but he could not rest or become idle. If he could not find something to help with, he double-checked the process to make sure he had it memorized. It took weeks of studying, and his school had suffered for it. Tomorrow he would take his finals early, and then he would rest. The time he would normally spend in school, he would spend here and at the library in Africa. He could sleep a little during the day, so Drake would not know he had been out of school a week early. Maybe that would help him make up for some of the sleep he had been deprived of, but he doubted that.

"Will it work?" Jacob asked nervously. Sarah and Rain had really put it together and understood the inner workings of the jumbled runes far better than he did.

Sarah shook her head, "It works." She didn't seem impressed though. "It's just messy."

"And fragile," Rain added.

Sarah hummed in agreement, "It takes a long time to apply, and it's very easy to stray or damage."

"But it works?" He asked again. "We're almost out of time. Will this do what I need it to do?"

Rain stood up and walked from their pile of careful research to her desk, "Yes, Jacob, it will work. I'm afraid you will need several hours to dedicate to setting up this incantation. And you mustn't forget that this technique isn't perfect; it doesn't do things automatically. You will have to find a way to push the demon through the portal, and you will have to close it behind him."

"Just like you showed me," he agreed, "I have that part down. I know what I must do."

"Just because you went through the motions of it, doesn't mean you know how," Rain said as she shot a serious glare from her burning gold eyes. "The real application of such magic is much more than just following the steps. It's like an accent to a language, and something this complex must be perfect."

Jacob nodded, "I understand."

Rain shook her head, "Be careful; it's very delicate." She nodded at the small leather book on the table. "It's ready. Don't tell a soul I let you walk out of this place with untested, restricted magic."

Jacob hadn't even thought about the rules he would be breaking by taking this kind of magic out of the castle. He reverently picked up the newly crafted spell and closed the book slowly. Sarah still stood beside him, "Jacob, be careful," she whispered.

He looked at his sister and smiled, "It will be okay; I'll bring father back safely."

She closed her eyes, "I meant you be careful. I have a bad feeling about this whole thing."

"I will bring us both back," he said, and then he gave her a strong hug, "Thank you for all the work you've done to help me."

"I wish there was more I could do," she answered, "but you're just too stubborn to let me."

"And you know why," Jacob replied. Sarah nodded and let him go.

Jacob turned to Dom, "Thanks for all your help, Dom. I'm really proud of you." He gave his brother a hug as well, and then he stood before his cousin.

"Julie, I'm sorry for getting you involved in this." She wasn't herself anymore, and it bothered Jacob that she suffered because of him. Every day her strength was diminishing and being replaced with something dark. Slowly she was becoming the haunting figure he had seen in his dream.

He embraced her, "I swear I will restore your strength; I will rid you of this curse."

Sometimes she would just remain silent.

The thought lingered in the back of his mind if it had been too late for Julie. Had the dream been a vision? Was that his choice? To be able to save only one? Had he chosen his father over his cousin without knowing? Would he have changed his mind if he had known? He shrugged the thought out of his mind. *I will save them both.*

Julie remained silent but managed to feebly return Jacob's hug. "It's almost over," Jacob said as he let her go.

Julie stared weakly and blankly at him. "Hurry," she whispered.

It pained him to see someone suffer like she was because of something he had done. He began to wonder if the technique he had used to pull Adramelech's spirit out of her had missed a piece. What if part of the demon was still in her?

The technique worked fine for Shadows, but maybe the Arch demon hadn't been fully removed.

He turned from Julie and walked to Rain's desk where she sat, watching from behind her stoic ever-young expression. "How will I ever thank you?" He asked.

"You are the Chosen, Jacob; you may use my services as you wish," she replied.

Jacob stood beside her, "I asked for your guidance; what you have done is far more than you were obligated to give. I stand in your debt."

She blinked, "We shall see once this magic has been put to the test." Rain remarked, "We have all worked hard and deserve a good night's rest." She looked up from her desk at Jacob, "Our hero most of all needs strength for what looms on the horizon."

"Your hero?" Jacob contemplated. "I'd be nowhere without you; the four of you have made this possible."

"And only you have the fortitude to face a demon to save another's life, for that you are the hero, not us," Rain replied.

Sarah and Dom nodded in agreement. Julie's awareness had been so suppressed that even if she knew what was being said, she didn't reply. It was almost like she was becoming a zombie.

Jacob did not take encouragement from that; he was alone again. When they were all working together, he felt like he was part of something that was greater than the sum of its parts. But once the task was complete, the sum was only equal to him—his abilities and skills were the limit of all their work, and he was feeling closer and closer to the end of his strength. If he failed, it would all have been in vain. He didn't like the responsibility, and he had never asked for it. And he was beginning to fear it would kill him. He shoved the thought aside; he was too tired to be depressed or wish it away or reply to Rain's honorific remark to him. So he left in weary silence.

He could have slept though his finals and done just fine; in hindsight it would have been a grand idea. Even without having studied his lessons for the past three weeks, he was more than prepared for his exams. And now he was done with school—forever. For him there would be nothing further, the work of his adult life was already cut out for him, assuming he would survive long enough to get comfortable calling himself an adult. If things kept going the way they were, he'd be fortunate to survive the summer.

The summer. Just a few weeks ago he was looking forward to spending the long summer days with Emily, and now he had barely spoken to her. He was busy, but that wasn't why; he wasn't convinced he could trust himself. He didn't mean to shut her out, but he wanted to protect her. Maybe once this was over, he could make it up to her; he would have to.

It was hot inside the volcano. The work was meticulous, and there was nobody to help him. Ress wished to assist him, but Jacob did not have the time or skill to teach him what had taken him the last month of constant study and practice to master. He worked and sweated to set up the spell, and all the time he could feel the demon breathing down his neck. All the preparatory spells were put in place, all the runes drawn. The mountain had been quarantined a year ago after the demon had killed the librarian, so Jacob had no issues with keeping people out of his business.

Jacob had finished all of his preparations and still had another day before his father would arrive. He made his way back to the portal to return to his home. He would have a whole day to rest and prepare his mind for what he was about to do. But his restlessness was sure to get the better of him; he worried that everything had gone too smoothly. It always felt like the work wasn't quite done.

He stepped through the portal and was snapped back to his library. The feeling of being hurled across the globe had become familiar and no longer fazed him. He went to the lower study; if he went home his father would realize that he had been out of school. Jacob didn't know what would be worse; if Drake found out Jacob had lied to him or if he decided to turn around and go back today. His scheduled date for exams was tomorrow, but he had taken them early and planned for tomorrow to be a free day.

He took a spot at a table beside the furnace and thought about how nice it would be to lay his head down and rest. For once he did not think about picking up one of his studies or delving into a new research or decrypting more of the lost languages. He was tired. For the first time he could remember, he was repulsed by the dry smell of the dusty books. The parchments that he was so fond of were the last things he wanted to see today. As the thought of dropping his head on the oak table dwindled from his thoughts, he found that he was nearly asleep and woke with a start. Then he gave in and slumped over to rest.

It wasn't long enough before he was awakened by his mother. He lazily lifted his eyes and saw his father was with her, and Rain and Roth and Julie. It was the first time in nearly four hundred years that a person outside of their bloodline had entered the secret halls, and Drake had to be escorted wherever he went.

Jacob sat up and then slowly stood wandering what time it was.

"Are you ready?" his father asked. "You have not been home. Do you need anything before we go? I don't intend on passing through that portal any more than I have to."

He wanted to say something, anything to stop his father from stepping through that portal. But he couldn't think of anything to protest. The new spell was in place, and there was no more work he needed to do. So why did he still have a very bad feeling about it?

"How long will we be gone?" Jacob asked.

Drake considered for a moment, "Three to five days. I'm not sure how much time it will take to study him."

Jacob wasn't sure what they would have to study, but he thought three to five days wasn't fair compared to the months he and the others put in to this project. But their method did circumvent one of the key steps in his father's plan.

He wished he had taken some time to at least speak to Emily before he left. It seemed like ages since they had spent any time together. She was worried, and he had done very little to ease her thoughts. Everything now was just proceeding so fast, he could not afford to drag her into something he did not yet understand. There were things he wanted to tell her, things she really should know, like the chance that he might not come back, or that if he did survive one more encounter with this demon, it could fundamentally change who he was.

"I'm ready," he said heavily after weighing his fears and regrets.

He was ready, as ready as he'd ever be. Jacob could remember a time when he wanted to be just like his father, as every small boy does. He admired what his father did, protecting people and throwing his life on the line for others. It had all happened so fast, Jacob wasn't sure when he had stepped out of the caves he used to crawl about in and into that role himself, but today he knew he was his father's son. And today this was his job. They descended into the lower chamber to depart. As they entered the dim room, Jacob felt something was wrong. The memory of the nightmare he had the last time he dreamed seemed to haunt this room. Roth stepped forward and uttered a short spell to activate the portal and then turned to them.

"Jacob, the Chosen One," he said. He was weak now; the might of his voice was less mighty, and the archaic dryness of his breath seemed stale and labored. "I give you my blessing as the one sent to redeem our blood. All of the Fallen shall look to you to deliver us from our fate. The blood of demons runs in our line, but there is no place for you among this family. Your blood is not tainted; claim us one day when you stand in Judgment."

Jacob nodded, "How are you certain?"

"I am certain that I am dying, Jacob. Aries promised me immortality until I met the Chosen, and my heart has been burdened since you first set foot on the board." Roth seemed at peace as if he had been awaiting his death—as if death was the last adventure left in his life, and he had been waiting unable to die for centuries.

Jacob looked at the old man and tried to fathom immortality. A dried and shriveled existence seemed wearisome. Even Rain's eternal youth seemed desperately lonely. So he wasn't the only one suffering in this clan. But Roth had made his own folly, and Rain had asked for her duties. Jacob never had a choice in the matter; it was thrust upon him, and he was expected to carry it or be crushed by it.

"Then I shall do my best," he replied.

Roth smiled and sighed, "Go now; our brothers in Africa have needed your help for a very long time."

Jacob stepped forward and his father followed him. As they entered the circle, a blue spark ignited in the center. Julie also followed, silent and wavering. Jacob turned to her and placed his hand on her shoulder. She looked up suddenly as if startled, suddenly aware of his presence.

"Julie, you don't have to come this time," he said to her, "I'll make everything better before I return. It's not safe for you to go like this."

Her eyes were weak. Jacob had watched her energy drain the past few weeks as they worked together. Her mind still worked, but it was fragile and was reduced to automated responses. Jacob feared that reintroducing her to this demon would stress her beyond what she could handle.

"But . . . I can't . . .," she said with a certain detachment, "I . . . will I die?"

Jacob looked puzzled at her, it was difficult to understand her now.

He felt a heavy hand on his shoulder, "Once a person meddles in this sort of thing, it cannot be undone." His father said, "It may be dangerous for her, but it would be far worse if we threw this beast into the fire before she had a chance to detach from it. She must come with us and bid farewell to the monster, or the demon could use her soul as a bridge or worse. Part of her soul might follow him into darkness."

Julie nodded and trembled, "It is inside me."

Again Jacob wondered if he had not removed the entire entity when he attempted to extract the demon from her the last time. What if everyone he had done that to suffered similarly? "Julie, do you understand what you have to do?"

She nodded and sobbed, "I hear him now."

"Can you do this?" Jacob asked.

"I . . . I don't have a choice," she whispered on the brink of tears. "I just want it to go away."

"I swear I will make it go away," Jacob reassured and then guided her in front of him toward the light.

He looked back and saw Drake stop for a moment. Lucile stepped forward and embraced him, knowing he did not intend to return, though she was hoping Jacob could work a miracle. She began to cry. "We knew this day would come," Drake said. His voice betrayed his heavy heart.

"I know," his mother whispered back. She collapsed at his feet and clung on to his hands as she buried her face in his knees and wept.

His father knelt down and embraced her again, "You swore you would be alright; I must do this." He picked her up and turned her face to his, "I have been glad for our time together. I have lived longer than I expected, and every day I have loved you."

"I never doubted it," Lucile opened her eyes, "I thought I was ready for this, but I lied to myself. I don't want to lose you yet."

Drake held her close and whispered something Jacob could not hear. As he watched, he was gripped by two thoughts; first, the urgency of his business to return with his father and second, that one day this moment would return and his father would still leave. One day this moment would be his; one day he would have to say goodbye and face his own death.

Drake relaxed and kissed her forehead, and then she looked up at him and kissed him for what she hoped wouldn't be the last time. She had faith in Jacob, but she was no fool; even if Jacob could do this, it was risky business.

Lucile stepped away, "Go before I stop you." She wiped free-flowing tears from her eyes as she struggled to let go of her husband's coat.

"Jacob, be careful," she said, "Do what you can, but I can't stand to lose you both."

Jacob nodded somberly, knowing what she meant. It was his intention to bring his dad back safely, but sometimes, often in this business, things did not go as planned.

Drake stepped up and joined Jacob and Julie around the glowing orb. The three of them stood in the center, and the light expanded and enveloped them. Jacob felt the familiar motion of the travel, and when the light faded, they were inside the volcano.

Jacob was hanging onto his cousin to support her. Drake, who had never experienced teleportation, was on his hands and knees fighting the disorientation and heaving from the unique experience.

"Do you feel that way all the time?" he asked as he finally caught his breath.

"It takes a while to get used to, but eventually you don't feel it anymore," Jacob answered.

He stood up straight and looked around, "I was asking Julie. This place is haunted."

Julie recoiled from the question, "All the time," she murmured.

"Listen to me very carefully," Drake said, "If you feel this thing near you, if you hear it breathing, you must tell it to go away."

"I tried—so many times before," she stammered.

Drake placed a hand on her shoulder, but her eyes did not rise to his, "It will fight you, but you must, no matter what, tell it to leave. Especially when I prepare to drag it back to Hell. If you fail to detach from it, it will pull part of you away with us."

Julie bit her lip and just closed her eyes.

"Do you understand?" Drake asked.

She nodded.

"I'd rather not stay too long," Jacob urged, "It seems we have already outstayed our welcome. Where do we get started?"

Three days' time passed in the blink of an eye. Jacob and Drake slept in shifts the last three nights they slept in the mountain. Jacob could not sleep at all, however; the presence of the demon was too strong. He could feel it breathing, and in the quiet hours, he swore he could hear its heart beating. Julie was much worse, though. She got more agitated the longer they stayed there, and she would randomly burst out screaming into the night.

During his shifts, while Drake was sleeping, he walked the dark tunnels that had been carved by magma flows and explored the maze. It just seemed like the perfect place for a demon to reside. He visited the chamber where they were to meet the demon, the same place they had met the last time. He studied the inscriptions he had made the week before to make sure he had them aligned properly and that none of them had been tampered with. Drake had not asked what they were, but Jacob was certain that his father knew where they came from. He wasn't familiar with the magic of Lucile's family, but he was familiar with the runes and crest that littered the floor of this chamber.

Every day that they spent there, he was reminded of the battles against Aries by the tightening of the phantom scars he had. There was something about the proximity to evil that made the wounds ache. A stab wound in his chest, a laceration from his ribs down to his thigh, and that agonizing burn on his entire arm from the ensnaring whip were the worst. But they were only memories, the wounds were never really there. It made him worry, but he didn't even let Drake know of the condition.

Finally, everything was set, Drake had figured out everything he needed to know about this demon, and Jacob was ready to override the plan and save his father's life. Of course, his father would have waited until the last moment to tell Jacob that he would have to deliver the final blow. It was a good thing he meant to rescue his father from his fate because there was no chance he would have the guts to kill him with his own hands. Julie's only job was to scream and yell for the beast to leave her alone and take whatever part of it that was still attached to her back to Hell with the rest of it. She had been doing that the last six hours. Jacob was ready to get this over with; he hated to see his cousin being tormented like this.

Also, his demon blood had been hot ever since they got here. That was one thing his father didn't know had been happening recently. His hidden darkness was starting to wake up, and being near a real demon for so long was agitating it. Jacob wasn't sure how much longer he could fight these demons before he became one.

They had all gathered in the chamber and Drake and Jacob were prepared for this battle. They had each ignited an incense burner. Jacob had his faithful sword, Jade, and the Light Shard dagger he had crafted in hand, and his father was summoning the demon to appear before them. This summons was a lot more intricate than the one Jacob had been taught, the one that insulted the creature and caused it to attach to Julie the last time he tried to challenge it.

The room was hot because of the lava flowing beneath them, but the air suddenly chilled. Drake had not yet finished the incantation, and the form of darkness manifested in their midst. Adramelech had appeared. His entire malevolence was hidden from view, but the absolute foulness of his presence was thick in the air.

"Jacob, be ready!" Drake exclaimed. He rushed into the shadow and screamed, holding the incense orb above his head. Jacob wasn't sure how this was going to work; all his father had told him was that he would have to complete the sacrifice. It seemed that tackling a full-fledged Demon was suicide enough that Jacob's part in that plan would be moot.

Then he saw his father's purpose. As he stood horrified, and in fear, he noticed the darkness being gathered into his father's body. Drake had forced the Demon to possess him. Julie was screaming every way she could for the Demon to leave her body. The darkness disappeared and Drake was on his knees trembling, "Do it!" He hastened, "Now . . . before it . . . before it gets out."

Jacob hurried to his father's side but not to kill him as instructed. He stopped and did a certain motion he had practiced, it was almost like a dance, and he muttered some phrases in the Fallen tongue. The smoke of the incense curled around him with his motions.

"Jacob, what are you doing; you must not hesitate." Drake commanded.

"Hold on, Dad. There's another way to do this." He had spent way too much time setting up his own alternative method to deport this evil, and he was not about to let it take his father. Jacob moved quickly and gave one final command and a rift opened in the air. There was a loud snap and a ripping sound when the rift appeared, and immense heat radiated from it. All the runes and inscriptions he had placed on the floor and walls lit up and glowed, each a different color. Jacob felt the rift trying to suck him in, and hoped it would be strong enough to pull the demon. He took Jade and ran her through his father's chest as he had done when he exorcised lesser spirits from many others. Something felt different about this one. Perhaps it was the magnitude of the evil he had stabbed. But he had not felt this abnormality when he pulled the demon from Julie the last time. He tried to pull the blade out, but it fought against him.

He twisted the blade and gave a mighty tug with his half-demon strength, and the blade yanked out, leaving his father's body unscathed. Jacob had meant to fling the demon toward the portal. Already committed to the motion, he saw not only Adramelech on the blade but also another entity. No, he had not touched the demon at all, the blade passed through the other entity, and that soul had clutched onto the monster. Before he could stop the motion, he realized he had not pulled the demon away from his father but had yanked his father's soul from his body. The two spirits flew toward the portal and were nearly engulfed by the rift. But Adramelech reached out and grabbed a hold of the world's side and caught them both. The air of the cave rushed into the void, and the incense burner from Drake's hand flew into the portal as the two spirits struggled to escape. The rift tried to close, but the creature refused to allow it and clawed his way back to the other side.

Forcing his way back through the portal, he extended a ghastly hand out to Drake's hollow body. As he pulled himself from the edge of the portal, the bond of Drake's spirit began to weaken and slip away. The demon reached and firmly anchored himself to the flesh. With his other arm, he flung the soul that clung to him away into the abyss, and the rift closed just as abruptly as it had opened with a tight hissing and scraping sound. The ground shook, and Jacob fell backward and landed on his cousin who had stopped screaming for the demon to go away at this point and clutched to Jacob for what little security she had left. Drake stood up with a motion that could not be human. The form of his father turned and looked at him with a hideous grimacing smile.

"No!" Jacob yelled as he scrambled out of Julie's grip and back to his feet.

"No! You bastard!" he screamed, and the demon blood in him surged. His fear was nearly annihilated, and he felt only anger.

The figure of his father contorted and rushed at him. Jacob acted on impulse, had his demon blood been more subdued, he would have been unable to do what he must. He lunged forward with Jade and plunged the sword into the hollow body. As he did, fire exploded in his arm as his flesh remembered the whip this Demon carried. Then he took the Light Shard and as he raised it, a light burst forth from the blade. He plunged through the skull of the flesh. The body flailed, and the demon recoiled.

Jacob's more human emotions took over for a moment, and he dropped to his knees at his father's body that he had just mutilated. Then there was a dark laughter, and his demon attitude quickly snapped back into him. Jacob turned to his cousin and glared at her petrified form sobbing behind him. "Run!" he said in a whisper that was almost a threat, almost laughter, and completely authoritative. The girl snapped out of her trance as if she had been daydreaming in school and bolted out of the chamber. Jacob could not be sure the demon would leave her alone or if part of it could still be attached to her, but he knew he didn't want to have it possess her again.

He turned into the darkness and bellowed a primitive yell that originated from some power deep inside him, but only his echoes returned his call. Part of him was thankful; he stood no chance against a full-fledged demon. But part of him was terrified; it could be lurking anywhere. He whirled around and checked his back and saw there was nothing. Then he felt the presence of the evil subside and dissipate as a hint of fading laughter crept through the rocks. The monster had escaped. His father had died for this? His demon strength drained out of him, and he collapsed on his face. No, that's not right; that's not how it was planned. He had not just failed to save his father; he had turned his sacrifice into vanity. And it was all because he had tried to use his own demon to get an advantage. How had things gone this way? The demon was still loose, and the only man he could turn to for help, his father, was gone. There were no words to express his grief and sense of loss and failure. Everything he feared had come to pass, and he alone had failed.

CHAPTER 24

This time as he stepped through the portal, he collapsed under the weight of the body in his arms. There was nobody to receive him because his return was not anticipated. Jacob struggled to rise, but his legs and arms refused. The burden of his grief and the body in his lap arrested his movement. Julie was silent, whether she had no words to say or still suffering from the demon, Jacob couldn't tell. She slowly walked off the platform and made her way out of the chamber. He just knelt there in mourning, slumped over, and wept. It would have been one thing if he had simply failed to protect his father, but it had been much worse. He had failed to deport the demon, and he was responsible for Drake's death. He laid on the portal angry with himself, cursing in disbelief. Never had he failed before. He had made mistakes, yes, but never failed. Some time passed before he was able to pull himself together and leave. Nothing had ever been so hard in his life as it was to bring his father's body home to his mother.

Though spring had returned and the sun was shining, the world seemed cold as he stood and watched the casket lowered into the earth. His father was a simple man and requested a simple pine box for a coffin. The rays of the sun fell on his face, but they brought no warmth. He stood beside his mother and brother and sister. Emily was standing among the few friends Drake had. She had been very sympathetic, but Jacob had been very silent. As the dirt was placed on the coffin Jacob struggled to hold back the tears. He watched his father being buried, and with each shovel of earth he felt more and more helpless and alone. Now he had to shoulder the curse alone, and it was his fault he was now alone. By the time the small pine box was no longer visible, his despair became complete and he turned and walked away.

Emily hesitated a moment and then hurried to catch him. Jacob had reached the far end of the cemetery by the time she reached him. He really wanted to be alone right now. As awful as that feeling was, it was the only thing he wanted at the moment.

"Jacob," Emily spoke; it was so nice to hear her voice. "I don't know what to say, but I'm always here to listen just like before."

Jacob turned to face her, this was the first time he had seen her since he completed his finals. It had been nearly two weeks now. He wanted to embrace her, but he couldn't bring himself to move or speak.

"Or we can just walk," Emily suggested and stepped closer. She took his hand and squeezed it. It comforted him; her touch was like medicine for his soul.

"I'm sorry," he whispered.

Emily frowned. "No, I understand," she replied, "He was your father. I would be the same way."

Jacob shook his head, "I can't do this." He said it as if he had been totally defeated.

"Can't do what?" she asked.

He looked up into her eyes and resisted the serenity he found in them, "I can't put you through this," he muttered, "I can't protect you like I should."

"Jacob, you're hurt right now, but you don't have to blame yourself," Emily said.

Jacob dropped her hand and stepped back, "I won't let you put yourself in danger by being near me. I love you too much. If I can't keep you safe, I have to let you go."

Emily's eyes fell to the ground, "Just because you're afraid?"

Jacob was glad she had turned her eyes down. He wasn't sure he could take it if he saw a tear on her face or to know he hurt her. "I am sorry. I wish I wasn't like this. I wish I was different."

"But I love you for who you are, not in spite of it, Jacob—because of it." She looked up and just stared at him helplessly.

Jacob felt needles in his chest when he saw the tears like the rain in her eyes; the pain she felt cut him as well. But there was nothing he could do. To wipe them away would only draw her closer to that which he was trying to save her from. He wasn't ready. He needed to be stronger before he could be there for her. "The person I am is changing, I have to go. It's the only thing I can do for you."

She wiped her eyes, "You've always been so selfless, Jacob. Think about yourself for once. Who is going to be there for you? Who will protect you from yourself?"

Nobody, nobody could ever be there for him. It was his curse, his burden. "I don't know, but I can protect you from me." He reached out for help once and almost killed Julie. Help was something he would never have. Jacob retracted his gaze and turned away silently and walked off. For a while he moped aimlessly though the paths in the graveyard. He wished things were simple like they had been when he was a child, crawling in the caves. The memory of what the world was like then with the cold rocks on his face and the cold rocks on his back, alone in the darkness with nothing but a faint light at the far end of the tunnel passed nostalgically through his emotional torment. He used to love being in the cramped, dark solitude. He was still alone in much more cramped, far darker solitude.

It must have been hours before anyone came looking for him. He hadn't noticed the sun beginning to set. The auburn sky filtered through the new leaves of the trees with the warm colors of spring. It was not comforting. Then he realized someone was walking behind him. He turned to see a man he had not been familiar with. This man wore the humble robes of a monk and a wooden cross hung from his neck.

"I'm terribly sorry, Jacob. I understand you must want some time to be alone, but I must speak with you," he began when he met Jacob's stare.

"Your father was a good friend of mine, and he spoke very highly of you. I do believe you'll do fine filling his place." He continued. "I'm Father Jonathan. I was assigned to mediate your father's needs to the church and offer him any council he requested. I would like to take a moment with you."

Jacob stepped toward him, "My father spoke very little of what you provided for us, but he did tell me I would find a guide when he was gone."

"This" he said as he extended a small black book to Jacob, "is his journal." Jonathan paused, "Well, now it's yours. You will find that the pages are full, but if you just turn the last page you will always have room to write notes to your progeny. This little tattered book has been in your family for many generations, and each of your fathers has written enough inside it to fill it ten times over. You will do the same."

Jacob received it curiously. He recognized the book and had held it many times before, but he never knew it was special. Why didn't Drake ever tell him? "Thanks," he replied as he ran his hand over the torn leather of the relic that belonged to his father.

"Turn to the last page first; your father left you a note there."

Jacob fumbled the book and slid it into his jacket pocket. "I'll do that."

The monk smiled, "Of course you will. If you should need anything, seek me out. I shall strive to serve you as well as I served your father."

Jacob nodded but said nothing. He couldn't digest it right now.

Jonathan stepped away, "Peace, brother Jacob. As I said when you're ready. There is no need to burden you today."

Then Jacob was alone again in the thin woods. He collapsed on his knees and then looked up through the green boughs at the amber-blue hues mixing in the sky and wondered how the rest of the world could seem so happy on a day like this. It was not long before he found his way back; he hadn't realized how far he had walked. Sluggishly, he drove himself home and sank into a deep slumber. He could not remember the last time he slept so soundly; there were no voices in his head, no images of demons or fire or the people he loved being tortured, just cold dark silence. And it was peaceful there.

When he woke in the morning, his mind felt more rested than it had in a long time, but his body was still reluctant to move. It was early, and the sun had just barely broken over the horizon. Despite his body's protest, he climbed out of bed and wandered outside. He made his way down the gentle hill that led to the rocky wooded area he used to explore when he was a child and sat beneath a familiar tree to try to sort out his thoughts. He looked around and noted how the landscape had changed since he last ventured this way. It had been years since he came down here. His eye caught a familiar crevasse in the rocky hill that he used to climb through, and he got up to examine it

The crack in the rock was a lot smaller than he remembered, but he thought if he really wanted to, he could crawl through it. Before he knew it, he was halfway in the cave, crawling on his stomach. He shrugged his way forward and pressed on. Things got tricky at first bend. There was an extra foot of him that he had to wiggle through now, and he no longer had the flexibility of a small boy. The second bend was a bit more challenging because part of his legs hadn't cleared the first bend yet. The tunnel was still faintly illuminated by the morning sun coming through the crevasse and shoving its way through the rocks as he had done, but as a child he normally carried a flashlight if he went this far in. He looked ahead, though, and saw another light that hadn't been there before. Even though it was cramped, he had to figure out what it was.

Jacob pressed his way through the tight spaces and found the small underground stream he used to dig in. A few feet upstream, there was a tiny opening he used to visit where he had room to stand up and move about. The light seemed to be coming from there. To get to that chamber he had to crawl up the stream. He placed one hand in the water and never remembered it being this cold before. The thought of turning back never occurred to him, just like it never occurred to him as a child. He shrugged his body in the icy water and pushed his way up the stream, pinned between two slabs of rock above and below him and soaked in the frigid current.

It seemed a lot further than it had in the past, but Jacob made it to the chamber. He pulled himself out of the cold water onto the stony underground beach. He didn't even notice the cold; he was dazzled by the light all around him. The walls had quartz in them and little flecks of fool's gold that he used to imagine was the real thing that made the chamber light up and sparkle. He sat down and rested his back against the stone behind him and gazed up. A rather large hole had appeared in the years since his last visit, and now sweet sunlight dripped down into his little hide-away.

He felt something pressing on his chest and realized his father's book was still in his jacket. He reached for it and opened it quickly to see if it had been damaged. It was completely soaked, but none of the ink was blemished. He flipped through the pages that stuck together with the moisture and marveled with relief that he hadn't destroyed the note that his father had left him. And with that memory, his curiosity pricked, and he flipped to the last page. There in his father's unmistakable hurried hand-writing was a note titled "My son, Jacob." He read the text that followed:

> Jacob, if you received this note then you know I have passed away. Do not mourn for me, as I have told you before this day would come. No doubt Jonathan gave you this notebook; it was kept by our fathers, and there is much wisdom in it. Jonathan is a good man, and he has helped

me take care of my family. You may trust him. Anytime you need to speak to him, you may go to the chapel where my remains were placed and find the abbot. Ask him, "What's the price on my head?" He will reply, "The wages of sin is death." And you must answer, "Dust to dust." He will know who you are, and he will find Jonathan for you.

Take courage, Jacob. This burden you bear is only for a while, and one day we will stand in the glory of one who is greater than any king of earth. You must persevere and run with endurance. I am very proud of you. You have become a caring, kind, vigorous, dedicated, driven young man. I could not be more pleased, and nothing you ever do could make me love you less.

Remember what I taught you and remember that you are stronger than I am; you are much stronger than I am. Remember that good always triumphs in the end.

Now one last thing I must warn you. I feared that telling you this before I passed might disable you from doing what you must, so forgive me. I have left you ill prepared for the upcoming struggle. I will return to the earth. You know of the pact of our ancestors that the demons could use our bodies once we perished. The bond in life was broken, but the bond in death is still intact. I'm sorry, Jacob, but please know that the image of me is only a specter and a hollow shell. You may be faced with this soon, or you may not encounter the illusion of me for years, but when you do, you must erase me permanently. I know how hard it is because I have done the same for my father, and he, his father. You are stronger than me, and I know you will bring me to my final rest. Do not fear the darkness because the sun will always rise.

Tell your mother I loved her every day, and tell Sarah and Dom they were bright stars in my dark sky; I love you all. Stay strong, my son, live happy and be blessed. Enjoy the things the Lord gives you and do not linger on trials and troubles because you will see that this life is merely a fleeting moment. There is no purpose in hanging on to either good or ill, for it will not follow you into eternity.

Be bold, Jacob,
Drake

The bitter reality hit him like a train. He was in this mess because he couldn't kill his father, and now he would have to relive that moment again. Jacob wanted to scream; why hadn't his father told him? That didn't matter; it wouldn't have made any difference. He suddenly felt smothered, he had to get out of this cramped space. Reaching for the light, he found that he was tall enough to reach the ceiling. Jacob thrust the small book back into his wet jacket and braced one leg against the wall behind him and then planted his hands against the opposite side. He brought his other leg up and wedged himself in the narrow shaft and reached up into the light. The top of the hole was just at his fingertips.

He was frantic, panicking, never had he ever been afraid of small spaces, but right now he desperately needed air. Jacob grasped the edge of the outside and found it was loose soil that gave under his weight, and he fell splashing into the cold water. He jumped back up and tried again. This time the loose dirt was gone and bare rock was closer to his reach.

Jacob struggled to get his other arm through and discovered that there was barely enough room to get his shoulders through. The tunnel he had crawled through to get here yielded more room than this tiny window. But that wasn't a concern for him now; he need open air, light, and the sky, and it was all right there at his fingertips.

He struggled, but he could not wiggle through, his frustration boiled into a fury, and something in him sparked. He struck the rock that blocked his exit, and it shattered into several small stones that rolled down the shaft and clobbered him in the face. They might as well have been made of cotton because he paid them no attention. The way was free now; he clamored up and out and rolled away from the hole and right off the side of the hill. His descent ended right in front of the crack he had entered through. Jacob lay on his back, panting to catch his breath and staring at the blue morning sky. He was going to be okay.

He raised his hand in front of his face and examined it. There was no bruise or mark from the impact that had crushed the boulder. And that gripped him with a new fear. He had not called on or felt his inner power in that moment. His hand, not the rock, should have been crushed. What was happening to him? He slowed his breathing and focused; he would overcome whatever was happening. Hadn't he already claimed that? He was a demon, but that was not going to stop him, though at times it certainly seemed that it would. Jacob had no idea how he was going to come out on top, but he had to.

After some time, his adrenalin flushed from his body, and the damp, muddy cloths became cold. He slowly got up and walked back up the grassy hill to his house. His mother was awake when he returned. S she was sitting in the dining room quietly reflecting. She looked up at Jacob and forced a smile but did not comment on the state of his clothes—unlike the last time he crawled out of the caves.

"I'm sorry," Jacob said as he removed the muddy shoes and stepped off the threshold.

"It doesn't bother me, Jacob; you're not a child anymore," she replied.

Jacob hung his head, "I meant about Dad. I thought I could help, but I just made it worse."

She looked up at him gently and shook her head, "You did what was right by you, and you did that for the right reasons. People make mistakes; my mistake was hoping."

"I tried; I don't know what went wrong. I thought I could be stronger, I thought I could beat it."

"No, Jacob, it wasn't you; I never let go of that hope." His mother was fighting hard to hold back her grief.

"He left me a message," Jacob said, "He said he would find rest." He wasn't sure if his mother knew what was going to happen to Drake before he found rest, and he thought it would be best to leave that out. "He wrote to me and told me to let you know that he loved you every day."

She smiled, "Yes, he often told me that. I just wasn't prepared to let go. I tried so hard to save him, and he told me not to worry. And then you came along, and I thought maybe there was still a chance." She sighed and closed her eyes as they were tearing up, "But he was right; there was nothing to do."

Jacob walked over to his mother and placed his hand on her shoulder. She fully embraced him in his muddy attire and wept into his shirt. "I wish there was something I could have done," Jacob repeated. "He told us not to mourn, but I can't see how. I don't know what to do anymore." Jacob had to choke down his own tears. So much had gone wrong and he seemed to be right in the middle of it all. Now, without his father, he had to face the world alone. And along with that, a whole new set of problems was just over the horizon.

End Book One

CPSIA information can be obtained at www.ICGtesting.com
Printed in the USA
LVOW08s0820020816

498653LV00001B/1/P